Warbird

Mark Batey

Published by Clink Street Publishing 2022

Copyright © Mark Batey 2022

First edition.

ISBN:
978-1-915229-16-8 - paperback
978-1-915229-17-5 - ebook

To Hannah, Charlotte and Sean

Contents

PART 1
SUMMER 1939

1   Zeppelin   13

2   Inside the nerve centre   25

3   Operation Bloodhound   35

4   The echo principle   45

5   Above Bawdsey   53

6   *Per Ardua Ad Astra*   65

7   Loose lips sink ships   73

8   The Odyssey   85

PART 2
WINTER/SPRING 1940

9   Rendezvous of the spymasters   97

10   Moonlit landings   107

11   Fifth Columnists?   121

12   Who goes there?   131

13   Dead drop   141

14   Reunion and separation   153

15   Assault and battery   167

16   Phantom Squad   185

17   Pact of steel   197

PART 3
SUMMER 1940

18 Scramble!   215

19 Quayside thunder   225

20 The ultimate judgement   241

21 The mask slips   253

22 Tripwire   261

23 Hawkskill   271

24 Crab Law   283

25 Goodbye Klara   297

Afterword: A new world order   309

About the author   317

Acknowledgement

For kind permission to include an extract from the 'finest hour' speech of 18 June 1940, the author thanks Curtis Brown and the Estate of Winston Churchill.

*"Life is given to each human being
For a very special purpose.
This secret each human being
Must discover for himself."*

Sri Chinmoy (1931 – 2007)

PART 1

SUMMER 1939

— 1 —

Zeppelin

Like a gigantic silver torpedo, the LZ130 *Graf Zeppelin* pierced the veil of cloud and emerged into a gleaming blue firmament on a north-westerly trajectory.

Early morning, Thursday 3 August. Precisely a month, as it transpired, before the declaration of war in Europe.

Klara Falke took her time dressing in her cabin. One of twenty berths on board, it was compact yet more comfortable than she and Curt had anticipated. Nonetheless, the carpet felt slightly damp and she donned her black Fogal stockings gladly. While she dressed, Klara reflected on the lift-off yesterday evening, executed so smoothly that she'd hardly even felt they were aloft.

But she had seen and heard everything. She'd asked the permission of the captain, Albert Sammt, to join him on the bridge while he piloted their take-off, and to her delight he'd agreed.

Built by the Zeppelin Company, the rigid, metal-framed LZ130 was 803 feet long, a mere seventy-nine feet shorter than the RMS *Titanic*, the largest ship ever built. When Klara boarded, the extent of it, close up, snatched her breath away. It was such a colossus that she could not even see the far end, which faded into the dusky horizon.

Astonishingly, the lift-off procedure was slick and quick. As soon as the ground crew released the mooring ropes, Captain Sammt ordered the venting of ballast and the throttling of all four engines – sixteen-cylinder Daimler-Benz diesels, adapted from those in high-speed motorboats. Each engine powered a three-bladed propellor, two mounted on either flank. He gave instructions to the helmsman at the wheel controlling the ship's heading; and to the elevation man, managing her pitch via a smaller wheel, his eyes glued to an overhead panel of quivering dials and flashing lights.

Immediately buoyant in the surrounding air, the zeppelin rose. On Captain Sammt's orders, the crewmen turned their wheels this way and that, guiding her deftly, nose first, into the evening sky.

"It feels more like floating than flying."

As if to acknowledge Klara's compliment, Sammt nudged the peak of his black cap. He stood on the starboard side of the bridge by a shelf with a telegraph machine and a Bakelite rotary-dial telephone. Below the shelf was a bicycle on a stand. Its pedals were connected to a small generator which, in the event of a power failure, would pump energy into an emergency radio set.

Sammt made space for his senior watch officer, Tobias Lehmann, who entered the bridge for his shift having completed a stern-to-bow inspection. He blew on his hands which tingled with cold. A qualified captain in his own right, Lehmann confirmed that the water ballast was evenly distributed along the keel. Klara watched Sammt discussing finer points of detail with him.

Kindly and paternal, Sammt was in his fifties. One side of his face was a wine-red patchwork of skin grafts. She realised that the scar across his forehead ran around his scalp and behind an ear. Under his cap, his thick hair was swept back, cloaking much of the scar tissue, while the bushy black eyebrows accentuated his authority.

As Lehmann took his position, Sammt turned, hands thrust deep in his pockets, to Klara. His wide eyes prompted her to follow him off the bridge.

The control car, welded to the underside near the bow, comprised three sections. The bridge, with large windows, occupied the forward portion. Next, a navigation room, where officers pored over tables of charts. There were also altimeters, gyro compasses and a telephone exchange with a dozen lines covering all zones of the ship. Two men and a woman, standing straight, rubbed the small of their backs after leaning over the charts for too long. Thirdly, in the aft space, an observation room – a small lounge.

"You may be interested," Sammt began, showing Klara to a seat in the lounge, "that directly above this control car is a dedicated radio room. Quite a large one, concealed inside the hull, adjacent to the crew quarters."

Klara looked up, inclined her head.

"I mean," he elaborated, "given that the purpose of this flight is espionage, you'll no doubt be spending time up there. A lot of extra equipment was installed last week."

"Good to know, thank you." A beat. How would he react to what she was about to ask? A deep breath. "Forgive me prying, captain, but did the inquiries into the *Hindenburg* catastrophe really get to the bottom of what happened?"

Sammt gently rubbed the cheek bearing the skin grafts. Both his hands were clad in thin black gloves, which Klara saw for the first time. He gazed out at the murky sky, smudges of cloud just visible below. They had lifted off a few minutes before 9 p.m. from the Zeppelin port on the southern tip of Frankfurt airbase. At midnight, they would overfly the city of Hildesheim, two hundred miles hence.

He pondered for a moment.

"A static spark ignited a whisp of hydrogen leaking from a gas cell near the ship's tail," he said. "That's what I believe at any rate, although perhaps not every conspiracy theorist agrees. Have you heard something new?"

After an uneventful trans-Atlantic crossing, fire erupted on the *Hindenburg* during her landing manoeuvres at Lakehurst naval airbase, New Jersey, on 6 May 1937. That was two years ago: the physical injuries had healed but how much distress, she wondered, did the mental scars still induce? Within seconds, flames had raced the length of the ship, turning the stricken giant into a raging inferno. The death toll reached thirty-five, one-third of those on board: thirteen passengers, twenty-one crew, and a hapless member of the American ground crew.

"I've heard nothing, I'm just curious. You were in the control car when disaster struck?"

"I was first officer, under the command of Max Pruss. A fine man. He too survived but with severe burns, much deeper than mine. I was lucky – I jumped fifteen feet to the ground without injury. Bent my legs, rolled over, a graze on my elbow, that was it. But then, before I could run clear, the entire burning frame came crashing down on top of me."

He swallowed hard, reliving the shocking ordeal. Klara, attentive, horrified, let him gather his thoughts.

"I was on my knees, the blazing wreckage around my shoulders. No way out, flames shooting everywhere. If I opened my eyes, they'd burn. I choked on the thick smoke – my face felt like it was melting off the skull. Then, perhaps, a miracle. I sensed a tiny breeze to one side. Was it really there? It was cool, not hot, so I crawled towards it through the wall of fire. What else could I do? Thank heavens, I made it out. Had I delayed seconds longer, well, who knows?"

The moon glowed in the night sky, a shimmering disc. Through the silence, the crackling of the living hell made Klara blanch.

"An ambulance whisked me off to the base infirmary. After an assessment I was transferred with most of the survivors to the nearest burns unit. I stayed in hospital for six weeks. My wounds were extensive, as you can see, but mercifully not bone deep."

While the echoes of his escape from a terrible death faded, Klara managed a little smile.

"Even after such an awful crash, wasn't it possible to secure non-flammable gas? Say, helium instead of hydrogen?"

Captain Sammt regarded her closely. He'd formed the distinct impression that this young woman, only a dozen years older than Ingeborg, his own twenty-year-old daughter, knew more about his career and the Zeppelin Company than she was letting on. But given the elite group of passengers on this flight, that was no surprise. He had half a feeling that he'd seen her somewhere before, but couldn't place her, and didn't want to come across as vague or rude. Anyway, she was bright and warm. A good listener, too. She'd shown a pleasing interest in his work, and he felt comfortable telling his story to her at his own pace. She held eye contact, which only encouraged him to talk more. He would have to watch his indiscretions, that was all.

"Well," he answered, "straight after the crash, Hugo thought he'd got the United States government to agree to supply helium. But..."

He was relieved when Klara took up the baton. "They reconsidered in light of the rising aggression of our National Socialist government?"

"*Genau*. Exactly." Now he wondered how much she knew of where his sympathies truly lay. "You're familiar with Hugo, or–?"

"Hugo Eckener. Worked in publicity, didn't he, before switching to operations. Succeeded the late Graf Ferdinand von Zeppelin as head of the company, which of course has recently been nationalised."

Yes, she'd done her homework. Sammt was impressed, perhaps even flattered. "Hugo and I believed – no, we *do* believe, passionately – that there's no prouder symbol of German engineering than her fleet of airships."

"This one is beautiful, really stunning," Klara concurred. "It's exciting just to be aboard."

She knew, but did not say, that Eckener had become *persona non grata* after the Nazis' ascent to power in 1933. He despised them and their vile schemes but held too high-profile a position for him just to disappear. Instead, it was forbidden for his name to appear in print.

Klara was sure that Sammt shared Eckener's rancorous opinion of the *Nationalsozialistische Deutsche Arbeiterpartei* – the NSDAP a.k.a. the Nazis. He had flatly refused to join the party when required to do so – but Eckener shielded him, kept him employed at the Zeppelin Company and ensured that he wasn't bothered by any of the police who persisted in keeping them under surveillance.

"The inflated vessel contains seven million cubic feet of gas," Sammt said. "Hydrogen is extremely effective – it provides more lift than helium, for one thing. Don't worry, you're quite safe, I promise."

The LZ130 *Graf Zeppelin* was the sister ship of the LZ129 *Hindenburg*, named after the late German president, Paul von Hindenburg. They were built from the same plans. With the LZ130 still under construction when the LZ129 exploded, work was halted. Among many safety-enhancing alterations, she was modified to use helium, on the supply of which the Americans had a stranglehold. And yet, ever since her first flight last September, commanded by Hugo Eckener, she had been inflated only with hydrogen and had never carried a paying public passenger.

"Let me ask *you* a question." Sammt pointed a gloved finger in her direction. "My youngest, Volker, is fifteen. He's an expert in all things."

"That's a teenager's job, isn't it?"

Sammt was serious. "He taunts me, claiming that I'll be the last zeppelin skipper. That these glorious birds have no future in war or peacetime. What do you think?"

Klara puffed out her cheeks. With Hermann W. Göring in command of the Luftwaffe, the expanding, modern German air force, anyone who spoke up in favour of dirigibles would have to be particularly courageous. Or foolhardy. "For missions such as this one," she said diplomatically, which would please Curt, "they're perfect."

Göring had been born into a wealthy, castle-owning family. He was an art collector and a *bon viveur*, but his most voracious appetites were for power and personal glory, in pursuit of which he was brutish and vindictive. Anyone who let him down would see him fly into a violent rage. He demanded simple answers to complex questions and shunned wordy reports. But through it all, at this time, he was '*Der Zweite*' – second-in-command of the Nazi party.

Sammt flashed a smile of gratitude. A thought struck him.

"As a young lad, I was fascinated by Charles Blondin, you know, the high-wire artist." He wondered whether she already knew this about him. If not, she must be asking herself where he was heading. "I was eight or nine when he passed away. It's amazing to think now that it was the better part of a century ago when he first tightrope-walked across the Niagara Falls gorge."

Blondin. Extraordinary Frenchman. Performed death-defying, heart-stopping feats.

"Believe it or not, I was so inspired by Blondin's skill in riding a bicycle along a high wire that I learned to slow-ride myself. My parents were astonished, but have you ever tried it, by any chance? I joined a club, persevered, became quite good, entered competitions."

He grinned at the childhood memories. This seemed new to her.

"What I learned most was balance. All these years later, I'm still grateful. You see, keeping a proper sense of balance, mentally and physically, has stood me in good stead." He rose to his feet.

"Long may it do so," she'd remarked before Captain Sammt took his leave and returned to the bridge.

Now, having finished dressing in her cabin on Thursday morning, Klara neatly stacked the two novels she had on the go on her bedside table. She put on a sparkling art deco pendant necklace and brushed her long blond hair, wishing it wasn't so thin. She hadn't had the length trimmed for six months and had recently noticed split ends. One of these days, she'd have it cut short.

Given Sammt's horrific experience in the incineration of the *Hindenburg*, she wondered how he'd felt stepping up to lead this, its sister ship, for the first time. She admired his composure, the ice in his veins, the quiet fortitude. Important qualities in her own line of work, too.

***

The *Graf Zeppelin* hit heavy turbulence in the morning air and every rivet in the frame shuddered. Abruptly, the nose tipped downwards. Passengers' stomachs lurched, drinks spilled. But the skilled crew on the bridge kept the ship on an even keel and, within seconds that seemed to drag on much longer, a smooth ride was restored.

Locking her cabin, Klara followed the corridor past a parade of closed doors. Most had plaques with numbers, one read PURSER. From the briefing dossier, she recalled that twenty-eight 'specialist' passengers were on board, in addition to the crew of forty-five.

The corridor led to a spacious, finely appointed lounge-diner. As she approached, the sound of a piano grew louder. Accomplished playing. A piano concerto – by Mendelssohn, she thought.

Like an hotel in the sky, the dining area had tables of four, laid for breakfast. It was not at all obvious, but the furniture was exceptionally light in weight. The tables and chairs were formed of tubular aluminium. Even the baby grand was a bespoke lightweight model presented by Blüthner. At the keyboard was one of the flight's mathematicians, Horst Ackermann. Brown suit, waistcoat, tie. The dossier identified him as a professor from Berlin, and Klara wondered whether the white smudges at his temples were chalk.

She avoided the tables of mathematicians, absorbed in their own company, mopping up orange juice, and made for one near a sloping window with two empty chairs.

"May I?" she asked, pulling back a chair. She was getting used to making practically no effort to move the furniture.

"*Natürlich. Bitte schön.*"

She did not recognise the speaker – his photograph was not in the dossier – but she knew the uniform. It was that of a *Hauptmann*, a Flight Lieutenant, in a *Jagdgeschwader*, a Luftwaffe fighter group.

But the older man, in his forties, sitting on the Flight Lieutenant's right – good heavens, she identified him at once.

"Herr Hess, it is a singular pleasure to meet you," she said confidently, then introduced herself.

He cleared his throat, clicked his heels, shook her hand. She accepted his offer to pour her some coffee. In her mind's eye, she reimagined the dossier entry.

Albert Hess. Born in Egypt. Father, Fritz, owned an import business in Alexandria. Albert was gassed and severely injured in the Great War of 1914–18, the *Weltkrieg*. He joined the Nazi party in the '20s, built up its connections in Cairo. Elder brother, Rudolf, had been Deputy Führer since 1933. After the Führer himself, Rudolf stood behind only Hermann Göring in the Nazis' pecking order and succession line.

"To what do we owe your esteemed presence on this mission, sir?"

Hess warmed to this woman immediately. Her inquisitive tone and bright-eyed enthusiasm made the question respectful, not remotely impertinent. She looked after herself – strong shoulders. But he could tell, too, that she carried inside her a tiger. It made her restless, hungry, always striving for more. I bet, he thought, that like many clever women she works exceptionally hard. While wondering whether the sheer burden of doing so ever suffocated her, he appreciated why she'd been accepted into the fast-expanding ranks of intelligence officers.

Hess ignored the raised eyebrow of the Flight Lieutenant at his side. He trusted his own first impression.

"Good question," he said. "I only wish I had an answer to match."

"We are here strictly as observers," the Flight Lieutenant cut in, "as directed by Reichsminister Göring, commander-in-chief of the Luftwaffe." There was a proud edge to his voice.

Hess now had a little more to say. "When the coming war is done," he declared between sips of black coffee, "I've been advised that I shall be named Governor General of Egypt. I suspect that assignments such as this one, and the reports to be compiled afterwards, are little tests along the way. Tests of my focus, managerial ability, loyalty. And as someone who has lived and worked away from the Fatherland, I may be able to offer a broader perspective on what happens in the next few hours, if all goes to plan."

"Just so," added the Flight Lieutenant.

Klara glanced out of the window. The zeppelin was flying over water – the North Sea, one of the coldest in the world – at a height of six thousand feet. Not long to go now.

"And you, sir? Strictly an observer?"

Was she teasing him? Surely not. But the Flight Lieutenant felt his cheeks had flushed, which he hated.

"Let me introduce myself. Karl-Heinz Weiss. I joined the army almost a decade ago, and began flying training in… yes, it was 1931. Three years later, I transferred to the Luftwaffe in JG279. Soon I became an adjutant and an instructor, which I enjoyed very much. In '37, I commanded a section of the Condor Legion supporting General Franco's Nationalists in the Spanish Civil War, flying Messerschmitt Bf 109s. I like to think it was useful experience for the air battles we must assuredly fight in the future, yes?"

"Unless peace terms are agreed," Klara said almost to herself.

"Karl-Heinz has been telling me that he scored five kills in Spain and was awarded the Spanish Cross," Hess said. He did not need to remind them that Franco had only emerged victorious earlier this year, nearly three years after the civil war began.

"I hope I can offer a pilot's viewpoint when the mission's findings are assessed, that is all."

Klara drained her coffee cup. "I'm sure your input will be highly–"

A door crashed and a boiling argument shattered the tame hum of the dining room. Two men spilled out of the smoking room in the corner opposite Klara's table.

It had seemed counter-intuitive to have a smoking room on the airship at all, but this one came with multiple safety features. A double-door airlock. An electric lighter available inside, no others to be taken in. The room kept at a higher pressure than the rest of the ship – monitored from a gauge on the bridge – so that no leaking hydrogen could find its way in.

A crew member stood guard outside the smoking room at all times, too. That morning, a freckle-faced cadet. He sprinted to a wall-mounted telephone and dialled the bridge, each turn of the disc agonisingly slow.

As far as Klara could tell, the argument was about, of all things, cigarettes. During the last decade, smoking had risen sharply among the German population and a public information campaign against it was in preparation. No doubt at that very moment it sat on the drawing boards of the overburdened propagandists working for Joseph Goebbels. Always eager to remain a trusted adviser to the Führer, Goebbels was adept at preventing the truth about any issue from seeping through his walls of disinformation.

But the nub of this clash was not the danger to health. Nor was it one man not sharing his pack with another.

The more aggressive participant was Ulrich Freitag, a Gestapo officer with a thick bovine neck and a clean-shaven, round pumpkin of a head. He was berating the other man for smoking a brand made by a foreign firm, most of whose board members were allegedly Jews.

Despising the racism, the other man nevertheless defended his choice chiefly for its flavour. But the Gestapo officer was not used to tolerating any kind of opposition and the man's protests bounced off him.

As Karl-Heinz buried his own pack of Trommler filterless cigarettes deeper into his trouser pocket, Klara stood and approached the pugilists, squaring up to each other, inches apart.

"Come back! What do you think you're doing?" Albert Hess, to no avail, hissed at her.

Captain Sammt entered the dining room and in a few strides was confronting the two men.

"Gentlemen, please. On this ship, my word is law. Be respectful, calm down, both of you, and return to your places." He could see the blood running hot in their veins.

As Sammt turned to the freckle-faced cadet, violence erupted.

Apparently further enraged at being lectured in a full room, Freitag swung a right hook at his opponent who was almost six feet tall but looked half Freitag's size. It was a ridiculously uneven match. The powerful blow caught him off guard – he'd been watching Sammt and sensed the punch coming a fraction too late.

Heavy and hard, the fist smashed into his temple, knocking him off balance. An aluminium chair cartwheeled away from a table as his heel clipped its leg. He staggered into Klara, almost grabbing her necklace, and pinned her against the dining room wall.

"Apologies," he gasped, the tip of his nose touching hers. She caught a sweet scent of after-shave lotion. His eyes were watering, hair tousled. His left cheekbone was a livid red. Freitag must be wearing a ring or have sharp fingernails as a cut had opened below the left eye, discharging blood into the corner of his mouth.

This man, Curt Schultz, was Klara's boss. She had seen him smoke and drink only occasionally when he was trying hard to impress or influence someone.

Freitag was not finished. He pushed past the cadet, hunting his wounded prey. It had not taken much to tip him over the edge. A human wrecking ball, his giant steps were full of purpose and menace.

He lashed out with a forearm, his fingers curled into a fist.

"Get out of my way," he snarled at Klara, who was righting the upended chair. His dark, sunken eyes were unsettling – they seemed to look straight through her without seeing her – and down her spine she felt the flesh crawl. "Don't make me teach you a lesson, too."

— 2 —

Inside the nerve centre

As the air commodore took his seat in the gallery, Linda's pulse quickened. The secret exercise she'd been looking forward to for days was suddenly, breathtakingly, under way.

Twenty-three-year-old twins, Linda and Gloria Hastings from Maida Vale, London, were extremely proud of their pressed, blue-grey uniforms. They often imagined their eternally courageous father wearing a similar one. He had lost his life in 1917, the year after they were born, in a dogfight over Pas-de-Calais with Baron Manfred von Richthofen, the combat ace of the German air force, famed for his Albatros D.III biplane, painted bright red.

Raised by their ever-loving mother, Marcia, who supplemented her work as a nurse with shifts at the local Lyons café, the girls yearned for adventure. Travel. Excitement. Escape.

Last year, 1938, the opportunity finally arose. On the same day, they negotiated time out of their mundane clerical jobs and enrolled with a Royal Air Force company in the Auxiliary Territorial Service.

"You go, I go," Gloria said. The ATS, a women's equivalent of the Territorial Army, offered them part-time training.

Then, two months ago, in June 1939, the Womens' Auxiliary Air Force was established to give additional support to the RAF. In anticipation of war, the king, George VI, gave the WAAF his seal of approval and the first recruitment posters were printed: 'Help the RAF / Join the WAAF'. Linda and Gloria were two of the many who volunteered at the outset. They envisaged their father waving them off with the biggest smile ever.

Today, Thursday 3 August, the sisters were participating in a simulation exercise at Bentley Priory, where they were thrilled to have started work this very week as WAAFs, having sailed through the demanding aptitude tests.

Bentley Priory, near Stanmore to the north-west of London, was home to Augustinian Friars in the twelfth century. In the eighteenth, it was rebuilt by the architect Sir John Soane as a magnificent stately home which successive owners further extended with their own imprints over the next hundred years.

In 1882, the estate was bought by a prosperous hotelier, Frederick Gordon, whose chain included the Grand and the Metropole in London's West End. Gordon had enjoyed much success by defying naysayers. Backing his own judgement that a country mansion on the outskirts of the capital would make a successful hotel, he built a railway line from the city and laid out a golf course. But this time, the hunch did not pay off. The venue failed to attract enough guests and Gordon made it his family home instead. He died of a heart attack, aged sixty-eight, in 1904. Four years later, the mansion reopened as a girls' school for seventy boarders, but this in turn closed after little more than a decade.

In 1926, the estate was split up, sold off in parcels. The main lot – the priory, a manor house in its grounds, plus forty acres of surrounding woodland – was acquired on the order of Sir Samuel Hoare, Secretary of State for Air, by the Air Ministry for £25,000. By May 1926, some training units had already moved in.

Ten years later, when RAF Fighter Command was created, Bentley Priory became its headquarters. From July 1936, it was the workplace of Air Chief Marshal Sir Hugh C. T. Dowding, the first commander-in-chief of Fighter Command, and his team of strategic planners.

This Thursday morning, the simulation exercise was stress-testing the air defence system devised by Dowding that was being installed around the country. It was nowhere near complete or ready yet, everyone understood that. But if the

RAF was to defeat the Luftwaffe in a fight to the finish, it was imperative that the multi-stranded system was robust.

Two large spaces in Bentley Priory were the focal points: the filter room in the main priory building, and the operations room in the nearby manor house. Linda Hastings had been assigned to the former, Gloria to the latter. The twins had started work at RAF Bentley Priory as clerks. By demonstrating their fast work, cool heads and aptitude for figures, they hoped to be transferred into the teams of plotters.

Linda was spellbound by the scale and pace of the activity all around her. The filter room functioned like a well-oiled machine in which all the cogs were inter-dependent. Sir Hugh's nickname may be 'Stuffy', she thought, having picked that up on day one, but he was a master delegator. Dozens of men and women were stationed at desks or on platforms, many in headphones. Others encircled a huge central table map. The chain of command was very clear: every person knew what to do and when.

Dozens more, including representatives of the army, navy and Observer Corps, were perched in the mezzanine gallery with a bird's eye view. A gigantic wall clock hung below the gallery, each five-minute segment shaded in its own colour. Self-evidently, time was of the essence.

It was all mightily impressive – and what a thrill to be here, in the thick of it, watching, taking notes, passing messages, learning. This was what they'd signed up for! Telephones rang, shrill and urgent, with growing frequency. They were answered immediately.

For the purposes of the exercise, RAF planes were representing Luftwaffe fleets. The height, bearing and speed of the fighters and bombers were tracked over the English Channel, across the coast and up the country. Reports came in from tracking stations and observation posts along England's south and east coastlines.

Tellers – the telephone operators – kept multiple streams of information flowing. Reports of the same aircraft from different sources were condensed into single tracks. When officers had cross-checked each item of new information, coloured counters were moved on the table map by plotters armed with magnetic rods. No voices were raised, no tempers frayed, just pure concentration.

Filter room staff telephoned activity summaries through to the operations room. There, a parallel team of plotters worked fast to keep their own table map of aircraft progress up to the minute.

It was in this room, the awe-struck Gloria appreciated, that Sir Hugh and his senior controllers monitored the intelligence and ensured that Fighter Command's sector stations – airfields – had the information they needed to decide locally which squadrons to scramble to intercept which raids.

If it worked as intended, Dowding's system would remove the enemy's element of surprise. The RAF would know what was coming, and could aim, assets permitting, to be in the right airspace at the right time. Gloria could not wait to get back to the priory's barracks, much later, to compare notes with Linda. The first phase of the exercise, with the planes still sweeping in, seemed to be going...

Suddenly, Gloria's engrossment was shattered by an air commodore bursting into the room and signalling frantically to two senior officers watching the table map. Something unexpected was causing turmoil. What the devil could have happened?

***

Less than five minutes later, a telephone rang on Sir Hugh Dowding's burr walnut desk. Pedestal drawers on each side, a worn leather top. He picked up at once and dismissed his secretary's apology for disturbing him. "That's fine, Joanne, send him in."

Dowding sat back and glanced at the simply framed, black and white photograph in the corner of his desk, next to the brimming in-tray. The portrait was twenty years old, although it looked more recent: he kept it out of direct sunlight. Her lovely face and wavy hair had not faded at all.

He'd married Clarice in February 1918. She was a major's daughter – her father, John, served in the Indian Army. She fizzed with *joie de vivre* and she'd made him unimaginably happy. He was an able skier and polo player, and she'd revelled in the social aspects of those occasions. She was a widow and brought with her a six-year-old daughter, Marjorie, from her first marriage. What delight there had been, he recalled, looking into her unblinking eyes, when their own son, Derek, was born in 1919.

Then, the following year, when she was only 35, Clarice died. Oh, the shock of that unexpected loss. The cruelty. The pain – he had never known pain like it. Every new morning it clobbered him in both the stomach and the heart.

She passed away in London on a Sunday, 27 June, and to this day he hated weekends. So what if they called him 'Stuffy'? Let them! Social engagements felt deplorably awkward without her company, and his solution was simply to avoid them.

Leaning on the vital support of his sister, Hilda, to bring up the two children, he devoted himself to a career in aviation. He was a self-taught pilot, who flew in combat in the Great War, after which he was accorded a permanent commission as an RAF Group Captain. He kept up his skiing and served for a year in the mid-'20s as president of the Ski Club of Great Britain. In 1930, he joined the Air Ministry, supervising supply and research. After four years, his intelligent, open-minded approach was rewarded with a knighthood and a promotion.

Just as the country's air defences were to be expanded, Dowding was placed at the heart of the effort, responsible for all the ministry's research and development work. Then, when the expanding RAF was reorganised in 1936 with fighter, bomber and coastal commands, he was put in charge of Fighter Command. Now, in 1939, the hugely experienced fifty-seven-year-old was perhaps at the peak of his powers.

Dowding examined the organogram laying out the structure upon which he had built Fighter Command. It was typed on a foolscap sheet whose bottom-right corner was dog-eared. There were presently four groups – four prongs on his organogram – each headed by an Air Vice-Marshal who reported directly to him:

10 Group, led by Sir Quentin Brand, defended the west and south-west of England. It currently had just a handful of operational squadrons.

11 Group, entrusted to his protégé, the New Zealander Keith Park, was – had to be – much larger. It covered London and the south-east of England, which were expected to bear the brunt of the Luftwaffe attacks.

12 Group, commanded by Trafford Leigh-Mallory, protected the area north of London. Leigh-Mallory was no stranger to family loss, either: his brother, George, had died after a bad fall on Mount Everest in 1924.

13 Group, under Richard Saul, was responsible for a large slice of the north of England and Scotland.

During the last couple of days, Dowding had pored over preliminary drafts of a rota to ensure that as many squadrons as possible spent part of their service in the south-east. In recent years, a high priority had been the development of fast, agile fighter aircraft, succeeding the biplanes of the past. The investment had yielded the Hawker Hurricane and the Supermarine Spitfire, but more of both those high-performance aircraft were sorely needed: at present, only a handful of squadrons had any Spits at all.

He'd also secured funding for the 'Chain Home' network of radio direction-finding stations along the coast – a cornerstone of his defence system. Developed in top secret, this network needed extending, too. It comprised two sets of masts. The first, three hundred and sixty feet tall, transmitted the radio pulses. The second, shorter at two hundred and forty feet, received back the waves reflected off incoming aircraft. The network used a moderately high-frequency range – 22–50 megahertz –

which its inventor, Robert Watson-Watt, whom Dowding had championed from the Air Ministry, insisted was their best shot.

Then there were the thousands of men and women, many of them teenagers, bless them, who had joined the Royal Observer Corps. They were essential for reporting on airborne intruders after they'd crossed the coast and passed the RDF stations. Tens of thousands more volunteers were required, each of whom would need police-led training to identify the size, height and composition of aircraft formations. They'd need binoculars and sextants, too.

And the GPO, splendid as its engineers had been, would have to install more telephone lines to connect each additional RDF station and observer post to the network. All told, the workload ahead was immense. He had no deadline to work to, but he sensed that the time before war broke out was shortening rapidly.

Yes, he had stuck his neck out to force through his system – combining the RDF stations, observer posts and telephone network – when there was simply no precedent for it. Yes, he knew that he'd put senior noses out of joint, made enemies among the 'Whitehall Warriors', the bureaucrats for whom he had so little time, and even among the upper echelons of the RAF. For some, his retirement could not come a day too soon.

But he believed in the system implacably. His reasoning was sound. Before the Nazis could contemplate invading Britain, they needed control of the skies. Britain had fewer pilots, so a greater interception rate was essential. The Dowding System would give early warning of German air raids and likely targets, and it was the best – no, the only – way to deter an invasion.

I do hope, he thought, looking again into Clarice's eyes, that I have done you proud.

A sharp rap on the door.

"You took your time," Dowding huffed as Air Commodore Bryan Worthington marched in.

Worthington had huge respect for the incisive ACM sitting behind the desk laden with folders, papers and telephones in front of the old fireplace. The pressure on Dowding's shoulders would have forced many people to buckle. Everything was planned, nothing was ready, nothing was certain. Often irascible, he did not suffer fools, yet the shadow of brilliance never left his side.

Worthington looked at Dowding's neat, slightly rakish moustache and finely combed hair. He was every inch the son of a Scottish prep school master, but was he really as cold and prickly as his outer shell implied? Rumour had it that he wore carpet slippers with his uniform, but a briefcase stood between the pedestals and Worthington could not see beneath the desk.

"Apologies for my tardiness. I wanted to double-check the data, sir."

"That's all right, Bryan," Dowding melted and waved the air commodore into a chair. Apparently, Worthington was still a fine opening batsman for his local Sunday side, which Dowding rather admired. "How is our simulation progressing? Seemed to start well enough."

"Consensus is, extremely well, sir. The ministry observers should be suitably impressed."

"As long as they continue to fund what's required, that's all that matters. Now, what's the flap?"

"Chain Home has picked up a rogue intruder, sir. It's not an RAF plane in the exercise. In fact, it doesn't look much like a plane at all."

Dowding held eye contact, said nothing.

"It seems far too large – it's huge – and it's travelling too slowly," Worthington elaborated. "Thirty knots, sometimes even less."

"A zeppelin?"

"That's our view, sir, yes." Evidently Worthington was concerned.

"Bearing?"

"Approaching the Suffolk coast over the North Sea."

"Bawdsey?"

"I'd say so, yes. We have a clear track of its progress from one RDF station to the next, and we expect confirmation from the live observers to start coming in at any minute."

Dowding rubbed his tired eyes.

"Dear God, Bryan, if the Nazis work out what we've been doing at Bawdsey, and its significance for our defences, well…"

"We expected a reconnaissance mission sooner or later, sir."

"Quite so," Dowding conceded, sat back. "Mustn't forget, some of the masts are visible from the other side of the Channel, after all."

"Do you want any remedial action, sir?"

"If we make a fuss, it'll only prove that the masts are important. No, we'll do as planned – let them look, and hope they don't deduce what they're seeing or hearing."

"It's awfully risky, sir."

"I know, Bryan." Dowding had quickly become irritable again. "But there's no alternative."

Worthington got to his feet.

"Oh, Bryan – don't lose sight of them, will you? And better let MI5 know that they're here, too."

"Very good, sir."

When Worthington had left, Dowding flung open his patio doors and stretched his legs on the terrace. His office overlooked a splendid Italian formal garden, laid out by a tasteful owner long before the Air Ministry acquired the priory. It was cloudy and warm, but the morning air was invigorating. Of course, even heavy cloud cover would be no barrier to the zeppelin's spy mission, if that's what it was.

A thought struck Dowding. Back at his desk, he telephoned his secretary.

"Joanne, get hold of Robert at RAF Bawdsey, would you? Most urgent. I'd like him to arrange a little shutdown for maintenance. I'm sure one must be due."

For one fleeting, delicious moment, Dowding sensed that Clarice had winked at him.

3

Operation Bloodhound

"This will hurt you more than it will me."

Klara Falke uttered the words to Curt Schultz in his cabin on the *Graf Zeppelin* as she dabbed his face with a cotton wool ball soaked in anti-septic solution, which a crew hand had fetched from a first aid box.

Schultz smarted. Was he exaggerating, playing for sympathy? He would have a black eye, a gashed cheek and a bruised stomach to show for the confrontation with Ulrich Freitag. Such a shame, Schultz's thick blond curls were gorgeous. She had to admit he was a handsome devil: lean, smooth skin, flinty eyes, lucky with the genes he'd inherited. And somehow, he always managed to smell fresh. She let him grip her left hand while she worked on his face with the right.

She knew he'd taken a shine to her, personally as well as professionally, almost as soon as she'd joined his team. She was a good team player, but she hoped his fondness wasn't overly obvious to their colleagues, that was all. She'd done nothing to encourage it – she wasn't seeking a relationship, certainly not one with her new boss – but she wondered whether she might have done more to discourage it. Undeniably, there was a spark, some magnetic attraction between them. Was it lust, or...? Well, if the spark led to a slow-burn relationship with room to grow, why shouldn't she remain open to that?

At least he hadn't asked about her family background – yet – so she hadn't been forced to lie.

Klara had joined Schultz's technical research unit in the Abwehr, the German secret service, ten months ago, during a rapid expansion in personnel. Already, the headcount topped a thousand. The unit was in a division – one of three – of the restructured Abwehr under the nominal charge of Colonel Hans Pieckenbrock. Klara was a liaison officer with a directory of contacts, in her case in the Luftwaffe, many of whom had come quickly to appreciate her concise communication skills, her fierce work ethic, her determination to make good on her promises.

She was enjoying being part of a community with shared goals and experiences. But regrettably, here in this building, she perceived an indistinct air of conspiracy, of division somehow corroding the prized togetherness. The whole was less than the sum of its many parts.

The briefing on the zeppelin mission had taken hours, in two different rooms. Schultz told her that she'd be accompanying him on board and gave as much background information as he could. Context, he said repeatedly, was all-important.

First, he took his Zenith gramophone player out of a cupboard in his office and played the vinyl recording of Brecht and Weil's play, *The Threepenny Opera*. As Klara learned, Schultz routinely put on a record during his briefings to spoil audio bugging.

"At least three separate intelligence organisations may be represented on the zeppelin," Schultz said. "You and I for the Abwehr. Plus, officers of the Gestapo, the secret state police, and the Sicherheitsdienst, the security service. Alas, this duplication is not unusual. Top-level meetings have taken place to clarify the intelligence and counterintelligence remits of each organisation, but I fear that trust is in woefully short supply."

Klara despised turf wars as self-defeating, a waste of energy. Chaos would never lag far behind a misdirected plan, and delusional, paranoid thinking would only exacerbate the tensions stalking every corridor. There seemed to be too many turf wars within the state apparatus already, due to the powers that be refusing to co-operate, and she could do without one that directly ensnared her.

She considered Schultz a dependable judge of character and believed she could learn much on his team – even if he came across as a mite too eager to be needed and liked. "The Sicherheitsdienst roots out opponents of the Nazi party, doesn't it?" she asked. "Does that imply that the loyalty of someone on the zeppelin is in question?"

Schultz turned his palms upwards and shrugged his shoulders.

"I hope not," he replied, "but you never know. These days, the Sicherheitsdienst gathers information on all sorts of matters. For every full-time agent, and there are thousands of them in Berlin, there must be a dozen informants."

"And the Gestapo has thousands, maybe tens of thousands, of agents sneaking about, too," Klara said to the vinyl strains of *Mack the Knife*. "Blind sycophants, some of them, no doubt. Is there anyone out there who is *not* an informant for one organisation or another?"

Schultz stared, deadly serious. "Be careful, Klara, be shrewd," he chided her through pursed lips. "You're earning a fine reputation and I'm happy that you've joined us, but don't give anyone a stick to beat you with. Not in Nazi Germany."

She looked him in the eye. "I'll try not to, sir."

"Dispense your trust wisely."

As a child, Klara had been introspective, diligent, imaginative. She and her sister, Katarina, had escaped by reading the Bible and other books, fact and fiction, of which their father had many. Looking back, his reading to her at bedtime had undoubtedly ignited her love of language. When times were dark, books made friendly company.

Katarina had inherited not only their late mother's high cheekbones and generous lips, but also, it seemed, her acute renal colic. Due to her kidney troubles, young Katarina had endured many hours of dialysis. Somehow, stories showed that there was always hope, always a way through. To their parents' delight, the sisters were very close. They tried to treat others well, as they would wish to be treated themselves – sometimes easier said than done and increasingly now at odds with the conduct of their own homeland authorities.

After a moment's reflection, Klara broadened the conversation. "May I ask what Admiral Canaris makes of all this? The overlap, I mean, the suspicion, the feuding between the intelligence communities. He must find it draining?"

Wilhelm Canaris was head of the Abwehr. His distinguished career in the Imperial German Navy began at the age of eighteen. A U-boat commander in the Great War, he came to the attention of the intelligence service because he spoke six languages. Now in his early fifties, he looked older, and had been known occasionally to pass himself off as a pensioner to go unnoticed.

"At first, Canaris backed the Third Reich," Schultz said matter-of-factly. "He was a staunch anti-Communist, for one thing. For another, he was committed to breaking the shackles of the Treaty of Versailles."

Klara knew, of course, that the Treaty of Versailles, signed in 1919 after the Great War had ended, forbade Germany from rearming. But there was a loophole. The Treaty's clauses on building civilian aircraft were less restrictive than those banning military machines. So, inevitably, throughout the 1920s, newly recruited military pilots were trained in civilian air clubs. Canaris toiled to ensure that the rearmament did not leak to the outside world.

It was not until February 1935 that the Führer publicly confirmed the existence of the new German air force. The world was worried, but by then the Luftwaffe had amassed 1,800 planes and ten times as many personnel. As soon as it was in the public domain, it grew even faster, under the supervision of Hermann Göring.

Ten months earlier, in April 1934, Göring had assigned oversight of the Gestapo to Heinrich Himmler, head of the Schutzstaffel (SS), the party's protection squad. He appointed Reinhard Heydrich, a former naval officer, to lead it. Heydrich was already head of the Sicherheitsdienst, the intelligence agency of the SS. So, for the last five years, to the chagrin of Canaris, Heydrich had called the shots at both the Sicherheitsdienst and the Gestapo.

"And now?" Klara prompted Schultz, hoping to be taken further into his professional confidence.

"Now, well…" Schultz blew out his cheeks. The music played on. "Canaris finds the Nazis too brutal, intolerant of dissent. He was deeply upset by the violence on Kristallnacht, believing that Germany had ruined not just the synagogues, but itself, too. In his heart and soul, he hates that German democracy is dead, as he sees it poisoned by a few persuasive politicians for their own ends, and he does not want another great war in Europe."

"He can't be alone in that, sir."

Schultz hesitated. "I… I find Canaris hard to read, to know exactly where he's coming from. But I think he's afraid, genuinely, of the horrors that the Gestapo, left to their own devices, will perpetrate."

"He won't be alone in that, either."

"And he worries that the children of Germany will have to cope with those horrors, atone for them, for generations to come."

Silence.

Schultz looked out of the office window. It was a dark, wet morning, disappointing in late July. Fingers crossed, he hoped he didn't catch a cold.

"There's even speculation," he notched up the gramophone volume, "that Canaris is part of an underground opposition."

"To the Nazis?"

"To the Führer."

Klara wondered about the Admiral's life expectancy. Aloud, softly: "I see why trust is the watchword, sir."

She did not elaborate at that time, but Klara had brought from her childhood a robust moral code which she upheld, despite the provocations that life tossed in her way.

"So, to our impending mission." Schultz's full attention was on Klara. On his desk was a manilla folder labelled 'LZ130', but he did not open it.

An intercom buzzed. Schultz turned down the gramophone. Leaning across his desk, he pressed a white switch.

"*Ja?*"

The voice of Brigitte, his secretary, sounded oddly distant, although her desk was merely yards from his door.

"General Martini is here to see you, sir."

"Perfect timing," Schultz observed, "as always."

"Conference room four, sir." The largest one.

"*Danke schön.*"

Click. The line went dead.

Wolfgang Martini stood to attention when Schultz and Klara entered the conference room on the floor above. Klara noticed the umbrella and battered attaché case behind him. Martini's cropped brown hair looked wet – whether from the rain or heavy lotion, she was unsure. Was this enough to explain his air of melancholy? The narrow moustache made him look rather like the Führer himself.

Martini had specialised in radio throughout his military career, which began at the age of nineteen, in March 1910, when he joined the 1st Telegraph Battalion of the German Army. By 1918, he was signals commander in the 11th Infantry Division. He worked as an army signals instructor for much of the '20s, transferring to the new Luftwaffe in 1933. Last year, 1938, his unrivalled expertise earned him a promotion to Major General and chief of the Luftwaffe's Signals Division. He reported in this role, which gave him responsibility for all radio-related matters, directly to Reichsminister Göring, commander of the Luftwaffe.

The three of them shook hands, then Schultz poured coffee from the tray Brigitte had organised. On the longest wall was a large steel clock from a Siemens factory which Schultz had salvaged, repaired and donated.

"Herr General," Schultz said in his most ingratiating manner, "you know my unit stands ready to assist in any way. How can we help you?"

Martini sighed, got straight to the point.

"We've been aware for some time of the tall masts erected by the British. With good binoculars, you can see a few of them on their coastline from our side of the Channel." A sip of coffee. "As you know, we have precious few agents in Britain. But through a variety of sources – aerial photography, one or two informants – we've come to believe that there may be many of these masts, though we're unsure how widespread."

"Sir, what sort of construction are they?" Klara pitched in. "Pylons? Broadcast antennae? Watchtowers, possibly?"

"From preliminary analysis, the masts are not optimal for sending or receiving radio pulses. Yet some of our intelligence suggests that this is what they are doing."

"And your hunch is that the intelligence is accurate." Schultz expressed his question as a statement.

Martini took a moment before replying. "It was a German physicist, Heinrich Hertz, who established that radio waves are a form of electro-magnetic radiation. That, like light, they are reflected by metal surfaces. He showed they could be transmitted across a laboratory."

"Hertz was around, what, fifty or so years ago?" Klara thought aloud.

"Just so," said Martini. "The 1880s."

"And in the half-century since then, many countries have advanced their applications of radio? For military or other purposes?"

"Of course." Martini forced a smile. "My instincts tell me that the masts are radio transmitters. And yet, I'm doubtful that the British, whose technologies are generally not far behind our own, would adopt a system like this. Our military radio uses VHF and UHF ranges, but these masts use lower frequencies, suggesting that the British are not so advanced. I find that hard to believe. Or perhaps, in my position, I can't afford to believe it. It doesn't really matter which."

"So, you want to expose the truth of what the British are doing."

Martini physically flinched at Schultz's use of the word 'truth'. What did it mean in the Third Reich, where differences and divisions were exploited unforgivingly with simple, populist slogans?

"I've been trying for some time to convince Reichsminister Göring of the imperative to understand the mysterious British masts." Martini looked crestfallen, as though he wanted to say more but held his tongue.

A crash of thunder outside and the pelt of heavier rain against the panes.

"Presumably, given the likelihood of war, time is of the essence," Klara hinted.

"With that in mind," Martini confirmed, "my Signals Division has been granted permission to use the LZ130 zeppelin for a reconnaissance flight."

"The LZ130 that has been mothballed for the last couple of years, sir?"

"I don't mind admitting, I requested a much broader approach with a dozen airships, each packed with radio detection equipment." Martini shrugged. "No luck. Nevertheless, I'm grateful to have this one chance, and it's essential to make the most of it."

He opened his briefcase, extracted a plump folder. It was stamped *Streng Geheim* – top secret – and *Unternehmen Bluthund* – Operation Bloodhound.

"Here are your briefing papers." He handed the bundle to Schultz. "I expect there will be two dozen people on the trip, in addition to the flight crew. The captain is Albert Sammt, an excellent man – you'll find a note on him in the dossier."

Bloodhounds are tireless creatures, Klara was thinking, with the ability to sniff out and follow scents to the end. How apposite a name for an eavesdropping mission on the British radio network.

Martini leaned forward. "You will be my ears and ears," he said earnestly. "Please ensure that, after the flight, you report directly to me."

***

Klara stacked the first aid kit by the washstand in Schultz's cabin on the LZ130.

"You'll live," she reassured him, and he thanked her for tending to his wounds.

"The mercurial Mr Freitag blurted something out when I was goading him," he said, a hint of satisfaction colouring his voice.

Hmm... Had Schultz been the original aggressor, provoking Freitag? Had he picked a fight with the brute deliberately to gain information?

"What was it?"

"He is an officer in Department G of the Gestapo."

"Department G..." Klara said to herself. He could almost hear the cogs whirring. Department D: overseas territories. Department E: counterintelligence... "Please remind me, sir, what does Department G do?"

"Officially, there is no Department G." Schultz patted his swollen eye. "But Admiral Canaris has long suspected its existence."

"Remit?"

"Special projects. Black ops."

"Who runs it? Do we know?"

"For the first year of its life, the Gestapo was led by Reichsminister Göring. Five years ago, with Himmler and Heydrich in charge, we suspect – no, we know – that he retained a clandestine unit inside the Gestapo, reporting only to him, to conduct his private investigations."

"So, Herr Göring effectively has a seat on the flight," Klara noted darkly. "Presumably he wants prior knowledge of what Canaris and Martini will learn from the mission?"

"Speaking of which," Schultz glanced at his tan-strapped wristwatch, "we'd better get to the radio room."

The room so called, situated above the airship's control car, was inadequately named. The label did not do justice to the spacious, high-tech audio laboratory that Klara and Schultz admired on entry. Work benches extending along the walls were laden with the most sophisticated radio receivers, battery-powered cathode ray tube screens, amplifiers and, in one corner, a panel of winch controls. Klara would have imagined this room belonged in science fiction, had she not seen for herself that it was science fact.

Huddled on swivel chairs in the centre were the electrical engineers, mathematicians and physicists – specialists in radio – who had been invited to join this prestigious, secret flight. Klara assumed that little pressure would have been necessary. General Martini's dossier contained digests on most of them. They were chatting excitedly to the machine operators who sat along the benches, twiddling dials, checking connections, altering settings, adjusting volumes.

The underbelly of the LZ130 was an inverted forest of aerials, of differing lengths, angled at varying degrees. In addition, there was a gondola – a cloud car – which a crewmember had started to winch down.

"*Ausgezeichnet!* Excellent!" cried Professor Schneider, standing up and letting his chair scrape across the floor for no reason other than to draw attention to himself. Sporting a buzz-cut and metal-framed spectacles, he had been hand-picked to implement a Nazi-approved curriculum at the Victor Weber University on Berlin's imposing boulevard, Unter den Linden. "Now let us see what the British are up to!"

As he sat down again, the door was flung open all the way back on its hinges. Exhibiting a superior smirk, all eyes on him, in strode Ulrich Freitag.

4

The echo principle

No small talk, no chit-chat.

Telephone conversations with Sir Hugh Dowding were invariably short, sharp, to the point, Robert Watson-Watt reflected as he replaced the receiver and scribbled on a pad. He could lay a safe bet on it – although he was trying to break that bad habit – and sure enough, this one had been no exception.

Bentley Priory near Stanmore, where Dowding was based, was a hundred miles away from Bawdsey village on the Suffolk coast. Watson-Watt's research had been accommodated in Bawdsey Manor for three-and-a-half years, since February 1936, and he would be sorry to vacate the premises when war broke out, although that was – rightly, he accepted – the plan.

Watson-Watt had many good reasons to be grateful to Dowding, a fellow Scot, ten years his senior. 'Stuffy' he might be to some, but his integrated defence plan, with radio technology at its heart, was inspired. It would keep Britain safe and free.

Dowding had telephoned with an unusual request, but Watson-Watt owed him so much that he wouldn't dream of letting the Air Chief Marshall down.

He glanced out of his window towards the Debden estuary. It was an overcast Thursday, 3 August. His fascination with the weather endured, but his true passion, his life's work, was wireless telegraphy. He removed his spectacles and polished the lenses.

Fortified with an engineering degree from Dundee, Watson-Watt had joined the Meteorological Office in Aldershot. During the Great War years, he investigated how radio waves might be used to detect thunderstorms. The Met Office relocated to Ditton Park near Slough, a site shared with the National Physical Laboratory, and before long, in 1927, the Met Office and NPL merged. A dedicated Radio Research Station was created, with Watson-Watt honoured to be appointed to lead it. His early devices were the size of sideboards, their shelves overflowing with copper cylinders, valves, dials and connecting wires.

In 1934, the year after the Nazis took power in Germany, the Director of Scientific Research in Hugh Dowding's department at the Air Ministry was an engineer named Harold Wimperis. He it was who formed a working party under the renowned physicist, Henry Tizard, to consider how scientific developments could bolster Britain's air defences. Wimperis asked Watson-Watt to present his theory on radio waves to the Tizard Committee.

It was a day no one present would ever forget. Watson-Watt was on scintillating form, but still, the committee's response to the presentation exceeded his wildest dreams. As he explained how radio waves could detect and locate incoming aircraft, he knew he had the committee in the palm of his hand.

His theory was straightforward. A transmitted pulse of radio waves would reflect off solid objects in its path – aircraft in the sky – and the echoes could be read on an oscilloscope, revealing the speed and direction in which those objects were travelling.

Tizard was an excellent administrator. His committee secured a budget from Sir Hugh Dowding to put Watson-Watt's theory to the test. On a bitterly cold Tuesday, 26 February 1935, in the Northamptonshire market town of Daventry, a BBC crew emitted radio beams from a short-wave transmitter. Working with wavebands used for broadcasting would, they all believed, secure the test from eavesdroppers. Three times, a twin-engine Heyford – the last heavy-bomber biplane operated by the RAF – flew from Farnborough airfield a straight course of eighty miles to within twenty miles of the transmitter.

The first run, at ten thousand feet, drew a blank. Nerves were shredded, glances exchanged. The reliability of the scheme, indeed its whole future, were, well, up in the air.

On the second run, something unprecedented happened. Something utterly wonderful, which melted the hearts of those who witnessed it. Displayed on the oscilloscope as blips of light, the time lag between the transmissions and the reflected signals could be seen and measured. With a time baseline applied, the distance between the Heyford and the transmitter could be recalculated as it changed. This was the first time an aeroplane had been detected and located in the sky.

Tizard felt vindicated; Dowding elated.

"The war will be won by the science, thoughtfully applied to operational requirements," Dowding lectured Watson-Watt, after which his support of the latter's work never faltered.

Committee member, Albert Rowe, christened Watson-Watt's revolutionary technology 'Radio Direction-Finding' – RDF. For a while at least, the name stuck. A patent application was submitted.

The committee shared rising concerns that Britain would be a target of airborne bombing by a resurgent Germany. Some were spooked by rumours that the Germans had mastered a 'death ray' to heat up aircraft and explode them in the sky. Watson-Watt was summoned: was such a weapon feasible? No, quite impractical, he concluded, requiring far too much energy. Don't believe all the gibberish you may behold in enemy transmissions, gentlemen.

Meanwhile, Watson-Watt's scientific assistant, Arnold 'Skip' Wilkins, committed to paper the complete set of calculations showing how radio waves could detect, rather than destroy, aircraft. Wilkins and Watson-Watt derived enormous satisfaction from the elegant ordering of calculations into theories, theories into demonstrations. Thankfully, these calculations soothed the jitters at the ministry.

Three months after the Daventry test, an experimental research station was established on the remote Orford Ness peninsula on the Suffolk coast. The huts may have been spartan, but the work ethic was ferocious. Dowding ensured that few people in the ministry were aware of the research and could not interfere – although he knew that, when they found out, they would hate him for it. In the utmost secrecy, Watson-Watt and Skip Wilkins led a small team of engineers – the 'boffins', as they were affectionately known – working as fast as possible, though never, apparently, as fast as Dowding wanted.

At least two radio antennae – a signal transmitter and an echo receiver – were needed for the system to work. With more antennae, the position and bearing of aircraft could be assessed more accurately over longer distances.

In June 1935, a fresh test confirmed that RDF could spot aircraft at a range of seventeen miles. By November, forty miles. New Year 1936, sixty, even when the aircraft was hidden in low cloud.

After nine months in Orford Ness, the boffins found their new base, in Bawdsey Manor a few miles to the south, enchanting. Rather like Bentley Priory, if the manor's walls could talk, what stories they'd tell.

A three-storey Victorian mansion, Bawdsey Manor had been built for Sir William Quilter, who bought the land from a farmer. Liberal MP for Sudbury for twenty-one years (1885–1906), Sir William was also a stockbroker and an art collector. The manor house, intended as a seaside family home from which he could indulge a passion for sailing, was greatly extended in 1895. He particularly liked the addition of the pointed Gothic towers, cleverly joined by a new, white frontage. Lady Quilter planned a garden, duck pond and cliff path in the one-hundred-and-sixty-acre grounds, which already included a farm and stables.

Twenty-five years after Sir William's death, the Air Ministry acquired the estate for undisclosed purposes. Few knew it was to be the secret location of the RDF research base. The Treasury quietly allocated £1 million for further development of the boffins' innovative work.

Watson-Watt could not have felt more fulfilled – although Dowding never let him forget that, ominously, a clock was ticking down to war. "Go faster, Robert, faster!"

***

In 1937, Bawdsey Manor was rebadged as RAF Bawdsey, part of 11 Group, Fighter Command. An RDF training school opened in a suite of high-ceilinged rooms on the ground floor, and it was thrilling for the boffins to see hundreds of women and men pass through before active service.

That spring, a convoy of cranes and flat-bed trucks rolled on to the estate. An area had been cleared, and a concrete base laid, for radio antennae. Tarpaulins removed, stacks of steel bars and timber beams were revealed. Four tall transmitter masts, made of steel, were erected, with wire strung between them for relaying the radio pulses. Separately, four timber masts, two-thirds of the height, were assembled to receive the echoes. Ladders and platforms just wide enough for one person were affixed up every mast.

RAF Bawdsey thus became the first link in the Chain Home network. The ministry signed off twenty stations, with Dover the next to open in July, Canewdon in August. That summer, Dowding demanded more test exercises, deploying Fighter Command squadrons. He congratulated Watson-Watt heartily when aircraft were tracked from one hundred miles, though still he wanted more.

As Chain Home expanded, often on remote farmland or coastal terrain commandeered for the purpose, a vast telephone network spread with it. GPO engineers – government employees, sworn to secrecy – laid ten lines to each RDF station, five routed through the Stanmore exchange, and as back-up in case of damage, five more routed through an exchange in Bushey, three miles away. Calls could be made between neighbouring stations as they tracked incoming aircraft and, at the same time, to the local Fighter Command HQ and to Bentley Priory. Each Chain Home station was given a dedicated filter officer at the priory, where everything came together.

Watson-Watt put his spectacles back on and sipped his tea. He had requested a cup when Mrs Chappell's refreshments trolley came round an hour ago, but it had gone cold. Ignoring a stack of German scientific journals, he picked up his *Financial Times* and scoured the columns of share prices, before scolding himself for succumbing to the temptation.

Yes, Dowding's defence plan, which they were constantly refining, was ingenious. Hats off to him, the network of RDF stations, observer posts and telephone connections was well thought-through and made clever use of the science.

And yet.

Watson-Watt was distracted again by a gull flapping against his office window. Earlier in the year he'd suspected there was a rooftop nest. He enjoyed observing the gulls' behaviour – resourceful, competitive, noisy – and found their presence soothing.

He had a gorgeous view, especially when the sun shone, along the coast towards Felixstowe. Those undergoing RDF training had, predictably, not taken long to discover the town's public houses. Watson-Watt himself liked an occasional wee dram in The Smugglers' Cave, reading his *Financial Times* or *Sporting Life* by the open fire before a stroll along the pier. Splendid for blowing away the cobwebs, lightening the dark rings of fatigue around his eyes. By road, Felixstowe was a forty-minute drive each way. But there was a direct option. You could take a ferry, really a large motorboat, operated by a Mr Charles Brinkley. He had lost his right hand in a dreadful accident and steered with a steel hook. In choppy conditions, it was terrifying.

And yet.

Chain Home was rudimentary. The masts were so clunky and obvious, sticking up like proverbial sore thumbs, that the Germans were bound to come snooping.

They did not rotate, either. They faced out to sea and that was it. They could only transmit to, and receive from, the space in front of them. Once aircraft had flown over, the system depended on the observers phoning in eye-witness updates. Otherwise, Fighter Command was blind.

The radio technology itself was not state-of-the-art. The pulse transmissions apparently used lower-frequency radio waves than emerging schemes in other countries. But for all its lack of sophistication, Watson-Watt knew with a profound sense of satisfaction that Chain Home *worked*.

They'd done it – the boffins had delivered to Dowding a practical solution. He'd persuaded Dowding that this was the very best they could do, even if they *might* be able to do better given, say, another year of research and testing. Build something operable now, and change the odds for Fighter Command's pilots, or wait for something ideal that may never materialise. Second best is better than nothing. As ever, Dowding had stuck by them, quietly delighted that the system could now spot aircraft up to one hundred and twenty miles away.

Straightening his tie, Watson-Watt left his office and descended a majestic low-tread staircase.

"Good morning, Mrs Brooks," he said as Jayne Brooks, the RDF training course supervisor, swept past him on her way up. Her full-length burgundy dress and cloche hat may have come from a Littlewoods catalogue, but they belonged to the 'silver screen goddesses' section and suited her beautifully. She looked more like Myrna Loy every time he saw her.

On the ground floor, a wood-panelled corridor led to the officers' mess and the security and housekeeping departments. In the opposite direction, an extensive library of recorded music, astonishingly up to date. The ministry had even agreed to install a mini-studio from which announcers could broadcast music as well as issue general instructions.

He left the manor and walked through the grounds, past the barracks block to a stone outbuilding converted into a workshop.

"Tammy? Are you there?"

From behind the workshop, hammer blows fell on a hard substance.

"Tammy!"

Thomas MacPherson, an indefatigable gentle giant, was the best mechanic Watson-Watt had ever encountered. If it had an engine, Tammy would get it going, nay bother. Watson-Watt wondered whether his home was as untidy as his workshop. Tammy was married to Alana and they lived in a bungalow off site. Alana was about to start her training as an RDF operator, which made Tammy intensely proud. Watson-Watt's mother, an ardent feminist, had left her son in no doubt of women's natural abilities, and he had stipulated that women should be recruited as radio operators for their concentration, patience and delicate touch on the sensitive equipment.

"Aye, sir."

Tammy emerged in blue overalls from the rear of the workshop, swinging a mallet. He cleared the sweat from his brow and stood to attention in front of RAF Bawdsey's much-respected superintendent.

"Sorry to interrupt your work, Tammy."

"Och, it's fine, sir. I was reshaping some stones from the cliff path. They're a bit worn and we dinna want any accidents. Now, how can I help you?"

"I'd like the entire section of Chain Home around here switched off at midnight tonight."

Tammy paused. Of course, the system was well maintained, checked and cleaned, but he had never before received an order like this.

"Are we expecting visitors, sir?"

"They're here already, Tammy. A zeppelin, almost certainly a reconnaissance flight."

"I see."

"There's a little exercise on at Bentley Priory today, otherwise I suppose we'd have been asked to carry out our special maintenance even sooner, if you get my drift."

"Nae problem, sir. Happy to oblige."

So saying, Tammy dropped his mallet and gazed up at the alabaster cloud, his brow heavily furrowed. Watson-Watt also noticed that both his fists were clenched.

5

Above Bawdsey

Klara felt the nose of the zeppelin dip as it brushed a swirling air current, and she placed her palm against the wall. Such was the concentration writ large on the faces of those in the crowded radio room that no one else seemed to bat an eyelid at this latest bout of turbulence.

Directly over RAF Bawdsey, Captain Sammt gave orders for the LZ130 to hover. They were above cloud cover but the gondola, lowered to the maximum, was suspended in clear air.

Klara wondered whether the gondola had already been sighted from the ground. Its aerials, scanners and cameras with telephoto lenses sent the radio receivers and cathode ray tube monitors into a frenzy of buzzing, beeping, blipping. So much high-pitched noise was reverberating in the operators' ears that most had, temporarily at least, slung their headphones around their necks.

Two professors, Ackermann and Schneider, specialists in mathematics and electrical engineering respectively, were in a corner, discussing the first readings. They talked animatedly, deploying their hands as much as their voices.

Click, click… Beep, click, click… Beep, click… What did all this acoustic activity mean?

Bruno Weber, an officer in the Sicherheitsdienst, was listening intently to their exchanges. He seemed particularly friendly with Professor Schneider, more than once clapping him on the back for encouragement.

Wolfgang Roth, a lecturer in engineering from Cologne, was poring over photographs of the Bawdsey Manor grounds.

A little grainy, they seemed to have been enlarged from images taken by a Suffolk estate agent in the early '30s. Roth conferred with a colleague on where the masts would appear if the photographs were taken today.

"It's a curious looking place, isn't it?" Roth observed. "Turrets, big windows, extensions. It resembles a higgledy-piggledy gingerbread house in a tale by the Brothers Grimm."

Ulrich Freitag moved towards Klara and Schultz, arms outstretched, penning them against a wall. "Sounds like somewhere Hansel and Gretel would belong," he sneered, noticing Klara's handiwork in patching up Schultz's facial wounds. "If I pushed them out of the airship, they could drop in for tea, *ja*?"

Klara felt, practically saw, Schultz's hackles rise. "You maniac," she heard him mutter through gritted teeth.

"Don't let him bait you, let it go," she whispered. "Sir."

When there was no response, Freitag looked scornfully down his nose. "See the Abwehr cower," he snarled so that only Klara and Schultz could hear. "How insecure and superficial it is. No wonder your General Martini does not support the German High Command's concept of Blitzkrieg – lightning war. He has no stomach to smash our enemies in fast campaigns, he is too weak!"

This time Klara could not hold him back.

"General Martini is a highly experienced, intelligent leader," Schultz snapped. "He believes that radio should play a key role in our air defences, that's all."

"Gimmicks! Distractions!" Freitag dismissed the response. "Attack over defence, that's the formula! Wars are won by professional soldiers, sailors, airmen engaging the enemy and winning!"

"That might have been the case in 1914," said Schultz, a little cooler. "But you'll find in the modern world…"

"That's enough," Klara asserted.

"Do as Gretel tells you," Freitag taunted, humiliating him in front of her. He kept up eye contact with Schultz, hardly even blinking.

Stefan Vogt, a fellow in physics at the renowned Technische Hochschule – technical college – which occupied much of Vienna's Karlsplatz, returned his headphones to the nearest operator. The bank of receivers was whirring, processing more data from the forest on the zeppelin's underbelly. Vogt turned to Wolfgang Roth and Hanna Lippert, a mathematician from Hamburg, and shared his thoughts.

After a few minutes, he crossed the room and relayed their opinions to Schneider and Ackermann. This prompted Schneider to begin a tour of the room, speaking in turn to every operator, every academic.

Klara was pleased to see Alfred Hess emerge from a huddle of bodies and approach her, sidestepping the obstacle that Freitag posed.

"I think they may be reaching a consensus," he said. "Of course, the more experts you have, the more points of view you get, so don't hold your breath."

"Who is that?" Klara asked, finding on the wall a framed portrait of a shaven-headed man with a bushy moustache. "Graf Zeppelin himself?"

Hess confirmed it. "Do you know how he got hooked on balloon flight in the first place? It's an extraordinary story. I bet not at all what you'd expect."

"Oh?" Klara's interest was piqued.

"He'd been to a military academy near Stuttgart and joined the army. When he was twenty-five, he travelled to America as a military observer. It was 1863 – the Civil War had begun a couple of years earlier. The president, Abraham Lincoln, personally signed a pass, enabling him to accompany the northern armies. Before long, he seized the opportunity to explore the wondrous American frontier beyond the war zone."

Hess broke off as a gaggle of engineers raised their voices in an increasingly excited discussion. The whole room was noisy – two dozen people packed in – and hot.

"It was in Minnesota, I believe," he continued, "that Ferdinand first clapped eyes on a lighter-than-air flying balloon, inflated with coal gas. It was used by soldiers for observation. Well, of course, he cajoled them into taking him up. They made a tethered ascent to seven hundred feet, he glimpsed the Earth from the air, a bird's eye view, and that was it, he was smitten. Most of the early zeppelin flights he piloted himself. Got a kick out of it every time."

"He'd be excited about this flight," Schultz noted.

"I think he would, yes," Hess reflected. "Anything that puts these airships to good use. The previous flight of this ship was for military observation too, over Czechoslovakia."

At that moment, Captain Sammt entered the radio room. In a wave, the crowd quietened.

"My colleagues, friends, ladies and gentlemen," Sammt announced, arms in the air, black eyebrows twitching. "We shall momentarily continue our journey north up the English coast. Tomorrow, on our return leg, we will overfly the Bawdsey complex again. Meanwhile, there is plenty to think about, yes?"

***

"Excuse me for being so bold," Karl-Heinz Weiss said to Klara, "but I'm sure I recognise you. You competed for Germany, didn't you? At the Berlin Olympics three years ago, am I right?"

It was shortly after noon on Friday 4 August. After hovering over RAF Bawdsey, Captain Sammt had guided the zeppelin up the Norfolk coast via Yorkshire to County Durham and Northumberland. They followed the trail of masts all the way to the Scottish borders, where it appeared to peter out, then wheeled through 180 degrees and headed south for Essex. Now, as promised, they were approaching Bawdsey for a second time.

In the radio room, Klara was distracted by two equipment operators consulting colleagues, all exchanging concerned glances, looking baffled. They rechecked the receivers, retuned the scanners, swapped their headphones.

"Very strange."

"Not what I expected."

"No signal at all?"

"Only silence."

Behind the operators, scratching their heads and chewing their nails, professors Schneider and Ackermann faced each other. Hanna Lippert, Stefan Vogt, Wolfgang Roth and Bruno Weber looked on.

"I'd say that settles it," said Schneider, pensive and grave.

"Conclusively," Ackermann replied.

Klara curled her blonde tresses behind her ears and watched the professors shake hands. Although they'd sounded decisive, neither man looked contented.

"Let's go to the lounge," Klara said to Weiss.

Lunch service was in full swing. But the atmosphere seemed subdued, quieter than Klara would have expected with every table occupied. They served themselves from the lavish spread – cold meats, sausages, pretzels, potato salad, lashings of sauerkraut – and joined Curt Schultz and Hanna Lippert who had taken two seats at a table for four.

"Hanna was just telling me," Schultz said as Klara and Weiss tucked into their meals, "last year she won the women's championship of the German Chess Federation."

"The final took place in Hamburg, where I live and work, so I had home advantage." In her graceful poise as well as her looks, Hanna reminded Klara of her sister, Katarina, whom she loved to the core of her bones.

"Then we have two esteemed German competitors at our table," Weiss declared, too loudly for Klara's comfort.

"Not really in my case," she said and gave an apologetic glance to Schultz. "Karl-Heinz recognised me."

"You have a keen eye, sir," said Schultz.

"A pilot's eye. Actually, it was the captain who tipped me off," Weiss confessed. "He told me it came to him suddenly an hour ago, having been on the tip of his tongue."

"It's true," Klara said, leaning in to encourage the others at the table to do likewise. "I represented Germany in Berlin three years ago, in the 25-metre rapid-fire pistol contest, the only shooting event for women at those games."

Klara relived the scene as if it were only yesterday. It would stay etched in her mind, in cold, hard stone, forever. A paper target with concentric circles was loaded into a rotating metal frame. It would turn ninety degrees to face her at a distance of twenty-five metres. The moment the firing time elapsed, it would twist back again. Round one. The partisan crowd roared so vehemently that its breath felt like heat on her back. She'd trained hard, knew she was ready. Calmly, she raised her right arm and fired five times with her unsupported hand, her left hand firmly behind her back.

"There was a field of twelve," Klara recalled. "After the first round, we had a second turn with five more shots, then the top six qualified for a final round."

"A shoot-out!" said Weiss with gusto.

Klara took a glug of orange juice, as did Schultz, who knew this story but was sure it was helpful for Klara to retell it, keep it out in the open.

"I made it to the final. So far, so good. You had to fire four shots, each within four seconds. I was in the lead after three shots." Klara stared at the table, avoiding eye contact. "But on my last one, for the gold, the hammer of my gun jammed and I was timed out. That was it. After all the training and practice, I finished fourth, just out of the medals."

The table fell silent as the diners imagined the gut-wrenching blow.

"A Russian girl won the gold," Klara concluded. "I liked her, was happy for her. The crowd hated me congratulating her. But my tears were short-lived. I sought new avenues to prove myself, make a mark."

"Which you've done brilliantly," Schultz added. He knew that Klara had spent some weeks after the Olympics taking long walks in Berlin's Grünewald forest park, tranquil and otherworldly. She achieved distance goals, restored her confidence, healed her head. That forest was part of her now, although she'd once confided that her primary escapes had been reading and sleep because then she didn't have to face the world.

"Berlin '36 was the Jesse Owens Olympics, wasn't it?" asked Hanna to a chorus of "*Ja, ja,*" from Schultz and Weiss. "He was the most successful athlete?"

"Yes – a black American the stand-out winner when the games were meant to symbolise to the world a resurgent Germany."

"Was it four gold medals he won?" Hanna again, thinking aloud.

Klara nodded. "Three in track races, the fourth in the long jump. He set a world record in the 4 x 100 metres sprint relay, you know. Even the Führer was impressed."

"Did you meet him, the Führer?" Weiss looked eager to know.

"Never. He vowed only to shake hands with German medallists and as it turned out, he didn't watch much of the sport. But I saw him once in the stadium. He happened to be there when Jesse Owens was presented with one of his golds. There was a huge roar from the crowd – ninety thousand, honouring his achievement – and the Führer waved to him from the grandstand. That was something, at least."

Schultz saw Weiss raise an eyebrow and hurried to say something. "It was hot and sunny that August in Berlin, wasn't it? Unlike this August here!" He gazed out of the lounge's sloping windows at the largely uninterrupted layer of cloud below.

At that moment, Albert Sammt swept into the lounge at the head of a phalanx including Schneider, Ackermann, Roth and Vogt. Ulrich Freitag brought up the rear. Ackermann perched on the edge of the piano stool, the others held the centre of the room.

"Ladies and gentlemen," Sammt called for order. "I'd like to thank you all for coming on this special flight for Operation Bloodhound. Did you know, this is the longest flight this airship has ever undertaken. When we arrive back home tonight, we'll have covered 2,600 miles."

Cue the applause. Klara had a poor line of sight to Freitag, but he did not appear to be clapping. Rising and falling on the balls of his feet, his sunken eyes darted about the room. Was he…? Yes, she felt sure, he was guarding someone. Who…?

"Let me introduce you now," Sammt was saying, "to the president of the University of Göttingen, Professor Doktor Lukas Osterhagen."

Some of the scientists looked impressed, applauded lustily. It occurred to Klara that they may not have known he was on the ship. He'd been included in General Martini's dossier, but this was the first time she'd laid eyes on him.

Osterhagen was short, not much over five feet, and portly. His complexion was so pale that he looked spectral, not quite human flesh and blood. Now in his mid-fifties, he was known to have been a German Nationalist since his teens. As the dossier recounted, he had established himself as the nation's pre-eminent physicist with an enviable sheaf of peer-reviewed research papers to his name.

He was standing towards the rear of the phalanx with Freitag as bodyguard, towering over him. The group parted to let him step forward. When he spoke, his voice was deep, soft, reassuring. It did not appear to match the body whence it came, but in his spare time Osterhagen was a gifted amateur operatic bass.

"I, too, thank you all for sharing your prodigious wisdom in such a fulsome way."

Klara was sure he already had the audience on side but wanted to flatter them anyway. This man was a seasoned performer.

"A consensus has been reached," Osterhagen declared to a murmur of approval. My most sincere congratulations to you all!" Smiles spread among his audience. "Yesterday, on our flight north, we detected static noise, crackling, whistling at the heart of our area of interest, Bawdsey, on the British coast. Today, on our second pass, there was nothing at all. What are we to make of this?"

Osterhagen looked about the lounge. All eyes were on him. He held the pause until they were desperate for more.

"Naturally, opinions varied," Osterhagen continued. "Who would expect anything else from such an expert gathering?" Self-conscious laughter. "But if we compare what we have heard to the emissions from German radio systems, used by the Wehrmacht and in other walks of life, well, there simply *is* no comparison. As you know, the equipment on this ship has scanned a spectrum of frequencies used in countries with radio technology. Apart from the static noise, ladies and gentlemen, we have literally drawn a blank."

"*Bravo! Stimmt!*" Hear! Hear! Voices in unison, volume rising.

"Therefore, these ugly masts are most likely part of the British national grid. It was sparking a bit on our first pass, yes? Heaven knows, if they truly expect to fight the new Germany, they will need all the power they can get!"

Laughter, applause, everyone belonging, no one left out. What a thrill to be on Professor Osterhagen's side, endorsing his vision, nothing but good can come of this.

"In conclusion, my cherished colleagues, there is no hazard here, no offensive weapon to threaten us. Nothing to disorder the inexorable progress of the Fatherland. Today, as I have noted, the masts were not even in use, not working. What sort of a scheme is that? I shall tell you. A worthless one, a contemptible one, a dead one!"

Loud cheers. Oh, the camaraderie, the shared relief. What a moment!

"Therefore…"

Another pause for effect. Pin-drop silence.

"We can be sure that the British do *not*, after all, have an early warning system, and this will be my report to Herr Göring."

The cheers were rapturous, unrestrained. No one wanted it to stop, or to be seen not taking part. They beamed at the star presenter who stood centre stage, shaking hands with those closest. Freitag looked smug.

Quietly, Klara draw Hanna Lippert aside.

"Well?"

Hanna opened her palms. She'd found Klara to be both interested and interesting, excellent company. "I'd say he was speaking for the majority. There's a handful, maybe more, who believe it could be a radio network, albeit not a very sophisticated one."

"They were shouted down?"

"Outmanoeuvred in the desire – no, the imperative – for a unified report on Operation Bloodhound. In a world without certainty, there was a need for certainty here."

"Nothing showed up on the scanners, just low-level buzzing," Klara pointed out. "Apparently."

"Nothing on the wavelengths we scanned – the very high and ultra-high ranges used in radio systems around the world. Although there are other bands in the spectrum, which the British may have chosen."

"And if they *are* some sort of radio mast?"

"On the available evidence, they probably aren't."

"But if they are?"

"Then the British have a head start. They will know what Luftwaffe aircraft are approaching their shores before they arrive. Our attacks will have zero element of surprise."

Klara mulled this briefly, then chatted to Hanna about her life beyond the classroom and chess board. It turned out, to her surprise, that they shared a passion for motorcycles. Hanna rode a Zündapp K600, a beautifully designed, powerful machine.

For her part, Hanna noticed what no one else had, that Klara's eyes carried the pain of past trauma. Not just her Olympic misfortune, something else, something deeper. But after this flight she may never see Klara again and decided not to probe.

Alfred Hess walked up. Behind him, Schultz was deep in conversation with Karl-Heinz Weiss, Bruno Weber and Albert Sammt, apparently concerning the lack of aerial photographs taken on this mission despite the leading-edge cameras on the gondola.

"You know the Führer has never trusted academics, don't you?" Hess said. "Too inclined to think for themselves. Won't swallow any old line the party feeds them."

"In the Führer's mind," Hanna pointed out, "Professor Doktor Osterhagen is an exception."

"It's true that he and the Führer are buddies," Hess conceded. "They have been for years."

Klara smiled thinly. "As a group, they haven't exactly put on their finest show of independence here, have they? I thought this was turning into a rally."

"Did you now? But you heard what the professor said, didn't you?"

This was, unmistakably, Freitag. The harsh sneer, the cold warning. For such a big man, he managed to move like a cat when he wanted to, stealthily yet fast. He was standing beside Klara, blocking her line of sight to Schultz. But the two men had been watching: Sammt and Schultz appeared mercifully quickly.

"Is everything in order here?" Sammt asked.

"Of course," Freitag pounced. "I was about to stress the importance of consistency, that's all. Each of us must take away Professor Osterhagen's message, no deviations. Discipline is essential. Is that clear?"

He glared at the group, daring defiance.

"Quite clear, thank you," said Hanna. Freitag ignored her.

"Hansel and Gretel," he spat out the names. "What about you? We speak with one voice. Do you understand?"

Schultz said nothing. He may have been weighing up his feedback to General Martini.

"Be absolutely sure. You wouldn't want me to hear that any corrections are required."

To Klara, Germany was a proud sporting nation: Max Schmeling, Luz Long and others were masters of their fields, committed to excellence, precision and fair play. Surely these values were eternal, not obsolete?

"I've got the message," she said, looking Freitag in the eye. He plodded away, disdain all over his face, and did not hear Klara add: "Rest assured, my actions after this trip will be perfectly appropriate." She might further have added: "I will not be your victim," but didn't.

"I heard something curious about Herr Freitag yesterday," Hanna said. "It surprised me. Under the skin, apparently, he's something of an Anglophile with a passion for British composers. He's been to concerts at the Queen's Hall in London – Elgar, Vaughan Williams, Britten. Can you believe that?"

The question drifted unanswered while the heady fizz of excitement hung in the air. As Albert Sammt peeled off to chat to a group by the window, it dawned on Klara and Schultz that the supernatural Lukas Osterhagen had vanished.

6

Per Ardua Ad Astra

He exited the Savoy through the revolving doors, enjoying a final flourish when the uniformed doorman, who had known his name for years, waved adieu. Sir Hugh Dowding swept past the Savoy Theatre, presenting Gilbert and Sullivan's comic opera, *The Gondoliers*, and turned right into the Strand.

Monday 7 August, 10.20 a.m. He'd breakfasted in luxury, overlooking the Thames with Robert Watson-Watt and Skip Wilkins. The three of them could have chatted for hours. They shared an immensely strong attention to detail, convinced that it reduced the chance of error, and a belief that knowing the background to any issue was essential to a full understanding of it. With sponges for memories, they neither forgot nor overlooked anything of consequence. They'd discussed not only the step-by-step roll-out of Chain Home, but also the ministry's plans to relocate the boffins in the event of war.

Now he welcomed the interlude to walk off his breakfast, and there was ample time to reach the ministry. Had it been an hour later, Dowding might have seen Winston Churchill march into the Savoy, homburg on his head, for an early lunch. Speculation was rife that he would soon return to front-line politics, perhaps succeeding Earl Stanhope as First Lord of the Admiralty in Neville Chamberlain's cabinet.

Before the Adelphi Theatre, which was hosting a Lorenz Hart musical, Dowding crossed the Strand, a grandiose boulevard humming with buses and cars, and headed north through Covent Garden. Clarice had acted on stage before they married. She'd adored being part of a creative company, enjoyed the camaraderie of actors and never tired of playing the same role in eight shows a week, despite the exhaustion.

He glanced at the faces he passed. It wasn't just the traffic that moved faster in London, people did too. So many men and women going about their daily business. So many jobs, families, loved ones, hopes and dreams.

Through an open window, a 78-r.p.m. disc played a sweet song by Gracie Fields. An elderly couple, each wearing a trilby, flagged down a double decker – white roof, red sides with adverts for handkerchiefs trumpeting 'Coughs and sneezes spread diseases'. Skirting a drinking fountain, they boarded in a pleasingly agile manner.

Even those old enough to possess first-hand knowledge of the 1914–18 war appeared oblivious to the threat of Nazi Germany not just to Britain but all of Europe. And yet Dowding had no doubt that every one of these citizens would grit their teeth and do whatever it took to get through the dark times ahead. What a curious nation this was – polite and reserved, doggedly determined, with a broad sense of humour and an acute sense of fair play to sustain it. May it last forever.

Currently under construction in Whitehall was a neo-classical, stone building with three internal courtyards, designed by Vincent Harris, architect of numerous town halls and libraries. How it would enhance the government offices, Dowding mused. Much delayed, it was to be the shared home of the Air Ministry and the Board of Trade.

For the time being, the Air Ministry remained in its location of the last couple of decades on Kingsway. Nearby, at the Holborn Empire, Max Miller, the 'Cheeky Chappie' music hall star, had taken up residence. Dowding crossed into Kingsway and as soon as a bus had moved off its stop, there it was: Adastral House. Its name, which he found absurdly clunky, came from the RAF's Latin motto, *Per Ardua Ad Astra*. Through adversity to the stars.

"Thank you, Jenkins," he beamed as the heavy door was pulled open from inside by a veteran of the first Ypres campaign who harboured a shrapnel wound in his thigh. Crossing the polished parquet floor of the Edwardian entrance hall, Dowding approached the reception desk.

"Please go straight up, Air Chief Marshal," the duty receptionist, Mollie, said with her customary efficiency. She had joined the staff when Dowding worked in the building.

He took the lift – still too wheezy and teeth-grindingly slow – to the top floor, the ninth, and walked along the familiar corridor to conference room one. The door was ajar. As he entered, Perkins and Trevanion, two of the ministry's most senior civil servants, seated at the long teak table, stood to attention. Dowding found them invariably sharper, better informed, than the ministers they advised.

The room was airy, bright and clean. You'd never think so much blood had been spilled – metaphorically – on this very carpet during his blazing rows with some of the ministry's mandarins. He didn't regret any of them. A means to an end, as he'd once told Watson-Watt. Provided that the end is the one you wanted all along, Watson-Watt had thought to himself with a glint in his eye.

Dowding sat at the table facing Perkins and Trevanion and knitted his fingers together. He must have a good ten years on each of them.

"The minister will join us shortly," Perkins began. He knew better than to try to fill Sir Hugh's time with small talk.

Dowding raised a trimmed eyebrow's worth of interest.

"Now that we're on the brink of war, he wants to discuss your state of readiness and what you think the government's immediate next steps ought to be. The 'peace for our time' promised by the Munich Agreement is about to be shattered into smithereens."

The PM, Neville Chamberlain, had been party to the four-power accord with the Führer, signed in his Munich headquarters last September. The Nazis were to be permitted to occupy Sudetenland, part of Czechoslovakia where millions of residents were of German origin. When France and Britain notified the Czech government that it could either accept the annexation or resist alone, it opted for the former.

Chamberlain also secured from the Führer a declaration that Britain and Germany would aim to resolve their differences through peaceful negotiation. On 30 September, the PM enjoyed a hero's welcome back in London, where he brandished a signed document expressing the desire of the British and German peoples 'never to go to war again'. Crowds at the airport and in Downing Street rejoiced as the threat of war, hanging over Europe for months while the Czech crisis brewed, seemed to have receded. But in March this year, 1939, the Nazis annexed the remainder of Czechoslovakia which they did not already occupy, and war slid ever closer.

"The Führer is hell-bent on aggression, destruction and bloodshed," Dowding commented plaintively. "Brute force must be laid low. So, war there will be. Who was it – George Santayana, I think – who said that only the dead have seen the end of war?"

Dowding understood how eager the British and French governments had been to avoid another clash with Germany. The two countries, which had promised military support to Poland, had reacted with consternation to the news that Hitler and Stalin had signed a German-Soviet non-aggression pact in August 1939. Privately, Dowding wondered how long it would last.

He was adamant that, if the Nazis were counting on the British suing for peace, they were making a grave miscalculation. Tyrants surrounded by yes-men were prone to blinkered errors, which could lead to their downfall. Perkins and Trevanion listened carefully as the ACM offered his opinions. They were familiar with his line of thinking yet hung on his every word.

"And the Nazis may just have made another miscalculation," Dowding informed them. "A huge misinterpretation of evidence which, if I'm right, could tip the scales in favour of RAF pilots in an air battle."

Silence. They were agog.

Trevanion asked: "Are you referring to last week's zeppelin spy mission over Bawdsey?"

"I am."

"MI5 have requested a full debrief."

"I imagined they would. We don't have the luxury of knowing for certain what the Germans made of Chain Home. But we did as much as we could to throw them off the scent. I'm hopeful we achieved that, but we can't exactly hide the masts, can we?"

"Indeed not, sir."

"When war breaks out, we must plan for the worst and assume that Chain Home will be an immediate, high-priority target. If it isn't attacked, the only reasonable deduction is that the Germans *did* misread the signals and did *not* grasp the network's significance. In a nutshell, gentlemen, it's as simple, and as terrifying, as that."

***

Friday 1 September. Linda Hastings zig-zagged the gear lever from top into third and slammed her right foot on the brake. In the passenger seat, her twin sister Gloria scoured the rapidly encroaching darkness for pedestrians who might take their lives into their hands by crossing the road. "Watch out – there!"

Less than a mile back, outside a post office, they'd witnessed a horrible accident. In the gloom, a small van had missed a bend, ploughed straight on and hit an old man. He'd been giving his terrier its early evening walk. The dog had scampered away, dragging its lead, but the owner, a retired shopkeeper, landed flat on his back and didn't move.

The sisters were on their way from Maida Vale back to Bentley Priory. Marcia, their dear mother, had been feeling unwell with a heavy cold – or that's what she'd said it was. But she was never ill and they were worried. Normally, they were not permitted to leave the grounds but, in the circumstances, both had today been granted compassionate leave. They'd intended to stay with mum until Sunday. But an urgent phone call, updating them on the day's events, had scrapped their plans.

At dawn that day, Friday, the Nazis had invaded Poland from the west, the first deployment of Blitzkrieg, cold-blooded and ruthless. Earlier in the week, the *Daily Telegraph* had run photographs of the build-up of tanks on the border. The Polish army was large but thinly spread and ill-equipped to face the might of modern Germany. It would not be alone in such a predicament.

Warsaw, a capital of great enterprise and culture, was surrounded, the garrison destroyed before it even hit its stride. Missiles rained down, followed by a deathly silence that clung to the smoke. While the besieged city burned – a hell on Earth – stunned parents wept for the future of their children, cold, frightened, hungry. No citizen was left unaffected. Would they ever see their homes, their friends and relatives again? If they sought refuge, where would they go? How long would they be away?

Preparations were made to turn Warsaw's Saski Palace, which had housed the general staff of the Polish army, into a new HQ for the Wehrmacht. A couple of weeks after the Nazis invaded, Soviet troops overran Poland from the east. The campaign would end three weeks later when Poland was annexed, its territory partitioned, a generation traumatised. Most ominously, what would be the fate of the three million Polish Jews, now confined to camps?

In Britain, the first official evacuations had been ordered, implementing plans compiled long ago. Under Operation Pied Piper, schools were closed and a huge social experiment launched. Evacuees were principally children and vulnerable adults, uprooted from towns and cities and despatched on trains and buses into the countryside, where they should be safer when the bombs fell. It was portrayed as a mother's duty to sew nametapes into her little one's clothing and then let him or her go.

From today, a blackout was enforced. The main difference from the blackouts of the Great War was that motor cars were now commonplace. And as Linda reflected ruefully as she changed down to second, having just in time spotted the white lines marking a junction, the roads were a dangerous – *lethal* – place to be after dark. No street lights. Traffic lights hooded, directed downwards. Shop signs switched off. All doors and windows covered. Not even lit matches or cigarettes. No headlamps allowed on vehicles, sidelights only, which in the pitch dark were inadequate.

You'd think they'd have reduced the speed limit, wouldn't you, Marcia had croaked from her sickbed while the girls mopped her brow, made hot drinks, brought clean handkerchiefs. Petrol rationing, to no more than two hundred miles of fuel per month, would soon shrink the number of private cars on the roads, and the government urged necessary journeys only, to be taken between 10 a.m. and 4 p.m. Meanwhile, until permitted drivers got used to the blackness, heavy braking and loud cursing were the new norms.

They were in a Hillman Minx Drophead Coupé. Gloria had arranged to borrow a car from the small Bentley Priory pool and was thrilled to have been allocated this one, despite it being the only one available. Dark blue, spacious glovebox, chromium-plated radiator grille that she felt sure would turn heads. Gloria had driven into central London early that morning, roof rolled down. Linda's turn to drive back.

If mum had been up to it, they'd have taken her to the pictures tomorrow, Saturday. Both sisters loved the larger-than-life escapism, the lives you could lead vicariously from the front stalls. For her part, Marcia was plainly delighted that her girls remained such close friends.

Linda and Gloria devoured every issue of *Picturegoer*, newly merged with *Film Weekly*. Clark Gable, Gary Cooper and James Stewart were their favourites, albeit in ever-changing orders of preference. But if an opportunity arose, they'd happily watch any talking picture – a Bette Davis, a Shirley Temple, a home-produced George Formby.

They'd thought their mum would enjoy *The Lady Vanishes* with Michael Redgrave and Margaret Lockwood, playing at the local Plaza. Poster-billed as 'a mystery express with comedy and chills', it had an 'A' certificate so there shouldn't be anything to make mum, or them, cringe in each other's company. It had been shot in nearby Islington Studios, yet they knew from *Picturegoer* that its lugubrious Cockney director, Alfred Hitchcock, was making such a name for himself that he'd soon pack his bags for Hollywood.

On the journey down that morning, the twins had discussed not only *The Lady Vanishes*, in which Mr Hitchcock apparently made a cameo appearance, but also *Goodbye Mr Chips* and *Gone with the Wind*, which were coming soon. They made bets on how far the queues outside the Plaza would stretch: thirty million tickets for the pictures were bought around the country every week.

But the Führer had put paid to the idea of going to the pictures or anywhere else this weekend. Gloria wondered how much longer the picture halls would stay open as she glanced at the centrally mounted speedometer. Linda was doing all of twenty-five m.p.h. Rightly so. It was getting darker by the minute and the rest of this trip, through the outskirts of north London and beyond, would be fraught with peril.

Had they seen it, the Pathé Gazette newsreel at the Plaza that evening squarely apportioned blame for the declaration of war. "The responsibility lies on the shoulders of one man," the voice-over blared. "By his latest act of aggression, Hitler has committed a crime not only against Poland, but against the whole human race."

— 7 —

Loose lips sink ships

Just after eight in the morning, yes, she was sure of it. The face of her wristwatch was tiny, but she felt self-conscious if she stared at it too hard.

The scents of leather, wood and engine oil fused in her nostrils, as they always did when she stepped into his car. After a minute or two the aroma faded: she simply got used to it.

Alana MacPherson felt nervous and excited in a first-day-at-school way. Which is exactly what today was. Monday 4 September – the long-arranged start of her training to be an RDF operator. The week's course was at Bawdsey Manor, her husband's place of work.

The MacPhersons lived in the market town of Woodbridge. It lay seven miles from Ipswich and ten, following the picturesque line of the River Debden, from the manor. The town had buildings dating back to the Tudor era. It was not pleasant to see townspeople hurrying about in tin helmets, but she supposed she'd better get used to it. Like many others, this was a town unsettled, on edge, where the uncertainty itself sapped energy.

After a windmill and a boatmaker's shed, they skirted a cordoned-off field which her husband, Tammy, grunted had been marked out for a military airfield. A team of lads was shovelling sand from a mound at the roadside into hessian sacks. Were those gas masks one of them was hanging over the fence? She detested the things. It was difficult to suck in enough air to breathe through the filter, and the rubbery stench, far worse than that of the car, made her retch. Nevertheless, the prospect of a gas attack was terrifying. Could one really happen here?

Alana wished the car gave a more comfortable ride. It was an Austin 7, the automobile that had reputedly brought the freedom of the open road within reach of the masses. Tammy's was an old 1932 model, but he wouldn't part with it. He loved to tinker under the bonnet and would take sections apart, only to reassemble them. This was, he claimed, the first mass-production vehicle with the clutch on the left, the brake in the middle and the accelerator on the right, a three-pedal layout he predicted would stick. It had a four-cylinder engine and a four-speed gearbox. Were he ever to drive it at Brooklands – a chance would be a fine thing! – it would top eighty. Perhaps he should adjust the lubrication system, just in case. One day, maybe, but not today.

Tammy was sombre. The morning was warm and dry, his face grey. He didn't even mention the football – Blackpool had won again and led the First Division.

The weekend's news was hardly unexpected. For many months, war had loomed. Politicians had postured, armies prepared, ordinary folk felt apprehensive. But now, with war declared, two decades after the last global conflict, he knew their lives were irrevocably changed. The Führer would only be stopped by force; this was a necessary war.

Since the Nazis had invaded Poland on Friday, the frenzy in political and diplomatic circles had not slackened. The British government stood resolutely behind Poland – after what had happened to Czechoslovakia and before that Austria, further Nazi warmongering could not stand – and an ultimatum was issued.

Yesterday, Sunday, at 11.15 a.m., the MacPhersons were among the millions huddled solemnly around their wireless sets when the BBC announcer intoned: "This is London. You will now hear a statement by the Prime Minister."

Mr Chamberlain sounded grave as he read his five-minute address from the Cabinet Room, 10 Downing Street.

Expectation had always weighed heavily upon his shoulders: his father, Joseph, was the self-made, loquacious Mayor of Birmingham who rose to be President of the Board of Trade in Gladstone's government.

"This morning," Chamberlain said into the microphone, "the British Ambassador in Berlin handed the German government a final note stating that, unless we heard from them by eleven o'clock that they were prepared at once to withdraw their troops from Poland, a state of war would exist between us. I have to tell you now that no such undertaking has been received and that consequently this country is at war with Germany."

Hours later, the French government declared war on Germany, its own ultimatum likewise ignored.

The PM's broadcast triggered a blizzard of public service announcements. All places of entertainment – dance halls, sports clubs, theatres, cinemas – were to close immediately as a precautionary measure until, the Home Office stated, 'the scale of the attack is judged'. The public was asked not to crowd together, except in church services and funerals, which could continue.

Air raids may come at any moment. Hand rattles would be the warning sound that poison gas had been used; hand bells the signal that the danger from the gas had passed. The capital's febrile atmosphere was exacerbated by air raid sirens, wailing just minutes after the PM finished his speech. The strident alarms stabbed terror into many hearts, especially those of parents clutching their children. They were a false alarm. Still, it took hours for those affected to relax. *Were the skies safe and clear? Would it be better to wait another ten minutes? Another hour?*

As some had speculated, Winston Churchill was appointed First Lord of the Admiralty – head of the Royal Navy – in Chamberlain's war cabinet. Churchill had vociferously opposed the PM's policy of appeasing the Nazis as 'an unmitigated disaster'; his prediction that war would come regardless had proved to be correct. Chamberlain could only assure the nation that there was nothing more he could have done. And amid fears of a German invasion, the first 150,000 soldiers of the British Expeditionary Force crossed the channel to France.

All too real yesterday, eight hours after war was declared, was the loss of the SS *Athenia*. A British steam liner, she was the first ship in the war to be sunk by a German submarine. She'd set sail from Liverpool for Montreal, carrying 1,103 civilians. Two hundred and fifty miles north-west of Ireland, the young commander of the U-30, Kapitanleutnant Fritz-Julius Lemp, mistook her for an armed cruiser. A torpedo struck the *Athenia*'s port side at 7.30 p.m. during the second sitting of dinner. Within minutes, passengers were queuing at the lifeboat stations. The lifeboats were plugged and launched, then floated for hours awaiting rescue ships. Nineteen crew, mainly from the engine room, and ninety-eight passengers perished, either blown up or drowned.

Alana's grim thoughts were punctured by the sight of three girls in an empty field to her left, taking it in turns to skip over a long rope. They were joyful, carefree, innocent. What on Earth did the future hold for them and their families?

Alana had ensured that she and Tammy ate their Sunday roast together, even if the beef and veg were overdone by the time they sat down. Mine was delicious, love, thank you, and the fruit cocktail will be too.

This morning he'd had very little for breakfast, a cup of tea and a scrap of toast, which wasn't like him. She caught his eye as he swung the wheel into a left turn, passing a postwoman and a horse-drawn milk cart. He managed a thin smile and looked ahead again.

***

Tammy's first intended job of the new week was to redirect the manor's television aerial. The reception was so poor that the walnut-boxed set was barely watchable. Perhaps he could reattach it high up on one of the RDF masts? In the event, the weak signal was irrelevant as the BBC suspended its fledgling television service when war was declared. The UK had barely 20,000 television sets, mainly in the south-east.

Meanwhile, licenses for wireless sets numbered nine million and counting. The government had made plans to close down the BBC: some had argued that broadcasting in wartime was undesirable. But wiser counsel prevailed. The BBC reorganised its output into a Forces Programme and a Home Service, which combined national and regional shows into one. Tammy and many others expected it would become an essential lifeline for people craving news, togetherness, good cheer.

Having dropped Alana off at the manor's entrance, he drove on past the barracks. As married couples tended to live off site, the block was used mainly by singles. Men and women had separate entrances and washrooms, but he'd wondered whether the planned segregation occurred in practice. Late in the evening, the manor's beautiful grounds and bench seats looking out to sea were well populated.

Before reaching the transmitter block, Tammy parked in the shelter he'd constructed near his workshop for the Austin 7. How would the shelter – or any on-site structure – withstand an air attack? He shuddered and went about the work he'd meant to tackle after the aerial.

Alana completed the training course registration process in double-quick time, not least because she knew the women at the sign-in desk. She pinned on her name badge, stepped into a sitting room where all the furniture was pushed back against the walls and poured herself a milky coffee at a white-clothed table.

So far, the trainees were nearly all women, of different ages. Most wore practical uniform slacks rather than skirts. Chatting in groups, they all seemed to know each other. She stood alone for a minute, sipping coffee, until a young woman in a grey suit and white blouse made a beeline for her.

"Oh, I'm so glad I'm not the only person who doesn't know anyone!" she gushed.

All heads turned, the room fell silent. Alana felt her face flush.

"How do you do? I'm Donna Hamilton, from Hackney. As you can see," she giggled, angling her name badge.

Donna's voice was piercingly high-pitched, but mercifully for Alana she moderated the volume. "I finished school a couple of months ago. Been working in my parents' corner shop since then. I'm all they've got. But I still want to do my bit, you know? What about you?"

Alana squinted at her watch and offered to get Donna some tea or coffee, while more participants trickled in. There must be twenty at least. She was rescued by a pair of double doors, which swung open, and they were ushered through. The adjoining room was cavernous, twice the size of the sitting room. There was no sign of it having been originally two rooms knocked into one. Why would anyone need a room this size? How would you heat it in winter?

A horseshoe of trestle tables pointed to a lectern and a blackboard. Every place had a pad and a pencil. In the middle of each table were flasks of water and stacks of paper cups.

"Come along, please, everyone, take a seat!"

The speaker, a tall, slim RAF officer in his fifties, scribbled his name on the blackboard in squeaky chalk: AC Bryan Worthington.

"Good morning and welcome." His voice touched all corners of the room. "I'm Air Commodore Bryan Worthington. Given the events of the weekend, I've come over from Bentley Priory, Fighter Command HQ, to introduce this session. After what seems an eternity of covert rearmament and ghastly rallies, Germany under the fist of Nazi rule has finally shown its hand." He glanced around the sombre, silent table. "I'll be here during your morning break to answer any questions about the declaration of war, what we anticipate next, and so on. One thing I'll say right off the bat…"

He paused as a red-faced latecomer bustled in and took a seat. They all stared at his name badge: Archie Livingstone.

"...Is we would not be surprised if this building and the RDF masts were the targets of an air attack in the coming days. Or even hours. Yes, I thought that might concentrate your minds. So, pay close attention to the emergency drills when you're briefed on them."

Worthington straightened his tie. "Now, this course is strictly confidential. It is also selective in so far as we insist upon special qualities in our RDF operators. It's not a role for everyone. Not all of you will make it through."

Donna Hamilton, sitting opposite Alana, sneezed and blew her nose.

Worthington stood aside. Behind him at the blackboard was a woman in a full-length blue dress. She had wavy, auburn hair that sat comfortably on her shoulders. Jayne Brooks – she chalked up her name – had first impressed Robert Watson-Watt when she worked for him a decade ago at the Radio Research Station. She was dedicated and articulate, a superb communicator, and he was pleased but unsurprised that she had surpassed herself as his RDF training supervisor. The calibre of operators passing the course was consistently excellent.

Having outlined a procedure to transfer to the reinforced basement if the sirens blared, Jayne Brooks moved swiftly on. "In order to provide early warning of an air attack, the Dowding system effectively controls British air space. Here's how."

Everyone around the horseshoe was as transfixed as the participants in previous courses: Jayne made all her lectures sound fresh and sharp. "The system uses a dedicated telephone network to gather information ASAP from our observers and Chain Home stations. It allows us to build a single picture of enemy aircraft formation strengths and likely destinations, and then direct our own aircraft and artillery against them."

Jayne proceeded to explain until satisfied that the participants had grasped the essentials of the Dowding system. As Bawdsey Manor was to be their home throughout the course, except for the handful who lived locally, she had everyone introduce him- or herself to the group before the first coffee break. Mid-afternoon, she invited questions. Unusually, a hand shot straight up.

Evan Finlayson spoke in a melodious voice. "Is there any danger," he began before belatedly filling a cup with water and wetting his lips, "that the radio waves will catch things in their path that aren't aircraft? Trees, perhaps?"

"An excellent question, Mr Finlayson," Jayne said, as if it were the first time it had ever come up. "Can anyone answer?"

If anyone could, they were not inclined to do so.

"Very well." Jayne didn't let the silence become awkward. "It's vital to separate our targets from the natural clutter. The repeated pulses of radio energy, travelling at the speed of light, allow us to detect motion in the air. Stationary objects can be filtered out."

Another hand was up almost before she'd stopped speaking.

"You said that objects can be detected moving towards or away from the masts." This from Juliette Gregg, a WAAF with a flair for organisation. "What about above or below? I mean, is it possible literally to fly under the beams?"

"In theory, yes. But don't forget, the receiver masts are lower than the transmitters. Incoming aircraft, over the English Channel or the North Sea, are unlikely to be so low that we miss them altogether. For the last few months, we've been in 24-hour watch mode."

Alana MacPherson asked: "Can the system be sure that it's tracking Nazi planes about to attack and not RAF planes returning home?"

Jayne Brooks smiled. "It's crucial, isn't it, to have a way of distinguishing friendly aircraft from hostiles. Happily, we do."

She paused while Betty from catering wheeled in some fresh water and loaded the empty flasks on to her trolley.

"It's called IFF – Identification Friend or Foe." Jayne gave the group a few seconds to write this down. "And I'm proud to say it was developed right here at Bawdsey. Our own aircraft are fitted with miniature, motorised transponders. They distort the reflected signals, so when they're viewed as blips on our screens, the oscillations of friendly aircraft differ greatly from those we're really tracking." Jayne mimed with her hands. "In the trials, it worked very well."

A few more questions came up. This is a good group, Jayne thought – attentive, eager, homing in on the key issues with which the boffins had wrestled during the frantic years of R&D.

The final question of the session was put by Celia Robson, another WAAF. "The boffins are clearly brilliant," she said to nods of accord around the horseshoe. "What's next? Is there more progress to be made with the RDF system or have they moved on to other projects, different technologies?"

"The short answer is both. But I'm afraid future workstreams are classified, as you might expect. Much of what's in development here – well, I'm not even aware of it, let alone briefed on it. But I can promise you, the teams remain as busy as ever. No one is resting on their laurels."

After the course, on Friday afternoon, 8 September, Celia Robson and Alana MacPherson pushed two tables together in The Smugglers' Cave, Felixstowe. They arranged six chairs around the double-sized table and sat facing one other.

Celia had made friends with Alana during the intense week of training. She was from Maidstone, where her father and fiancé both worked as gardeners at Leeds Castle. The wedding reception was booked there next May. Both women's hair, correctly pinned above the collar throughout the day, was now brushed long and loose.

"He's in his element, isn't he?" Celia grinned, nodding discretely to her left, where Archie Livingstone was ordering drinks at the bar. In fact, Archie was in a friendly conversation with the barmaid, who was new to her job and seemed to be enjoying the extra tuition.

The National Services (Armed Forces) Act, passed by parliament last Sunday, the day war was declared, required men aged 18–41 to register for service. Bar counters were increasingly staffed by women, one of many roles they were stepping into.

"Ah, there they are!"

Donna Hamilton's voice pierced the room like a whistle blast. She had arrived with Susannah Innes and Juliette Gregg. The three of them joined Alana and Celia at the table, Susannah having placed their drinks order with Archie. The air was smoky and she coughed deeply as she sat down.

Alana had seen and heard very little of Susannah during the week. She wore horn-rimmed spectacles and had a mole on her right cheek. She was one of only two participants who did not pass the course. They'd been given a test paper and a practical exercise – reading a cathode ray tube screen full of blips – on Thursday afternoon, and Jayne Brooks had notified them of their grades on Friday morning.

Archie brought a tray of drinks and sat down by Susannah.

"You seem to have made a good friend at the bar," Celia teased him. "I can always turn mine into a double wedding if you like."

"Very droll," said Archie, not laughing. Thankfully the barmaid had moved out of earshot.

He was the other person to fail the course but hoped to enrol again on the next edition. There was probably a small quota who had to fail every time – that was baked into the process, wasn't it? Surely it was an irritating technicality, not a real setback?

"Well, here's to us!" Celia called a toast. "Good luck, everyone!"

"Chin, chin!"

"Lovely to meet you all!"

"What a week – best of luck!"

Within minutes, Archie was back at the bar, ordering a second round. An ARP warden interrupted his renewed conversation with the barmaid, who pointed him to the landlord. Not long afterwards the warden was pinning notices – so freshly printed that Archie could smell the ink – on the noticeboards. If an air raid siren sounds, they stated, either leave immediately and take shelter, or remain at your own risk.

Archie didn't think for long: with beer still just thruppence a pint, he'd stay, thank you very much.

"It's so nice that we've been able to celebrate – and commiserate – like this," Donna was saying, her voice hitting the entire lounge. "It's so important to banish all the doom and gloom, continue living our lives, isn't it?"

They clinked glasses again. Alana knew Tammy would not be feeling the same optimism. Regardless, the group was soon chatting merrily, discussing aspects of their lives like old friends.

Archie nudged Susannah and they peeled off for the dart board beside the fireplace. He was surprised to lose the first game in less than ten minutes. Susannah scored double sixteen to finish at the first attempt.

"Best of three!"

He ordered their third round of drinks.

"Your turn to throw first." Susannah took a swig of wine, cold and dry, savouring the complex taste. Her expression had crystallised into – what was it? – anger, resentment, abandon?

"Archie," she said, watching him aim at double top.

He focused hard, scored single five.

"Do you remember on our first day, when Myrna Loy said the boffins were working on new developments in radio technology. What was she was referring to, did you pick up any inkling?"

Archie sniggered. He was beginning to feel warm and mellow, the alcohol burning the edges off his senses. Before he could compose himself, a shrill voice sliced through the cosy fug.

"Susannah, please!" Donna Hamilton was on her feet. "You know we can't discuss the course like that! What are you thinking? Careless talk costs lives!"

Alana wished the floor would open up and swallow her. Even the landlord, who was accustomed to people temporarily based at RAF Bawdsey letting off steam, stopped pulling a pint and stared. After what seemed an eternity, but was only a few seconds, the hubbub was restored. Laughter, jangling coins, clinking glasses, good-humoured chatter. Archie concentrated on his darts but was disappointed by his opening score of twenty-six.

No one noticed him, but seated at the back of the lounge, partly obscured by the bar counter, was a man with thinning hair, wearing a black suit and a light grey pullover concealing his braces. He was alone, sipping a frothy pint, a copy of the *Daily Telegraph* held in front of his face. He kept very still, did not turn a page for several minutes, even breathed inaudibly. But he was tuned in to every word, and he understood the value of the exchange he'd overheard between the woman called Susannah and the man now throwing darts. If he'd had any doubts, the strident intervention by one of the women at the table confirmed its significance.

An hour later, the afternoon sunshine still warm, Alana bid farewell to her five colleagues. By this time, the man with the *Telegraph* had slipped out of The Smugglers' Cave and made a call from the telephone kiosk forty yards down the road.

8

The Odyssey

"Don't mention it," he muttered bitterly and tip-tapped his way down Chapman Street, pulling up his collar against the autumn chill.

The woman, who had dropped her gas mask, marched straight on, head down, in the opposite direction without thanking him for picking it up. He'd hooked it on the end of his walking stick, flicked it into the air and caught it in his left hand. If she'd seen his neat trick, it hadn't impressed her, but it was the lack of common courtesy that rankled.

He'd always been an outsider. Never quite fitted in or belonged. What was it about him that kept people on their guard?

One thing he knew for certain: he'd had an unusual career path. Just the way things had worked out, rolling with the punches. From school, he followed his father into shipbuilding, a mainstay of Tyneside life. His father spent his entire career as a welder at Stannard's – the Stannard Green Shipbuilding & Iron Company. His grandfather was a tugboatman, and he was sure that *his* father was a fisherman. The family had relied on boats of one form or another for its livelihood for generations.

He'd shown up for work with his father on that first day. No interview. He was simply taken on as an apprentice shipwright. Go to yonder tool-shed, speak to the riveters, good luck. He soon learned respect for the many trades – they never missed a deadline at Stannard's – and he wasn't shy of hard graft.

His relationship with his father fluctuated but seldom reached cordial. The old man drank too much by far, and fists would fly all too often when he made it home, just five minutes from the shipyard. When his mother died of tuberculosis, his father swallowed more beer than ever to numb the pain of loss. He stayed out later, and they never had a conversation about their common grief or what she'd meant to them.

Throughout his apprenticeship, Stannard's and the other yards had full order books, mainly with tankers and colliers which transported coal to London and back within five days. He'd never forget the clanking din of the busy yard, nor the awesome sight of the overhead gantries and trolley cranes. An iron landscape of tremendous man-made machines, against which the men themselves were tiny worker ants.

He was fitting out the bridge of a new tanker when the life-changing freak accident occurred. One of the four chains attaching a girder to a hook on a crane snapped in mid-air and the girder dropped. He was standing in the wrong place at the wrong time. His tibia and fibula were smashed – he'd never known agony like it, before or since. Unfortunately, the tibia, the larger of the two bones, did not set properly, and his limp remained a daily reminder of the episode.

His father did not visit him in hospital, but he read voraciously, as though his life depended on it. He devoured Agatha Christie's *Murder on the Orient Express* twice, the second time recognising more clues and tasting its under-lying brilliance.

A first novel by George Orwell, *Burmese Days*, showed public attitudes souring to British colonial rule, portrayed as inhuman and corrupt.

From Aldous Huxley's tale of a capitalist dystopia – chilling it was, too – *Brave New World*, the idea that 'words go through everything… you read and you're pierced' kept whirling in his head. Storytelling was amazingly powerful: it could change how people thought, felt, acted. He gleaned that being an outsider, however unpleasant, was nothing new, and that rules were there to be bent, provided you knew how to get away with it.

On his discharge, he was unable to return to frontline shipbuilding. Stannard's shuffled him into an office role, arranging the weekly pay packets. When his line manager retired, he was given more responsibility and began to warm to his administrative duties.

But Stannards' order book was running dry. Some colleagues blamed the Wall Street Crash, which the year before had wrecked the American economy and, with it, many ordinary people's lives. In Britain, winter 1931 was the most wretched season with a quarter of the workforce – three million people – unemployed.

It was Aunt Carol, his father's younger sister who had also felt the palm of his hand, who threw him a lifeline. Not just a lifeline, a whole new livelihood, six years ago, in 1933. He jumped at it, but his father severed all contact. There was no conversation, just an understanding that they were now leading separate lives, and neither of them made any diplomatic move towards reconciliation.

Aunt Carol and Uncle Charles, a.k.a. Mr and Mrs Rycroft, ran a picture hall, the Odyssey, in Chapman Street in the west end of Newcastle upon Tyne. Although there were two dozen other cinemas in the city, including one in the very next street, the locals could not get their fill of the silver screen. Some came to every main feature, at least once, choosing the same seat each time.

Uncle Charles was an entrepreneurial fruit merchant. In 1929, he formed a new company with a capital of £15,000 in £1 shares. The following year, the Odyssey was opened by the city's Lord Mayor. Originally a variety theatre, the building was shelled out and refurbished from top to bottom. It now had 1,265 seats, a comfortable circle lounge upstairs, and a free car park. It also sported a cutting-edge Western Electric sound system. The usherettes loved wearing their blue skirts and blouses as they felt like air hostesses. The more so, perhaps, when they were standing near the splendidly realistic palm trees in the majestic, red-carpet foyer.

The Odyssey's staff – usherettes, projectionists, lamp boys, cleaners and sellers of tickets, magazines, cloakroom space and all manner of refreshments – had welcomed the new office manager cordially enough, not least because he was related to the owners. But he was always the outlander, introverted, not a theatrical person at all, a shipbuilder, a fish out of water.

While he checked the advertisements for the Odyssey in the *Evening Chronicle*, he followed the mostly grim news of the shipbuilding industry. Palmers' yard in Jarrow had closed in 1933, making thousands jobless and penniless.

Monday morning, 5 October 1936. With Charles Rycroft's permission, he'd gone bright and early to see the men start their Jarrow March. Some of his former Stannard's colleagues would be taking part. Eight months ago, Stannard's had gone to part-time working – shipyard, blast furnaces, engine works, the lot. Sure enough, he'd seen a group of Stannard's men, but they shunned him. As soon as the going got tough, he'd jumped ship, looked after number one. Well, they didn't need him then, and they didn't need him now.

Two hundred black-suited pilgrims set off earnestly that day, their flat caps shielding them from the wind and rain. They carried placards and banners and, in an oak casket, a petition of 12,000 signatures. What they sought from the government was capital investment, so that industry and jobs could return to Jarrow. They were delighted with the support, sympathy and hot food they received on the long march south. It took until the end of the month to reach London, only for Stanley Baldwin's government to reject any intervention at all.

And yet only the most insensitive soul could fail to read the shift in public attitudes, in favour of greater investment in welfare. Winston Churchill, for one, noted the prevailing mood. As it happened, with war looming, the shipyards that remained were soon inundated with orders for warships. Rearmament was under way.

He reached the Odyssey and hobbled, eyes watering in the wind, down a side alley to the staff entrance. The two-by-four lift was waiting for him, cage doors open.

On the top floor: a suite of offices. Next to them, the projection room housed two Cinemeccanica machines through which the large reels of 35mm celluloid unspooled at a rate of twenty-four frames per second. Usually, five or six reels made up a feature-length film. The images cast on the screen, which was supplied by Andrew Harkness of Borehamwood, gave the most magical illusion of movement, suffused with glorious colours and synchronised sound. There had never been an immersive experience like it and they advertised the venue as 'The Wonder Screen of the North'.

"Good morning, Mr Jarvis."

Lorraine Dawson, a member of the technical team, put her head round his office door. He'd noticed recently that she was wearing an engagement ring, but neither of them had mentioned it, and it felt as though the moment had passed.

He looked up from his desk, where he'd flipped over his daily calendar: Friday 22 September.

"I'm making a cuppa for Gordon," said Lorraine, referring to her boss, the Odyssey's fearsome chief projectionist. "Can I get one for you?"

A rare show of kindness. No doubt the good mood in the office was occasioned by the reopening of the cinema today for the first time since the declaration of war.

"Thank you. Milk, no sugar in mine." Immediately he wished he'd injected more gratitude into his reply. He smiled but she'd already gone.

She really knew nothing about Harry Jarvis, Lorraine thought while the kettle boiled in the staff kitchenette. Which was odd as he'd been at the Odyssey longer than she had, and she'd worked there for more than three years. He seemed introspective, disillusioned, not much interested in his colleagues. He must be teetering on the brink of forty, but he never spoke of a family or friends. He never talked of anything very much. There was a sadness, a coldness in his eyes, they'd all seen it, it never seemed to leave him. But he must be doing a decent job... She wondered what he *thought* about all day long, what went through his head. She'd heard lurid suspicions voiced among her colleagues in projection, but really, did they have any evidence? Were they just being spiteful?

Harry Jarvis was cross-checking the schedule of films to be shown at the Odyssey against the list of 35mm prints that had been delivered. Yes, all received. He double-checked the running times against the mandatory closure time of 10 p.m. Films were presented continuously with no separate performance times, so customers could come and go as they pleased.

The Odyssey had not opened since Monday, 4 September. They'd all feared a long period of enforced closure under Home Office orders. But the backlash began the moment the screens went dark. A letter from George Bernard Shaw, published in the *Times* on Tuesday 5 September, called the shutdown 'a masterstroke of unimaginative stupidity'.

When the orders were relaxed, Harry knew that cinemagoing would be the country's greatest escape. He was not surprised that the government had identified picture halls as a channel to instruct as well as entertain the masses, especially young workers who were hard to reach via advertising in newspapers.

No children's films were scheduled among the forthcoming attractions. The Odyssey had a joyous track record of packed-out Saturday morning shows of short films, cowboy adventures and animations, punctuated by sing-a-longs or turns on stage. Admittedly, they often had to rope in the cleaners to help keep order. But with children being evacuated and many schools closed, that opportunity was fading. What other groups could he think of whom the Odyssey might entice?

As Lorraine put a steaming mug of tea on his desk, his telephone rang. Edith on the switchboard connected an outside caller.

"Thank you," he grunted. "Hello?"

Lorraine pulled his door closed and took her tray to the projection room. She was still not used to wearing her engagement ring, delighted as she was with it, and became particularly aware of it with her fingers bunched together, holding the tray. She couldn't yet contemplate making a wedding dress for herself, but her older brother Donald, an RAF pilot, had promised her a white silk parachute which she intended to tailor into shape.

"That is Mr Harry Jarvis?" asked the clipped male voice in Harry's ear. Was it the line or was there a slight accent? Harry's pulse quickened.

"Speaking. What can I do for you?"

"I am calling from Department G, you may have heard of us. We would like to make occasional use of your picture hall for the private meetings of a film society. Do you understand? What do you think of this?"

Harry had been expecting the call. It had come sooner than anticipated.

"I'll be pleased to take that forward with you. We should meet to discuss the details."

"I look forward to meeting you, Mr Jarvis. My name is Ulrich Freitag."

***

Linda Hastings replaced the handset of the payphone in RAF Bentley Priory's entrance hall. She and Gloria, who had stayed close by, listening to the conversation, stepped outside for some fresh air. They saluted an officer who passed them in the doorway. There was still enough light in the sky for a short stroll before black-out.

"I think mum is right to make plans for Christmas," Gloria said cheerfully. "How did she sound?"

"Back to her good old self. Must have been a nasty bug she picked up at work."

"We've just got to make the most of all being together," Gloria went on. "Heaven knows what Christmas next year will be like."

Many young evacuees would stay separated from their parents this December. Luxury goods would be hard to find, even basic foodstuffs were becoming scarce. Women were encouraged to wear flat shoes, conserving wood, and to buy light- or self-coloured clothing to save dye for military uniforms. Furthermore, the twins knew that the Ministry of

Food was honing its plans for rationing, to start in the New Year. Every man, woman and child would receive a ration book with coupons for butter, sugar, bacon... They had already been printed. Before long, most things would be on the ration.

"You know, depending on how much time off we get at Christmas, I'd wondered about volunteering at St. Martin-in-the-Fields," Linda announced. "They're setting up a canteen in the crypt. They'll be looking for people to make or serve food, maybe put up decorations. What do you reckon?"

"You go, I go," said Gloria happily. "It'll be lovely to see Aunt Alana, too. It's been ages and I'm determined to beat her at charades this year."

The twins' Aunt Alana was the beloved younger sister – seven years younger, to be precise – of their mother, Marcia. Aunt Alana lived near Ipswich, but Uncle Tammy was always happy to drive. The twins liked to borrow his Austin 7, having both learned to drive in it.

When it came, Christmas Day 1939 yielded a spree of special programmes on the BBC Home Service. A centrepiece was a reassuring, nine-minute speech by the king, George VI. It was so popular that it embedded these annual royal broadcasts, initiated in 1932 by George V, in the nation's hearts and minds.

"The festival which we know as Christmas," he began, "is..." a little stutter, but his mass audience respected him, wanted to hear him "... above all a festival of peace and of the home. Among all free peoples, the love of peace is profound, for this alone gives security to the home. But true peace is in the hearts of men, and it is the tragedy of this time that there are powerful countries whose whole direction and policy are based on aggression and the suppression of all that we hold dear for mankind."

This was also the speech that cemented the conviction that the war was entirely just, fought against a wickedness that, come what may, had to be defeated.

Thus far, the war had been 'phoney'. The expected air attacks had not materialised, much to the relief of Sir Hugh Dowding and Robert Watson-Watt. The Nazi propaganda machine claimed that the British aircraft carrier, HMS *Ark Royal,* sank when the Luftwaffe swooped on the naval base at Scapa Flow, Orkney. Panic convulsed those in Bentley Priory until it was established that the claims were, thank God, pure hokum.

"Come on," Linda said, clutching her sister's arm. "Let's go back. It's getting chilly and *ITMA*'s on soon."

It's That Man Again was a Home Service sketch show, bristling with topical jokes. The central character was played by one of their favourites, Tommy Handley, whose cast of comedians included Hattie Jacques and Deryck Guyler.

Arm in arm, Linda and Gloria re-entered the priory, mimicking in unison *ITMA*'s recurring catchphrases: "I don't mind if I do... Ta ta for now!"

PART 2

WINTER/ SPRING 1940

9

Rendezvous of the spymasters

Linda and Gloria Hastings appreciated something of the high-level intrigue and stressful planning that had percolated for many months on the British side of the war, and they envisaged similar machinations in Germany. But they'd have been held spellbound by a particular event in Hamburg, of which only a few people were ever aware, soon after *Neujahr* 1940.

It began unostentatiously.

Squatting down, a frail man stroked the backs of the two neatly trimmed, white poodles. The contact seemed to rejuvenate him, stave off the cruel inevitability of old age. He like dogs, missed not having one of his own.

"Come on, leave the gentleman alone!"

The slender lady walking the poodles saw that they were fascinated by a scent on the man's hands. Dragging them away, she missed the little smile that the man permitted himself.

Minutes earlier, he had emerged from the S-Bahn, Hamburg's electrified railway. Built three decades ago, it still looked clean and new. During the seven-stop ride from his hotel, he'd sat opposite a blind veteran of the 1914–18 war, who had a beautiful guide dog, a golden Labrador, and he'd not been able to resist petting her while she panted.

He went on his way, shuffling past the ancient trees that lined the Outer Alster. This was one of two vast lakes in the centre of the city. He imagined, in the summer months, hordes of local families, couples, parties, out boating, canoeing, rowing. Paddling, perhaps. Today, with a dash of winter sleet in the air, it was not busy. Wrapped up warm, he kept his hands in his pockets.

Soon he recognised his destination. A grand villa overlooking the lake, it had once belonged to one of the elite ruling families of the Hanseatic cities of Bremen, Lübeck and Hamburg. They regarded themselves as a cut above other European nobility. But modern-day Hamburg was a thriving industrial port. After Berlin, it was Germany's largest conurbation.

A silver plaque engraved *Hotel an der Nordsee* was the only sign of the villa's current use. It had five opulent suites, each with round-the-clock valet service, and four conference rooms with one-way glass in the windows that no one could see through.

In he shambled. Miraculously standing taller now, he passed a row of telephone cabins and a security guard at the base of a luxuriant Christmas tree, and presented himself at reception. His name was Schäfer – they could barely hear his voice – and he was here to meet Herr Zimmermann.

Ah, yes. Welcome to *Hotel an der Nordsee*, we've been expecting you, sir. We trust you will be most comfortable here. Gunther, our longest-serving pageboy, will escort you to the conference room.

"My dear friend, how are you? Happy New Year!"

As soon as Gunther had pocketed his tip and closed the door behind him, the newly arrived guest flung his arms wide apart. He had no idea, alas, that Gunther was a Gestapo informant who recognised him from photographs with well-concealed amazement, and that he remained outside the room for several minutes before stepping into one of the telephone cabins. His job may be menial, most guests not paying him any attention, but capitalising on this golden opportunity would nudge his name a rung or two further up the ladder.

The guest's real name was not Schäfer. It was Canaris. He was Admiral Wilhelm Canaris, chief of the Abwehr, Germany's secret intelligence service.

His host was not Herr Zimmermann, although that was the name in which the room had been booked. His real name was

Herbert Wichmann. Each military district of Germany had its own branch of the Abwehr, responsible for local espionage, sabotage and counterintelligence. The largest regional station – *Abwehrstelle* or Ast for short – was located here in Hamburg and Wichmann was in charge.

"Happy New Year to you, too!"

Having embraced, the comrades helped themselves to coffee from a side table. There were pastries, which they left alone. The walls were pure white. On a recessed shelf stood a polished bronze sculpture of two idealised human bodies embracing. Looted from a discerning Jewish owner, Canaris suspected. The only other decoration was a framed horizontal flag with a red background and a central white circle containing a black swastika. The appropriated symbol of the hypothetical Aryan race.

It was Thursday 4 January. The two friends had not met in person since the Blitzkrieg campaign that had overwhelmed Warsaw four months ago, although they maintained frequent contact by other means. They shared a background in the navy and Canaris knew that, after a successful invasion of Britain, Wichmann was due to be appointed head of a new Abwehr branch in London.

They sat at the highly polished table. Canaris set down his coffee cup, crossed his legs.

"So, Göring is to be promoted," he lamented. "To Field Marshal."

"You know he's finally getting his way with the zeppelins?" In the air, Wichmann slashed a forefinger across his throat.

"I'd heard."

That spring, on Göring's orders, both the LZ130 *Graf Zeppelin* and the incomplete frame of the LZ131, a third Hindenburg-class airship, would be dismantled. The end of an era in which zeppelins ruled the skies, the mountain of scrap carted off for new warplanes.

Wichmann watched his friend while they sipped their coffee. Canaris, much as he liked him, had always been something of an enigma. He'd helped to prepare the expansion plans for the Third Reich, and yet in 1938 he tried to persuade the Führer not to invade Czechoslovakia. He professed his loyalty, yet he found the growing number of reports from Abwehr officers of massacres by the SS and Gestapo to be so disturbing that he channelled intelligence on the atrocities to the Vatican via the Catholic Resistance in Berlin. Wichmann knew him to be erudite, yet that morning he appeared brittle. He was unshaven, unkempt, presumably part of his cover: the grey stubble aged him beyond his early fifties.

Wichmann himself cut an impeccable figure. Pressed dark suit with striped tie, short dark hair slicked back, small eyes that were deep pools of liquid. But he, too, at heart, despised what the Nazis stood for, their tactics, the lasting harm they would inflict on his beloved Germany.

The last time he and Canaris had met, they'd discussed reports from agents in Sudetenland and other parts of Czechoslovakia, predicting ultimate disaster for the Fatherland. A cadre of spies was coalescing around Canaris with the aim of preventing Nazi invasions of other countries, warding off what they perceived as a global conflict which could only further damage their country. Heaven help them if the Führer got wind of their exchanges.

"How are your United States operations proceeding?" Wichmann asked. "To your satisfaction, I hope?"

"So, so." Canaris inclined a hand this way and that. "We have agents working in most of America's armaments manufacturers. They did well to get through the recruitment stages, yes? We will arrange for one or two to be exposed soon, which will enable us to open a dialogue with the US government about the extent of our infiltration."

"And about tactics to counter the Nazi regime both before and after the Americans enter the war?"

"*Genau*. Exactly. We must keep a focus on the longer term."

"What will the Americans do to the infiltrators they identify? Execute them?"

A beat. "We will try our utmost to prevent that," Canaris replied with a shrug of such callous indifference that it sent a chill down Wichmann's spine. He had rarely seen Canaris's hardest edge surface, and did not regard him as a fanatic, yet moments like this reminded him that it was always there. "They knew the risks. Nothing was assumed or left to their imaginations."

Which would be cold comfort to the agents sacrificed, Wichmann reflected. Had his friend made his living from fabrication and falsehoods for so long that his soul was going rotten? He steered the conversation towards the topic he knew Canaris had wanted privately, out of their offices, to discuss.

"The plans for further invasions by the Wehrmacht in the continent of Europe," he said carefully. "How do you read those?"

Canaris made a steeple out of his hands, rested his chin on his fingertips. "Our army numbers one and a half million men," he replied, thinking aloud. "Ninety-eight divisions, well trained, well armed. I'd say the war machine is in excellent shape."

"It is," Wichmann agreed, "but the nations we attack will not trust a word we say, not after Czechoslovakia and Poland. They mightn't be as heavily armed as we are, but they'll fight like tigers."

"According to the planning directives, Scandinavia will be next. Norway tried to stay neutral, but such were the tensions in Europe that it had to rebuild its army. The investment was too little, too late. In two or three months from now, our warships and paratroopers will occupy Oslo and Copenhagen, I'm sure of it. That curious Norwegian fascist, Quisling, is supporting the Führer from the sidelines, but he won't get much recognition from us. He'd sell his own mother if he thought it would do him a smidgen of good."

"For the Führer, taking Norway makes good sense," Wichmann maintained. "The North Atlantic fjords will make ideal submarine bases."

"It's the iron ore, the coal supplies, that will be most valuable," Canaris pointed out. "And then, after Scandinavia,

France and the low countries. We will have overwhelming air superiority, and the intelligence indicates that their weaponry is outmoded. None of them has rearmed as Germany has." He separated his palms and topped up the coffee cups.

"Let's say everything goes to plan, as I'm sure it will." Wichmann swallowed a mouthful of coffee. "After these victories, my friend, comes Great Britain?"

"It must follow the fall of France, as night follows day. The British declared war at the same time and, as you say, any diplomatic moves we make for peace will lack credibility. There are still those in Berlin who believe the British government will never let it come to war, that there will be a last-minute truce. I confess I'm not one of them."

"Our intelligence capability in Britain is still below par?"

"We have fewer agents there than in France, Belgium, Holland and elsewhere," Canaris confirmed. The longer the conversation went on, the younger he sounded. "Our British network must be expanded – fast. We need more detailed local knowledge and connections, a fuller understanding of their preparedness."

"How long would you say we have?"

"A few months, no more."

"The German High Command, when they approve the landing operation against Britain, will they also approve an intelligence-gathering mission before we land on their shores?"

"I am counting on it," Canaris said, delighted that Wichmann was thinking along the same lines. "But as we know only too well, the German intelligence system is a multi-headed monster. It is so hungry, it likes to eat itself. Himmler, Heydrich, Göring, any of them would slit my throat in the blink of an eye."

"Mine too, my friend." Wichmann examined the dregs in his cup.

"I can't be certain," Canaris continued, "but I suspect Göring has tried to steal a march on the Abwehr by sending his own people into Britain already. We will hear, at best, an edited version of their activities."

"That's intolerable. So, what do you recommend?"

"We must play a dual game." Was there any other kind in Canaris's armoury? "On the one hand, we must support an official reconnaissance operation in Britain, when the High Command approves it. Given its importance, I will do my utmost to have it placed under the control of the biggest regional bureau in the Abwehr. I trust the head of that bureau will be willing to accept the extra responsibility?"

"Thank you. I shall." Wichmann's head bowed in compliance.

"On the other hand, it's essential that this operation does *not* succeed," Canaris emphasised, looking his friend in the eye. "Of course, no failure will lead to our door. As in the US, the problems that befall the agents, leading to their exposure and arrest in Britain, must be choreographed meticulously. But through – what shall we say? – an unconnected series of missteps, no good intelligence will reach the other agencies in Berlin. They will be as confused as we shall be delighted."

"And meanwhile...?" Wichmann paused as footsteps – Gunther again – were just audible outside the door, then silence.

"There must be an *unofficial* operation, before the official reconnaissance begins. The Abwehr will initiate its own intelligence-gathering mission to discover what is really happening in Britain, reporting only to us. Forewarned is forearmed, yes?"

"I like it, my friend!"

Wichmann reached for the plate of pastries. Since rationing had started in Germany, he'd consumed too many bland meals of meatless sausages. "Perhaps we might collaborate with another Ast, so that there are, to use the British phrase, too many cooks spoiling the broth. The more strata the better, no one will know who is in charge."

Canaris smiled for the first time since arriving in Hamburg. "Time is of the essence," he warned. "We must urgently deploy a team of elite Abwehr operatives into Britain. Let's start by looking at those who speak fluent English. I'm sure Ralf can help."

Wichmann, who knew Ralf, decided against a pastry after all. He glanced at his Rolex. "There's not a moment to lose."

***

In his office at RAF Bawdsey, Robert Watson-Watt switched off the wireless news. He scooped his jacket from the chair back, draped it around his shoulders, then walked through to the narrow staircase that led to the red turret on the corner of the manor house.

The halls and corridors were quieter since most of the boffins had moved out last autumn. After almost three wonderful years of hustle and bustle, he wasn't used to it yet.

Concerns that Bawdsey would be an early Nazi target had been heightened by the zeppelin spy mission. He'd agreed plans for the boffins working on research projects to be dispersed – to Aberdeenshire, Flintshire and Northumberland – with a much-reduced cohort remaining in situ with the on-going training programme. But no air raids had come – not yet at least – and Sir Hugh Dowding shared his huge relief that the Germans appeared to have misread the significance of Chain Home.

One single incident had troubled them during the relocation. Fleets of commercial furniture vans were hired to transport the boffins' apparatus – screens, tuners, receivers, machine tools, benches – to their destinations. An MI5 officer had insisted on accompanying them to Northumberland in his own car, a grey Ford 8. As it happened, the trucks heading north up the east coast were buzzed for fifteen nerve-shredding minutes by a Messerschmitt Bf 109. It had two machine guns, 7.92mm calibre, each able to fire more than a thousand rounds per minute. It followed them closely, peppered the road ahead, delaying their journey. Had the pilot been aiming for the road or the lead truck? Had he split from a larger formation of Me109s? Was this a random encounter, or planned? He flew off causing no further damage and they did not find out.

They had not wasted a minute of the Phoney War, four months to date. The Chain Home network had been extended, more observers recruited and trained, extra GPO lines installed. The whole system was becoming more robust and reliable. And Dowding had furnished his squadrons with new aircraft.

Although it was modernising rapidly, the Kriegsmarine did not yet have the strength to do battle with the Royal Navy, one of the world's largest navies and the bedrock of Britain's military strength. Nevertheless, merchant shipping, bringing vital provisions to Britain across the English Channel and Atlantic Ocean, was a constant target. Last autumn, German U-boats and destroyers had laid mines, thousands of them, around the British coast. The Treaty of Versailles had not only forced Germany to surrender its Great War submarines but forbade it from manufacturing new ones. When war was declared, Germany had 57 U-boats, fewer than thirty with the range to operate in the Atlantic – but, the Führer having brushed the treaty aside, orders were in place for hundreds more.

At the top of the turret steps, Watson-Watt knocked on the metal-studded wooden door. He could feel his heart pumping faster after the climb and wiped a bloom of sweat from his brow.

"Come in!"

He entered the large workshop, where five men in white coats were working. It was toasty-warm: a wood fire was bookended by mounds of logs. One of the men gave a hearty wave.

"Take a seat, sir, I'll be with you in two shakes." This was Frank Ridley, the boffin whom Watson-Watt had come to see for their first Monday progress meeting of the year.

From his swivel chair, Watson-Watt surveyed the room. Daylight streamed in through slits in the stone walls. The roller-skate was still up there on a shelf, overshadowing the protractors, rulers and set-squares. It had been a Christmas gift for Ridley's twelve-year-old daughter, Jacquie, from her Uncle Arthur, Frank's brother.

Arthur was in the merchant navy. En route last month from Liverpool to New York, the crew of his ship, the SS *Marlin*, had sighted off the starboard bow the fizzing wake of a torpedo. The captain managed to take enough evasive action – the empty ship was riding high in the water on this outward leg – for the torpedo to strike a glancing blow. It exploded at the stern, holing the *Marlin* but not fatally. She was sailing as part of a small convoy of six vessels – various formations were being trialled

– and most of the crew transferred to the *Earl of Beaconsfield* with no loss of life. He squeezed in a brief visit to FAO Schwarz on Fifth Avenue and bought Caran d'Ache crayons and roller-skates for his daughter and niece, both evacuated to Cumbria.

On the return leg, sailing fully laden in a larger convoy escorted by a Royal Navy warship, the *Marlin* was attacked again. It was not hit, but the warship scattered depth-charge canisters off the stern. Two thunderous explosions later, the U-boat surfaced, small and agile but badly damaged, evidently leaking. Like a steel coffin, it sank slowly, inexorably, with heaven knew how many men still alive inside. Watson-Watt banished thoughts of their fate from his mind.

The roller-skates had been well used. Frank had brought this one in, hoping that Tammy MacPherson would find time to repair a buckled chassis. The informal atmosphere, the spirit of debate and co-operation, itself helped to make Bawdsey a fertile source of new ideas.

Frank finished the calculations with which he'd been wrestling and locked them in a drawer. He and his team had been charged with miniaturising an RDF system to function inside an aircraft. Airborne Interception (AI), as they were provisionally calling it, would deliver information directly to flight crews. They'd conducted prototype tests on a Bristol Blenheim and would do more on the new Bristol Beaufighter. Exciting, highly motivated times in the turret.

Watson-Watt kept files on what purported to be another secret project occupying this team of boffins. It concerned the development of a pilotless glider, remote-controlled via short-wave guidance signals, which could be launched from a flying aircraft. In fact, the team never progressed any such glider beyond the drawing board – the files were retained as a decoy in case of leaks or, worst case, invasion.

Finally, Frank came to sit with his supervisor and the two men put their heads together. Frank launched into his oral status report, as sharp-witted as ever, while Watson-Watt, cheeks reddening in the warmth, made mental notes to raise at the end.

10

Moonlit landings

"She seems very nice, dear, very pleasant," Mrs Purnell said into the telephone handset. Recently installed, it was much used. "Oh, about thirty, that's all."

The thirty-two-year-old woman dressed in black paused at the top of the stairs, a smile between her dimpled cheeks, and listened to the telephone conversation in the hall below. She kept statue-still so that the creaking floorboards in the old farmhouse did not betray her.

"She's a sort of supply teacher... Miss Fletcher... Came to this area with so many bairns evacuated from Newcastle and Gateshead, and more due to leave... Aye, she reckons there'll be thousands more evacuees in the next few weeks, however unpopular it may be... What's that? Oh no, dear, no trouble at all. She's taken the bedsit at the top of the house... Very quiet. I think she keeps the curtains drawn all day as well as at night. Mind you, it's pitch dark by four o'clock, so day and night merge into one another at this time of year, don't they?"

The woman padded downstairs, carrying a pair of black leather boots and sandwiches wrapped in greaseproof paper. Through the spindles she had a clear view of her landlady's varicose veins.

Mrs Purnell finished her conversation with Mrs Crawford, a life-long friend who worked in a railway station booking office. They ended on some choice remarks about the points system for food rationing, newly introduced. Mrs Purnell polished on her sleeve the framed photograph of her son Gary – so dapper, wasn't he, in his army uniform – that stood proudly on the telephone shelf.

She smiled at her lodger on the bottom stair, pulling on her boots. "Let me fetch a bag for your sandwiches, dear." She scurried into the kitchen to rustle up a stiff brown paper bag.

"Thank you," her lodger said. "I won't be late back. But as you know, I love my motorcycle!"

There was the merest hint of an accent in the lodger's voice, an edge suggesting she wasn't local. But she was well spoken and courteous, and they never heard a peep out of her. From the family's home, Silverbeck Farm in Northumberland, England's most northerly county, Mrs Purnell had never travelled farther than the Scottish Highlands for an agricultural show and a short holiday, and she didn't want to pry, appear unworldly or rude, when the young teacher was unfailingly prompt with her rent. Besides, there'd be plenty of evenings to blather – the new school term had begun only a week ago. This was 14 January, a Sunday, almost 2 p.m.

"You enjoy your snack, dear, don't let me hold you up. It's a free country – still!"

The lodger said cheerio and turned along the lino-covered corridor to the back door. An oval mirror covered a tear in the floral wallpaper, and she caught a glimpse of herself as she passed.

She still wasn't used to this new look, Klara Falke thought to herself, although it suited her well enough.

It was the radical haircut that dramatically altered her appearance, rather than the subtler changes to her make-up and clothing. Her long blonde tresses, which had reached down her back since she was a teenager, were gone. Now her hair rested above the collar, pinned back at the sides, with a parting and a burst of curls on top. To achieve this, she'd wear curlers all night; thankfully, they no longer disrupted her sleep.

Klara didn't break her stride – you're Miss Fletcher, schoolteacher, now: live the cover, it must be second nature – and was soon in the yard, the cold air pinching her cheeks. Past the washhouse, occupied by a farmhand, she opened one of the barn doors. The odour of manure clogged her mouth. This section of the barn, without cattle, was a cart store. From its slot between a hay wain and a barrow, she wheeled her Norton ES2 into the yard and extracted a few hay strands from the front wheel.

Avidly, Klara followed the sports news. Norton motorcycles had won numerous Grands Prix and Isle of Man TT races in the '30s, and she liked the sporty look of the ES2 with a half-litre engine. This one came in black with an alluring chrome fuel tank, large enough for a 150-mile range, and chrome exhaust. It was a 1939 model with a dual seat, for which she'd paid £74 in cash – untraceable – to a Newcastle dealer. He'd said that the model was to be suspended for the duration of the war while Norton made motorcycles for the army, so she'd better snap it up.

She flipped open the leather pannier on the right of the rear wheel, inserted the sandwiches and took out a green headscarf. She tied this on her head with a reef knot and tucked in the ends. That's it, ready to go. As Klara kick-started the engine, the ES2 whirred into life, and she worked her way through the four-speed transmission on the open road.

Hanna Lippert would enjoy riding this motorcycle, she thought, seeing a ghost of Hanna's face in the speedometer. Curt Schultz, too: he liked all things mechanical, vehicles, gadgets, clocks. He'd briefed her fastidiously in his office in Berlin. The assignment, and her role in it, came 'on the direct orders of Admiral Canaris'. She should be very proud, seize the opportunity. Who knew where it may lead?

Had he sounded a mite jealous? Not really. He'd made it clear that he himself may follow her to Britain – Operation Trawl was a complex one, top secret, with numerous phases. Perhaps the edge in his voice was due to regret that they'd be parted for months. For Klara, it was a good test of whether the spark of romance was ever going to flare into a meaningful relationship. She'd only left Germany a couple of weeks ago, just before Christmas, but so far, she'd not missed him anything like enough.

Under cover of darkness, a fishing smack had brought her through cold, jerky waters to the Northumberland coast. She carried two suitcases, one containing clothes with English labels and a wad of used Bank of England notes. The other had equipment she might find useful. The documents issued to her – British passport, identity card, driver's licence – were in her cover name, Miss Evelyn Fletcher, born in Doncaster, 17 May 1909. The thirty-two-page passport, with four out of five years' validity remaining, showed a few entry and exit stamps for European countries. It looked, felt, smelled genuine and had given her confidence the moment she saw it.

The drop-off point was the harbour in the growing village of Amble, which owed its prosperity not only to fishing and farming but, increasingly, the export of coal. Rich seams were mined in nearby Broomhill, Radcliffe and Togston, and a branch line brought the full wagons to be unloaded. The line intersected with the road to RAF Acklington, which Klara had read was a busy Fighter Command station.

Amble harbour, at the mouth of the River Coquet, had two piers. Along the southern pier were chunky timber staithes, five of them, from which the coal was discharged into gaping collier holds below.

Shortly after midnight, the fishing smack moored against the southern pier. Bitterly cold, Klara climbed a ladder to the top. It was slow-going in the dark, but she made it without slipping with first one and then the other suitcase.

She had memorised her route to perfection. Despite the black-out, she knew how far to walk, where to turn. By moonlight, she picked her way past the staithes and crossed a side road leading to a brickworks whose kilns fired thousands of clay blocks every day. In the distance, a pithead and lift assembly towered above the roofs of the miners' bathhouse and locker room. Beyond a terrace of cottages built for quarrymen and shipwrights, she reached the bottom of Queen Street, the village's Victorian high street, dominated by Co-operative Society stores. Many Co-op customers would be dividend members, filling books with stamps according to their purchases.

Sure enough, parked outside the first Co-op store was a Rover 10 saloon. It did not flash its lights or sound a horn. But when the driver saw her, he stepped out and polished the windscreen with a yellow chamois.

Introducing himself simply as 'Alf', he was well into his sixties. One side of his face was etched with scars, reminiscent of the zeppelin's Captain Sammt. Alf slid her cases along the back seat while she climbed into the front. He drove the thirty miles south to Newcastle with very few other cars on the road. At one crossroads, a fox hightailed it into their path to gorge on roadkill, but Klara screamed when she saw its bright eyes. Alf swerved and the fox bolted.

He was an observant driver and she relaxed. She didn't see him look at her even once. He said little at first, but when he did speak, he didn't breach her cover for a moment. Was this a test? Could the car possibly be bugged with one of those listening devices that intelligence agencies were using? Or did he simply not want to be distracted?

"When do you start at your new school?"

"Next term, early next month."

"As a supply teacher, are you joining because of the larger class sizes? Due to the evacuees, I mean."

"That's part of it, yes. I'm also replacing a science teacher who's been given leave of absence to work on aircraft design."

"I see," said Alf, executing a left. "Presumably parents are more confident now about kids going to school? It's three months since the war was announced and not much seems to have happened."

"Long may that last."

He let that comment pass. "What about those who haven't been evacuated? With so many schools closed, the remaining kids have lost their education, their school milk, their midday meals. What are they supposed to do all day? Run riot and catch scabies?"

"I think more will be evacuated in the coming weeks, another phase, but I've no details yet."

"If you ask me, kids should stay in school until they're fifteen or sixteen." Alf's voice tailed off. "We shouldn't force them into adulthood too soon."

She heartily agreed. As any teacher would, she added.

There was something about this woman, Alf reflected. He'd known it very quickly. She made him want to talk, to say more as the journey progressed, despite him not intending to do so. He'd known this only rarely and he must take care.

They halted at a red light. A black Wolseley with a 'Police' sign and a siren on the roof stopped behind them, its engine purring. Separately, both Alf and Klara half-expected an officer to tap on their window, but they took deep breaths and let the interminable seconds tick by. When the lights changed, Alf moved off at a snail's pace. The police car overtook and vanished into the darkness.

Five minutes later, they turned off Milburn Avenue into Cookson Street in a leafy Newcastle suburb. He pulled up outside a Victorian villa named 'Sycamore Grove B&B'.

"This is where you'll be staying tonight, what's left of it. Don't worry about it being the middle of the night. Duncan – he's the proprietor – is expecting you. He's a friend of the film society that meets at the Odyssey – you're familiar with it?"

Klara nodded. As they got out, she asked: "I take it you're in the film society, too, Alf?"

He did not answer directly but said: "I believe it's the principal network of sympathisers and contacts in the region." He sounded rather proud of its status.

Klara nodded again, said nothing.

Was that a light in a top-floor window across the street? Something had flashed in the corner of Alf's eye and he was concerned. Glancing up, he saw nothing in the blackness except the rippling tendrils of his own breath.

He dragged her cases off the back seat, then reached into the glovebox. He withdrew a brass AA badge for a radiator grille and buffed it on his sleeve.

"The characters engraved at the bottom are not the membership number," he told her. "Can you make them out? They're a telephone number."

With automatic exchanges and dial telephones rolling out across the country, more and more telephone numbers comprised seven digits. Three letters forming a local area code preceded four numbers for a specific property. Angling the badge in her palm, Klara read: NEW1815.

"That's the number to call for the film society. Got it? Don't repeat it under any circumstances." The grip he suddenly had on her wrist was vice-like.

"I've got it, thanks."

Alf tossed the badge into the glovebox and hauled her cases up the granite steps to the front door. He didn't knock or ring, simply pushed the door, which opened into a hallway sparsely decorated with streamers and tinsel but no lights. A sulphurous smell of onions lingered.

"Hello and welcome." A male voice spoke as a door off the hallway creaked open. A grey-haired man with a pencil moustache and rimless spectacles appeared and took the cases from Alf, who relinquished them gratefully and flexed his fingers.

"Duncan?"

"That's me, Duncan Caldwell, pleased to meet you." His teeth were nicotine yellow.

"Evelyn Fletcher. Sorry to arrive at such an ungodly hour."

"You've actually made good time. And it's very British to apologise to strangers on first meeting them, so well done."

Alf wished her good luck, bade her farewell. Having shaken his hand, Klara followed Duncan into the room from which he'd appeared. It was a lounge, mottled walls, with paintings of ships and trains hanging from the picture rail. A wireless set overshadowed the sideboard on which it sat. The bulky three-piece suite was forest green, the patterned carpet predominantly brown. Klara imagined the room being gloomy even in daylight without the curtains closed. It reeked of stale tobacco.

"Can I get you anything before I fetch your room key?" he asked. "You've been travelling for hours, you must need a drink?"

Klara sank into one of the single chairs and realised she was exhausted. "That's very kind. A glass of water, please."

He whistled shrilly as he left the room.

"How many other guests are staying tonight?" she asked when he returned.

"All eight rooms are occupied. It's a long-established B&B in an ideal location for the city." He paused. "You're the only *special* guest at present, if you get my drift, but I've had one or two others. I've assured the film society that it's a service I'll gladly offer."

"Well, your hospitality is much appreciated."

Regardless of the hour, Duncan clearly wanted to converse while she sipped her water. "You know, the way I see the Führer," he said, watching a house spider scuttle under a table, "is he just gets on with it. He cuts through your day-to-day politics with a strong answer for every issue. No nonsense, no argument. That approach appeals to me, which is why I support the film society. I must say, it's very fulfilling, I hope you'll agree."

He rubbed his leathery palms together, the action of which triggered a cough, made his chest heave. His lungs must be as black as soot.

"Thank you for your openness," Klara said while he got his breath back. She drained her glass and yawned. It was well after 2 a.m.

Duncan fished a key out of his pocket. "Here you are. I'll bring up your suitcases. First floor, on the left. Have a comfortable rest."

In fact, Klara recalled, accelerating out of a corner on her ES2, the bed had felt hard and lumpy, as if she were lying on the wooden frame with no mattress. She was distracted by a large cobweb in the ceiling cornice – and it wouldn't have surprised her if there were cockroaches, too. She'd had an hour's sleep at most, but no matter, there was work to do. A busy person is a happy person, she'd been instructed from kindergarten.

That Sunday afternoon, 14 January, she rode north through undulating pastureland, glancing every so often to her right at the sapphire-blue sea. It was a region of ancient, resilient countryside, whose rich coal seams had made it an engine of the Industrial Revolution. She clattered over a level crossing, its gates chained across the tracks, giving road users the right of way. A signal box, standing guard in a clearing, looked unoccupied.

After five miles, she headed for the quiet fishing village of Boulmer. Black-and-white gulls, ever alert, perched on the rooftops of the stone cottages. The air tasted salty. Blue and red cobles lay beached along the sand dunes, ready to head out at dawn. At the roadside, among handbarrows and fishing lines, a couple of youngsters disentangled their conker strings.

Two elderly men, taking on the work of their enlisted sons, heaped empty lobster baskets on to a flatbed lorry. They looked up from the tailgate as the motorcycle flashed by. Klara waved keenly as if she recognised them, and they waved back, hesitantly, by which time she was well past. Local lass, nowt to bother with there, howay, heaps more baskets to load.

In Berlin, Klara's briefing dossier on Operation Trawl had included a tentative list of RAF airfields throughout north-east England. Very little background information. There was clearly no organised network of agents and informants for Abwehr officers to run, although now, belatedly, that was beginning to change.

Woolsington airfield was apparently used for commercial flights as well as RAF training sorties, but no confirmation either way. Acklington and Boulmer – operational, no details. Further south, Thornaby and Croft had airstrips that could be used for bombers – but were they? Against the listing for Ouston was written: *For fighters?* Brunton and Eshott had: *Potential sites marked out or under construction?* So it went on, all very sketchy. She had a lot of ground to cover.

From memory, there must be a left turn soon. Klara slowed down. Nothing else was on the road. Dozens of gulls and crows in the bare trees twisted their necks to watch the interloper's progress. Yes, here it was, concealed by hedgerows.

The wintry daylight was fading, and the wind getting up, as Klara turned into a single-lane track, curling through a field in which a handful of horses grazed. At the end of the lane stood a six-foot-high, barbed-wire fence. Was it electrified? It didn't look so, but careful, it would be razor-sharp. A stony path beside the fence seemed new. Klara flicked the handlebars and followed the path, picking her way over the uneven surface until she came to a gate, cut into the fence. Padlocked.

She stopped, lowered the stand as a gust of wind tried its hardest to blow her over. She took a pair of lightweight military binoculars from the pannier and removed the lens caps.

Slowly she scanned the site. Two runways, grassy, not worn bare. At the far end: four Hawker Mark 1 Hurricane fighters – she knew them at once. The fence encompassed the whole, rather small airfield – RAF Boulmer. She was at its northerly edge. Almost within reach inside the fence, an unmanned Lewis machine gun was mounted on a tripod. This was anti-aircraft ordnance from the Great War, not the most fearsome threat in today's world.

She climbed back on the ES2, adopting a low riding position, and followed the fence around its western and southern flanks. Through the binoculars, she made out half a dozen Nissen huts, a wooden control tower, a couple of black saloon cars and another Lewis gun.

3.25 p.m. Darkness gathering, sunset within the hour. The top half of the ES2's headlight was masked with tape. Klara was about to move on when a jeep with four men appeared from behind a hut. She tracked it with the binoculars as it headed out to the Hurricanes. The airmen dismounted, jogged to the nearest plane and...

What? Klara could not believe her eyes! She gulped, forced the binoculars into her eye sockets to steady them in the wind.

The men literally picked up the Hurricane and plonked it down a few yards further afield, pointing the other way. They went to the second plane and carried it to a different position, too.

These Hurricanes were *plywood!* Plywood and canvas. No metal, no engines, no fuel. Excellent, life-size, two-dimensional replicas.

Klara had taken them for the real thing, not given them a second glance, even when magnified. She'd seen what she expected to see. But here they were, being manhandled as props.

It took a couple of minutes to shift all four, then the jeep was on its way back to the hut. Anyone seeing the planes before and after would think they had flown today, landed and parked up in different spots. They would believe the airfield was active, conducting real operations.

In truth, as Klara had discovered, RAF Boulmer was a decoy.

***

3.45 p.m. Head down, teeth gritted, Klara gunned the ES2 towards the village of Acklington, ten miles from Boulmer. She was wide awake, pumped with adrenaline. The qualities she'd refined in her shooting career – speed of thought, spatial awareness, alertness – came to the fore as reflex actions.

She was certain RAF Acklington was a working airfield, even though Boulmer was a fake. In her dossier it was the only one with any background notes to speak of.

In 1916, sixty-three acres of farmland south of the village, known as Southfields, were requisitioned for 36 Squadron, but the site was discontinued after the Great War. By January 1938, a new airstrip had opened on an adjacent field, which by April was occupied by No.7 Armament Training Camp. In September, the training school was relocated to an RAF base in Dorset. RAF Acklington was handed over to 13 Group, Fighter Command.

That dossier record had seemed, even on a first read, to be a rare nugget of good intelligence. But *what was happening at Acklington* that was so secret, so vital to protect, that the RAF, the army, MI5, whoever, had gone to the trouble of constructing a decoy airfield, presumably to deflect air attacks, ten miles away?

The ES2's headlight cast a yellow semi-circle on the black asphalt ahead. The road twisted, sometimes doubling back on itself, and she never exceeded forty.

Acklington village comprised a row of cottages on either side of the road, a church, a cattle shed and a railway station down an embankment, dominated by its signal box. Klara leant into the turn that took her down a lane, a ditch running alongside it. A farm and a blacksmith's stall both appeared deserted.

But not quite. Here was a tractor coming the other way, driven by a woman in a green sweater and corduroy trousers. Klara veered perilously close to the ditch to let the tractor chug past. Riding on, she made out the remote RAF station through occasional gaps in the hedge and trees. Though faint and shadowy in the darkness – it was now after 4 p.m. – this was a much larger concern than the decoy site at Boulmer. It was a village in its own right. The intelligence assessment had been correct: RAF Acklington was very much in operation.

Observing the main entrance, Klara halted the ES2, switched off the light and wheeled it behind the thickest tree trunk she could find. It was breezy and the temperature was still falling, but Klara was used to winters in Berlin where the rivers froze over, so this was no hardship.

She opened the left-side pannier and took out a hessian sack. From it came three items: a pair of long binoculars, an infrared lamp with chest-straps, and a battery unit to wear on her back. She connected them, forming a single piece of apparatus.

Curt Schultz, always proud of German scientists, had told her of their latest breakthrough in *Nachtsichtigkeit* – night vision. The Russians had invested in this technology, but the Nazis had no intention of being left behind by a nation of communists. They were determined that Germany would set the pace in more spheres than 'Radio Detection and Ranging' – for which RADAR, the American acronym, caught on everywhere, supplanting RDF and other labels.

In February 1933, the month after the Nazis seized power, a secret meeting of the CEOs of Germany's biggest industrial firms, many of them household names, was convened at Hermann Göring's official residence in Berlin. It was a time of global economic depression. Twenty or more executives attended, Schultz had told Klara; none declined.

Göring welcomed them lustily, oblivious to his chronic halitosis, before introducing the Führer himself, who spoke for ninety minutes. Yes, ninety! The Führer and Der Zweite were both impulsive men, but this presentation was carefully planned.

The Führer reassured the businessmen of his fundamental belief in private property, which went down well, then cited the Darwinian mantra, 'the survival of the fittest'. Just as in any business sector, the lesser being swallowed up by the greater is the natural way, isn't it? So, to defeat communism, the Nazis *must* have unyielding authority, total power, and more *must* be invested in rearming Germany.

He told them that, until he became Chancellor in January 1933, he'd spent five months living and working on the top floor of Berlin's Hotel Kaiserhof. Joseph Goebbels – his master propagandist, always eager to remain a trusted adviser – invited him home as he feared the communists in the hotel kitchen would poison the Führer's food.

Follow Goebbels' example, the Führer urged them: if something needs doing, do it. Take nothing for granted: assumption is the mother of all foul-ups. He was pleased to see them nodding and smiling. They were with him, and he was going down better than Göring, which made his success all the sweeter.

Göring took the floor again to discuss the federal elections, due on 5 March, at which a landslide victory for the NSDAP could only be achieved with a massive injection of funds. Presumably, Klara said sourly, the vicious attacks by Nazi Brownshirts on political opponents were swept under the extravagant carpet?

"*Sieg heil!* Hail victory!" Indeed, the meeting had concluded with everyone standing together, arms outstretched in Nazi salutes.

The CEOs donated two million Reichsmarks to party coffers. At the federal elections, the NSDAP won 288 seats, an increase of ninety-two, but secured only a minority share – 43.9% – of the popular vote. Nevertheless, the Führer – who, as Chancellor before the elections, remained so afterwards – passed an Enabling Act before March was out, granting himself absolute power.

Succumbing to his narcissism, he had not, since then, permitted any further elections. Government ministries began to work with very little direction or co-ordination. Above the fray, the Führer saw it as his life's purpose to guide the Fatherland to victory: no, ifs, no buts, no ground given. And mindful of biting economic sanctions at the disposal of enemy countries, he was concerned to make his own land as self-sufficient as possible.

AEG, one of the corporations represented at the secret meeting, had developed the prototype night vision device, now on loan to the Abwehr. An array of applications by the armed forces and secret services was envisaged, but a rigorous testing programme was required. Your feedback, please, as soon as your mission is over.

Klara strapped on the apparatus. It was surprisingly comfortable, not biting into her shoulders as much as she'd feared. She must have connected the components correctly because, within seconds of her switching on, a green image materialised before her eyes. Using natural infrared light, the lenses enabled its operator to see in near-darkness.

Crouching low, Klara gazed at the fighter aircraft parked at the end of the runway, well over a dozen of them, and at the cluster of low buildings beyond. To the right stood a formation of masts, two sets of four, matching those visible from across the Channel. Bunched close together, they resembled the pylons being built by the country's Central Electricity Board to power its new national grid – but there were no thick electricity cables suspended between them. This *had* to be a radar system!

Above her head, Klara became aware of thrumming, getting louder. A Rolls-Royce 12-cylinder Merlin engine.

As she looked up, a Supermarine Spitfire – nose high, wheels down, elliptical wing steady, orange navigational light flashing – passed overhead and dipped very gracefully into land.

— 11 —

Fifth Columnists?

Eyes closed, Lorraine Dawson lolled on the settee in his living room, half-listening to the Home Service. A variety show had started. The announcer had guaranteed that, with Arthur Askey, Diana Morrison, Charlie Chester and a gaggle of others, it would be 'full of mirth'.

A rarity: Lorraine had a few minutes to herself. Her fiancé, Jonathan Hedley, was walking his mother to the tram stop for her journey home, south of the river in Gateshead. Mrs Hedley had spent the afternoon at her son's two-up two-down in Newcastle and Lorraine had joined them, as she often did on Sundays if she had no shift at the Odyssey. She'd baked a small Victoria sponge for Mrs Hedley, whose sweet tooth had rather taken to her future daughter-in-law.

Lorraine would depart soon for her own flat. She rented one in a three-year-old block whose cellar served as an air raid shelter. Half a dozen stops on a trolley bus, that was all. Before bed, she'd do a bit more sewing on her wedding dress. So far, touch wood, it was shaping up well.

Lorraine let the strange events of the last forty-eight hours replay in her mind. Had she done the right thing, or put two and two together and made a mountain out of a molehill? What would her colleagues and the Odyssey's owners make of it if – no, when – they found out?

Two days ago, on Friday 12 January, she'd made a cuppa for Gordon, chief projectionist, and one for Harry Jarvis, whose limp always seemed more pronounced in winter. When she took the tea to Harry's office, he was nowhere to be seen but the door was wide open. He can't have gone far, she reasoned, walking in.

As she picked up the empty mug on his desk, her eye was caught by a pamphlet with a large emblem on its masthead. Harry's mug had covered it up – deliberately? – but the exposed white circle containing a jagged red lightning bolt was unmistakable.

For a moment, Lorraine froze. She replaced the empty mug on the exact spot and put the fresh tea alongside it.

"What in God's name are you doing?" Harry Jarvis stood crimson-faced in the doorway, clutching the frame. "How dare you–?"

"I was just bringing your tea. Look, there it is. I'm leaving, OK?"

"Oh – all right. Thank you." His thin smile radiated no warmth or gratitude. As she passed close to him on her way out, she imagined – or did she feel? – his hot breath on the back of her neck.

Yesterday – Saturday – morning, she met Jonathan at a John Collier store. She'd offered to help him pick an all-in-one 'siren suit' that could be pulled on swiftly over his nightwear. He'd been teased at the station when it emerged in conversation that he didn't possess one.

Jonathan was a constable in Newcastle upon Tyne City Police. Last autumn, he'd sold his own car, a rattling Morris Cowley, to buy her an engagement ring. Being betrothed to this gorgeous woman made him feel more blissfully happy and secure than he'd ever thought possible. He was also teased at work about the seemingly permanent spring in his step.

He'd listened intently when they sat down in his living room after their mercifully successful shopping trip. She told him three things about Harry Jarvis, a manager at the Odyssey. Number one. In the last few months – since September – Harry had been receiving small boxes of film reels, the sort used for trailers and cartoons.

Well, it is a cinema, he'd said sceptically, and she punched him on the arm.

"Normally, these little segments are sent to the projection room as soon as they arrive," she explained. "What good can they be to anyone else? We have to splice them into the programme on our Steenbeck."

He raised a quizzical eyebrow.

"It's an editing table," she answered and tucked her legs under her body. "Recently, a lot of short reels have come addressed personally to Harry, and none of them has made it to the projection room. Weird, eh?"

"Go on." His body language indicated that he wasn't convinced.

"Number two. Something else that began last September. Harry rents the cinema out, late at night or very early mornings, to a film society."

Big deal! "Erm... Are they watching films? How many people?"

"We don't know. He shuts down any conversation about it. There doesn't seem to be any paperwork on file – they arrange their own projectionist if they need one, so none of the staff has attended any of the meetings, as far as I know."

"Just Harry?"

"Just Harry."

"Could they be watching the reels he's been sent?"

"Feasibly, yes. But they can only last a couple of minutes each, they're not part of a feature film."

"Were they all sent from the same source? The same person? A film company?"

"You'd have to ask him that, constable." Now she stroked his arm. "But I'd say they've come from different places. Or people. The boxes look different each time."

"And no one knows who's attending the meetings?"

Lorraine shrugged her shoulders.

"OK. You said there were three points?"

"The first two might be perfectly innocent, unrelated, with decent explanations," she said. "But put them together with number three. Yesterday, I noticed a BUF pamphlet on Harry's desk."

"The British Union of Fascists?"

"The one and only. I know some people don't take them seriously, but I think their logo is scary. I wasn't supposed to see it, obviously, and he hit the roof when he found me in his office. He seems to take them very seriously indeed. He'd gone to the loo, and I was taking him a fresh brew. There was handwriting on the pamphlet. Someone had used it to write him a message."

"You didn't read it?"

"No chance."

Jonathan scratched his head. She could see behind his eyes, his mind was whirring.

The BUF was formed in 1932 by Oswald Mosley, a gifted orator apparently inspired by the Italian dictator, Mussolini. It brought together various far-right groups into a single anti-communist, protectionist, nationalist network. Jonathan knew that the voices in government calling for the BUF to be banned were rising in number and volume.

He looked Lorraine in the eye, held her hand.

"Darling, thanks for telling me all this. You were dead right to do so. Let's not leap to any premature conclusions, but from what you've said, you might have a Fifth Columnist in your ranks."

'Fifth Columnist' – a Spanish Civil War term, which she'd heard him use before.

"Harry – a subversive agent? Acting under our noses to aid the Germans?" She frowned. "What do you want me to do?"

"Nothing!" He was emphatic. "There might be nothing to this, but don't breathe a word. Don't ask questions, don't let on that you've informed me."

"No fear! Besides, I don't think Harry will want me setting foot in his office again any time soon."

"Please be careful, darling. But keep your eyes peeled. Tell me if anything else strikes you as odd or suspicious."

His bride-to-be looked at him lovingly. "And what are you going to do?"

"Refer it to my sergeant. But there's a team in MI5, the security service, working day and night to investigate potential Nazi sympathisers, Fifth Columnists, who may be helping to prepare the ground for a German invasion."

Harry Jarvis? She knew he was a loner, perhaps he was naïve too. But could he really be part of a faction conspiring against Britain?

Jonathan was still speaking. "I'll see the sarge on Monday morning. It's his call, but I think, for good order, we should add Mr Jarvis to MI5's burgeoning case load as soon as humanly possible."

***

That Sunday afternoon, 14 January, a grey Ford 8 came to a halt and parked in Milburn Avenue, a tree-lined, residential street in Newcastle. Two huge buildings towered above the houses: a Victorian bathhouse and an eight-hundred-seat picture hall, the Carlton, on the corner with Cookson Street in which the Sycamore Grove B&B was situated. A Turners' photographic store cowered between the behemoths, a government poster in its window exhorting: 'Make do and mend'.

Christopher Talbot parked outside Turners for the clear view of the bathhouse. He was waiting to pick up Lucy, his daughter, who had been practising for a swimming gala. At twelve she'd not been evacuated; they were unsure whether she'd be called for evacuation at all.

Two middle-aged men from the Newcastle Home Guard picked their way down the bathhouse steps, chanting a local folk song, *The Blaydon Races*. They'd probably used the place to get a shower, Talbot decided as he watched their backs recede up the avenue to be swallowed by the afternoon darkness.

Talbot had joined MI5 last year, when the service was belatedly granted investment in the run-up to war. He'd moved across from the Special Branch of Newcastle City Police, where he was a Detective Inspector based at the city-centre headquarters in Pilgrim Street, which also accommodated a magistrates' court and a fire station.

Lucy believed he still worked for the police. He'd spent a couple of weeks in London – 'on a big case' – when he joined MI5 and had found the organisation to be demoralised, under-staffed and seemingly ill-prepared, given the tensions in the world, to play its part in the coming war.

Perhaps Vernon Kell, the quietly spoken army captain who founded the security service three decades ago had stayed at the helm too long? From Sandhurst, Kell served in the South Staffordshire Regiment in Russia and China, where he and his wife, Constance, lived through the so-called Boxer Rebellion that sought to rid the land of foreigners. In 1902, back in London, he was made a staff captain at the War Office. An excellent linguist, he worked there with distinction as a German intelligence analyst.

October 1909. The War Office picked Kell jointly to run the new Secret Service Bureau. He led the domestic section, protecting the country with counterintelligence measures, while Captain Mansfield Smith-Cumming headed the foreign section, operating overseas. Soon, the two sections split into separate organisations: the security service, MI5, and the secret intelligence service, MI6.

Known within the confined MI5 office as 'K', Kell hit the ground running. He contacted chief constables, asking them to identify potential foreign spies in their region. A catch-all Official Secrets Act was shepherded through parliament in just one day by the supportive Home Secretary, Winston Churchill. It enabled those suspected of disclosing information unlawfully to be arrested, their mail intercepted. Needs must?

1914. K masterminded the capture of twenty-two spies identified as working in the UK for Imperial Germany. This operation dealt such a paralysing blow to German intelligence that it struggled to recover. But, after 1918, cost-cutting so reduced the size of MI5 that its own existence was threatened. In the 1930s, it found new purpose, to counter subversion by communists and fascists.

By September 1939, Talbot knew that K, newly promoted to Major-General, was well into his sixties and serving on a rolling one-year contract. His deputy, Eric Holt-Innes, also ex-army, was a similar age. Having excelled in the 1914–18 war, MI5 now appeared tired and wrong-footed by the conduct and intentions of Nazi Germany. Perhaps it was because the leaders had experienced the horrors of that war, which lived on inside them, that they simply could not countenance another. The entire service numbered just thirty officers, including Talbot himself in the north-east, plus a hundred administrative staff.

Since war was declared, MI5 had prioritised two programmes: internment and vetting. 70,000 Germans and Austrians resident in Britain last September were declared 'enemy aliens'. Internment tribunals began under the aegis of the Home Office. Aliens were assigned to one of three categories: (A) to be interred; (B) exempt from internment but subject to other restrictions; or (C) exempt from any restriction. The vast majority were placed in category C, including most of the 55,000 Jewish refugees who had come to the UK for safety, escaping persecution.

In the internment camps, in Liverpool, London, Glasgow, Sutton Coldfield and on the Isle of Wight, detainees undertook farm labour and garment making, and staged their own entertainments. Thousands were released as soon as a more sophisticated vetting procedure was devised. Some were shipped overseas. Yet fears of saboteurs and spies lingered among the public, politicians and media.

Just as suspicion thrived on conflict, so security was vital for public confidence, Talbot thought to himself. Two sides of the same coin. He almost wished this Phoney War would cascade into actual combat, just to bring an end to the ugly climate of paranoia that hung over the country like a poison cloud.

MI5 was so inundated with vetting requests, many apparently spurious, that the under-powered machine was in danger of clamming up. Yet every single referral had to be investigated, reported on, filed away.

Strumming his fingers on the steering wheel, Talbot cast an eye on the photographic store. Above it was a two-storey flat, on the top floor of which was an office room where the live-in manager, Terence Bradley, cashed up and did all his paperwork. The rear window overlooked the next street, with a clear view in winter through the bare trees.

Bradley had observed guests arriving at the B&B at the dead of night, dropped off by the same car, a Rover 10. The first time, he'd done nothing about it. The second time might have been a coincidence, however unlikely. When it happened a third time, well, that was a pattern, wasn't it, and surely his duty was to act? On this occasion, he'd managed to jot down the Rover's six-digit registration number.

All such cases in the region were sent to Talbot, who was expected to deal with them efficiently. The good news was, he'd been given some help. MI5 was taking on additional officers and he was delighted to have met his new colleague already. I'm newly single, the recruit had explained quite unnecessarily, and ready for a fresh challenge, which was essential. They'd made a positive start, tracing the registered owner of the Rover 10, tracking his pattern of journeys.

It wasn't all vetting and rooting out ill-wishers. Talbot had been briefed on the significance of the new research facility next to RAF Acklington, and he'd escorted the convoy of boffins and their equipment from RAF Bawdsey, which they were vacating as it was considered a high-risk shelling target. An Me109 had buzzed the convoy and strafed the road before flying off. Whatever orders the pilot was following, Talbot figured that the Nazis would know that the work conducted at Bawdsey was continuing elsewhere, some of it on his patch in the north-east.

He was still drumming on the wheel when Lucy bounded down the bathhouse steps and knocked on the car window. Parenting had taught him many things, including humility. This clever twelve-year-old, on the cusp of her teens, was very much her own person with her own interests and talents. Front crawl might be one, getting dried was not. Her hair was wringing wet, but her sunny disposition and wide grin melted his heart every time. He gladly set aside his thoughts of security work and for the next few hours that Sunday afternoon, during a riot of board games, he endeavoured to be the best dad he could possibly be.

— 12 —

Who goes there?

Although the Spitfire had taxied out of sight, Klara was sure that its windscreen had a state-of-the-art anti-glare shield. During night-flying it prevented the pilot being dazzled by the glowing exhausts of other aircraft.

Where had the Spitfire been? she pondered, dismantling the night vision device and bundling it into the pannier. A practice or training flight? Short-range reconnaissance? This was the closest she'd ever come to a Spitfire and, she had to admit, she'd never seen a marvel of engineering so seductively beautiful.

Klara was about to remount the ES2 when a thought struck her. Better safe than sorry. She smoothed the brown paper bag neatly around her sandwiches, forming a square block, then wrote three short lines on the top and replaced it in the pannier.

She rode to the main entrance and halted at a white pole. From a wooden guardhouse, twenty feet long, she heard raised voices: two or more men arguing. Next to the guardhouse was the station's sickbay, outside which was a rack of bicycles. Every building seemed to have a Tannoy speaker above its door.

She'd been waiting at the barrier only a few seconds when a man emerged from the guardhouse, straightening his tie. The name strip on his chest read: LIVINGSTONE.

Archie Livingstone approached the motorcycle courier. A woman... Some strands of blonde hair had escaped from under her headscarf, one had settled at the corner of her mouth. More and more couriers were women; normally he waved them straight through. The possibility of this courier relying on the very fact that women were generally trusted rather than suspected, their passes not checked, by men at gateposts had not occurred to him.

Klara had experienced moments of intense pressure before, but she now realised that, were she deemed to be trespassing on RAF property, she would be arrested.

"Good afternoon, how may I help?"

"Afternoon." Be nonchalant. "Small package to deliver." She blew on her hands, looked ahead expectantly and revved the engine.

"It's not cold!" Archie protested, moving to the handle at the end of the pole. "You wait until the middle of the night – the graveyard shift here is no fun at all!"

He flashed a smile. I bet this man can be a real charmer, Klara thought. He's handsome and he knows it, and probably believes that that entitles him to get on in life.

"I'll just make my delivery and be on my way."

Archie was about to raise the barrier when another man appeared in the guardhouse doorway, torch in hand.

"Sergeant Harris," he introduced himself loudly, glaring at Archie. Klara's heart sank. "I haven't seen you here before, have I? Your identity card, please."

Harris tapped the torch against his leg and the bright beam swung on the ground like a metronome.

"Of course." Klara thought Archie had blushed and taken a step or two back. Fishing in a pocket, she retrieved a driver's license and an ID card. "You can examine both, if you like?"

Harris handed the torch to Archie, who directed the beam on the sergeant's hands.

It was compulsory for adults and children to carry a National Registration Identity Card, in case homes were bombed and families separated. Evelyn Fletcher's ID card had a yellow cover. Inside was her name and address, handwritten in capitals. An official circular stamp in the corner was slightly smudged, but no matter.

The driver's license had a red cover with a county council emblem. The inside spread, which Harris opened, showed the holder's name and address, naturally matching those on the ID card, together with a date, a five-digit license number and two signatures, one the town clerk's, the other Evelyn's.

Satisfied that the documents were genuine, Harris returned them. Plaudits to the masterly team that had provided them. Archie redirected the torch, avoiding the eyes.

"Where have you come from?" Harris demanded.

So, he wasn't finished yet.

"I'm a Wren." Did that answer his question?

The Women's Royal Naval Service, whose members were known as Wrens, was formed for the Great War and revived last year. All women in the navy, except nurses, were Wrens – telegraphists, plotters, clerks, cooks, electricians, many more vital trades.

Harris was awaiting a fuller explanation. "When did you join the Wrens, Miss Fletcher?"

"Last year, sir. Got the details at a local employment exchange. I wrote to the Admiralty, as they suggested, filled in my application, did my training at Finchley. Didn't think it was possible to march so far in two months."

"I'm sure," Harris said, sounding more relaxed. If he was using her to set an example, and score points over the hapless Livingstone, she hoped that by now she'd done enough to temper him. "By the way, what's your accent?"

"Oh, I'm often asked that!" Klara didn't miss a beat. "College in Geneva, sir. When I'm not filling in with occasional driving jobs, I'm usually to be found translating enemy signals."

"Very good, Miss Fletcher." Harris stepped closer and patted the pannier closest to him.

"Do you... want me to open it, sir?"

Harris had second thoughts. He knew the package was none of his business and did not wish to overstep the mark. The courier had been unfailingly co-operative. Via this little display of authority, he trusted that he'd made his point about security at the gate.

"That won't be necessary. Carry on, Miss Fletcher."

Harris indicated to Archie, who lifted the pole.

Klara rode into RAF Acklington. The lane broadened into a tarmac road, wide enough for large vehicles. She went slowly, drawing minimal attention. Fingerboards gave directions. Neat rows of wooden huts which served as barracks were complemented by an armoury, an officers' mess, a large NAAFI and other outbuildings. Some had smoke gushing from black pipes poking out of their roofs. There must be hundreds of people on this station. Dozens were streaming in the same direction for afternoon tea, served between 4 and 5 p.m.

The runway to Klara's left had a group of Spitfires parked up, and more could be seen in a hangar, doors wide open, in a siding. Maintenance work was in progress on the windscreen of one plane, perhaps the one that had just landed.

Klara followed the road to a single-storey building with a DESPATCH sign by its double doors. A NAAFI van was parked outside, by an open crate of what she recognised as fabric shooting targets. Roped to aeroplanes, they were used for airborne firing practice.

Pulling up, she was relieved to find no line of sight to the gate post, so she could not be observed by Sergeant Harris. The double doors swung open. Out strode two men engrossed in conversation, each with a cigarette attached to his lower lip. According to the insignia on their arms, they were flight sergeants.

"Football in Poland has been outlawed since the invasion," one bemoaned. "Some matches took place secretly in Warsaw and Poznan, but the Nazis were informed and raided the stadiums."

"What happened to the players?" his colleague wondered. "Carted off to concentration camps? I must ask Maz – he'll know all about it."

"Good excuse for a beer with him, on my book."

Klara kept her head low. She read the name tabs on their breast pockets: MALLINSON and PIKE. Members, she assumed, of a squadron on its tour of duty.

Something else caught her eye. Once the flight sergeants were yards away, she squeezed the accelerator and rode around the side of the building. When the double doors had opened, she had – very briefly, but it was enough – seen straight through to a back window. Through this, in the gloom, she'd made out another cluster of buildings previously unnoticed. Cars were parked outside, lots of them, even on a Sunday afternoon, but she couldn't be sure of the distance – were these buildings even within the airbase perimeter? Could they hold a clue to the airbase's apparent secrets?

Two WAAFs, Juliette Gregg and Celia Robson, emerged from a hut and walked straight towards her. Klara's heart skipped a beat but they were more concerned with the next dance they were organising in a hall above a Co-op store in Amble, three miles away, and how many locals they'd be able to accommodate. They headed off for tea.

Far too many people were about for Klara to linger, and she brought her recce to a close, returning to the barrier. This time, she didn't see Sergeant Harris, but Archie Livingstone raised the pole with a cheery wave. Klara saluted, rode on.

She forked left and headed for the hive of activity she'd observed through the despatch block windows. As she'd suspected, it lay beyond the airbase boundary, in the next field. There was a detached house with a couple of outbuildings, just off the airstrip's flight path. And another construction, too... What was it?

With her binoculars, she soon ascertained that it wasn't a building. It was an entrance to a mine, with a low pithead housing a lift that descended into the shaft. Klara would check on her maps, but she was sure that the mines near Acklington had closed.

"Aye, aye, who goes there?" A moment later, less aggressively: "Are you lost? Do you need any help?"

A male voice, elderly, hoarse, with underlying determination.

Klara lowered the binoculars and faced him. Home Guard. Unarmed. She'd heard no footsteps. He'd have been concealed by trees – on surveillance duty around the mysterious mine head?

"Thank you, but no, I'm fine."

"I thought there might be something wrong."

"Not at all. Actually, I was about to have a bite to eat. They gave me a sandwich in the airbase when I said I hadn't eaten all day."

"Oh?"

"I've just delivered a parcel, you see, so we used the same wrapper. Kind of them to share a bit of scran."

Klara lifted the brown paper bag out of the pannier and showed it to the Home Guard private – no stripes – for just a second. Long enough for him to glimpse the airbase address that she'd written on it.

"Very well, provided you're not in any kind of trouble. There's nothing to see here, so move along please, as soon as you can."

So saying, the private walked away, stretching his weary limbs.

Nothing to see here? She was new to this site, but every moment Klara spent there suggested otherwise. She opened the bag and finally bit into the tinned meat sandwich. Grey bread, no butter. Dry and chewy, the meat was unrecognisable as such.

Time to head back to Silverbeck, but with one more stop on the way. Klara needed to make a telephone call.

***

Midnight had tolled when the latest meeting of the film society was called to order in the Odyssey. It was now the small hours of Monday 15 January. Harry Jarvis provided a pot of coffee, brewed as always from a packet he kept locked in his office cupboard, not from the one in the staff kitchenette.

The mood was lively, expectant. Those present were happy to be in the company of like-minded individuals from all walks of life, all manner of backgrounds, especially with the undeniable frisson of meeting *in secret*. What would they say if they were caught? Were they doing anything wrong? They were gathered in the Odyssey's rear circle, with space to mingle behind the back row of seats.

Today, for the first time, attendance topped twenty. Three people had arrived for their first meeting – and he'd taken a call yesterday afternoon from a Miss Evelyn Fletcher, who had sounded eager to join next time. That word of the group's existence was spreading was exciting on the one hand, challenging on the other: it increased the risk of a leak, of exposure, although Harry had made himself an escape plan.

The newcomers, two men and a woman, were all in their fifties. Over coffee, the woman, Sonia Stobart, told Harry her story, much of which had happened in a maelstrom since New Year. A tremor in her wrist caused her coffee cup to shake until she steadied it with her other hand.

"I was born in Gateshead, but when I was very young, still at school, we moved to Hamburg. My father worked for a German bank, you see. In 1912, when I was twenty-five, I married the chef in my favourite place to eat out, close to the Alster."

She risked a sip of coffee. "In March 1916, Gustav, my husband, was killed in the German attack on Verdun. So much slaughter. When Gustav died, I'd just found out that I was pregnant with Matilda, our daughter, who did well and became an optician with her own clientele in Hamburg."

"So far, so good." Harry covered for her while Sonia put down her cup and picked up her handbag.

"A fortnight ago, immediately after New Year, two men paid me a visit. They were perfectly courteous, but their instructions were chilling. I was to return to England, provide information to help the Abwehr, or life would become extremely difficult for my daughter and her business. I have been here for six days," she said, lowering her voice. "Money is no problem – they gave me plenty of cash. And do you know what, I've rather enjoyed snooping around, taking photographs, making notes. Coastal defences, arms depots, you name it. I take it I can have material forwarded to Germany via this group?"

"Of course," Harry replied. "We're always delighted to help with that."

Sonia hauled a bulging white envelope from her handbag. "These are the fruits of my first six days," she said. "There will be more, I promise." She held it close to her chest.

"I'm sure Matilda will be fine," Harry said, taking the hint. "Have you heard from her since you've been here?"

Sonia shook her head despondently.

"That can be arranged. Leave it with me."

She handed over the envelope.

Behind them, Warren Sixsmith, another of the newcomers, was admiring the huge, windowless auditorium that could not be snooped on from outside. He chatted to the third newcomer, Jack Redfern, a recently retired ironmonger. Then Warren lit a cigarette and went in search of an ashtray, while Jack asked Harry how he got his limp.

About an hour ago, Harry had been in the cinema foyer, inserting a Laurel and Hardy poster into a frame, when he heard five staccato knocks – the last three twice as quick as the first two – on a glass door below the entrance canopy.

A man in his sixties was standing there, the ends of his scarf blowing in the wind. In the shadows behind him, at the kerb, rested a Triumph 5H motorcycle.

"Hello, Alf," Harry said politely. "That motorcycle's yours?" He peered through the darkness, left and right. No one in the street.

Alf nodded.

"Anything happened to your Rover? Not an accident, I hope."

"Nothing like that. Just a feeling. Thought I'd change vehicles on the courier runs for a while."

"Fair enough."

Alf handed over two boxes, each six inches square, an inch thick. They were plastered with film icons – strips of celluloid, director chairs, arc lights, megaphones.

Harry thanked him, then added as an afterthought: "You brought Evelyn Fletcher in last month, didn't you?"

Alf nodded again, said nothing.

"What did you make of her?"

"I enjoyed her company." What was Harry fishing for? From the way he spoke, he didn't know Alf's true identity, which suited Alf just fine. "She has a knack – people will want to open up to her, befriend her."

In the pit of his stomach, Harry couldn't avoid feeling jealous of this woman. He ached for an ounce of the benign affability that she apparently exuded in abundance.

"Thank you."

Alf got on the Triumph, while Harry locked up and went to his office. Inside the first box was a report on a new generation of British Army tanks being tested secretly on the North York Moors. In the second, a map marking harbour defences and military barracks in eastern Scotland. He hoped the film society members would bring additional intelligence for the group to sense-check. Harry himself would ensure they were sent on to Berlin.

He always looked forward to the members arriving. He was never sure exactly who would attend each session, but as long as his core of regulars were present, well, that was fine.

When they'd had their fill of coffee, he usually sat them down and gave an eloquent speech. It meant a lot to have them hanging on his every word: he'd never known such respect before. He started by reminding them of the need for secrecy.

"Most people promise not to tell, but they do." He looked them one by one in the eye. Alice Young, among the first to have joined the group, tended to bite her nails at moments such as this. "We can't tolerate broken promises, can we? Not when our lives depend on discretion."

If only they knew how true that was, Harry reflected. They would not like to incur the murderous wrath of Ulrich Freitag, who had assured Harry, the last time they'd spoken by telephone, that he would attend the group's next meeting, at which Evelyn Fletcher would make her first appearance. It had sounded more like a threat than a promise.

13

Dead drop

The bittersweet irony of his job – indeed, his life – depending on him travelling in a Junkers aircraft, when he'd had a hand in killing the founder of the company, had not escaped Ulrich Freitag.

Here he was on a Ju-52, with its sixty-foot wingspan and distinctive corrugated aluminium finish that looked ahead of its time. Based in Dessau, eastern Germany, Junkers had built thousands of these planes: by the mid-'30s, the Ju-52 was a mainstay of many airlines. It had three propellors, one on each low-slung wing, the other on the black-tipped nose. It could carry seventeen passengers or, without the seats, three tons of freight.

This flight had a sparse load. Apart from the experienced pilot, who knew his passenger reported directly to Reichsmarschall Göring, Freitag was the only person on board. The pilot had kept it to himself, but he was thrilled to have been entrusted with such an important trip. When he'd sworn never to disclose his passenger's identity, he'd meant it.

Freitag's rucksack, hooked on to the jump harness, contained his Walther pistol in a leather holster. He'd insisted on selecting his own spare parachute and was now rechecking the one he intended to use – chute, suspension lines, harness – in case he felt the need to swap them over.

You can't be too careful, he reminded himself. Only last week, a colleague in Department G, highly trained as a *Fallschirmjäger* in an SS parachute regiment created by Himmler himself, had dropped into tall trees near Ravenscar and snapped his neck.

Hugo Junkers had only himself to blame for his demise. Freitag hoped his wife, Therese, and their children appreciated that, although he hadn't met any of them and never would. If only the stubborn old man had co-operated when the Nazis came to power and helped with the vital work of rearming Germany – but he'd flatly refused. *Dummkopf!* Naturally, he had been threatened with imprisonment for high treason if he didn't hand ownership of his companies to the NSDAP. But even then, Junkers held out and was kept under house arrest for months.

Freitag was baffled by the pointless obstinacy. Five years ago, in February 1935, he was one of a covert unit despatched to Junkers's home in Bavaria to secure all his shares in the company once and for all. Perhaps the negotiations had got a little hot-tempered, too physical? Perhaps Junkers had suffered a heart attack? Perhaps Freitag had over-used the poker during their fireside chats? It was all beginning to blur in his memory. Whatever the cause, Junkers had died on his seventy-sixth birthday and the Nazis gained total control of his company. So, job done.

Freitag finished repacking the parachute. It was fine, no need to change them over.

He was eager to renew his acquaintance with Harry Jarvis, if only to discover how the group of like-minded folk had developed under the 'film society' guise. Off-hand, Freitag could think of no better place for the group to meet than a picture house: an everyday building with few windows and a large auditorium where you could see all around. *Perfekt.*

The first reports they'd sent in were promising, adequate detail, gradually shading in a more sophisticated picture of civilian and military life. This is what Department G wanted from them and other such groups of agents and sympathisers around the country. Göring wanted Department G, and no one else, to take the lead in briefing the invasion planners. Following intelligence from a reliable source in a Hamburg hotel, they had decided to muscle in on the Abwehr's Operation

Trawl. But Freitag had to take care: the Abwehr must believe that they retained control of these groups, and that Department G's presence was invisible.

He hadn't formed a high opinion of Jarvis himself. Like many traitors, the man was profoundly unhappy. His spying for Germany owed as much to his dissatisfaction with his own life as it did to his support of the Nazis. No matter, provided the network grew, yielded useful intelligence, repaid the investment…

Freitag wondered how the group would react to his attempts to galvanise them into action. To undertake not only intelligence gathering, essential as that was, but direct acts of sabotage to damage British infrastructure, undermine public confidence. The north-east group had the optimal skillset. It comprised builders, farmers, chemists, press correspondents, guesthouse proprietors – precisely the experience he needed – and more. High time for them to step up and realise their true potential.

"*Schottland!*"

The pilot yelled their location through the open cockpit doorway.

Freitag's dark eyes narrowed. The next communication would come when they reached his drop zone. Under cover of darkness, he would jump from 9,000 feet, freefalling for half a minute before tugging the ripcord at 6,000 feet. The parachute would be fully deployed by 5,000. At no more than a hundred feet from the ground, he would release the harness and grip the webbing, letting go at just ten feet. Knees and ankles pressed tightly together, knees bent a little, legs tense to absorb the impact of the Scottish Highlands' heathered moors. The canopy would float away, drawing any enemy fire that might possibly be there.

Although the freefall was short and exhilarating, Freitag did not like being at the mercy of the elements. He avoided dwelling in the past or fretting about events he could not change. In the present, he liked to exert complete control. He had his orders and his methods. He was sure the Odyssey's film society would bend to his purpose. Nothing would stop him.

He walked to the side of the plane and braced himself for the blast of icy wind when he slid open the door.

***

Alice Young, who had not missed a single film society meeting, considered the most recent one to have been the best so far. This pleased her, calmed her restlessness. Progressively, there was more activity for the group – and now for her individually – to undertake. If that made her a kind of activist, at her age, well, she was thrilled.

She wondered whether the easy conversation she'd struck up with Walter Dodds would lead anywhere. He was the third generation of his family to live and work on a farm, which rotated livestock and arable crops on its meadows, to the west of Newcastle. He'd lost his wife prematurely, now he was on his own.

Photography was a hobby, he'd said, not that he had much time to pursue it. He'd come with a set of black and white prints of some Chain Home stations – from a distance – on the coast. He'd developed them himself, so no one else could possibly have seen them, which Harry Jarvis had commended as an excellent idea. He'd asked Walter to write on the back of each print the precise location and when it was taken.

Alice had got talking to Walter afterwards. They'd moved down to the front of the circle and leaned over the balcony, imagining they were forty years younger, firing dried peas from pea-shooters at kids in the stalls. How they'd giggled, before sitting down when some of the others stared.

"You know, the Führer adores the cinema," Alice told Walter. "He shows films to his guests after dinner, and I've read that he has lots of film people, actors and so on, among his circle of friends."

"Have you seen *Metropolis*?" Walter looked at her with his pale blue eyes. "It was first out a dozen or so years ago."

"Fritz Lang made it. I've seen it twice."

"Apparently the Führer is a great fan of it," Walter said. "You know, he strikes me as a champion, who won't take no for an answer. A man of the people, despite what the newsreels would have us believe."

"You can tell that from the plain uniform he wears," Alice agreed. "What he stands for, as far as I can tell, is unity. A classless new order, an end to starvation, sky-high inflation and unfairness. Darling, who could disagree?" She'd never voiced such apparently treacherous opinions before. She felt liberated, excited. She hoped Walter didn't guess that her vivid imagination enabled her to live more happily in her fantasy world than in reality. She'd travelled far in her mind, much less in person.

"When you put it like that…" Walter shrugged.

Alice had seemed such a sweet person, but desperately lonely. It was clear that a deep-rooted grudge festered within her and that she retained a starry-eyed, utopian view of the Third Reich. The apparent clarity of an us-versus-them, for-or-against ideology appealed to her so stoutly that it left no room for the grey areas that haunted everyday life. She didn't seem to be as motivated by money – discreet payments from Harry – as he and other members of the group undoubtedly were.

He said quietly: "I'd love to have glamorous film people as my friends. The visions, the places they create on the screen are incredible, so real, I'd be fascinated to know how they do it."

He gazed around the auditorium. Alice snapped him out of his reverie by clasping his hand on the armrest. Her grip was surprisingly strong.

"You can be my friend," she gushed. "And, darling, I'll be yours if you'll let me. You know, I went to drama school in London, years ago now. Some wonderful people there, lots of wild ideas. I did well, won a prize in my first year, played a lovely range of parts on stage. Supporting roles, mostly, but it's one reason why I like this film society. It's lovely to feel as though I belong again."

In turn, Walter gave her hand a friendly squeeze. It felt like a little bird. His own hands were paws, large and hairy, and his fingertips, bless him, were as coarse as sandpaper.

"I'm afraid that my promising early shoots didn't blossom," Alice recalled ruefully. She didn't pull her hand away. "A couple of plays on the trot received poor notices – critics can be so vicious – and the parts dried up. I would see younger actresses being cast in roles I knew I could do perfectly well, but darling, no one wanted to know."

"I'm sorry," Walter muttered simply. Yes, she felt alienated, bearing the hurt and humiliation of rejection to this day.

"I don't mind telling you, there were times when I was pretty desperate, near the edge. But you muddle through, because you have to, don't you? And today, when I hear about another country promoting respect and obedience, well, the idea of it warms the cockles, it really does. This is different from the last war. Somehow I wanted to show my support while I've still got my health, do you see?"

Walter had said sweetly that he understood, truly he did. Perhaps she would see him, talk to him again, next time? He'd said he hoped so, before excusing himself to have a word with another group member, Neil Sinclair, who had worked for thirty years for the same firm of builders.

Alice wondered whether it was Neil who had managed to get hold of the key that weighed so heavily in her coat pocket now as she leant into the biting wind that swirled in all directions on the Tyne Bridge. She was relishing the role in which she'd been cast at that film society meeting and was determined not to let the group down. Hobbling with a walking stick, with which she'd rehearsed at home yesterday evening, curtains tightly drawn, she crossed the bridge, shuffling slowly along its wide pavement. She headed south, the city of Newcastle behind her, towards Gateshead.

Alice well remembered the razzamatazz of the Tyne Bridge opening. It was only a dozen years ago – not long after *Metropolis* had come out – in October 1928. Movietone News filmed it. The king, George V, and Queen Mary were guests of honour, backed by thousands of cheering schoolchildren. They'd been allowed out of class for the occasion, so no wonder they cheered.

Already spanning the river was a Swing Bridge for vehicles and a High-Level Bridge for road and rail, both from the previous century. But the newly christened Tyne Bridge really was a miracle of modern engineering. A parabolic arch, built of steel girders clamped together by 750,000 rivets, finished in the 'Greenwood' shade of light green from a paint supplier in Gateshead. The arch stretched 1,200 feet long and almost two hundred feet high – closer to three hundred when measured from the water below. The bridge had rapidly come to symbolise the city itself.

Alice shuddered when she thought of the construction workers, who had not even had safety ropes. Yet only one, Nathaniel Collins, a thirty-three-year-old scaffolder and family man from South Shields, lost his life during the building phase, which lasted two-and-a-half years. The same design and construction firms were engaged on the much larger Sydney Harbour Bridge in Australia, which was begun before, but would be completed after, the Tyne Bridge.

Two lanes of traffic flowed in each direction, but this afternoon, darkness already descending over the great industrial city, it was not busy, which helped to relax her. Alice had expected it to be relatively quiet: the number of private cars on the roads was rising, but many young adults who were the drivers in the household were now away preparing for war. More pedestrians were walking north than south, so wrapped up against the wind that they paid her no attention. Just this once, that suited her fine. High up in the framework, pairs of kittiwakes were forming a breeding colony, where they would stay until August.

For this performance, Alice was wearing spectacles. A prop pair with plain glass, she'd kept them from her short run, years ago, as Berta the maid in a long-forgotten production of *Hedda*

Gabler. She'd put on gloves and a headscarf, the darkest one she could find, and a brown overcoat, fully buttoned up. It flapped around her knees but kept her body warm.

She was making for the south-west tower, one of four granite columns, two at each end, that anchored the bridge into the quaysides. Recessed into each tower at pavement level were metal-studded doors. The towers had been designed as warehouse space. Five floors had been envisaged in each tower with a lift to connect them to quayside level. But plans changed before the bridge opened and the storage spaces were never fitted out. No lift was installed in the south towers, but Alice had been told one was working on the north side.

She reached her tower and peered beyond it, through the twilight, at the rows of brick terraces in Gateshead. A wooden gate leading to a cemetery fought against its hinges, while the bare trees at the cemetery's edge leant in and out with every whim of the wind. She listened for a moment in awe to the silvery brown river, flowing with eternal purpose below. A bell clanged on a collier as it chugged under the bridge, heading inland.

Leaning her stick against the doors, Alice took out the key that Harry Jarvis had given to her, in private, when he'd explained the act required of her, right down to her character, costume, make-up, deportment. She'd interpreted his direction faithfully, hoping for many encores.

Having checked no one was close by, she inserted the chunky steel key – an incongruously gothic touch on such a contemporary bridge – into the lock. To her surprise, it turned easily, with barely a click in the wind. She picked up her stick, pushed the right-hand door and stepped inside.

Pitch black.

The light-switch was where she'd been briefed – on the left, just inside the door – and a single bulb, hanging from the tower's rafters, lit up. It swung on a blast of air, lobbing shadows up and down the walls.

Alice closed the door. A spider crawled over her left foot, pursued by its own shadow. She gathered her wits. The space was daunting, much larger than she'd imagined. The internal walls were bare granite, several blocks thick. She was standing on wooden floorboards which groaned with every pace and smelled damp. A wooden staircase on the far wall snaked all the way down from the rafters through the inserted stories to the quayside. The floorboards stopped short of the far corner on her right: the intended location of the lift shaft.

She tried to unscrew the flat top of her walking stick anti-clockwise. It did not budge. She removed her right glove and twisted it clockwise as hard as she could. No joy either. Another go, turning both ways. After a few agonising seconds, a crack and the top spun off, exposing a hollow core. It was not a stick, but a tube. Inside was a roll of foolscap pages, full of typewritten text, stapled top left.

Alice put her glove back on. Beside the light-switch, just as she'd been told, was a wooden shelf. Blowing off a cloud of dust, she extracted the papers and laid them on the shelf. She screwed the cap back on the stick, switched off the light, heaved open the door. A couple was walking past arm in arm, lost in each other's company. They did not look round, walked straight on, foreheads leaning into the wind.

She let them get a dozen paces away, then crept out onto the pavement. Still very few cars or people on the move. She locked the door, pocketed the key and enveloped herself in the folds of her coat.

She headed south into Gateshead. Wait – were those footsteps approaching from behind? Her blood running cold, she hesitated, awaited the clamp of a hand on her shoulder.

None came.

Alice shivered, watched the breath stream from her nostrils. There was that sound again – kittiwakes, perhaps, flapping on the girders?

Stay calm. You've achieved your part of the dead drop without a hitch. Bravo! A well-deserved round of applause at the next film society meeting? Keeping in character, Alice shuffled on.

She'd been gone less than five minutes when a grey Ford 8 stopped by the same tower. A passenger jumped out, took out his own key and let himself in. Without switching on the light, he seized the roll of papers from the shelf and replaced it with a similar roll of typed pages from an inside pocket. He tucked the originals in his pocket and withdrew, locking the door behind him. No sooner had he climbed back in the car than his colleague drove off, ten seconds after pulling up.

"Job done!" Warren Sixsmith said, his heart racing. He looked at the driver, Christopher Talbot, his line manager in MI5, with whom he had forged an excellent working relationship since taking up this posting a fortnight ago. Talbot was methodical, a clear thinker and communicator, and Sixsmith had every confidence in him. That said, he did seem to think he was a stunt driver on a film set every now and then.

"I must get this key back to the picture house. There were bunches of them, but I'll feel more comfortable when it's returned. I'd like Alice to go on believing she can confide in me."

"That's important," Talbot agreed. "I must say, I'm delighted at the way you've infiltrated that so-called film society."

He took a left at the end of the bridge, turned the car round to face north and pulled into the kerb.

"Look ahead!" He crouched low in his seat. "See?"

Sixsmith stared. In the darkness he saw little with any clarity, but there, perhaps twenty yards in front, climbing nimbly onto the passenger seat of a Rover 10, was Alice Young. Her driver, a man in his sixties, closed her door, got in and drove off.

"Keep your eyes on the tower," Talbot told Sixsmith. "We must witness the pick-up."

Five minutes elapsed. Six.

Talbot, who had been putting his thoughts in order, spoke up. "Bear with me, Warren. What do you make of this scenario? First, an inquisitive neighbour reports a suspicious pattern of arrivals at a guest house in Newcastle. Next, a police request to vet a manager at a picture house nearby. He's receiving information in packages resembling film reel boxes. The information he gets is discussed in that picture house at meetings of malcontents, anti-communists, Nazi sympathisers. A cell of Fifth Columnists in our midst, it's fair to say?"

Sixsmith did not avert his gaze from the bridge. "Some have their own contacts who help conduct reconnaissance, take photographs, you name it. Put it all together over a period of time and there's a good deal of valuable intelligence for an enemy preparing to invade."

"And the car that has just picked up Alice is the same one that drops people off at the guest house in the middle–"

"Bingo!" Sixsmith cried.

Talbot leaned across, stared at the tower. A black-suited man was entering. No car, so he must have walked, at least part of the way. Seconds later, out he came, stuffing the papers into a pocket. Pausing only to lock the door, he vanished into the darkness.

"There he goes," Talbot said softly. "The Collector, let's call him. I hope he believes that the dead drop was genuine."

"And that the material we planted is *bona fide* intelligence," Sixsmith added, "not an MI5 substitute."

It was months later when MI5 deduced that the Collector was the same, black-suited man who had hung on every word of the conversation between Susannah Innes and Archie Livingstone in The Smugglers' Cave, and that he had a long-standing connection to the driver, Alf.

14

Reunion and separation

The smoke billowing from the copper-rimmed chimney on the sleek, coal-powered locomotive engulfed the front of the train as it rolled, right on schedule, into Alnwick station in central Northumberland. The early afternoon of Friday 16 February was swept by a cold breeze despite the winter sunshine. The locomotive, *The Duchess*, was a mighty steam engine whose sheer size impressed Klara. She felt in awe of those who had built it, realising a wonderfully ambitious dream.

Alnwick was the terminus of a four-mile branch line from Alnmouth, the station on the east coast line, three hundred miles from London, which offered northbound passengers their first view of the sea. Alnwick was a surprisingly grand Victorian station – perhaps so designed, on reflection, given the VIPs who visited the nearby castle? The concourse had been adapted for the times: the pillars and platform edges were painted white to reflect the light, and all the lampshades stopped light shining upwards.

The Duchess had scarcely sighed to a halt at the buffers when one by one, in quick-fire succession, the carriage doors slammed back on their hinges. Some carriages had blue lights which were being tested at night-time but appeared rather eerie in daylight; others had their blinds drawn.

Klara looked on as a torrent of children, some very young, others in their teens, streamed out, crowding the platform. Each of them carried a case or holdall, a few clutched blankets and pillows too. Most of the evacuees would be placed with families; some of the older ones would be selected for farm labour or billeted in hostels. There, they would receive three cooked meals a day – probably more, she thought, than they'd get at home.

A whistle blew twice, the children fell into line. Every exhaled breath sent a plume of vapour into the air, while some stamped their feet, creating drum-beat rhythms. A few, bless them, looked in desperate need of a toilet.

"Hello, stranger."

Klara looked left and there he was, at her side. She had only known for eight days that he was coming. She hadn't seen him for a couple of months – immediately she thought his face looked thinner, he'd lost weight.

For Curt Schultz, the joy of seeing her again surpassed the pain of parting. Grinning broadly, he put down his suitcase. As they embraced, she was aware that he was hugging her harder than she was hugging him. Did he mean it or was he just acting his cover to the hilt? Despite the long journey, he still managed to smell as fresh as ever.

When they separated, she looked him in the eye. "How are you, Simon? How was the journey?"

"Well worth it." The smile had not left his face. He'd seen her shorter haircut only the once before she left Berlin. It exposed the beautiful nape of her neck, which she'd let him touch in his office, and he hoped she would again. Short hair suited her, although he'd need a little time to get used to it. Likewise, his cover name of Simon.

She was no longer watching him. Her eyes were scanning the concourse, which was teeming with uniformed servicemen, children, women waiting patiently. The youngsters who had poked their heads out of the train windows had grey, soot-flecked faces for their trouble. From the guard's van, a man in railway uniform strode through the carriages, checking that every compartment was empty. He shook the arm of a soldier sleeping in a luggage rack above the padded bench seats.

"It was standing room only," Schultz said. "I was in that carriage there, two from the end. I rested my head on the window, shut my eyes and listened, listened, listened."

"Good." Klara lowered her voice. "They like discussing the weather, don't they? Even if there isn't any."

"The cold came up quite a bit, yes, along with worries about rationing and air raids. Dance parties and films, too – they enjoy a night at the pictures."

Klara walked slowly towards the booking office window, which had a view across the concourse. The lines of children were being processed by a team of women armed with clipboards, seated at a trestle table by a wall of sandbags. One woman had a whistle strung around her neck.

"This is the latest wave of evacuations," Klara told Curt. "Many children are taken from the target areas of the industrial cities to the relative safety of the countryside."

"This throng came from Newcastle, changed trains with me at Alnmouth. Lots of the youngsters had fun comparing the new pyjamas that each of them seemed to have brought." He shrugged.

"Given my cover occupation as a supply teacher, I wanted to be here today not just to meet you – my, er, brother – off the train, but to be seen by a Mrs Barker in the booking office."

"Mrs Barker?"

"She doesn't know me, but she's a close friend of my landlady at Silverbeck, and she'll put two and two together when she notices me. They talk most days on the telephone. It'll reaffirm my legend."

"In the paranoia of the Phoney War," Curt whispered conspiratorially, "that's a smart idea."

Klara felt a tug on her coat. She turned, at first saw nothing, then looked down on to a small boy's cap.

He was standing very close, gripping her. His eyes were red, his cheeks streaked with tears, not only from the cold, but he looked well-kempt. At his side was a brown suitcase, much too big and heavy for him.

Klara crouched down on her haunches and gently cupped a hand on his shoulder. "What's your name, young man?"

He had two attempts before any words emerged. "K – Kevin." His two front teeth were much larger than the rest.

"Well, hello, Kevin, nice to meet you. Are you here on your own? Any brothers or sisters?"

Kevin shook his head, chin trembling. He was six or seven years old, Klara's age when the Great War broke out.

"That's all right. It's often easier when there's only one of you. Have you registered – checked in – over there? Once they have your name, the kind ladies will be able to help you. That's what they're here for."

Kevin tugged her coat again. "But you look like my mummy. Can't I go home with you?"

"Oh, my dear boy, that's not possible." A lump began to solidify in Klara's throat. "I'm not here to take any boys or girls – I can't."

The traumatised child's eyes pleaded, filled with tears.

"There's no room where I live," Klara explained. "No spare bed, no toys, no books that you'd like. Besides, there'll be a family looking forward to welcoming you very much, and I couldn't disappoint them. Shall we go together to make sure the ladies have everything they need?"

Kevin, who had been studying his shoes, looked around. He seemed frightened by a throng of soldiers at a catering kiosk which was serving discounted drinks to people in uniform. He reached into a pocket and pulled out by its ears a much-loved plush donkey, which he cuddled with one hand, heaving up his suitcase with the other.

"Can't I go home with you?" he repeated. "I don't need any toys."

Klara's heart nearly broke. She had never had to confront the raw human reality of an evacuation before. Off-hand, she could not recall the last time she had wept, but within a minute this young boy, uprooted and craving stability and love, had touched her deeply. He'd given her a tiny insight into the cost of this wretched war – which, in this country, hadn't even started yet. Her eyes prickled with hot tears, which she did not want Curt Schultz to see.

She took Kevin's hand, squeezed it, and led him to the table, where the ladies still had dozens of evacuated children to allocate to a host family. They had been joined by a local chaplain, helping them comfort the younger ones.

"I want to work on a farm!" Klara heard a petite girl say in her loudest, Shirley Temple voice.

"Well, my dear," retorted a lady at the table, "you'll have to marry a farmer, won't you!"

As it happened, a couple of farmers were watching the registrations, scratching their chins while they weighed up the taller lads. But it was the exchange with the petite girl that made her bristle. Having competed in her late twenties in the Olympic Games, Klara could never accept being told that anything lay beyond her grasp. She hid her indignation well, but really, was that the most inspirational advice for a young girl who had expressed an ambition?

Thankfully, another lady had seen Klara trying to console Kevin and came forward, clipboard at the ready, to offer a helping hand. Gently, Klara unfurled his little fingers and bade him Godspeed.

"Goodbye, dear Kevin, and good luck!"

When Kevin glanced over his shoulder, Klara had already turned away. He'll be fine, she told herself, they all will. Children adapt quickly, resiliently, cope with stress. Kevin was handsome enough, he was sure to be picked early. She fixed on a smile and had a last look back: Kevin, talking to the chaplain, didn't see her.

Klara swallowed hard, dried her eyes.

"Let's go," she said to Curt.

She'd parked the ES2 off the main road that led into Alnwick town centre. A hundred yards away was the Playhouse, now fifteen years old, a popular picture house with two hundred and fifty seats. Tonight, it was showing a Will Hay comedy.

Klara sat up front on the dual seat, leaving space behind for Curt, who gripped the panniers. The school, St. Hilda's Grammar, where Klara had told Mrs Purnell that she, Evelyn Fletcher, was teaching had just broken up for half-term and she'd be meeting Simon, her older brother, off the train at Alnwick. No, she wasn't sure how long he'd be visiting, but it would be nice to have him nearby, wouldn't it?

Twenty minutes later, Klara brought the Norton to a halt on a hillside path overlooking RAF Acklington. She chose a spot behind thick tree cover before handing the binoculars to Curt. Little Kevin had not left the forefront of her mind. She prayed he would settle quickly in a new family home, find his place in the changing world.

"That RAF base is the most significant one in this area," she said. The airfield sprawled below them, people in uniform coming and going between the buildings and huts. To the north-west, a railway line scythed through the fields. She told Curt about the other airfields she'd visited and her discovery that RAF Boulmer was a decoy.

"Now," she continued while he gazed at the Spitfires. "Look to the right – slowly. Near the airbase, a manor house and what looks like a mineshaft. Got it?"

"I must say, it's rather a small mine." Curt tightened the focus. "Still in use?"

"Look at all the cars parked at the house," Klara said. "I've spent hours watching this site and the patterns of movement. Dozens of people work there. Some go into the house, do a day's work, go home. Others take the lift at the pithead, descend into the mine and emerge hours later."

"But they're not miners? It isn't actually a mine?"

"The men and women who go down there are dressed as civilians. A few RAF officers, but mostly civilians. They come out without a speck of coal-dust. There's some secret work going on down there, nothing to do with coal. So secret, in fact, that the decoy airfield was constructed to deflect the Luftwaffe."

"That's good work," Curt complimented her again. "I've missed you so much."

Klara said nothing. He seemed eager to make up for lost time; she wasn't so sure.

"How much of all this have you reported back to Berlin?"

"None," she replied. "Not yet, anyway. I'd prefer to build a complete picture, get my story straight. What do you think?"

"Well, the planning for Operation Sealion, the invasion of Britain, and Operation Lena, the Abwehr's pre-invasion reconnaissance, is progressing well. Both operations will be implemented this year, no question. We're part of Operation Trawl, the advance party. If you have good intelligence, you must feed it back. It will be expected of you."

"I'm making progress in my own way, at my own pace," she defended herself. "I hope my work will be of use."

"Of course it will." His desire to protect her burned fiercely. "And I'll help you."

"Now you're here, what will your priorities be?"

"Having a close look at those radar installations on the coast," he said. "General Martini is uneasy, but Göring remains adamant that the case is closed."

"Operation Bloodhound the last word on British radar? With plans for the invasion still on the drawing board? I doubt it." Klara paused, having sensed movement in the grass. Two white horses grazed nonchalantly down the gentle slope, as if she and Curt weren't there.

"I know what you'll say," she said, "but may I ask—"

"Fire away." He had another good look through the binoculars at the suspicious mine.

"I'm attending my first meeting of the film society next week." Klara wrapped her arms around her body against a biting gust. "They'll want to know what I'm working on, what I hope to contribute as a newcomer. How much should I reveal in that forum?"

"All of it. If they suspect you're holding out, your position is weakened, you'll be on the back foot. So, do yourself justice," Curt lowered the binoculars, "and don't make yourself a marked woman."

Sitting in his Ford 8 at the detached house, Christopher Talbot was distracted by a piercing glint of sunlight, which came from the hill in front of him. He'd been flicking through a folder of correspondence. One memo requested a protocol change regarding the Boulmer airstrip, which he made a mental note to check later. For now, his full attention was on the hillside.

There it was again, the same momentary flash of a light-reflecting lens. Someone was up there, amongst the trees, using a camera or field glasses. He saw no other movement.

Talbot fired the engine and drove fast to the foot of the hillock. He waited five, ten, another five minutes. Nothing, just a pair of white horses, nuzzling each other. If anyone had been there, they had now gone.

***

Apparently, the roof had leaked overnight in a torrential downpour, which dislodged tiles and hurled loose branches into the gutters. Water had seeped through in two places and dripped on the carpet and seats in the rear circle. Without exception, no one was to go up there.

When the film society members arrived for their session on Tuesday night, 20 February, Harry Jarvis ushered them to the front of the stalls. They had coffee between the first row of seats and the stage. Some felt this space was better than the rear circle – not so many stairs to climb, for a start – yet peer as they might, none of them spotted a leak in the ceiling.

Harry was standing in the foyer, keeping watch on the unlocked glass door when Klara walked up. He introduced himself over a handshake.

"A pleasure to meet you," he said, although it did not sound as though he meant it. His eyes were dim. "At last."

"I've had a busy few weeks," Klara said quietly. Was someone else lurking in the darkness in this huge lobby? She could not be sure, but she'd thought there were footsteps in the corner. "Scouting airfields and some naval bases. Gathering as much knowledge as I can. I might as well tell you, one focus is on an old mine near Acklington airbase." That was, she hoped, enough to prove she had a lot on her plate and was happy to share it with him. A good contributor, an asset to the group.

"Splendid." Harry stood closer to her than she felt he needed to. She took a pace back, brushed against a palm tree. "We have a tried and tested dead-drop method of passing information to our friends in Germany, so let us know—"

"Hello there!"

Harry was interrupted by the arrival of a man in a tailored dark blue suit. He introduced himself to Klara as Warren Sixsmith.

"Ah, we've been looking forward to you joining us," he said breezily. "If there's anything I can do, show you the ropes, come and find me." He looked her in the eye. "Any time."

While Harry awaited other arrivals, Klara let Warren Sixsmith guide her from foyer to auditorium, where a dozen people were chatting animatedly. By now, they were familiar with each other, most having attended several meetings. Klara was the one who needed to break the ice, and Warren stayed at her side, presenting her first to Alice Young, who was anticipating another dead drop on the Tyne Bridge, and Walter Dodds, the farmer, who was showing a photograph of his latest litter of Border Collies to enraptured colleagues.

Jack Redfern, the retired ironmonger, was talking to a stocky man named Bob Cracknell. He had a crooked nose, broken years ago. When Jack was speaking, Bob turned his head as he had no sight in his right eye. Sonia Stobart, with a crisp white envelope tucked under one arm, joined them and revealed her happiness yesterday when a letter arrived from her daughter.

Sixsmith was urbane, thoughtful and dapper, Klara thought. But then every man looks good in a well-fitting suit and crisp white shirt. She would later discover that his mother was a seamstress who had taught all her children how to iron fast. He had a tiny gap between his front teeth, and long eyelashes that made his eyes look bigger. He listened before speaking, a trait that endeared anyone to her. Yet she realised at once that she was not the complete focus of his attention. He maintained a restless eye on their surroundings – who was talking to whom, who was coming and going.

Nearly time for the meeting to start – now, where was Harry? Still greeting people in the foyer? Klara thanked Sixsmith and went to get some coffee from the trays at the end of the stage. A light in her peripheral vision made her look up – and her blood curdled.

She risked a second glance, kept walking, head down, towards the coffee. In the wall above the rear circle were three glass portholes: the projection room. Two portholes had a Cinemeccanica projector behind them, primed to beam flickering images on the screen.

In the centre window were two faces, surveying the group members as they congregated. One was Harry Jarvis. The second man, at his side, had a large, completely bald head. It was, unmistakably, Ulrich Freitag.

Klara poured herself some coffee, hands steady despite the hairs on the back of her neck standing on end. She poured another cupful for an elderly man who shuffled up behind her.

"There you go," she said kindly. "Can you manage?"

Handing over the coffee on which the man warmed his palms, she kept the projection window in view. Was Freitag jabbing a finger against the pane directly at her?

Inside the projection room, Harry Jarvis was feeling less awkward in this man's company than he'd feared. He was relieved to have discovered Freitag's unexpected interest in Benjamin Britten's music, as he was able to comment, however briefly, on the scores Britten had composed for documentary films, which pleased the big German.

"What do you know of that woman, the one pouring coffee now?" Freitag asked. He had not clapped his sunken eyes on Gretel since the spy flight in the zeppelin, but he did not want her to know he was in Britain. Not yet, at least.

"I met her for the first time twenty minutes ago," Jarvis revealed. "I know practically nothing about her."

They moved inside, away from the porthole. They did not see Klara put down her cup and stride up the aisle to the doors at the rear of the stalls. From the deserted foyer, she climbed the staircase to the circle level, then a lino-covered back staircase that coiled around a lift shaft to the top floor where the projectors were housed. Within a minute, she was listening at the door. With no other sounds, she caught enough to get the gist of the muffled exchange.

Harry Jarvis was explaining why he did not compile dossiers on the film society members. "Discretion is essential for this network to be effective. A file of records is a trail of evidence, which I neither want nor need. I'm afraid that secrets burn holes until they get out. So, I discuss, convey, only what I need to. The lower the chances of a leak, the better for us all."

Freitag's voice: "I follow your logic." Klara expected there to be a 'but', but none came, or if it did, she didn't hear it. Instead, Freitag returned to his previous point. "That woman pouring the coffee—"

"Her cover is a schoolteacher. Alf – you know him, of course? – told me that. He warmed to her. What she's doing in reality…" Harry cast his mind back, what was it she'd said just minutes ago? "… she's keeping a disused mine in Acklington under surveillance. She must be on to something – on a first impression, she strikes me as competent and capable." He remembered his acidic feelings of jealousy towards this woman but swallowed them down in a gulp.

"I don't like her. I don't trust her…." The words were mumbled.

"So, you know her then? How…?"

Klara wondered whether Freitag would see red at the cross-examination, knock Harry Jarvis to the floor. But he let his voice, not his fists, do the talking.

"As you yourself said, the fewer people who are in on our secrets, the happier I am."

Klara was infuriated that she missed the next exchange. Then she picked up Freitag again.

"You must not let her work in…" What was that word? Isolation? "You must assign someone you trust, maybe one of the others down there, to shadow this woman. She should not know they are there. But if secrets are unearthed in Acklington, I want to know what they are."

Klara's throat had run dry. She dared not cough, make any sound at all.

"Those are my orders. Do you understand?" Freitag's voice was raised. The Freitag she knew. Harry Jarvis had not resisted his domination of the group, but it did no harm to remind him who was top dog.

Klara was hanging on for Jarvis's reply when, five yards ahead, another door opened.

The startled face of Jack Redfern, ex-ironmonger, appeared. Rather than making a scene, accusing Klara as she'd dreaded, he patently felt he was one who owed an explanation and held a finger to his lips.

"I make duplicate keys for Harry," he whispered. "All sorts of them. Just putting a new batch in here. No one to know."

"Of course," Klara whispered back. *Ex-ironmonger? Less of the 'ex'.*

"And I've been asked to see the big German fellow later – some task or other he wants done. No rest for the wicked, eh?"

Redfern came out of the room, followed as if they were conjoined by Neil Sinclair, who closed the door silently, not even a click. On the way down, they nodded fleetingly to another member of the group, coming up. Perhaps it was this distraction that made Sinclair miss a stair and almost lose his footing. He landed with a thud on the next stair down – and in that instant the conversation in the projection room stopped dead.

The blue-suited man climbing the stairs reached the top. He signalled to Klara and whispered: "Come on, Evelyn, now! If they find you here…"

The projection room door cracked open, a sliver of light edged around it. No more voices. Either Jarvis or Freitag was about to appear. The light spread across the floor…

Klara reached the stairs in six tiptoed paces and followed the man down. Neither of them breathed until they were in the circle lounge on the floor below. They listened for footsteps.

Warren Sixsmith's tone was hushed but very urgent. "Evelyn, please listen, we might only have a few seconds. I'm an officer in MI5. I can prove it to you, but for now you must trust me." *Trust him?* A rapid glance around. "It's all clear. Come at once."

·

15

Assault and battery

Tonight was the night, Bob Cracknell told himself. Wednesday night, 20 March. His night. Harry had told him that the big German had approved it.

Bob had spent the past month – ever since the last film society meeting – making plans, observing his prey. She hadn't noticed him, he was sure of it. And he was ready, with all his notes memorised, he really was. If not now, when?

Bob had been born into a fairground family. Aged ten, after his mam died, he worked full-time for his father, a travelling showman. From March, throughout the eight-month season, they pitched their carousel and swingboats for a week at a time at fairs from coast to coast. He loved the sights, sounds, smells of a hectic fairground, the intoxicating blend of delight and trepidation on the punters' faces.

This was his way of life until, one winter, his father developed a cough that clung to his chest until it squeezed the life out of him. At fifteen, Bob found himself alone and angry, grieving for his dad. The following season, he sold the carousel and swingboats, but kept the old man's van and the little caravan it towed, which had been their home these last five years. He heard that one of the old-time boxers working in Sharkey's Boxing Booth was retiring and he badgered Gerry Sharkey into take him on as a new pugilist.

"Marquis of Queensberry rules," Gerry had stressed. "And don't punch the locals too hard, we want them to come back. Spot any raw talent, I'll cut you in if they turn pro!"

For a dozen years, Bob took on all comers in Sharkey's boxing ring. He found that he fervently disliked his challengers and enjoyed thumping them with impunity. Most who fancied their chances ended up on their backs within two rounds, and he earned the moniker 'Crusher Cracknell'. The wider his reputation spread, the fiercer the opponents who showed up. It was in Bognor Regis that, eventually, he suffered the worst pounding. When he slumped to the canvas, his battered nose was all but flat and his right eye so badly damaged that he had practically no sight in it.

Crusher's career was over. He retired from boxing and put to practical use the knowledge gained over the years maintaining his dad's van by joining Swanson's garage in the east end of his home town, Newcastle.

He kept an eye on the lads hired to operate the fuel pumps and wipe the windscreens, and he ensured that the forecourt was tidy. He repaired cars and vans, large and small, sending the contented owners into the little office to settle up. Every financial transaction was in the hands of the proprietor, Maurice Swanson, who worked around the clock. He was in the office when Bob arrived early in the morning, and he was there when Bob left in the evening.

Last Monday, everything changed. Maurice had told Bob out of the blue, with no apparent regret or emotion, that the business was going bust. No reserves to pay suppliers, but he would leave early today and withdraw enough cash to see Bob and the lads right for that month.

In shock, Bob had said little. But of course, that was the last he'd seen of Maurice. In hindsight, should he have challenged him, extracted some sort of guarantee, before watching him drive off? Maurice had not shown up for work on Tuesday or any day since, and his home telephone – assuming he'd given the correct number – was not answered.

Not for the first time, Bob felt that life had dealt him a cruel hand. This time, he could unburden himself by directing blame on to Maurice individually and, by extension, Jewish people as a whole. In some quarters, this seemed quite fashionable.

But Bob's anti-Semitism, dredged from the swamp of his prejudice, was born of ignorance. Maurice Swanson was not a Jew. Bob had simply assumed it, and assumption can spawn many wrongs. Maurice was a man of no faith and, as it turned out, precious little morality either. With more garages opening in the area, he cleared out the account and made off with a new woman, leaving his colleagues in the lurch. If Bob ever laid eyes on him again…

Sensing an opportunity, Harry Jarvis had stepped in. He promised to help financially for services rendered. And there happened to be a job he wanted carried out, for which he thought Bob was ideally suited.

Bob was jolted back to the here and now by the dark green four-door Singer turning into the street. It was approaching 7 p.m. on 20 March. He didn't know the woman's name – it hadn't mattered so far – but he knew her routine inside out.

He'd begun his assignment by keeping watch on the manor house and the mine by RAF Acklington. For days on end, he studied the comings and goings, identifying who worked in which location at what hours, when they arrived and departed. Any who regularly came or went in groups were rejected. He'd sifted out three people – all women – as potential marks. All travelled alone, none seemed to socialise much.

He followed one of them home. She lived on her own, and as far as he could tell from listening in the shadows, she made herself an evening meal, read a bit, went to bed.

The second woman was also on her own but wore a wedding ring and spent many evenings in the company of her neighbours. Her husband was away, he assumed, in the armed forces.

But this woman, driving the Singer, the third of the three, seemed perfect. He thought she might be Jewish to boot. Her home was a cottage in Morpeth, a town ten miles south of the airbase. She shared it with her children – two boys, eight to ten years old – and an older woman, her mother, obviously, who spent most days and some nights with them. She was there when the children came home from school. Again, no husband was present: if he was alive, he too must be in the armed forces.

Parked across the street, Bob counted the seconds, as he'd done on several previous evenings. It was a fast routine. She switched off, jumped out and let herself in. She closed the front door with her heel, and he imagined the reunion with the boys in the parlour or kitchen. They'd go up to bed soon.

Bob waited half an hour. Just in case her mother went out, a friend popped round, or a neighbour came home. It was dark and quiet, but tonight this street was his playground. Trying not to disturb the stillness, he crept up to the Singer. A last check: no one in sight, no eyes peeping through the blackouts. Just a gull on a lamppost, jerking its neck, watching his every move.

Dropping to the ground, he executed an agile roll under the Singer without grazing his knees or elbows. He ended on his back with the car's underbelly inches above his face. No sweat, second nature for a mechanic. From his coat, he withdrew a screwdriver and a wrench, wrapped in cloth.

Bob knew precisely what he was doing, and in less than two minutes, it was done. His pulse was racing when he stood up, but a warm glow inflated his body. This task would secure the affirmation and acceptance he deserved.

By dawn the next morning, Bob was back, parked along the street, this time in the bullnose Morris Minor van with the garage livery. He suspected it was an old Royal Mail van, repainted black, but he'd never put Swanson on the spot.

He didn't need to be there quite so early. The woman habitually departed at eight. But this morning, nothing could be left to chance.

8.10 a.m. He hoped she wasn't much longer, he was cold and stiff, wanted exercise.

She emerged formally dressed, as always, large handbag brushing her stockinged thigh. She tossed it on to the passenger seat, turned the ignition key and – nothing.

She tried again. No spark, no splutter as the engine sprang to life. Oh, Lord, what could be the matter? It was running fine last night.

Bob watched her scowl, check the time, make another attempt to start. Come on, third time lucky. Nothing.

He timed his move to split-second perfection. Driving with the passenger-side window already lowered, he halted alongside the stricken Singer.

"Having trouble, madam?" he shouted. "Anything I can do?"

The woman got out, saw the garage name painted on the black van and approached the open window.

"You're from this garage – are you actually a mechanic?"

"I am."

"Do you have any time right now? I mean, you're on your way–"

"Yes, I'm going to another job, but I'm early for once and it's no trouble." A local accent.

"Well, I'd be extremely grateful." How fortunate was this! "The car's been OK, but this morning, a few moments ago, it wouldn't start."

"Why don't I take a look? It might be something trivial."

"Thank you so much."

Bob pulled in behind the Singer and brought out a heavy blue-steel toolbox.

"A Godsend that you were passing," she said. "Your timing couldn't have been more perfect if–"

"As I said, I'm calling on a client nearby. Now, let's get to it."

He flipped open one side of the hood above the radiator grille and rolled under the engine, which was exactly as he'd left it. Thirty seconds – ignition coil reconnected. Another minute – rotor restored tightly into distributor cap.

He saw her consult her watch again, but by now she'd accepted a delay. He picked a small hacksaw and dragged the blade across the handle of his wrench, hoping she'd hear the grating sound. He was sure she couldn't see what he was doing. After a few taps on the oil pan for good measure, he stood and made a show of wiping his dry brow.

This man has a particularly thick, muscly neck, she noted. And his torso and upper arms filled the jacket he was wearing, the buttons straining to contain him. His nose was broken, and his grimy fingernails were bitten as short as they'd go.

171

She imagined he could cut a most intimidating figure if he wanted to.

"Give it a try now," he said with complete confidence.

To her relief and delight, the engine fired first time. As good as new.

"What do I owe you?"

He hesitated, embarrassed.

"Oh, come on, it's your professional time. You can't mend my car for nothing, I won't hear of it."

He smiled thinly. "That's very good of you." He walked towards the house. "Let's sort it out inside, if that's acceptable?"

"Perfectly." Unseemly to settle on the pavement. On reflection, she'd have expected him to put the wrench and hacksaw back in the toolbox. Instead, he slipped them into a deep pocket inside his jacket, which weighed that side down.

She led him into the front room, through a narrow hall with framed postcards of English cricketers. He recognised Len Hutton and Wally Hammond.

"My sons share a bedroom. Their tastes in pretty much everything, including sport, are diametrically opposed, so I let my elder son have space in the hall for his idols."

"Hutton's knock of 364 against Australia a couple of years ago was sensational. I seem to remember he was just twenty-two." Bob was mightily pleased with himself.

"Do come in," she said, waving him into an easy chair. "If my son hears you say that, you'll have a friend for life and he'll be late for school."

Bob left the door open and sat down facing her directly.

"He's upstairs now, is he?"

"Both of my sons and my mother. She'll see to their breakfast."

Confirmation of what he already knew.

"You'll want to get to your client, and I need to be at work." She paused. "But you've been very kind. Would you like a cup of tea? It's the least–"

"No, I'm fine, Mrs..." He took out a notebook and stubby pencil.

"Maxwell," she lied. "Betty Maxwell."

She noticed that he wrote slowly, printing one letter at a time.

"And of course, I know the address, don't I? We're here! The house number's 31, isn't it?"

"That's right."

"You said you have two children?"

For the first time, a worm of doubt wriggled in her mind, showed itself in her eyes.

"Yes, but what does—"

He held an index finger to his lips.

Oh, Lord. Her mouth went bone-dry. Suddenly everything was wrong. Could she remember the garage name on the side of his van?

After a torturous silence, Bob put away his notebook.

"I need some information," he said coldly. "One way or another, you'll tell me, so please make it straightforward for both of us and co-operate. I'll be gone before you know it."

"Who are you?" Betty's anger was a front: she was terrified. "It's – it's obvious now that you weren't in the street by chance. But you're in my house, keeping me from my work. I'd like an explanation."

"I am a mechanic," Bob said. "Your car is fixed – for now."

"What – what does that mean? For now?"

"Next time you get in, perhaps with your sons in the back, who knows, your brakes might fail."

Betty stayed silent. Every fibre in her body was screaming that this big, battered man could kill her. There was a sadness in his eyes, a longing for a kind of fulfilment that she was, presumably, expected to provide. Convinced his threat was real, she started to tremble.

"Your engine might explode," he went on. "You never know, stranger things have happened where petrol is concerned. You want to be very careful."

Betty said nothing. Was that a creak on the stairs, leading from the hall to the bedrooms? Oh God, she hoped they all stayed upstairs, out of harm's way, a while longer. She'd made the boys promise to share a bath before dressing for school. And to mop the floor afterwards.

This man appeared to have heard nothing, but then he was unfamiliar with the noises the house made. She must cover them, keep his attention locked in this room.

"So, you disabled my car – very early, or last night, was it? – and you put on your little performance this morning in order to have this private conversation with me. Is that right?"

He tapped the wrench on the side of his chair, then on his left palm.

"Obviously you mean business. But I can't help with car engines, I don't–"

"Don't be stupid!" He stood, took a pace forward and beat the wrench harder into his hand. "We know where you work."

Obviously, he wanted to know about her work, what else? She'd realised that as soon as he turned the tables on her. But if he hurt her family…

"Who is 'we'?" She steeled herself and risked his wrath once again.

"Never you mind," he snarled, and launched into the speech he'd rehearsed many times in the last week. "You work in Acklington, next to the RAF base. There are two places of interest – one is the manor house where you usually work. The other is the underground silo, converted from an old mine, where dozens of people are kept busy, yes?"

Betty's gaze fell to the floor. She only glanced up as he stopped talking. He took another step closer, the wrench clamped in his fingers so tightly that his knuckles had drained of blood.

"Last autumn," he continued, "shortly after war was declared, a convoy of trucks from RAF Bawdsey came up here to Acklington. We believe that some research projects have transferred to that mysterious site of yours, protected by the RAF squadrons and a decoy airbase a few miles away at Boulmer."

Her head was spinning. How long had Boulmer been blown? Who was this man? A sleeper agent? Could he be working for German intelligence? She was sure he could read in her face that all he'd said was correct. If she denied it, what might he do to her boys?

"What we want to know is the exact nature of the research. It's to do with radar, isn't it, secret applications, next-generation testing – but you're going to provide full details."

He stood over her, satisfied that the encounter was progressing as planned. Another couple of minutes and he should be on his way.

"May I know your name, please?" she asked, masking her alarm.

"Never you mind. Who I am doesn't matter."

"Are you Mr Swanley? Smedley?" The name on the van eluded her. "What should I call you? I mean, if we're to do business–"

"We *will* do business, I've made that clear. You have today, and today only, to write a specification of the radar research at Acklington and fill a folder with as much evidence of it as you can. Do not say a word to anyone. I shall be in touch later today. You will not know when, but I assure you–"

Bob suddenly realised that the expression on Betty Maxwell's face had altered. She was no longer looking at him, but *past* him, at something behind him. Or someone. She began speaking loudly, far too loudly, to conceal the approaching footsteps. What was…?

Bob never saw his assailant. The ten-year-old boy, barefoot, hair dripping from the bathtub, came towards him on his right side, where his vision was impaired, and he was half a second slower to react.

Before he knew it, the cricket bat had smashed into his skull. As Betty stood and opened her arms to her child, the wrench slipped from his fingers, an excruciating pain filled his head to bursting point and everything went black.

***

PC Jonathan Hedley of Newcastle City Police had been looking forward to meeting Christopher Talbot ever since the sergeant had assigned him to this case. His immediate reaction, alas, had been disappointment. Jonathan wasn't quite sure what he'd been expecting, but there was nothing exceptional or outstanding about Talbot at all. Quite the reverse. He was unassuming. His attire was, well, ordinary. He just blended in. Perhaps, his fiancée, Lorraine, later pointed out, this is what spies *should* do – look ordinary, while surreptitiously observing everything around them.

The sarge had told him to assist Mr Talbot with a line of enquiry that was essentially police work. His specific orders had come from Talbot himself.

It was 10 a.m. on Good Friday, 22 March. Both he and Lorraine were pleased to be working this weekend, adding over-time to their wedding coffers. He crossed the forecourt of Swanson's deserted garage to the little office, built inside a corrugated iron-roofed workshop on the backlot. The workshop was pitted with trenches where the mechanics worked, and a hydraulic lift seemed to be used to store tyres. Only one car was in the workshop, its bonnet open, not a soul working on it.

Strips of brown tape dangled from inside the office window where a blackout sheet had been torn off, and Jonathan could see movement inside. He knocked on the office door, entered without waiting.

The space inside was abustle. Three men in overalls froze, rabbits trapped in headlights. Two had been rifling through filing cabinets; the third, seated at a battered wooden desk, was searching in the drawers.

"Good morning, gentlemen," Jonathan said, taking charge. "PC Hedley, City Police."

"Have you found Mr Swanson?" One of the men at the filing cabinet blurted this out to the evident consternation of the other two.

"Mr Swanson?" Jonathan asked, curiosity piqued. "The owner?"

"He's away, er, a short break, that's all."

"I see." Jonathan made a mental note of Swanson's disappearance and took the names of the three men. "It was Mr Cracknell I was looking for. Is he coming in today?"

"What's wrong, officer?"

"I didn't say anything was wrong," Jonathan said in a level tone. These men were on edge, scared. He wondered what had happened here, but he had an immediate matter to pursue. "We believe Mr Cracknell can assist with an on-going enquiry. It's important that I talk to him." None of the men moved a muscle. "As soon as possible."

The man at the desk looked downcast, defeated, and glanced at his colleagues, who shrugged. If the police were involved and they chose not to co-operate, their situation could only get worse. They'd implicate themselves in something – they knew not what – that they had nothing to do with. None of them wanted the long arm of the law poking into their sideline activities as local spivs.

"Mr Cracknell telephoned yesterday afternoon. He'd taken the van to repair a client's car first thing, a few miles away, and never returned. Not like him at all, a workaholic. Then, a call later on. He sounded awful. Never known him so bad, barely recognised the voice."

"Where was he when he telephoned?"

"At home, I think. I didn't ask, but he keeps this pair of budgies and I could hear them chirping."

"Very well." Jonathan approached the desk. The man flinched, sat back. "I need Mr Cracknell's home address, then I'll be on my way."

Not wanting to delay PC Hedley's departure, one of the men plucked a sheet from the second drawer of his cabinet and handed it over.

Jonathan copied Cracknell's address into his notebook and returned the sheet.

"When Mr Swanson and Mr Cracknell are away at the same time," he asked, "who is in charge? Do you work shifts, take things in turn? How does it work?"

Something close to desperation swelled in their eyes. It was clearly rare for Swanson and Cracknell to be absent at once. Their staff were disorientated, seeking answers in the files, and daunted at the sight of a policeman.

"We hold the fort between us," the man at the desk answered.

"Thank you for your help, gentlemen." Jonathan took a business card from his top pocket. "If any of you thinks of anything else, or if Mr Swanson should reappear, please contact me." He placed the card on the desk with a snap and bade them farewell.

Outside, Christopher Talbot started his Ford 8 the moment he saw PC Hedley emerge. He'd accelerated away before Hedley had closed the door.

"It's chaos in there. Headless chickens. They have my sympathy."

"So, where are we heading?" Talbot asked, giving way to a bus.

Hedley read out the address. "It's only a couple of miles."

Talbot took the first exit off the next roundabout and drove through long streets of terraced houses with occasional shops and churches.

"Here we are." Turning right, he slowed to read the house numbers. One had a washing line in its front garden, white shirts flapping dementedly. He pulled in by a house with smoke billowing from its chimney. "It's that one with the brown front door."

From the opposite direction, a man with a shock of chestnut-brown hair pushed a handcart laden with fruit, vegetables and, perhaps because it was Easter, fresh eggs which, Hedley noted, were not on the ration.

"Not yet, anyway," Talbot cautioned. "As soon as enough dried egg powder is available, I expect fresh eggs will be rationed, too. One a week?"

"My fiancée uses a lot of eggs in her baking," Hedley said. "She's such a lovely baker, when she has time."

Talbot wasn't listening. He was watching the vendor wheel his squeaky cart from door to door. It was amazing that no produce fell off.

The man knocked twice on Bob Cracknell's door. A pause. He'd given up and was walking away when the door cracked open.

"That's him," Hedley confirmed. "No sign of the garage van nearby. Lord, look at those bandages!"

"Well, if my head had been treated as a cricket ball, I'd be wanting a bit of TLC too!" With that, Talbot took a small envelope from the back seat and tucked it into a pocket.

He turned to the young constable, who had shown such eagerness to deal with the suspected cell of Fifth Columnists. "I'm going to have a chat with Mr Cracknell. Injured as he is, he's still a strong man in a tight corner. He might well bolt. Would you keep a close watch in case he comes out fighting?"

Hedley, uneasy, did not protest. He simply said: "Good luck."

Before getting out, Talbot waited until the vendor was two doors further down. Straightening his jacket, he knocked on Cracknell's door.

"I thought I told you I didn't want…" he heard Cracknell moan, the voice more weary than angry. The door opened, wider this time, as Cracknell was sure he knew who was there.

"Oh," he said, seeing a stranger. "I… Well…" He struggled to gather his thoughts. "Yes? You're not selling anything, are you?"

"I do have an offer for you, Mr Cracknell."

"An offer? I don't know you, do I? Who – how do you know my name?"

"Let's talk inside. It won't take long – no longer than your visit the other day to Mrs Maxwell."

Bob closed his eyes. Shutting out the light soothed his throbbing head. He'd been half-expecting someone to come, but he felt so dreadful that he hadn't really concentrated on anything. He wasn't even sure how he'd got back home. The hours after he was whacked on the skull remained a blank.

Bitterly he said: "You'd better come in," and led the way into a sitting room about seven yards square, with a chimney breast encroaching. A hooded cage with a pair of budgies stood in one of the alcoves. A coal fire crackled in the hearth and the little house felt snug.

Bob began to sway and held out his arms for balance, but the nausea passed.

"You're police?" he rasped, face pale.

There was still fire in his belly, Talbot rather admired that, but he was no longer concerned that Cracknell would run for it.

"Sort of. Talbot is the name." He sat down.

Cracknell had a black eye, a swollen lip and thick layers of bandages swathing the top of his head. He walked gingerly, as if balancing on his shoulders a head that might split at any moment. He sat on a two-seater settee and winced as he tucked a pillow behind his neck.

"Well, Mr Talbot, what's this about? Do I have a choice whether or not to accept your offer?"

"Oh, there are always choices in life," Talbot said lightly. "Let me set out the position and you can see what you think."

Cracknell sank into his pillow, eyes closed.

"You've been leading a hectic double life," the sort-of copper began. "By day, a hard-working mechanic at Swanson's garage."

Cracknell's eyes opened, wide and fiery at the mention of Swanson's name.

"By night, an active member of a Nazi-supporting cell masquerading as a film society."

Cracknell's eyes opened wider. If he realised at that moment that news of the film society had leaked, he could not know that the infiltrator, working for MI5, was Warren Sixsmith.

Talbot went on: "You tricked your way into the house of the woman you know as Mrs Maxwell to demand her inside knowledge of secret work apparently going on in Acklington. You intended to channel that information through the film society to people in Germany planning the invasion of Britain."

"So you say." It was no more than a whisper.

"There'll be ample witnesses giving testimony before your trip to the gallows."

"The gallows?"

"In the last century, people convicted of treason were hung, drawn and quartered. Nowadays, the penalty is simply hanging. Fewer entrails to mop up afterwards."

Cracknell looked very brittle. In their cage, the budgies chirped and trilled, chattering to themselves. "What's her real name, then, Betty Maxwell?"

Ignoring the question, Talbot said: "You weren't to know that her eldest is a future opening batsman. You have a concussion, some nasty bruises, but you'll live. When Mrs Maxwell contacted me, I arranged for you to be examined and patched up. You probably don't remember, do you? Once the doctor had left, you slipped away, as we thought you might, an injured workman, but you were never going far. Your van is still parked in the Maxwells' street, and of course it was no problem to find your address."

Cracknell assumed he'd crawled into a bus or a taxi to get home. To his knowledge, his address was on file at his bank and at the garage.

"Why did Mrs Maxwell contact *you*?"

"I've been keeping watch on her place of work. They all know who I am, why I'm there. I hope they find it reassuring."

Cracknell, regaining his composure, considered this. "Say I deny everything and a case goes to court, your witnesses would have to take the stand, speak publicly, be exposed to cross-examination. You wouldn't want that, would you, Mr Talbot?"

"Nor, I think, would you like us to get word to your lords and masters in Berlin that you can't keep your mouth shut, that you're a leak in the Newcastle cell."

"I've never squealed on anyone."

"I'm talking about the perception, not the reality. The seeding of distrust. If you think a cricket bat hurts, wait until the Brownshirts decide to interrogate you."

Cracknell looked as though he wanted to swing a punch, the old Crusher coming back. But a pained expression spread across his face as if the skin were blotting paper, and he rubbed his temples.

"So that's my choice, is it?" His voice was nasal. "Either the hangman's noose or a day of reckoning with the Gestapo and their friends? A choice of two death penalties."

"That seems a fair summary."

Cracknell stared at his visitor. "You know, I may not have had your start in life. I may have worked with my hands, not my IQ, but at least I'm not the monster that you've become. How in Hades do you sleep at night?"

The rage boiling inside Bob Cracknell was plain to see, even in his diminished, concussed state. For a moment, Talbot thought of his daughter, Lucy, fast approaching her thirteenth birthday. If she knew how her dad really earned his living, some of the actions he took in the name of national security, would she still be proud of him? He blinked the doubt away, focused on the broken man in front of him.

"If you'll forgive me," Talbot replied, "I won't measure my ethics against the extreme hatred and mistaken superiority of a Nazi sympathiser. Unrestricted power is a fantasy, you know, even if it's propped up for a while by bribery and corruption. But listen, here's the good news." He paused. "I can offer you a way out of your dilemma. For what it's worth, I've never been a supporter of the death penalty, any more than I imagine right at this minute you are."

"Much obliged," Cracknell grunted.

Talbot took the envelope from his pocket. "Simple. We add another dimension to the double life you're already leading. You continue to attend the film society meetings, but the information you supply comes from me."

Talbot laid the envelope on the arm of his chair and gave it a tap. Cracknell half-opened his eyes.

"And if I deliver your misinformation, you'll ensure that I escape death?"

"An admirable outcome all round, I'd say."

Cracknell said nothing. Talbot returned the envelope to his pocket. As a juicy carrot, it had served its purpose for the time being.

"We'll be in touch again in a few days, before the next meeting," he told Cracknell. "Meanwhile, you rest up, drink plenty of water and keep your head still."

"Yes, doctor." Cracknell's sarcasm was sour.

"And as you'd expect, if you breathe a word of this deal to anyone at all, then rest assured, it's cancelled."

"I've told you, I don't squeal."

"Well, let me leave you to make your peace with what we've discussed." Talbot was about to leave when the meeting took an unexpected turn.

The exchange had served to sharpen Cracknell's crafty wits and, for better or worse, he found Talbot to be a plausible speaker. An idea had struck him. Could there be an opportunity to turn some tables? Now or never.

"One moment, Mr Talbot. Wait, please."

Cracknell grunted and heaved himself up, slotting the pillow behind his back.

"Yes?" His tone had been markedly conciliatory, quite a conversion, and Talbot was surprised by what he said next.

"Do you have a few more minutes? While you're here, before I change my mind, why don't I tell you a few home truths about Maurice Swanson?"

16

Phantom Squad

Noon, Easter Sunday, 24 March. Robert Watson-Watt and Margaret, his wife of twenty-four years, left their house in Sheen Lane, Richmond-upon-Thames, and waved to the Pattersons opposite, who were returning home with their dog, Sheba. Robert and Margaret walked arm in arm to the junction with Queen's Road, which they followed down to Richmond Park.

They'd moved to Sheen Lane a year ago and loved the house, the neighbourhood, the leafy spaces of south-west London. They couldn't bear to contemplate Luftwaffe bombs pulverising the area in weeks, months, who knew when?

Easter – a time of rebirth and renewal, forgiveness and the ultimate triumph of hope. How propitious. But, he wondered, is that how he – they both – would remember *this* Easter?

He owed Margaret an apology. It was delicate, awkward; he felt a change of scenery, some fresh air, might help. An investment he'd made eight months ago in a start-up, manufacturing farm equipment, had not paid off. The company had run out of liquidity and gone bust, taking his investment, which his family could ill afford, with it. Rather than discuss the implications properly, he'd spent an hour that Sunday morning on an urgent call with the Air Ministry.

Out of sight of their street, Margaret unhooked her arm. Yes, he definitely had some making up to do. If only his commercial acumen matched his scientific prowess…

An army staff car rumbled past. A Humber Snipe, khaki-green. The near-side back window was down, and Watson-

Watt recognised the sole, pipe-smoking passenger: 'Hoppy'. Lieutenant-Colonel George Hopkinson, commander of the GHQ Liaison Regiment.

Watson-Watt knew the car's destination: the Georgian mansion on the park's highest peak. It was named Pembroke Lodge after the Countess of Pembroke, an early tenant, who loved the place so much that she beguiled the king, George III, into granting it to her. Having improved and extended the property, she died there at the grand old age of ninety-three.

As a base, the GHQ Liaison Regiment had requisitioned the nearby Richmond Hill Hotel. For its officers' mess and billet, including Hoppy's quarters, it had wisely commandeered Pembroke Lodge.

The regiment had been formed recently, soon after the fall of Poland. Its purpose was to pinpoint the battlefield positions of Allied and enemy forces. Risk assessments and target identifications worth the paper they were written on depended on the speedy flow of accurate information. At first, the plan was to eavesdrop on radio transmissions from the field to estimate the sender's location. Many of the regiment's operators and linguists had been trained by the Royal Signals in wireless communications and cipher.

Hoppy had further developed the regimental plan. Motorcycle riders using miniature radio sets would send back coded messages from right under the enemy's nose. Known as the 'Phantom Squad', they were already active in France. All one hundred and fifty officers and 1,250 other ranks wore on their upper right arms the black felt square containing a white P which Watson-Watt had recognised on Hoppy.

He and Margaret were now in Richmond Park. Winter's grip had loosened and the freshly surfaced wildflowers made a sumptuous display. They passed a cemetery and an over-sized anti-aircraft gun hemmed in by a square wall of sandbags. Walking south, they reached a favourite bench, which they were pleased to find unoccupied as there were plenty of folk about. They sat down, stretched out their legs.

For the first time that day, Robert began to relax. He took off his glasses, polished the lenses, let his shoulders sag. The knots of tension and regret began very slightly to unwind.

Margaret was as delighted as ever to see fallow deer – does and antlered bucks – stroll across the parkland in front of them. Three hundred years ago, the royal court was shifted nine miles from a plague-stricken Westminster to Richmond, where this new park was laid out on the hill for the hunting of red and fallow deer. It remained one of the most spacious parks in the country. Last autumn, Margaret had watched the rutting males fight brutally over the herd's females, belching to claim their territory. Now, a solitary female paused, no more than ten yards away, gazing directly at her. A prepossessing young doe, pale brown pelt with white spots along her back, on which not a hair moved.

Margaret smiled, wondering if the doe was in calf, and whispered: "Hello there!" New life entering the world, oblivious to the gathering war clouds? There was something reassuring, yet deeply troubling, about it. "Stay safe, you beauty."

Robert put on his glasses. At the park's southern extremity, occupying forty acres, was an army camp where infantry recruits were put through their paces. A few hundred yards around the perimeter, sandbags surrounded a temporary bomb disposal centre to a height of six feet. As far as he knew, there had been no explosions – yet.

"How was your morning call with the ministry?" Margaret was asking.

He decided to level with her, to declare perhaps more than he should. "They've had a nasty shock in the last few days. A cell of Nazi supporters tried to intimidate a local woman who'd joined my project team in Acklington."

"Is she all right?"

"Well, a ghastly experience, very shaken, but she and her eldest son overcame the intruder – on this occasion."

"That's good to hear." Margaret sounded unconvinced.

"The action against her was unsophisticated. Its real purpose may have been to frighten her, to disrupt her work, not necessarily to extract secrets. But the ministry is understandably keen to learn about the network of German agents and who is calling the shots."

Two women strolled by. They were singing quietly to themselves the song that perfectly expressed the longing of loved ones separated by the war. Margaret thought she'd first heard Vera Lynn perform *We'll Meet Again* last year on Bert Ambrose's radio show.

"She should have her own show, you know."

"I didn't notice – who was she?"

"Not the passers-by, Vera Lynn. That was her song."

"Oh, well, I'm sure it's just a matter of time."

Margaret looked at him hard. "So, what are they working on in Acklington that is such a threat?"

His wife was always quick to put two and two together to make four. He stared ahead, beyond the deer and the rabbits that capered around their hooves to the tranquil parkland stretching into the distance, and he lowered his voice.

"Two strands of research, categorised most-secret, both being developed in conjunction with the Americans."

At university in Dundee, Robert had befriended Sam Linklater, a law student from Saratoga, New York, with whom he shared an interest in horse racing. Sam went on to work in counterintelligence at the FBI and, extraordinarily, had become a valued contact in Robert's professional life too. To date, Margaret had never met him.

"And they're going well?"

"I believe so. Both projects involve high-frequency radar. Far higher than we use for Chain Home." She was watching him. Ah well, in for a penny. "The first concerns ultra-high microwave frequencies. We're trying to establish whether they'll enable us to get a fix on aircraft hundreds of miles away, for offensive or defensive purposes."

"Is that the project the woman who was attacked was working on?"

"It is, yes. The site has a big space underground – it used to be a mine – and to be on the safe side, we thought it best that the microwave research is conducted down there." The Treasury had been remarkably swift to sanction the fit-out, but he didn't bring up the cost. "Actually, she was involved both above and below ground level, but for most people it's one or the other."

"And the second project?"

"Testing whether radar can measure ocean waves, again hundreds of miles away."

"And that's useful?"

"Extremely, if it works. Surface currents can give advance warning of dangerous events like oil leaks or tidal waves."

"It all sounds terribly clever." For the first time, Margaret's voice rang with enthusiasm. "I hope it comes good, dear, your experiments usually do. But you will keep the researchers safe, won't you?"

"MI5 are on the case, supported by the police." Indeed, security on the site had been tightened and work rotas changed. The team leader known as Betty Maxwell had been given a few days' leave.

Margaret looked away, said nothing. Her husband had a huge amount on his plate that she really knew nothing about.

Well, this is as good a time as any, he thought. Straightening his tie, Robert launched into an apology for the loss of the money he'd invested – in good faith – in the farm equipment venture.

The sun, which had been radiating some early spring warmth, slipped from view behind a swell of cloud.

***

Easter Monday afternoon, 25 March. Klara and Curt walked down the gentle slope of Queen Street in the centre of Amble, Northumberland, heading for the harbour. The shops and schools were closed but plenty of people were milling about, watched over by gulls on the rooftops. Klara had plaited her hair and draped a thin coat over her shoulders. It was, perhaps, the most carefree day she'd had in months.

She thought often of the evacuee, Kevin, and of that night, a month ago, when Warren Sixsmith had whisked her away from the Odyssey's projection room. She would never know how close she came to being discovered.

Sixsmith had confided, in the desperate heat of the moment, that he was an undercover MI5 officer. Who else knew? she wondered. She'd admitted to wanting to know more about Freitag's intentions for the group, which was why she'd sneaked away to listen at the door. But that was all she'd said.

Sixsmith had replied that Freitag wanted the group to exert a more disruptive influence, as well as providing intelligence. Which rang true: this was the Freitag she knew. She'd sensed Sixsmith staring, trying to read her mind, so she'd thanked him for his assistance, and they'd arranged to meet again the following week, away from the Odyssey.

She'd said nothing about this to Curt. The perfect moment never arose, and she felt it better to keep Sixsmith's identity a secret – for the time being. As ever, Klara preferred to listen, ask questions, absorb the replies, rather than answer them herself.

Besides, she'd started to enjoy having Curt around. In the last few weeks, they'd spent most days together, undertaking more reconnaissance of the region's airfields. He seemed to be regaining his lost weight. She'd got used to him riding behind her on the ES2, the delicious frisson of his hands around her waist. At first, she'd felt flustered, but gradually strengthened and thrilled by the simple human contact.

When they stopped to eat or refuel, they'd derive great satisfaction from passing themselves off as a couple from Austria – thank heaven, three years ago, they'd escaped persecution! – or as a South African pilot with his girlfriend, about to embark on training with the RAF. A blend of confidence and quick-witted charm had got them through, and it was gratifying to know they could make their covers and accents gel.

She'd return each evening to Silverbeck, even during the school Easter holidays. Once, she'd introduced her big brother Simon to Mrs Purnell, and they'd talked of Kevin, whom Mrs Barker had seen her comforting at Alnwick station.

Was Curt satisfying a simple longing for companionship, of which she'd enjoyed so little before he arrived? Or was there more to it, that she was not ready to admit to herself, let alone him? She was fond of him, yes, respected him. But if the foundations of a lasting relationship were shared love and truth, she didn't feel they were close to it, and she was even less sure that the time was right.

He'd said he wanted intimacy and hoped she'd feel the same way very soon. So, she didn't have long to unravel her feelings. But there was so much about her that Curt didn't understand, that she hadn't told him. Were there streaks of guilt entangled in her feelings, too?

Today, she hoped they could enjoy a few hours of gentle relaxation as Evelyn and Simon. Was that too much to ask on a bank holiday? She resisted the impulse to hook her arm through his as they walked by the spot where Alf had met her in his car, and on past the RNLI lifeboat station which had opened last year when the one at nearby Hauxley closed down.

They reached the section of the harbour where the fishing boats were moored. The wall was crowded, the atmosphere friendly. Klara and Curt lost themselves in the throng, gazing out to distant Coquet Island, a breeding sanctuary for roseate terns, Arctic terns, puffins, many more. They were both wearing binoculars – birdwatchers, for sure. They waved to a little steamboat, the *Longstone*, her single smokestack billowing in the centre of the deck. It was surrounded by bench seats for a dozen people, all occupied. While the sound of the lapping waves was a tingling pleasure, she hoped the skipper of the *Longstone* had sufficient knowledge of the fast-changing coastal currents.

They walked through the crowd as far as they could go to the end of the harbour wall, filling their lungs with briny air. A merchant ship headed south, about three miles out. A pair of Spitfires banked overhead, flying low in close formation, perhaps on a training sortie from Acklington. Along the harbour wall, every head craned upwards, and murmurs of appreciation rippled through the crowd. She might have imagined it, but Klara could have sworn the second Spitfire tipped its wings in acknowledgement.

"Have you thought what you might do after the war?" Curt asked. He put an arm around her back and, without asking, softly rubbed the nape of her neck.

She waited for a young family to pass before answering his question with one of her own. "What shape will Berlin be in after the war? Empowered under a victorious Führer, or a bankrupt ruin on her knees?

Schultz was about to chastise her for expressing her second possible outcome, but her eyes seemed far away and he changed his mind. "In Berlin or anywhere you go," he said, "I hope there will be a place for me too, that we can go forward together."

"I know, I know." She cut him short before, even in the open air, she began to feel claustrophobic. She flashed a consolation smile, which he readily returned. "Come on," she said. "Let's—"

The peace was shattered by the deafening boom of an explosion, which assaulted their whole bodies. Klara and Curt took involuntary steps forward, disorientated. A split second before she heard the blast, a glaring yellow flash speared the corner of Klara's eye. She looked for the source while other adults and children screamed, cried, picked themselves up.

No one seemed physically hurt. No blood stains on clothing, no dust clouds soiling the air. Fingers were pointing out to sea. Some of those who, seconds earlier, had been strolling along the harbour wall were now ogling an horrific scene playing out on the angry water.

The *Longstone* had blown up. Her back broken by the blast, she was sinking into a pool of flames. Fiery smoke gushed from her funnel. Two, three bodies were visible in the water, but they were on fire, thrashing about, ducking below the surface, emerging blackened, still burning. A couple of those on board who had been blown free were swimming for the harbour, their clothes torn. Klara could not help but recall Albert Sammt's haunting ordeal on the blazing *Hindenburg*.

"Quick – help them!"

"Get the lifebuoys! Find some rope!"

While the calls came thick and fast, Curt shrouded Klara in his arms, shielding her from whatever might come.

He propped her up, looked into her eyes. "Are you all right? No injuries?"

She avoided his gaze. "Fine. You too?"

"Ears ringing," he shouted in order to hear his own words, "otherwise good."

So saying, Curt ran along the pier to round up items that might help. He dragged a net and a long stick to the shoreline.

The bell to summon the lifeboat crew was clanging. The blue doors of the station were open and the boat itself was emerging on to its slipway.

Klara watched the blazing wreck, almost totally submerged. The sea was boiling and gulls hovered over the site, squealing possessively. Two more survivors had swum clear, but she reckoned that at least half of those on the *Longstone* had perished. Dear God, what carnage!

She'd realised that the boat had touched a magnetic mine, tethered below the surface. Packed with enough explosive to split open a much larger vessel, it would have been attracted by the steel hull. The *Longstone* had no chance.

The first two survivors reached the harbour. They found their footing and waded ashore, shaking from top to toe. A police constable ran towards them carrying a blanket, which they shared gratefully.

Klara was astounded to see a young man with a notice reading PRESS pinned to the back of his blazer. He was sprinting along the harbour wall, unfolding an Eastman Kodak camera with red bellows. How did he get here so quickly? She tracked him with her binoculars but did not recognise him.

At her side again, but looking very shaken, Curt double-checked that she was well. He kissed her hand – *I'm here for you.* His voice wobbled as he said: "You know my heart leaps every time I see you. The idea of you not being–"

"Come on."

The lifeboat had reached the survivors and she led him from the commotion. They walked briskly, pensively, towards Queen Street. Numerous people dashed in the opposite direction towards the harbour – distressed relatives, friends of those who had set out on the *Longstone*? In the heart of the town, just ahead, clusters of people tried desperately to confirm who had been on board. How many visitors, how many locals? The police would be knocking on their doors all too soon.

"This way," Klara said. Nudging Curt's arm, she led him into a side road, a church dominating the far end, which formed a T-junction with the street where she'd parked the ES2. A short cut.

Curiously, there was no one else in the road. There were stone cottages, little shops, a building materials store. Very few lights were on and the natural light in the sky was fading. A stray terrier scampered by, tail between his legs, nose to the ground.

Suddenly, the sound of their footsteps was drowned out by the roar of a car engine and a vicious squeal of tyres. Curt reacted first, turned, saw the black car speeding unerringly towards them. The bars on its radiator grille resembled giant fangs.

"Run!" he screamed. Klara matched him stride for stride. The monster was looming, devouring the ground by the second. They raced on, keeping close to the house fronts.

"Faster, Klara! Sprint to that wall!"

The engine, in low gear, screamed louder.

"Jump!"

As Curt yelled the command, he half-shoved Klara over the waist-high stone wall encasing the church plot. She cleared it easily, landing on a cushion of long grass.

Curt stayed a second longer and the black car was upon him. The bumper hit the back of his right leg as he vaulted across the wall. There was a collision: he heard the near-side tyre-arch scrape along the stones, leaving a streak of paint.

The car careered on, reached the end of the road, brake lights glowing. Instead of turning left or right, it reversed towards them.

This was no ghastly accident, no intoxicated or joy-riding driver. Oh Lord, this was deliberate, an attempt to murder them both in cold blood. Having thought they'd witnessed all the dreadful deaths this day had in store, now it was their own lives under attack.

Freitag? He's a psychopath, capable of extreme violence, Klara thought, but she didn't recognise the car.

"Keep low!" Curt hissed, rubbing his right leg. "Did you happen to see the driver? Anyone else inside?"

"No," Klara replied, crouching at the wall, head below the parapet.

"I'm sure there was a man in the passenger seat," Curt gasped. "Spectacles, grey hair, a thin moustache, I can't be sure."

Could it possibly be... that sounded like... the proprietor of Sycamore Grove, Duncan Caldwell? Klara's blood ran cold when she thought of his nicotine-yellow teeth and her restless night at the B&B.

The car crawled past them in reverse. Was the crazed onslaught over? It halted, then came forwards more sedately.

"Remember... loyalty... next time!"

They were both convinced they heard the muffled threat, or snippets of it, spat out at them, and yet the car windows and doors stayed shut.

Curt helped her up, dusted off their clothing. His leg was bruised, but no broken bones. Klara's hands were still trembling five minutes later when she started up the Norton and rode out of Amble to Silverbeck.

Having left the motorcycle in the barn and removed their boots, Klara and Curt were padding along the hall to the stairs when Mrs Purnell appeared in the kitchenette doorway, holding aloft a foolscap envelope as if it were a dead rat.

"This came for you earlier, dear – Easter Monday of all days." Was it irritation, suspicion or purely curiosity adding an edge to Mrs Purnell's voice? "Hand-delivered. Fellow in a grey car, that's all I know. He left it on the step and drove off at a real lick. Do you know who he was?"

"Oh, a teacher colleague, most probably," Klara said lightly. She hoped there was no tremor in her voice, no sense of how she was really feeling. "We often exchange lesson plans, you see, especially if there's been little time to prepare for a particular age group. Good use of the gap between terms."

Curt climbed the stairs, hoping it would encourage Mrs Purnell to let the matter drop. It did not.

"He didn't look like he was just passing to me, seemed in a frightful hurry. Is there anything you're not telling me, dear?" Mrs Purnell took a step closer to Klara. "Which school was it you said you teach at?"

17

Pact of steel

Three weeks later – mid-morning, Wednesday 17 April – Klara found herself sitting on the exposed, bramble-flecked remains of a once-mighty Roman fort in the Northumberland countryside. Curt Schultz was not present. But two men sat opposite her in silence, enthralled by what she was finally divulging.

"They knew all along that I came from a religious family," Klara said. "But they didn't follow up during the recruitment process. The Abwehr was expanding fast. Their focus was on language and inter-personal skills, aptitude, analysis, that sort of thing. Once I was hired, I never mentioned my family background. Nor did anyone else." She shrugged. "That's all there is to it, really."

That morning, the two men had driven west of Newcastle to a location between Hexham and Haltwhistle. Having parked off-road, they walked the final stretch to an escarpment crowned by the timeworn remains of the fort.

In AD 122, a Roman army constructed a wall out of locally quarried stone stretching all the way from Irish Sea to North Sea, Bowness to Wallsend, seventy-three miles across the country. Their colossal achievement would mark the north-west frontier of the Roman empire for three centuries. But there was more to it: along the way, they added mile-castles and great forts. This one, *Vercovicium* – Housesteads – contained its own hospital as well as barracks, lavatories, stables and grain store.

The Housesteads fort lay on the crest of a rocky ridge. As far as the eye could see, the landscape was untamed, resilient, pristinely beautiful. Even for Northumberland, it was an uncommonly clear, crisp day. Sheep and cattle dotted the peaceful pastures, the lush grass tinged with summer's yellow. Housemartins and swallows nested in the beech trees, which made their ancient presence felt by rustling in the wind.

They sat on a knee-high corner of the fort's outer wall, affording them the broadest view of their surroundings. Basic tradecraft, Talbot had said when he selected the spot. They'd been waiting barely ten minutes when they saw her approaching, unexpectedly from the west, binoculars around her neck, sketchbook in hand, headscarf fluttering.

One of them, who knew Klara from previous occasions, leapt to his feet and stepped forward to shake her hand.

"My guardian angel," Klara said, referring to Warren Sixsmith helping her evade capture in the Odyssey.

"Lovely to see you, too," Sixsmith beamed. "May I introduce my gaffer, Christopher Talbot?"

Talbot stood. "Miss Evelyn Fletcher, supply teacher for young evacuees, I believe?"

"Klara Falke's my real name. The British identity was MI5's invention, although the Nazis who arranged my travel here assumed it had been devised in Berlin. The cover has stood me in pretty good stead – until your reckless driving aroused the suspicions of my landlady."

Ever alert, Klara scrutinised the walkers exploring the remains or striding by on long hikes. She was satisfied, no one within earshot.

"My apologies." This was Talbot sounding contrite. "Occasionally I drive rather... enthusiastically. MI5 runs courses in London, instructing... Well, least said, soonest mended, eh?"

Sixsmith came to his rescue: "You know, Hadrian's Wall was so much more than a border protecting the empire from the Picts and Scots to the north. It created a space where different peoples could meet to barter, trade or exchange news. Which makes it the perfect location for this meeting, doesn't it?"

Klara smiled. It was in fact one of many recent meetings, with different people, that she'd approached with a mixture of excitement and trepidation.

Who is Sixsmith trying to impress, as if I don't know? Talbot wondered. "You must have been shaken to your bones by the attack on Easter Monday," he said. "No repetition, I take it?"

"Not yet."

"Try not to let it distract you too much," Talbot went on, a physician calming his patient. "The aim was probably to scare the wits out of you, rather than kill you, we've seen that elsewhere on this case. Maybe someone wants you to keep out of their way?"

"It took me a week to stop jumping at my own shadow," Klara confessed. The partly-heard threat from the battering ram of a car – "Remember... loyalty... next time!" – had played over and over in her mind. Could it have been Caldwell's odious voice? She shrugged the weight of it from her shoulders. "But what doesn't kill you makes you stronger, isn't that right?" She didn't look like she needed their affirmation. "It'll take more than a crude attempt like that to stop me in my tracks."

Talbot believed her. He would later discuss with Sixsmith that Klara had probably inherited her steely resolve from her father. But neither of them underestimated the reserves of courage required to reject fascism and defect from her homeland.

"Why don't we start with your childhood?" he nudged, as tight-knit swallows banked above their heads. Had scraps of food been left behind? Or were they circling in on worms, flies, moths on the ramparts?

Klara explained that her father was a Lutheran pastor. He led services based on the teachings of the German monk, Martin Luther, who in the sixteenth century had condemned the excesses of the Roman Catholic Church. His followers, branded Protestants, split from the Catholics, triggering the Reformation. Klara had always been taught that the Bible was the true source of divine knowledge and that redemption from sins could only come from God's grace.

Nazism was, of course, a far cry from a Christian movement, but Pastor Falke was aghast that the Lutheran Church apparently collaborated with the NSDAP in the 1920s and '30s. He joined the Quakers, a faith group founded in the Protestant tradition, which held that the light of God exists in every individual. A full relationship with God is open to those whose lives are guided by that light. In Berlin, Pastor Falke spoke out against the Nazis and on several occasions was beaten to a pulp by vigilante thugs in the *Sturmabteilung* – the Brownshirts. Talbot could imagine how traumatic the young Klara had found those experiences.

Her elder sister, Katarina, had flown the nest, married Harald. The longest entry in Klara's diary – deferred when she joined the Abwehr – described the lovely wedding ceremony.

Harald worked for Winkler AG, a firm supplying minerals to the construction sector. He'd joined the Communist Party, which he regarded as the only one capable of opposing the NSDAP and its vile ideal of an Aryan utopia. He and his new wife secretly helped Jews to escape persecution in Germany via Switzerland and, later, Belgium. Their routes were precious and few.

Ever self-reliant, Klara forged her own path, never saying 'no' when an opportunity presented itself. It is through our actions that we reveal ourselves, she judged. Having excelled in the sport of shooting, she enrolled as a spy. The Abwehr's organisational structures and self-esteem suited her well. When Talbot asked about vetting procedures, she said that, if a connection was made to Pastor Falke, the other qualities she brought had persuaded the Abwehr to ignore it and admit her anyway.

After a brief silence, Sixsmith commented: "You must have done a most convincing interview."

What are you like? Talbot thought, nearly rolling his eyes.

"They were expanding, looking for new people," Klara said simply.

Talbot brought her back to her childhood. "You haven't mentioned your mother," he probed gently.

Klara blushed. "She died when I was twelve."

Talbot winced. That was Lucy's age – old enough to understand everything.

"Left my father, all of us, utterly bereft. Loss is always part of life, but how could our lives go on day after day without this woman we all adored? I promised her, holding her hand before she slipped away, even as she was full of sleep and my heart ruptured, that something good would come of that sorrow, some lasting triumph from the exquisite agony. And I meant it." She held their gaze. "Ever since then, I've not been afraid to die, you know. My mum is always with me."

Silence, demolished by Sixsmith. "Then she'll know that you're the very best of her. There's no shame in dying, is there? The only shame is in not living your life to the full."

The words I live by, Klara reflected, rewarding the connection between them with an ephemeral smile. Talbot, meanwhile, looked much happier.

A pair of housemartins, black above, white below, glided overhead, defying gravity. A male and a female, Sixsmith wondered, nesting together?

He gave Klara a prompt. "When we met after the last film society session, you mentioned that you'd flown on a zeppelin over England last year. Lots of radar tracking equipment, is that right?" He exchanged glances with Talbot, whom he'd updated during the drive from Newcastle.

Curiously, despite the raw nerves, Klara was enjoying her discourse with these British espionage officers. They seemed fundamentally honest and concerned for her security. Sixsmith, in particular, had kind eyes – unlike Harry Jarvis. This was, she realised, a rare occasion when she felt safe. Or – the sudden thought struck her like a lightning bolt – were they manipulating her, trying to trap her, perhaps set her up?

As if on cue, Sixsmith leapt to his feet and picked up a shepherd's crook which had slipped from the fingers of a passer-by, a woman with a dog. A simple act of courtesy and kindness, of which she would like more in her life.

She refocused on their conversation.

"Yes, that's right. What an airship she was, *prächtig!* Magnificent! We got back to Germany after the mission on 4 August, a Friday, late evening. To my disbelief, despite the brains trust involved, nothing about British radar was discovered. But there was an incident on that flight which, for me, was the final straw. One glimpse too many of Nazi brutality, and that was it. Something snapped inside, made me act faster than I'd probably have done otherwise." Klara peered into the middle distance. "Within a fortnight, I'd arranged a meeting with Sir Nevile Henderson. You know him?"

"The British Ambassador in Berlin," Talbot answered. "Since April 1937."

"Just so," Klara approved. "Chamberlain, who became prime minister a couple of months after that, was desperate to have some kind of working relationship with the Führer. As it turned out, I reckon Henderson was a bigger fan of appeasement than Chamberlain himself. He was a devotee of the Munich Agreement and, to my astonishment, openly friendly towards Hermann Göring."

An expression of revulsion distorted her face.

"When I asked Henderson about it, he said, well, Göring rather admired the buccaneering spirit of the British – that was his explanation. He was in poor health, but I got the impression that Henderson had spent much of last summer trying to persuade Göring and the Führer not to attack Poland. He knew, of course, that this would be a jackboot too far for the British and the French, that they'd declare war."

"The Blitzkrieg campaigns must have been devastating for Henderson," Talbot observed. "And what must he think now, with Norway and Denmark capitulating to the Nazis only last week?"

The drumbeat of all-out war is thudding ever louder, he thought wretchedly. Once more, he swept Lucy from his mind.

Gazing up at the endless skyscape, Klara was distracted by a party of blue-jacketed hikers who marched by, paying scant attention to the ruins.

"You told Henderson last August that you wanted to defect to British Intelligence?" Sixsmith jogged her memory again.

"Essentially, yes. My soul hurt, you see, and I had to do something." She moistened her lips, holding their gaze while they mulled this over. "Things happened very quickly. The following week, just before the end of August, I was back in Wilhelmstrasse for a session Henderson had organised with a battalion of liaison officers. More like an interrogation. Was I for real? What were my motives? You can imagine it. I didn't see Henderson this time – apparently, he was having a shouting match with the Führer and his foreign minister, von Ribbentrop!"

For a moment, the three of them pictured that scene as an eagle, majestic predator, plummeted from above, talons poised.

"Very soon afterwards," Klara resumed, "I flew to London for similar debriefings with MI6. As far as the Abwehr in Berlin was concerned, I was taking a break to care for my father who'd suffered a stroke. In fact, both my parents had already passed away, but it wasn't enough of a priority for anyone to check. Curt Schultz believed me, had my back, which helped."

"Your sister, Katarina," Talbot said. "Is she still in Berlin?"

Klara nodded. With a high-pitched shriek, the eagle was away. "Still helping Harald to get Jews out. Occasionally she gives one of them a letter addressed to me, to be posted from the country they arrive in, which is lovely. We understood that it would be a long time until we saw each other again, but of course I miss her."

"What about Schultz?" Sixsmith asked. "He's been over here for a while now, hasn't he?"

"Under cover as my brother. He always seemed reputable, supported my appointment. He's unaware of my defection, of course, and it must stay that way."

"You don't think he suspects anything?"

"I hope not. Curt might connect his self-worth to the number of people who fawn over him, but that aside, he's thoughtful and clever. Still, I'm sure he doesn't know that I've sworn a new allegiance. The real reason he's here – or part of it, I'm sure – is to keep an eye on me. No one trusts anyone in Berlin."

Sixsmith and Talbot exchanges glances.

"What intelligence have you remitted to Berlin?" Talbot enquired. "Can you give us an inkling of what the invasion planners are working with?"

"I've sent as little as possible – maybe too little. But when I have, the content has been provided by my case officers in MI6 and MI5."

"Both services?"

"I still liaise with both, yes. Communication is half the solution to every problem, gentlemen. I realise that my situation is rather – what – abnormal."

"Alas, we're not living in normal times, are we?" Talbot countered.

"A few weeks ago, I sent a bogus file on British military aircraft production. It put the emphasis on bombers rather than the new-generation fighters. I don't know how it will have been received. I did not report that RAF Boulmer is a decoy site. But I did suggest that MI5 asks the RAF to shunt the replica aircraft around a lot more, to imply more activity, look more natural. In the coming months, the Abwehr and other agencies will send more people into Britain, not fewer, so better be prepared."

A bell rang in Talbot's mind. "I got a copy of that memo about Boulmer. I even checked that it was acted upon, you'll be pleased to hear."

Klara grinned.

"You're spinning a lot of plates, Klara, aren't you?" Talbot sounded concerned. Everything he'd been told about this woman, and his own first impression on meeting her today, pointed to her scrupulousness. Yet living multiple lives in tangled webs was never easy. And the act of day-by-day endurance could itself be heroic. "You're bound to find traps at every turn. How are you coping with it all? How do you feel in yourself?"

"I'm well, thank you for asking. Things are clear to me – I know what I'm doing and why. My father switched his loyalties just to survive, so in our family my situation is nothing new. You learn to compartmentalise everything very carefully."

"And your daily workload?"

"Curt and I have been touring coastal defence installations in recent weeks, building up eye-witness accounts. It's important to be seen to be playing the game, isn't it?"

Talbot smiled, said nothing.

"I try to ensure Mrs Purnell sees me apparently marking homework, that sort of thing, in term-time. Often, what I'm actually doing is translating intercepted material for MI6 or the British Army. There's no shortage of secret work. I think Mrs Purnell's mind is at ease – but when you dropped off your papers, she thought I'd been exposed as a blackout looter or something equally appalling!"

"Another film society meeting soon," Sixsmith said. "You'll be attending?"

He smiled when Klara nodded. Later, when they walked to the car, he'd have a private word with her, tell her he understood this double life would test her to the limits. But the enemy of his enemy was his friend, and she was very much his friend. She must keep positive thoughts front of mind – look forward to a reunion one day with Katarina, perhaps?

After a contemplative pause, Talbot said to Klara: "As you'll know, an enormous amount of time in the spy game is spent watching and waiting. Sometimes we perform an infiltration task, or a protection role, or we identify agents to turn to work for us. I've been thinking during some recent periods of watching and waiting…"

He let a couple of ramblers with a Jack Russell stride out of earshot. "… The presence of this man Freitag concerns me deeply. He seems to come and go, but he's plotting something, perhaps involving your film society network. It'll be significant, potentially very damaging."

At a slight rustle, Talbot looked up. The eagle was back, a mouse in its claws.

"I'm eager to discover what that something is," he said to Klara. "Warren briefs me on Freitag's appearances in the Odyssey, but I'd love to learn more from you first-hand. What can you tell me about him?"

**

"He feels, I'd say, a profound sense of a destiny fulfilled," ACM Sir Hugh Dowding said into the telephone handset. "By the way, how is Margaret?"

"She's fine, thank you." Robert Watson-Watt set aside a study of potential military applications of infrared radiation received from the boffins in Flintshire. "All's well after my recent recklessness. She sends much love."

"Reciprocated, of course," Dowding said, then returned to his interpretation of the new PM's feelings. "It's barely three weeks since he moved into number ten, but so much seems to have happened."

He paused when Joanne, his secretary, entered. She placed a correspondence folder in his in-tray and asked whether he'd like a tea. He shook his head.

Today was Thursday 30 May. The Phoney War had finally erupted into an all-too-real one on 10 May, when the Wehrmacht unleashed Blitzkrieg on Northern Europe. The campaign was proficiently executed, the force overwhelming, leaving the Allies outmanoeuvred. Luxembourg and Holland fell quickly, the German plan being to absorb them into the Reich. Belgium had surrendered just a couple of days ago, on 28 May. The battle for France, which the Germans had attacked in a pincer movement from north and south, was raging still. In Britain, the public mood was sombre, riddled with forebodings that refused to scatter.

Neville Chamberlain — austere as ever, dark suit, starched collar — lost a confidence vote in the House of Commons on

10 May. In his resignation speech, broadcast on the wireless, he explained: "Early this morning, without warning or excuse, Hitler added another to the horrible crimes which already disgrace his name... In all history, no other man has been responsible for such a hideous total of human suffering and misery as he."

The king entrusted Winston Churchill to step up as prime minister. Churchill headed a cross-party government that sought to present a united front to the advancing enemy. Chamberlain served in his war cabinet. On 13 May, in his maiden speech as PM, Churchill told the Commons that he had nothing to offer except blood, toil, tears and sweat.

"Let's pray that's enough," Margaret had said to Robert when the speech was reported on the news.

Now, it had turned six on the sunny evening of 30 May. Dowding and Watson-Watt were in their offices in Bentley Priory and Bawdsey respectively, and Watson-Watt asked: "What's the latest with Operation Dynamo?"

The military disaster that had seen many thousands of British and Allied troops surrounded and forced to retreat to Dunkirk on France's north-west coast seemed a distant memory. All that mattered was the extent to which a most unlikely evacuation of soldiers from Dunkirk's beaches and harbour could be delivered.

"I hardly dare say it," Dowding replied, "but since Sunday evening, when the armada of little boats began to take men off, a miracle is unfolding across the channel. Truly. Some boats are bringing their passengers to our shores, turning round and heading straight back out to pick up more!"

"How long can it go on?"

"At this rate, God willing, more than 300,000 will have been rescued and the beaches cleared within the week." Dowding paused as if he could not believe it himself. He rubbed his temples and admired Clarice's wavy hair in the picture on his desk. "France herself I'd give a further week – by all accounts, the fighting is very fierce – but by mid-June, mark my words, Robert, Nazi tanks will be rolling along the Champs-Elysées."

When Watson-Watt said nothing, Dowding continued: "I've been sent daily summaries of the retreat, which my secretary reads too, as her brothers are both out there. Lots of incidents stick in the mind. Just this morning, I was reading of a corporal and some privates, trapped in a French village by the sudden German advance. When the corporal was shot in the leg by a sniper, a private made a dash to save him, drag him away. The sniper was up in a tree and had a clean shot, unfortunately, which tore the lad's throat out. That was the end of both him and his corporal."

"Poor souls," Watson-Watt muttered. "Their poor families."

"They were serving in the Royal Northumberland Fusiliers. Gave all they had to the cause. Alas, far too many never made it back to Dunkirk."

"There's been some action in Northumberland itself recently," Watson-Watt said. He recounted the intimidation of Betty Maxwell. "To add insult to injury, the Germans seek to corrode our morale by manipulating press reports that emphasise their achievements. Meanwhile, I'm glad to say that MI5 is further expanding its teams."

"That reminds me," noted Dowding, "I have another morsel of cheerful news in amongst all the blood and gore."

"Pray tell."

"This hasn't been announced officially yet, so you didn't hear it from me, but the PM has ordered the formation of a Special Operations Executive to conduct espionage in occupied Europe and support the local resistance."

"Dirty tricks brigade, eh?"

"Thousands of people are joining. Some departments are merging. It'll operate under the aegis of the Economic War Ministry."

Watson-Watt wondered whether any of this was the good news. But no.

"In amongst all the equipment and vehicles left abandoned by our soldiers," Dowding was saying, "I've requested that the SOE's first priority is to plant some old radar equipment. Low-grade, short-range kit, do you see? When the Nazis find it among all the ordnance strewn at roadsides, I hope they'll treat it as further proof that we have no modern radar system in this country."

Watson-Watt gasped at his friend's cunning. "Well done!"

How to keep the good news flowing? Having recently escorted the new PM on a tour of radar-equipped RAF stations in southern England, he said warmly: "You must feel exhilarated by the expansion of Chain Home too."

"Well, CH has clicked into place this summer, which is a great relief, not a moment too soon. But you know, it's not just the network, what matters is making timely use of the incoming evidence." Dowding ran his fingers through his hair. "I regard the battle for Britain as having started last September when hostilities were declared. We've been working round the clock to prepare for the onslaught. I just hope we've done enough."

"I read in a transcript a few weeks ago a sweeping statement by Göring that the Luftwaffe would take merely a fortnight to smash the RAF."

"Which means, if it's true, they'll be heavily reliant on their fighters. Fewer bombers, at least in the initial stages."

"So, lots of dogfights with Messerschmitts?"

"That's it," Dowding affirmed. "I'd already calculated that would be their strategy. Our own aircraft production has switched from bombers to fighters."

"I know you had to soak up monumental pressure from Paris and London for more fighters to be sent over to the battle in France."

Dowding dispelled this with a shrug. "I simply had to conserve the bulk of our brand new fleet," he said. "Some Spits and Hurricanes have fought the Luftwaffe for the first time over Dunkirk this month. A baptism of fire for the pilots – no bad thing – but despite a few losses, I'm assured that spirits are high."

"What did you deploy in France, then? Blenheims?"

"Blenheims, Lysanders, Gladiators. But credit where it's due, Beaverbrook has been doing a fine job. You really should get to know him, you'd get on well."

As Watson-Watt knew, Dowding was referring to Lord Beaverbrook – Max Aitken – the Canadian-born newspaper proprietor, recently named Minister of Aircraft Production. The Air Ministry had expressed concerns about the initial slow rate of production of Spitfires, more complex than the slightly older Hurricanes, but Beaverbrook had held his nerve. Reportedly more than a thousand aircraft of all types had been built that month, May, five hundred of them fighters to be added to Fighter Command's stock.

"I'm hoping we'll have fifty-plus squadrons when the air battle comes," Dowding said, running through the numbers with which he wrestled daily. "We might get up to 3,000 working planes in all. But given pilot shortages and reserves, we'd expect say seven hundred operational fighters, facing a thousand or more in the Luftwaffe. They have many more bombers, too. Whatever happens, we'll be outnumbered."

"But you've got high morale and your superb defence system, that gives you an edge, doesn't it?"

"Never forget, the pilots are worth immeasurably more than the planes. We can never have enough pilots. Our entire crusade is hanging by a thread, and if we lose, the consequences will be irreversible."

"What about the Italians?" In Watson-Watt's mind was the so-called Pact of Steel, signed a year ago by Hitler and Mussolini to formalise an agreement they originally struck on political and military co-operation in 1936. "They have a large air force, don't they?"

"On paper, maybe." A pause. "We had a lengthy discussion about this in my last meeting at the ministry. I don't believe Italy's air force will be much help to the Luftwaffe. There are no night fighters, no long-range aircraft, no modern production methods. Besides, the Italians haven't declared war on us yet."

"They will though, won't they?"

Dowding permitted himself a smile. "My guess? They'll do it at the eleventh hour, when France falls – some time next month – and the war in Europe seems to be over. Ciano,

Mussolini's foreign minister, wants to keep his country out of the war altogether, but I think he'll be overruled. Their wretched conscripts will be forced to fight for a cause they don't believe in."

"A recipe for disaster." Watson-Watt's voice was tinged with regret. Italy was such a beautiful country. He greatly admired the inventive work of Guglielmo Marconi, who had died in Rome a couple of years ago. How many Italian lives would be lost in this horrendous war? 100,000? Half a million? He shut his eyes.

"I think… Oh, sorry, Robert, one moment, please."

Dowding cupped his fingers over the handset and gave Joanne his undivided attention. From her urgent expression, he knew immediately why she had come.

"I'll have to go, Robert, but thank you for the call. The PM is hanging on the other line."

PART 3

SUMMER 1940

— 18 —

Scramble!

Thursday 15 August. The prevailing high pressure had served up a gorgeous summer's day with light cumulus clouds scattered across a deep-blue sky. Noon came and went. At RAF Acklington, many people basked and relaxed.

The clanging bell shattered the tranquillity, jolted the pilots into action. The very moment it pealed, the rush was on. Cups and kettles forsaken... Snooker cues, table tennis bats dropped... Cards, newspapers, paperbacks abandoned... Jackets, helmets, goggles grabbed... Parachute packs and Mae Wests – inflatable life-vests – strapped on... all during the short, breathless dash to the neat rows of Spitfires.

Ground crew assisted the pilots into the cockpits; some snatched a moment to top up the oil. Seconds later, the reassuring rumble of the Merlin engines and the first propellors spinning into life.

As soon as the Spitfires' throttles were opened for take-off, they quivered in anticipation. The pilots applied their rudders to left and right to hold them in a straight line. Once airborne, within seconds of each other, they were truly in their element, their powerful engines giving the smoothest of rides even at high speed – 350 m.p.h. was about the max in these Mark IXs.

72 Squadron, Fighter Command, was airborne less than eight minutes after being scrambled. The Dowding System had provided advance warning of incoming enemy aircraft: the initial spot, deemed to be a formation of twenty planes ninety miles away over the North Sea, was logged at 12.08 p.m.

Linda Hastings, one of the WAAF's most proficient plotters, was on shift in 13 Group, Fighter Command's underground headquarters in Kenton Bar, Newcastle. She was leading a team of ten, tracing the raid on the plotting table under the watchful gaze of the controllers.

The counters on the map held added significance for Linda. The dear boyfriend she'd met in the city a month ago – what a whirlwind romance, even her twin Gloria hadn't met him yet! – was an RAF pilot. She'd never forget the heart-fluttering charge from opening that first letter of his. Now, the life of her loved one was in play on the table and Linda's chest tightened, as if in a vice, whenever she thought of it.

The map showed all of Scotland and England north of the Humber. Only last week, the defence of Liverpool, Manchester and Birmingham had transferred to a newly formed 9 Group, so the focus here was on raids from the east, crossing the North Sea.

Linda was crystal clear, as she knew Gloria, still working at Bentley Priory, was too. Britain was the last nation standing between the Führer and total control of Europe. In the early hours of 14 June, Nazi jackboots had trampled through Paris – a spectacular victory, just as 'Stuffy' Dowding had foretold. The swastika would soon be raised in Jersey, too. The long-awaited attack on mainland Britain must be imminent.

On 18 June, the Hastings and MacPherson families were among the millions who listened to Mr Churchill's half-hour speech. An invigorating rallying cry, he read it live on the wireless at 9 p.m., reiterating what he'd said in the Commons earlier in the day: "The Battle of France is over. I expect that the Battle of Britain is about to begin. Upon this battle depends the survival of Christian civilisation... Hitler knows that he will have to break us in this island or lose the war... Let us therefore brace ourselves to our duties and so bear ourselves that, if the British Empire and its Commonwealth last for a thousand years, men will still say, this was their finest hour."

Linda found the PM's words inspired her all summer long. Years later, on VE Day, together with Gloria and their fiancés, swept along on a delirious tide of relief and happiness, Linda would look back on the summer of 1940 and better understand the shifting phases of the Battle of Britain. Now, without the benefit of hindsight, she was concentrating doggedly, taking each hour, no, each minute as it came, with no knowledge of what the next might bring.

The air battle had begun in the second week of July. The first phase comprised the *Kanalkampf* – bombing attacks on convoys in the English Channel to decimate supplies and morale. The very fact that the RAF was circling in wait to intercept practically every incursion finally convinced Hermann Göring and Wolfgang Martini that the British had, after all, installed an early warning system.

So, the chain of primitive masts *did* constitute a type of defensive radar, protecting the coastline. Puce with rage, Göring played down the ghastly intelligence blunder. But how could all those 'experts' on the zeppelin have been so inept? Had he not ordered them to be all-embracing, sweep every frequency?

With the existence of British radar evident, Göring changed tack. He agreed with the Führer that the Luftwaffe should use its advantage in outnumbering the RAF to achieve a knockout victory as soon as possible. This was the week when the battle entered a new, more intense, phase.

Tuesday 13 August, two days ago, was already being dubbed *Adlertag* – the Day of the Eagle. Luftwaffe attacks were directed at no fewer than nine Fighter Command airfields and radar stations, principally in the south, covered by 11 Group.

In the event, some of the firepower intended to be unleashed on *Adlertag* was recalled. The weather turned out to be significantly worse, with lower cloud, than the forecasts used by Göring's planners had promised. He vented his malodorous spleen upon them, too.

Although more than 1,400 sorties were launched on that day against airfields and aircraft factories, the devastation was limited. Chain Home stations that did sustain damage were not operational for a few hours while repairs were completed. Only one, on the Isle of Wight, was out of action for a substantial period, ten days in all. Radar vans were welcomed there as temporary replacements.

To Dowding's profound disinterest, both sides' propaganda units minimised their own casualties, releasing no details, while brazenly exaggerating the enemy's losses. Information had rapidly become an unwanted front in the war. He preferred to rely on facts from the field, which indicated that the RAF had lost thirteen aircraft on *Adlertag*. The Luftwaffe tally was forty-five.

The fingers of Linda's right hand drummed a staccato beat on the handle of her little wooden rake, poised at the edge of the giant map. Come on, what was the latest?

She felt the rising tension of the radar operators in the receiver room, one floor below, hunched over their screens, eyes boring into every blip traversing the glass. One blip might signify a single warplane or a group bunched together. How many? How high?

Come on...

Tapping her headphones, Linda glanced at the board with columns of white light bulbs, installed to show the readiness of every squadron in the region. 72 Squadron with a dozen Spitfires was already airborne – when might the others be called upon?

It was a sign of the vast scale of the day's attack that even 13 Group, in the north, was being tested. Linda moved a few coloured counters, placed them with great precision, her heart pounding. She sensed nodding from the bigwigs in the gallery, but she did not look at them.

12.30 p.m. The reports from the east-coast Chain Home stations were changing. The size of the enemy formation that 72 Squadron was intercepting had risen by half to thirty or more, a mix of Heinkel bombers and Messerschmitt fighters, now thirty-five miles out to sea. What were their targets? 13 Group had never known an attack such as this. Until now.

At the head of 72 Squadron was Acting Squadron Leader Edward 'Ted' Graham, who hailed from Ebbw Vale. After boarding school in Somerset where, he reckoned, his leadership qualities were awakened, he worked for a building firm. In summer 1934, soon after his twenty-third birthday, he fulfilled an ambition, enlisting in the RAF Reserve and embarking on flying training in Bristol. He joined the RAF itself the following year and in February 1937 was posted to 72 Squadron when it re-formed after a hiatus in the wake of the Great War.

In April 1939, the squadron was outfitted with Supermarine Spitfires, replacing the aged fleet of Gloster Gladiator biplanes. Ted's skills as both pilot and leader did not pass unnoticed. He'd been named 'B' flight commander by the time the squadron rotated to Acklington. They'd spent the spring months of the Phoney War flying defensive patrols over local towns, harbours, farmland.

In the first week of June this year, they relocated to Gravesend to support the astonishing evacuation of Dunkirk by patrolling its crowded beaches. For the last couple of months, they'd been back in Acklington, biding their time, helping to keep the airfield and the adjacent complex secure. Ted had been advised to expect another relocation, to RAF Biggin Hill, at the end of the month. Although today's Luftwaffe raid was a nasty surprise, he and his squadron were ready.

Ted glanced to port and starboard. Two of his sergeants, Mallinson and Pike, were at his wingtips. His Spitfire was a nose ahead, the point of a pyramid flying at 170 m.p.h. Ted adored flying Spits. And they seemed to enjoy being flown, always wanted to stay up, do more. He grinned at his wingmen, who promptly peeled off – "So long, skipper!" they muttered into their helmet mouthpieces – and took up new positions flanking colleagues close behind.

Ted led them up the coast to Bamburgh, where a majestic castle – once the royal seat of Northumbria's kings – had stood on a rocky escarpment high above the sea for more than 1,400 years. Bamburgh's golden beach was desecrated with anti-tank measures to disrupt the most impassioned invasion: huge coils of barbed wire, buried mines and, at regular intervals along the dunes, guard posts known as pillboxes: concrete cubes with slits for rifles and machine guns. The pillboxes were manned by the Home Guard who, Ted was convinced, would give no quarter. He thought he saw some gun barrels twitching in the sunlight, the only hint of human life on the entire shore.

At Bamburgh, the Spitfires banked to starboard and climbed out to sea. They flew over the chain of Farne Islands, jagged specks of rock where, a hundred years earlier, the lighthouse keeper William Darling and his twenty-two-year-old daughter, Grace, had rowed out in mountainous seas to rescue the survivors of a wrecked steamship. This afternoon, Ted reflected, conditions were flat calm: the modern-day lifeboat crews could rest easy.

On he flew, bearing east, to intercept the raiders. It was not long before he spotted in the distance a swarm of stiff-limbed black and grey insects against the blue and white haze.

As he alerted his colleagues – "Tally ho! Bandits, twelve o'clock!" – Ted realised that the estimates of the size of the raid had undershot, severely, the reality. Tight, V-shaped formations, each aircraft emblazoned with a black Balkenkreuz emblem, were approaching the coast. Heavily armed Heinkel III bombers, some Junkers 88s too, guarded by yellow-nosed Me109 fighters with machine guns in the propellor shaft and on their wings.

Dear God, this was massive. It was not one squadron, it was an entire fleet. All in all, a hundred planes, maybe more.

Just above his instrument panel of a dozen dials, Ted's eyes settled on a small button: the on/off switch for his gun sights. He pulled back the central stick and the Spitfire, responding immediately, climbed higher.

***

At the same moment, Hauptmann Karl-Heinz Weiss was checking the compass on the dashboard of his Me109. The multiple formations, comprising the bulk of Luftflotte – Air

Fleet – 5, were on a south-west trajectory. Having crossed the North Sea, they were approaching the Farne Islands and beginning their sweep in towards the industrial powerhouse conurbations of north-east England.

Last night, at the Luftwaffe's Stavanger airbase in occupied Norway, Hans-Jürgen Stumpff, Luftflotte 5's chief of staff, had led a packed briefing. It was clear that Generaloberst Stumpff liked Stavanger. With its old town of wooden houses encircling a sublime cathedral, it resembled many fine cities in Germany. The Führer had approved a rapid building programme to improve Norway's aging infrastructure: he admired what he saw as the racial purity of his Nordic brethren and yearned to absorb them into the Third Reich.

The Generaloberst had begun his career in the German army. Now past fifty, he'd stayed fit and slim, and looked immaculate in his uniform. He was punctilious in his manners and precise in his use of language.

He reminded his audience of pilots of the Luftwaffe's aims, set by Reichsmarschall Göring: Pummel Britain into submission; target its aircraft production and industry; level its ground defences; destroy the RAF. Germany being stronger than Britain, it was inevitable that the mastery of Europe would soon be complete.

Tomorrow's huge 'flank assault' would overwhelm the British defences in the north-east. To ensure victory, Luftflotte 5 would be deployed in two thrusts. The principal attack, on the industries of Tyneside and Wearside, would be followed by another on the aerodromes of Yorkshire. With strikes on multiple fronts, they would not know where to look next. *Alles klar?* Everything clear? Had his oratory truly inspired them?

The briefing, well received, had lasted an hour. A hail of applause carried the Generaloberst out of the hall.

This morning, 15 August, Karl-Heinz Weiss had enjoyed a leisurely breakfast, washed down with just one cup of coffee rather than his usual two. Pre-flight checks were completed in good time. The airfield at Sola on Norway's south coast had been revamped since April when the German paratroopers seized control. It housed an extended base for seaplanes, an enlarged hangar and a two-mile taxiway to the abutting airfield at Stavanger.

The cockpit of the Me109, like others designed by Willy Messerschmitt, was a snug fit around Karl-Heinz Weiss's body. He felt as though he was wearing the aircraft rather than sitting inside it. He pitied his colleagues flying the Heinkel bombers. Cumbersome beasts, especially with full payloads, they were devilishly difficult to handle and notoriously uncomfortable. Not that he would share such views openly, to anyone.

Despite their collective bravado at the briefing, Weiss knew many pilots detested the thought of crossing the sea. Germany being principally a land country, not a small island like Britain, their warplanes were designed for short-range sorties, not flights hundreds of miles over water. How long could they stay over England before having to return to refuel? The longer the flight, the more fuel the bombers would need, so the lower their capacity to carry bombs.

Karl-Heinz himself felt this mission was well within the limits of his E-series Me109, upgraded with a more powerful engine. He was in his tenth year as a pilot. Three years ago, he'd been awarded the Spanish Cross for his five kills in the Civil War. The RAF wouldn't lay a glove on him.

The one concern that nagged him had nothing to do with the Messerschmitt's performance. It was the British use of radar. He blamed the academics for the misinterpretation of the signals detected on the LZ-130. When that Olympic shooter, Klara, had taken the liberty of expressing doubts, the Gestapo had stepped in to silence her. Nothing he could have done.

Nevertheless, it was apparent that the British had used their radar system advantageously in the *Kanalkampf* phase of the Battle of Britain. The presence of Luftflotte 5 would be detected momentarily and an RAF response scrambled. Karl-Heinz hoped they sent Spitfires. He ached to test himself, to outrun the very best.

Ted Graham continued to climb, leading his squadron past 16,000 feet, 20,000 feet, into the clouds. They were 4,000 feet above the incoming raiders. Ted realised why the initial analysis had so under-estimated the scale of this attack. The three formations were practically lashed together in their V shapes. And some Me109s, flying behind the He111s, were fitted with supplementary fuel tanks, slung below the fuselage, which made them look more like bombers than fighters. Determining accurate numbers was well-nigh impossible.

Ted peered through his canopy in all directions. The whole of 72 Squadron was behind him, watching through thin cloud the enormous swarm of Heinkels and Messerschmitts draw closer by the second.

Quayside thunder

In the smoky, subterranean operations room at Kenton Bar, Linda Hastings nudged a counter forward on the giant map. She hooked another one, brought it a fraction closer to the first. In the front row of the gallery, near the officers from Coastal Command and the Admiralty who smoked incessantly, she was aware that Air Vice Marshal Richard Saul, salt and pepper hair, black eyebrows, was scrutinising her every move.

Born in Dublin, Saul retained his Irish lilt, the soft vowels music to the ears. He was modest, kept a lower profile than, say, Keith Park, the ebullient AVM in charge of 11 Group. But he was bold and brave and had earned a DFC – Distinguished Flying Cross – for his exploits in the Great War. He'd played a lot of rugby and hockey for the RAF, and still enjoyed tennis, although this summer there'd been precious little time to play. Not just due to the start of the war, either. Last year, his wife Edna, whom Linda had met once at a reception and liked tremendously, had given birth to their daughter, Judith. They'd married relatively late, Richard being now forty-nine. Like every parent, he must wonder what kind of world would be left for the next generation.

Saul was admired, by Linda and others, as an architect of Fighter Command. Before taking over 13 Group, he worked for Sir Hugh Dowding, planning the organisation's structure. 13 Group, responsible for Scotland and the north of England, was always envisaged as a relatively quiet zone, where squadrons exhausted by the pressures of protecting the south-east could be posted for R&R – rest and recuperation. He had planned a series of rotations for Dowding's consideration.

Today, unexpectedly, his mettle would be tested. It was already clear that the Luftwaffe was unleashing its heaviest attacks of the battle so far, targeting many places around Britain, including in the north-east. Well, so be it. Alongside Park, Brand and Leigh-Mallory, Richard Saul was not going to be found wanting. Quite the reverse. His squadrons, heavily outnumbered though they were, would be more than a match for whatever Hans-Jürgen Stumpff slung his way.

Saul glanced at the columns of white light bulbs: 72 Squadron had been scrambled to intercept the enemy off the Farne Islands, but aircraft were still available in 79, 605 and 607 squadrons. He would deploy only Spitfires and Hurricanes: the remaining Blenheims and Defiants could not withstand the new-generation Messerschmitts, and to compound the challenge he had a few planes away in Northern Ireland.

Saul's tactical brain whirred swiftly, undistracted by the clickety-clack of teleprinter machines on a desk below. He leaned forward, narrowed his eyes and gazed across the grid-lined expanse of the North Sea.

Seaward of the Farnes, Ted Graham's band of Spits was closing on the armada of escorted bombers at a rate of eight miles per minute. Aided by broken cloud cover, they had an excellent bird's eye view.

Ted issued instructions into the radio mic: "Form two groups, repeat, two groups, red team, blue team. Red team – follow Sammy to attack the Heinkels. Blue team – follow me versus the Messerschmitts. Select your own targets. Take care and good luck. Over and out."

"Roger, skipper. Over and out," came the chorus of upbeat acknowledgements. They'd refined their tactics in a host of practice scenarios, although none of them had met such a massive force as this.

Ted took a deep breath: the moment had come. "Blue team, dive!"

Throttles pressed, sticks forward, engines roared their approval.

Karl-Heinz Weiss heard the roar before he saw the Spitfires overhead. He thought he'd glimpsed a tiny group of aircraft in the distance a few minutes ago – had to be the RAF – but it disappeared behind cloud and he saw no reason to break formation. Come what may, the mission must be accomplished.

He realised his palms were sweating. Especially at low levels, Spitfires were faster, and had a smaller turning circle, than any Luftwaffe aircraft. As well as their agility, Spitfires possessed great destructive power with eight machine guns across the wingspan. Ever since the battle over France that spring, the last thing any German pilot wanted to hear was: "There's a Spitfire on your tail!"

Suddenly, they were buzzing everywhere, over, under, in front, behind. How many were they? Surely not just one squadron?

Weiss took evasive action, banking steeply, then climbing to take stock. The calm sky had mutated into a flash-bang blizzard of noisy action as a fierce dogfight developed. Spitfires and Messerschmitts – yes, far more Messerschmitts – flew at full pelt in every direction, spurts of bullets criss-crossing their paths.

One stream of bullets raced over Weiss, hitting nothing. Instinctively, he ducked, but was more determined than ever to set up a target and force it down.

Flames erupted from the wing and tail of one Me109. Its pilot – Hugo Umbach was his name, Weiss liked him – was watching the fire on his wing. When his head turned, his face was a mask of terror. Despite the seatbelt pressing him down, his whole body jerked upwards as more bullets slammed through the cockpit's metal skin as if it were mere flesh. Umbach's plane tilted downwards at 300 m.p.h., the engine screaming all the way to a bone-crushing collision with the sea. Amidst plumes of smoke and spray, it disappeared. Umbach had not parachuted out.

A hail of bullets ripped into another Me109. High-octane glycol gushed from its cooling system, the black ooze coating the canopy and seeping inside. Within seconds, the trickle became a flood. Desperate to land somewhere, anywhere, before the boiling engine disintegrated, the pilot had no chance to do so. He closed his eyes, accepted his fate. One further machine-gun burst and his plane exploded in mid-air, showering burning debris on the waves, which swallowed it hungrily, leaving a smoky hangover.

Red team leader, Fred 'Sammy' Sampson, was guiding his half-dozen Spits into attack on the mass of Heinkels. Scores of them, sluggish Goliaths, presented a broad target. Flying fast, Sammy got to within a hundred yards before opening fire, backed up by one of the squadron's two Polish aces, Kacper W. Maszkowski, known to all as 'Maz'. Agonisingly slowly, one He 111 sank in the air and headed nose first for the sea. The four men who bailed out made it safely to Bamburgh beach, where the Home Guard awaited them. Sammy and Maz would both claim that Heinkel 'kill'.

Moments after the first Heinkel crashed, the entire formation crumbled. Most of the Me109s formed defensive clusters on their own, leaving inadequate cover for the bombers. To gain extra speed, some Me109s ditched their external fuel tanks – rashly, Maz thought – letting them plummet into the sea with the ferocity of 1,000-pound bombs.

The Heinkels, Ted and Sammy realised, were now splitting into two groups. Was this pre-planned, or improvised given the forceful RAF attack? The second group stayed out to sea, possibly intent on reaching targets further south, in Yorkshire?

Karl-Heinz kept his head and accompanied the first gaggle of bombers, thirty strong, that flew along the coastline. They were, after all, not far from their industrial marks on Tyneside and Wearside. Among copious targets, the briefing had highlighted the Vickers Armstrong plant – in reality, a long-established chain of enormous factories occupying swathes of Newcastle's docks area. In those sheds were created tank parts, armaments, machine tools, warships. It was important that they were obliterated and today, Karl-Heinz was determined, would be the day.

He checked his rear-view mirror. Clear. In the top corner of his canopy, a sudden blur. A single Spitfire swooped over the Heinkels, cannons firing. Black smoke spewed from the belly of one bomber as the Spitfire darted away, pursued by an Me109 which fired at its tail but missed.

"Go get him!" Karl-Heinz urged his fellow pilot, then cursed as he saw the stricken bomber tumble out of control from the sky. It broke into pieces when it crashed on the waves, but he was sure he glimpsed the crew clambering on to a wing. *Viel Glück, meine Freunde!* Good luck, my friends!

Maz had his sights set on another Heinkel. He was about to fire when a volley of bullets perforated his starboard side, splintering part of his canopy and fracturing the IFF transponder. A stinging pain in his right thigh made him glance down. A flesh wound was leaking blood into his trousers.

At once Maz took evasive action, teeth clenched, arms outstretched, pitching the Spitfire's nose down hard. He braced himself for the 'negative G' sensation, like racing down a slope in the big dipper at Blackpool Pleasure Beach, where he and his wife and two pals had spent a Saturday in June.

He was acutely aware of a snag with the Merlin engine. In negative G – when the plane accelerated downwards faster than it would freefall – fuel was forced up to the top of the chamber, flooding the carburettor, drowning the supercharger and shutting down the fuel-starved engine. This was not, he knew, an issue for the enemy: the Messerschmitts' fuel-injected engines did not suffer the same problem.

Thankfully, an outstanding engineer from Hampshire named Beatrice 'Tilly' Shilling had come up with a solution: a small brass restrictor disc, like a washer. It had a hole precisely wide enough to admit fuel into the engine without flooding it. Tilly, who was also a successful motorcycle racer, delivered packs of restrictors to Fighter Command airfields herself. The fix could be made easily in situ. At Acklington, she thought the young man at the gatehouse was instantly smitten with her. She disliked bureaucracy, excessive formality, and willingly shared a joke with him while he gazed puppy-like into her eyes. Then she sped away to her next destination, his dream obliterated in a cloud of dust.

Happily, Maz knew that his Spitfire was one of the first to have been fitted with the restrictor and, in his fractured English, he'd teased Archie Livingstone about his moment to cherish with Tilly Shilling. He blinked away the memory, confident that his engine would not splutter or stall.

And it didn't.

Maz eased the stick up and the Spitfire came smoothly out of the dive. She did everything asked of her, never complained. He tore a wadge of cotton wool from the first aid box at his side and unbuckled his belt. He laid the cotton wool on his thigh wound and pulled the belt tight around his leg as a tourniquet. Grimacing, he eased the stick further back, looked out over the proud nose and re-joined the fray.

Peter Hatcher – whose middle initials were T. and O., hence his nickname 'PTO' – flew his Spitfire underneath the Yorkshire-bound Heinkels, trying to split them up. He saw ahead two Me109s, tried to pepper them with gunfire, but realised that his port-side machine guns had jammed.

He flew close to the Me109 on his starboard side and fired again, point blank range. Smoke burst from its damaged engine and momentarily flames licked the fabric of both wings. The smell of cordite filled PTO's nostrils as the pilot ejected, his parachute flapping open just as his burning plane bellyflopped on to the sea and exploded. PTO would never get used to the ear-splitting din of real-life explosions.

Already banking away, PTO cheered himself with the thought of the little photograph of his lovely new girlfriend, which had hardly left his person since she'd given it to him on their second date. She'd signed the reverse – *Linda xxx* – and even now the scent was intoxicating.

Concentrate, he urged himself. He kept firing at the Heinkels, but his port-side guns refused to fire. Bullets were spat at him from all directions – his tailfin took direct hits –

but he retained control. He'd trained in Southern Rhodesia on Tiger Moths and Harvards, and the Spitfire felt rock-solid. He would see Linda again soon.

How many Spitfires are in this dogfight? Karl-Heinz wondered again, weaving his Me109 left and right, avoiding flying straight. The Me109s must outnumber them three to one, but it felt like there was no such advantage. The view in Berlin that British air power was inferior was complacent, baseless.

PTO's Spitfire suddenly filled his mirror. Karl-Heinz's thumb caressed the trigger button that fired his rear-facing machine gun. Steady now... that's it, keep her in line...

Linda Hastings slid a counter on the table map away from her. *Please keep him safe.* She strained to hear the latest reports in her headphones. Telephonists described the shifting picture to opposite numbers at RAF Bentley Priory, where the national picture came together. They all knew this was a much bigger attack than first envisaged – and it was far from over.

Please give him strength. Please bring him back.

Linda glanced at AVM Richard Saul, deep in conversation with the officers on either side of him. He scribbled some numbers and arrows on a pad and handed the sheet to a messenger – one was never far away.

No turning back now. Having played every card in his hand, Saul rubbed a twinge in his neck. 13 Group was at full stretch, as never before. He'd deployed 605 and 607 squadrons to protect the industries of Tyneside and Wearside respectively. 79 Squadron, also based at RAF Acklington, was to cover the airfields between Acklington and Newcastle. A communiqué was sent to Leigh-Mallory's 12 Group, requesting reinforcements to defend the airfields and coalmines of South Yorkshire.

On the table map below Saul, a second group of incoming enemy aircraft had been identified. They were still crossing the North Sea from Scandinavia, bearing south-west, to make landfall south of Newcastle. This group – smaller than the first – seemed to comprise Junkers 88 twin-engine bombers, nimble workhorses of the air fleet, and some angular Stukas – single-engine Ju-87s

– that many in the Luftwaffe had considered obsolete, only to change their minds when the 'little bombers' proved their worth, dive-bombing at will in the Spanish Civil War. Stukas were also feared for their pinpoint accuracy – a good hit tended to land no more than fifteen feet from the centre of its target.

Darling, where are you now?

Over the North Sea, the dogfight continued at breakneck pace. Like angry hornets, Spitfires and Messerschmitts buzzed amongst one another, aiming or evading gunfire.

To Bernhard Franzisket, a popular Heinkel pilot, the RAF roundels on Spitfires were demonic eyes, the outer blue sclera containing a white iris and red pupil. This, as it turned out, was his final, tormented thought: his canopy was sprayed with bullets from above, his headphones were sliced in two and his chest was drilled with black holes. As Franzisket gasped, vision blurring, limbs losing feeling, his torso turned a sticky red. His crewmates bailed out, but his lifeless body remained strapped in place when the Heinkel collided, port wing first, with the sea.

That's curtains, he's had it! Sammy thought grimly, counting his own blessings as he soared away.

The loss of this Heinkel, the sixth Luftwaffe aircraft to be shot down in the skirmish, had a devastating effect. Perhaps it was the loss of Franzisket himself that crushed his colleagues' spirits. Perhaps it was the nagging fear of flying beyond the limit of fuel capacity. Or had the RAF's formidable opposition exposed their lack of a proper contingency plan?

The Germans' concerns melded into over-riding fear for their own lives. The fleet's morale was shot. Yes, of course, the Luftwaffe had sustained losses in recent times, Karl-Heinz reflected. The Nazis could never have achieved domination of Europe unscathed. But this small island nation puzzled him. Why hadn't it negotiated a peace treaty, as some in Berlin had seemed so sure it would? He'd assumed the Bulldog Spirit, of which he'd heard tell, was a myth, but…

To his frustration, a radio call to 'regroup' was misunderstood – or knowingly misinterpreted? – by many in the air fleet. A dozen or more Me109s slotted into a new formation, heading east, back across the North Sea. At least as many unprotected He111s banked to port and headed east, too. Most with bombs remaining jettisoned them to lighten the load. A few of them exploded, catapulting seawater to the heavens, outraging the gulls. The distance was four hundred miles, nearly two hours of flying low over the waves. The reception awaiting them would be withering, but at least they were returning, men and machines, in one piece.

Maz, ignoring his throbbing leg, looped his Spitfire around the eastbound aircraft, reminding them of his presence. He felt like a good English sheepdog, herding an errant flock towards its pen, and his heart swelled with pride.

Ted Graham was pursuing an E-series Me109. It was giving cover to a pair of Stuka dive-bombers, newly arrived in the second wave. He'd been tracking this Me109 for several minutes. In the nick of time, he'd fired on it to help PTO evade its rear machine gun, and PTO was now chasing other targets. A lucky charm must be protecting him today, PTO chuckled.

Something about this German pilot raised Ted's hackles – and his respect. The way he was allowing – yes, actually allowing – Ted to get him in his sights, near enough to see the row of victory markings on the tailfin, then weaving out of harm's way as he was about to fire – it was as if some telepathic link was binding them together.

Well, if he wants an aerial duel, I'm not going to decline the gauntlet, Ted assured himself and flew on, the call of duty burning fiercely inside him.

***

Karl-Heinz Weiss led him a merry dance south towards Newcastle. Ted was sure he saw a crowd of coalminers, ending or starting a shift, waving their caps as he chased the Messerschmitt down. In his mind's eye, he raised a salute back to the pitmen.

Air raid sirens tolled city-wide. In the Odyssey, no one could find Harry Jarvis – who had seen him last? He'd come in that morning, hadn't he? A duty manager in black tie stepped on stage, waited until the booing subsided, then gave every customer a choice. Either remain in your seats or go home immediately and wait in your shelters for the danger to pass. Most people stayed put and the film – Samuel Goldwyn's production of *Wuthering Heights* – flickered on.

Over the city, a cluster of Heinkels encountered a crop of barrage balloons, tethered with steel cables. Without consulting him, Harry Jarvis's Aunt Carol had agreed that one should be attached to the roof of the Odyssey. The Heinkels tried to gain altitude to overfly them, but two did not begin their ascent soon enough and their wingtips struck the cables.

The impacts caused the cables to be released simultaneously from both their anchor position and the balloons themselves. The loose cable ends trailed behind the two aircraft. The further they flew, the flatter the cables became, curled around the wingtips. When they touched the top and bottom of the wings, small bombs hooked on the cables were detonated. The explosions damaged the wings beyond repair.

One Heinkel crash-landed in a park in Gateshead, creating a fireball that claimed five lives: an elderly couple was lost to their children and grandchildren, and three unevacuated pupils would not re-join their classmates in September.

The other Heinkel became the stuff of local legend. Many more people would claim to have witnessed its mid-afternoon landing than were present at the time.

The aircraft had lost thrust and was gliding, losing height. With very little time to pick a landing spot, the pilot opted to ditch on the river. He had never trained for such an eventuality, but wisely kept the wings level, air vents closed, landing gear up. In he came, surprisingly slowly but whining loudly, touching the surface of the water downstream from the Tyne Bridge. As every schoolchild would soon know, the pilot had an unusual surname, for which he had cursed his paternal ancestors all his life. It was Leichenhaufen, which translated literally as 'a pile of corpses'.

From the Heinkel's belly, a giant swell of water surged eastwards, overflowing the banks and forcing every boat to bob furiously up and down. It was an extremely tight fit: the wingspan was marginally shorter than the width of the river, and the tip of the port wing scythed through a freight vessel, the *Aurora*, which sank within a minute. Barely thirty minutes earlier, its cargo of cereal grain had finished unloading.

The water landing slowed the huge aeroplane. Leichenhaufen steered dead straight, straining to keep the nose up. Still afloat, the plane was dragged to a halt when the same wing chomped into a wooden ferryboat, moored on the north quay.

The flight crew was apprehended, and the river unblocked with pickaxes, saws and ropes made instantly available from the quayside factories. Crowds began to gather on the riverbank and bridges: tales of the bomber on the river – 'the talk of the Tyne' – would cascade through generations. The few who had cameras were rewarded with astounding photographs, which populated numerous exhibitions.

Ted Graham swung his Spitfire to starboard, avoiding a torrent of bullets from the Me109's rear gun. Dear God, that was close, he cautioned himself. The German had kept mostly to the east end of the city, frequently adjusting height but not relinquishing his course – or his target. It must be the Vickers Armstrong armaments plant, Ted decided. He spread the word through his radio.

As if it had overheard, a Ju-87 Stuka dive-bomber appeared in his field of vision, flying lower than him, perhaps half a mile ahead. Ted pictured the fear and panic on the ground as the sirens wailed: "Howay kids, crawl doon and divvent forget your pullovers!" He knew that many families made do with makeshift shelters in their basement or back yard, stocked with candles, water and blankets. Some folk had hauled their beds downstairs for faster access at night.

PTO's voice crackled on the radio. He and a colleague, pilot officer Aldred, had followed two Heinkels south of Newcastle to the Durham coalfield. They'd unleashed a shower of stick bombs on to a colliery. The pithead shaft, quickly ablaze, resembled an inverted rocket. There must have been fatalities, they couldn't tell how many. They'd strafed the Heinkels with gunfire and both aircraft came down, one in woodland, where it exploded, the other in a built-up area, ripping the roof off an end-of-terrace two-up, two-down as if it were a sardine can. It then cascaded through an allotment patch and became ensnared in a barbed-wire fence. The wreckage was surrounded by locals armed with pitchforks.

"Roger that," Ted said, zig-zagging his way after the Me109.

As they banked to follow the line of the river, Ted saw not one, but two Stukas ahead. The German pilot had held him off, enabling the little bombers to approach their targets.

There they were, climbing steeply in readiness for their trademark drop. The first Stuka reached its apex, tilting forwards into a terrifying nose-dive. Its engine howled as it reached vertical, getting unbelievably close to the ground before pulling up, up and away. Just as the Stuka was headed skywards again, the pilot released his payload: a single 250kg bomb.

It might have been a gust of wind or a flock of gulls, but the Stuka veered slightly to starboard just as the bomb was despatched. While the plane roared skywards, the bomb missed the roof of the Vickers Armstrong factory, falling to the right and exploding on impact with the quay.

Clouds of concrete debris, flames and smoke swelled up, blackening the afternoon air. Workers in overalls scurried from the factory, spluttering and coughing.

The Me109 held its position between the Spitfire and the second Stuka, which now began its own climb. Stick forward, it tipped into its death-defying dive. From anti-aircraft cannons on the ground, two streams of tracer bullets soared up. They tore into the canopy and upper side of the diving Stuka's fuselage – to no apparent effect. The pilot continued his vertiginous descent and released his bomb at the lowest point.

It landed between the Vickers Armstrong complex and a Stannards warehouse. The explosion knocked doors off their hinges and shattered windows in both buildings. The quay's surface was cratered.

Ted observed that a section of Stannards' roof had caved in. But the Stuka never made its ascent after dropping the bomb. It continued straight down and crashed head-long into the quay, causing a second earth-shaking explosion. The fireballs merged into one. Thick smoke spiralled into the sky as the *boom* reverberated. It was heard miles away.

The Me109 banked to port, making for the city centre. Another burst of tracer bullets spewed from an anti-aircraft gun, peppering the wings and tailfin of the first Stuka. It disintegrated in mid-air. A crumpled ball of smouldering wreckage smashed on to the quay by the Stannards warehouse and rolled on to a tugboat roped to a pair of bollards. Ted watched the tugboat lunge crazily as the water around it fizzed.

Where was the Me109? Oh, God. He'd taken his eyes off it for, what, two, three seconds? Nothing to port…

Ted's mirror was filled with the yellow nose and propellor of the Me109. Now for the first time he had reflected sight of the face of Karl-Heinz Weiss. All he knew about this man was that he was an outstanding pilot, indefatigable and cunning.

Ted ducked and bobbed but could not shake the German off. He saw his thumbs move to the machine gun firing buttons. For the first time in his life, Ted believed that he was facing not merely a dangerous foe, but his own mortality.

I am dead, I really am dead…

He was reassured to find that he was not afraid. He had long believed in a loving God who would not desert him at the end of his life. He'd witnessed the reality of death as a young child, when the body of his newly departed grandfather had lain overnight, stone cold, on their kitchen table in Ebbw Vale, and he heard his grandfather's voice now, pressing him to act, respond, shape his own destiny.

Ted slowed, applied full rudder to starboard and pulled the stick back. His Spitfire performed a perfect flick roll – a 360-degree sideways turn – and the Me109 shot past him.

Ted centralised the rudder, pushed the stick forward to recover from the roll. Thank God, these acrobatic Spitfires would do anything in the air!

The Me109 was back in front, in his sights. Without delay, Ted thumbed his firing button – and nothing happened. Was he out of ammo? Mechanism jammed? Perhaps this really was his date with destiny.

He heard a Merlin engine roar alongside him. It was Maz, smiling as always despite a pained expression and bloodied fingers on his controls. He flew past Ted to the Me109's port side, and inched closer to it, closer still, until his starboard wingtip was under the German's port wing.

Then Maz banked hard to port. His starboard wing, rising sharply, flicked the Me109's port wing into the air, causing the whole plane to flip over. It cartwheeled for what seemed an eternity, over and over, but was probably only five seconds. Time enough for Maz to line up behind the Me109. As soon as it recovered and flew straight, he let rip with his machine guns. The rear of the Messerschmitt, including the entire tailfin, disintegrated.

For a head-spinning moment, Karl-Heinz did not realise the extent of the damage. He flew on, trying to evade the Spitfires, but his controls would not respond. He sensed that he was losing altitude but to bail out would be suicidal.

A huge expanse of parkland – Newcastle's Town Moor – stretched before him. It covered a thousand acres, more space than New York's Central Park, much more than London's Hyde Park. Every June, one of the world's largest travelling funfairs – 'the Hoppings' – occupied a meagre slice of it. Crusher Cracknell had boxed more rounds on this land than he cared to remember.

Grateful for the open space, Weiss tried to miss the trees and lakes. He crash-landed on a grassy slope that would be popular in winter. His shattered Me109 slid all the way down the bumpy incline, coming to rest near a bandstand, where two middle-aged members of the Home Guard were cheerfully leafing through a Ministry of Food recipe pamphlet, *Eating for Victory*. So preoccupied were they that they didn't notice the astute, bloody-nosed German pilot extracting the Me109's fuel-injection pump and quietly setting fire to it. He lit the fire with his Trommler cigarettes. Before he was captured, he managed to toss the Me109's complete handbook into the flames, too.

Maz and Ted flew north to base, RAF Acklington. Ted made radio contact with his colleagues: every member of the squadron responded, exhausted, gratified, overwhelmed. They could hardly believe their triumph, the sheer size of the enemy fleet they'd left in disarray. Surely now the prospect of a full-scale invasion from Norway or Denmark was degraded? They'd have a good knees-up in the NAAFI tonight to decompress.

Again, Maz and Ted noticed the matchstick citizens of Newcastle on the ground, cheering themselves hoarse as the Spitfires passed. As was his wont, Ted rocked his wings.

— 20 —

The ultimate judgement

Four days later, in RAF Bentley Priory, Sir Hugh Dowding rubbed his neck, flexed his shoulders. He spent so much of each day on the telephone, the handset cradled under his chin, that in the afternoons he frequently suffered muscle spasms.

Monday 19 August, 2.45 p.m. From his comfortable office in Adastral House, the air minister had rung for an update. Given the events of the previous week, Dowding feared it had the makings of a particularly lengthy call.

"Well, thank you, minister. My system proved equal to the task, but may I say that congratulations are a tad premature. You see, we were fortunate last Tuesday that inclement weather curtailed the attacks on some airfields, but they more than made up for it on Thursday, didn't they?"

Dowding stretched his legs so that his carpet slippers tipped the far corner of the desk.

"You're correct, minister. In Berlin, it's already referred to as Black Thursday – the 15th. By all accounts, the heaviest fighting of the air battle so far. Yes, indeed, the Luftwaffe flew a multitude of sorties, more than two thousand, we estimate, from Norway and France, against many targets. I'm sorry, what was that? Oh, to our knowledge, they lost seventy-five aircraft on Thursday alone. Every group in Fighter Command saw action."

The minister read from a report in his hand. The ink ribbon had been fading when the flimsy page was typed, and he angled it into the sunlight streaming through his west-facing window. He asked Dowding to verify the text.

"I can confirm that 13 Group, led by Richard Saul, had an outstanding day, minister. No, I wouldn't call it a miracle, but they did emerge more or less unscathed, one or two pilot injuries, relatively minor damage to some aircraft. Yes, they'll all fly again. Very considerable damage was inflicted on Air Fleet 5, an entire fleet shattered. It departed with its tail between its legs, having caused minimal damage to our industrial assets."

Dowding listened, breathed deeply to calm his impatience. "That's correct, minister. Not a single working day lost in Newcastle or Sunderland. You can certainly say, if you wish, that the fourteen Hurricanes of 607 Squadron shielded Sunderland most effectively. What's that? Oh, that squadron belongs to the Auxiliary Air Force – yes, the so-called 'fillers' – stationed at RAF Usworth near Sunderland. First class, I concur."

The minister's voice pattered in Dowding's ear.

"I must say, I hadn't seen the like of it." The Air Chief Marshall's voice rose half an octave. "The photographs are quite spectacular… The wingspan right across the river occupied a double-page spread in the paper… Yes, I believe special editions were rushed out… Oh, good, I'm glad he liked it. But you know the Heinkel was promptly broken up, minor inconvenience to shipping. Beyond a doubt, terribly good for morale."

Dowding poured a tumbler of water from a jug provided twenty minutes ago by Joanne, whose eyes were markedly red and puffy. He'd been on the telephone to Trevanion, a senior civil servant, for a few minutes before the minister's call, and he didn't feel he'd thanked her properly, which rankled.

"A Spitfire squadron from Catterick saw them off," Dowding said into the handset, referring to the section of Luftflotte 5 that had targeted Yorkshire's airfields on Black Thursday. "We may conclude that we weren't at all overwhelmed, as we surmise their principal objective to have been. They are unaccustomed to anything other than lightning-fast victories, so I'd say we dealt them a psychological blow as well as a physical one."

A pause.

"Oh, I'm sure they were all delighted, minister, it was much appreciated." Dowding had been asked about the PM's visit to RAF Uxbridge, part of 11 Group, last Friday, 16 August.

"It was even more timely, given the events of yesterday," he added. The Luftwaffe had unleashed furious firepower on RAF targets in southern England yesterday, Sunday 18 August. Retaliation for Black Thursday, or premeditated? Dowding tended towards the latter. Fighter Command had lost sixty-eight aircraft, the Luftwaffe just as many. A ghastly day, remorselessly grim news. Joanne, still visibly distressed twenty-four hours later, was awaiting news of her neighbour, a pilot missing in action.

Dowding had taken a call from the curate of Biggin Hill in Kent, a prime target that had sustained heavy bombing. He was also chaplain to the RAF station there, and he was fuming.

"Those who don't respect the Lord's Day," the chaplain barked regarding yesterday's fatal attacks, "those who sin egregiously and treat the Lord's name irreverently will one day have to face the ultimate judgement. There's no escaping it – they should not be deluded into thinking they have the Lord's blessings."

Notwithstanding the fire and brimstone, Dowding thanked him for his moral clarity before hanging up.

"Do I think we're in for much more of this?"

Dowding repeated the minister's question, giving himself a few extra seconds to consider his response. "I don't have a crystal ball, minister, but let me put it this way. The Luftwaffe has some fine aircraft, and as you know, they outnumber us materially. The sun is set to shine for the next week, so Robert tells me – he's still a most reliable weather forecaster, you know. But because the Nazis have not yet achieved their objective, we must put up as many planes as we can – yes, new ones are essential – and bring fresh pilots through training. It's the only way we can stand up to them."

Dowding swallowed some water, ran his tongue along his lower lip.

"I think they will continue their aggression for as long as they believe they can win air superiority... Laying the path for invasion. Meanwhile, I do expect we're in for a lot more of it, as you so delicately put it, minister."

Silence on the line. Dowding awaited further questions; none came.

Though counting the seconds until he could get back to work, he had one more point to ram home. "Are you still there, minister? Good. They'll want to retaliate, of course, for bombing raids we make in Germany. Last week was, I suspect, merely a taste of the Blitzkrieg that lies ahead. They'll be determined to knock the fighting spirit out of us. So, to my mind, there will never be a better time for German agents to sabotage Chain Home. I'll wager they mount an operation in the very near future. What do you say, minister?"

There was no immediate response. Neither man could have known then how accurate Dowding's prediction would turn out to be. And yet, although he'd never told him in as many words, the minister did appreciate that without the brilliant inventiveness of the ACM's secret system, without the early-warning intelligence that was bolstering her defences, Britain would be conquered and overrun, as sure as eggs is eggs.

***

Mrs Purnell saw the grey Ford 8 pull up outside the farmhouse. It was familiar... where had she seen it before?

She was leaving the barn carrying a tray of eggs as two dark-suited men got out of the car and approached her front door. Having lost sight of them, she cut across the yard, re-entering the house via the back door. She was putting the eggs away in her kitchenette when firm knocks reverberated from the front. She didn't feel much like it but went to answer.

With the door ajar, Mrs Purnell recalled in a flash where she'd seen the car. Five months ago, when it sped away from this very door, leaving a package on the step. But these men were not schoolteachers, as Evelyn had claimed, no way.

"Hello, Mrs Purnell."

They even knew her name. Who *were* they? Something official. She opened the door wider.

Christopher Talbot introduced himself and Warren Sixsmith. For the reassurance it was worth, he presented his ID. "We're from the British security service. There's nothing wrong – nothing at all to worry about. We've come to see Evelyn."

Mrs Purnell was wearing a full-length black dress, a string of silver pearls around her neck. Her face was white, her eyes sunken in their sockets. The hand that gripped the door frame trembled.

Mrs Purnell's attire prompted Talbot to continue. "May I say how sorry we are for your tragic loss."

She wondered how many times these hard-headed men would speak words such as those, concerning soldiers they didn't know and would never meet, before this dreadful war was done.

Her only son, Gary, had joined the Royal Northumberland Fusiliers. She had been informed of his courage and quick death in a carefully written letter on regimental notepaper. Detached from their colleagues making their way to Dunkirk, Gary had tried to rescue his corporal, wounded in the leg in the village square of Valéry-les-Roses. As he did so, he had been shot by a sniper, killed outright, did not suffer. Simply met his fate in the line of duty. She should be extremely proud.

Mrs Purnell was grieving for her lost son, of course – the handsome young devil that he was – but also for a long life of promise, love, adventure that would not be lived. She'd always said that the best day of her life was the day her son was born. How sickeningly unnatural it felt that she should outlive him. How would she ever come to terms with it?

She realised that her hand on the door frame was shaking more obviously and hid it behind her back.

"Thank you," she said, practically a whisper. She did not wish to talk to them about Gary, she might break altogether. "You know, I knew something was awry with Evelyn when I telephoned St. Hilda's where she said she taught and they told me she'd only filled in there for a week. I can imagine her being good with the bairns – but one week! I'd had suspicions for some time, mind you. Oh, I admit, I've grown fond of her, she's a likeable lass, although I don't much care for that brother of hers. Simon, they call him. They made me out to be a fool when I spoke to the lady in the school office, and you don't forget that in a hurry, do you?"

"Have you done anything about your discovery? Confronted Evelyn herself?" Sixsmith enquired gently.

Shaking her head, Mrs Purnell said: "I haven't seen her for a while. That's how it goes, especially during the spells when she takes off on that noisy motorcycle of hers."

"Is she at home, by any chance?" asked Talbot.

"No. I'm not sure exactly when I last saw her, to be honest."

"The motorcycle is gone?"

"Must be a few days now. Unusual."

Talbot gave Mrs Purnell a printed card. He looked serious. "If she returns, please call me on that number. Any time. It would help us a great deal."

Mrs Purnell inspected it at arm's length. Talbot was unsure whether she was long-sighted or had serious misgivings or both.

When he and Sixsmith turned to leave, Mrs Purnell summoned them back.

"Who *is* Evelyn? If she's not a teacher, what does she do?"

Talbot forced a smile. "As I said, there's no cause for alarm, please don't worry. Evelyn has spoken highly of you. She's fond of you, as you are of her. We've spent more and more time with her recently. She's a good friend, and if I may say so, a very brave person, too." He nearly added "like your son", but decided against it.

Mrs Purnell stood firm, said nothing. They were evasive, not telling her the whole story, that was obvious, but she'd had all she was going to get. It struck her for the first time that Simon might not actually be Evelyn's brother. She only had their word for it, which didn't seem to count for much. Evelyn had been living under her roof for months – oh my, was that even *her* real name?

"Do you have anyone with you at this dreadful time?" Sixsmith asked. "Not your farm hands who are always busy. I mean a relative or friend, someone to keep you company?"

"Andrea Crawford, a friend from Alnwick, is staying with me, bless her."

Talbot drove away, at first in silence. Then, one of the two men sitting in the back of the car, whom Mrs Purnell had not noticed, spoke up.

"So, Klara is missing, yes?"

Captain Nils Larsen stared at the back of the heads of the MI5 officers in the front, their hair slicked down above their white collars. He glanced at his colleague, Lieutenant Tor Jensen, to his right. He had not meant it to be a rhetorical question, but no one answered. Perhaps they simply couldn't bear to do so aloud.

Larsen and Jensen were officers in the Norwegian Intelligence Service. In late April, soon after the Nazi invasion, they had been given – in no uncertain terms – an assignment from a new chain of command. They were to travel to Britain, purchase maps, and confirm in detail the state of the principal roads, bridges and railway lines in the north-east. Other officers were being selected to cover other parts of the country.

As soon as they had berthed in Newcastle, Larsen and Jensen handed themselves in to the police, stating – truthfully – that they wanted no truck with the Nazis and hated what was happening to their country. The police had been efficient, vowed to help, knew who to talk to on their behalf. After weeks of repetitive meetings and interviews, they were eventually accepted as the genuine article and promised wartime postings in the British intelligence community.

They were delighted to accept. A month ago, they'd been attached to Christopher Talbot's unit in the north-east branch of the security service. Talbot and Sixsmith had evidently worked so closely together that they could read each other's thoughts: their rapport was excellent. They had cool, clear minds, these Englishmen. They were reserved but charming. They had integrity and would absolutely not give up.

It turned out that Larsen's daughter, Sigrid, was the same age as Talbot's daughter, Lucy. But they spoke of practically nothing other than work, work, work. From the outset, they'd seemed genuinely grateful to have two extra pairs of experienced hands, and Larsen was gratified to be working with them. For his future career, a stint seconded to Britain's MI5, no less, could be an exceptional springboard.

Warren Sixsmith had briefed Talbot, Larsen and Jensen on the latest film society forum. It had taken place in the Odyssey, overnight as usual, last month, July, chaired by Harry Jarvis. Ulrich Freitag, whose control of the group tightened at every session, had said it would be their final gathering before a summer break, and he'd be in touch regarding future dates. Sixsmith had found Jarvis strangely reticent about when they might reconvene. Perhaps the war made everyone take one day at a time.

The vital development was Freitag's selection of five members of the group to help him prepare for what he called Operation Funk, a summer project. What qualities did the five – two women, three men – possess? Although Warren was not picked, and not party to the individual briefings, he made a show of helping Alice Young, one of the quintet, to don her yellow summer coat when the group dispersed from the foyer into the night. She'd been muttering something about hair dye, going blonde, which may have been a hark back to her days on the stage. Oftentimes tricky to tell with Alice.

It was Captain Larsen who recognised at once the potential significance of the codename 'Funk' when they'd discussed it the following day. In English, he said, the word meant a state of bewilderment or fogginess, didn't it? But it was also a German word for radio. A *Funkturm* was a radio mast, such as might be found in any German city.

A puzzle clicked into place in Talbot's mind. "Freitag's mission is to sabotage Chain Home before the invasion. Of course it is! He's been planning it for months, it must be imminent."

"Did you say Mrs Young spoke of hair dye?" This question came from Jensen.

Sixsmith nodded, replaying in his mind the moment in the picture house foyer.

"Well, it may be a coincidence," Jensen said, noting Talbot's expression which screamed that he did not believe in coincidences, "but hydrogen peroxide – hair bleach – is an oxidising agent. It can accelerate burning in explosions, yes?"

His words struck fear into Sixsmith. "My God, you're right! What do you need to make a bomb? A combustible substance, an oxidiser, a detonator…"

"A timer of some sort, too, say an alarm clock, to trigger the detonation when the seconds run out." Jensen mouthed the sound of a blast.

"Let's take a step back." Talbot looked at Sixsmith. "Remind me, please, who were the five people selected by Freitag? Go on, run through them."

"One, Walter Dodds, a farmer." Sixsmith counted the names on his fingers. "Two, Jack Redfern, an ironmonger, recently retired but still cuts keys for Harry Jarvis. Three, Crusher Cracknell, you know all about him. Four, Sonia Stobart, and five, Alice Young."

"So, we have a farmer, an ironmonger and a garage mechanic. Of the two women, one will do anything to protect her daughter. The other is a chameleon able to act any role Freitag requires."

"Exactly," said Sixsmith. "If you needed to get hold of petrol, some oil cans, chemicals, batteries, timers, all that sort of bomb-making paraphernalia, that little band of five can source everything you need."

"And given their occupations, no one would think there's anything out of the ordinary," Talbot added.

"Why is the farmer significant?" Jensen asked. "What's the connection?"

"Fertiliser," Talbot replied. "Ammonium nitrate is used in insecticides and fertilisers, so it's entirely appropriate for farmers to order supplies of it. Generally comes in sacks of white crystals. It's another strong oxidising agent, and when mixed with fuel, it can be extremely hazardous."

"Nothing needs to be imported, either," Larsen observed. "Everything procured locally by perfectly chosen individuals who may not even grasp the scope of what they're collectively doing."

"Freitag knows," Talbot said grimly, "that's for sure."

He had shared their thinking with Klara at the next in what had become an on-going series of meetings with her after the initial, revelatory one at Hadrian's Wall. They arranged them on different days at different locations, but they were always useful sounding-board discussions. Klara had felt that their deduction rang true, and it was just the kind of 'black ops' activity that would spring from Department G.

She had shared the deduction with Curt Schultz, positioning it as her own idea, no mention of MI5. As natural as it seemed to discuss her opinions with him, she immediately regretted it. She had taken pains to compartmentalise her life, as she'd put it, and this felt as though she'd crossed a line.

As it happened, Schultz had said very little, lost in thought, as if the weight of the world had landed on his shoulders. Like her, he was not at all surprised by the existence, and presumed purpose, of Freitag's operation.

Talbot had intended to ask Klara whether she or Curt had had any further thoughts about the operation. Their latest meeting had been scheduled for yesterday afternoon, Sunday 18 August. They were to meet at the cottage in Bamburgh where Grace Darling was born and take a stroll around St. Aidan's churchyard where Grace and other members of her family lay buried.

But for once, Klara had not turned up.

Normally she was a model of punctuality. Talbot and Sixsmith had waited an hour before leaving the village, but a knot of concern had constricted their stomachs ever since. No message had been left for them. Now, twenty-four hours later, even at her lodgings, there was no trace of her. She had, as Captain Larsen suggested a few minutes ago, vanished.

As far as they knew, Curt Schultz was missing, too.

Feeling an urge to drive faster, Talbot reined himself in. The last thing they needed was to draw attention to themselves. His hunch was to check the local Chain Home stations. The nearest masts to the farm were at RAF Acklington, amongst the most northerly sites in the network. Surely as good a place as any to start? Yes, Sixsmith had agreed.

Within minutes, the hunch paid off. They turned off the main road towards the air base, advancing slowly. Fewer than fifty yards from the junction, lying in the roadside ditch, was the Norton ES2. Captain Larsen spotted it first and called out to Talbot to stop.

The handlebars and rear wheel were buckled, both panniers ripped apart, empty. The large headlight was smashed, fragments of glass scattered close by. Staring at the wrecked machine, Sixsmith felt the thud of the impact on his own body. His eyes settled on the front wheel revolving in the afternoon breeze, clicking at every turn. A tyre tread was gouged in the soil. The scene of the crash, whatever its cause, yielded no signs of life.

The mask slips

Later that afternoon, Monday 19 August. Daylight was fading as Ulrich Freitag drove the bullnose Morris Minor van, his right foot pumping the accelerator clumsily. He glanced at the passenger seat, whose occupant had lit a cigarette but did not look like he was enjoying it. He let it burn, the ash accumulating on the tip.

With RAF Acklington five miles behind, they were travelling south towards Widdrington, Druridge Bay, Lynemouth. So far, so good, Freitag thought to himself, the operation was on schedule, going to plan. It needed to: a huge amount was at stake. He'd heard personally from Reichsmarschall Göring that the Luftwaffe would make widespread bombing raids on British cities and airfields for at least the next two weeks.

They passed a flatbed lorry, heading in the opposite direction, stacked with empty baskets, nets and pots. The two fishermen chatting in the cab would head out to sea in the small hours of tomorrow and return with a bounteous fresh catch.

As the offside front tyre clattered through a wicked pothole, the whole van shook. While Freitag cursed, an inch of ash dropped into his colleague's lap. In the back, Klara Falke stirred, opened her eyes. They felt gummy, as though they badly wanted to stay closed. Where was she? She rubbed her eyes, which came into focus on a low ceiling, inches above her head. Metal. Animated, rocking from side to side.

She was lying on a blanket that smelled musty. In a moving van. She wriggled free of a folded-down steel trolley, digging into her back. Unexpectedly she felt thirsty and hungry. She stretched her legs – and her feet collided with something hard. Four black oil drums stood in the corner. Each had a panel near the top, six inches square, attached with screws. This concerned Klara, but for the moment she was consumed by the two men in the front. With no barrier to separate the brown leather front seats from the open space in the rear, she was close to the back of their heads and knew with a jolt who they both were.

The memory of the accident surged back. She recalled Curt Schultz on the saddle behind her, fingernails clawing into her waist at the sight of the bullnose van approaching them from the other side of the road.

Why had it made him so tense? It was where it should be and would pass by on their right as normal.

But this was far from normal. The van turned towards them, accelerated, came straight for them like a torpedo. *What the...?* Had Curt *known* it was going to do this? Was she delusional or was it the same vindictive driver, Caldwell, who had almost mown them down in Amble? If so, this 'accident' was pre-arranged...

Forced to take evasive action, Klara ended up in the roadside ditch, the ES2's front wheel taking the brunt of the crash. Curt, she was sure, had already leapt clear. She'd bumped the side of her head and felt groggy. She tried to look up and – *yes, that's right* – she'd seen a man on a bicycle go past. Then came a rapier-sharp pain and she blacked out. How long ago was that? It seemed only minutes, but...

Between the two men's heads, Klara saw the tractor at the same time as they did. It suddenly pulled out of a lane, concealed by hedgerows, and was broadside across the road a few yards ahead. Slamming on the brakes, Freitag yanked the steering wheel to the left. The van's tyres screeched. The tractor was turning to align with the road, and the van must have missed it by a whisker. A young lad, school age, was driving and he gave a conciliatory wave to their rear doors.

Freitag heaved a sigh of relief, ran a hand over his pumpkin head. Glancing back to check the oil drums, he saw that Klara was awake, sitting up, staring at him. He nudged the man to his left, who flicked his cigarette out of the window and swivelled round.

"Good evening," Curt Schultz said while Freitag drove less hurriedly. "How are you feeling?" He sounded genuinely concerned.

Ignoring the question, she asked: "What was it you said to me before we met General Martini? 'Be careful who you trust'? Now I see what you had in mind." Of course, she reminded herself, Curt did not – must not – know that she was employed by MI5.

"Klara, I–"

"Do you know when he started working for Department G?" Freitag glanced over his shoulder, elbowed Curt out. "Twelve months ago, in the smoking room on the zeppelin! Do you recall? I hope, Gretel, that you didn't think we were really arguing about cigarettes!"

He tossed back his head and laughed.

Curt's eyes were closed. This was not how he'd wanted this delicate discussion with Klara to unfold, but Freitag could not resist goading her, controlling her.

"I'm sorry," Curt said to Klara. The guilt may have been gnawing at his insides, but his simple apology did not ring true.

"Why?" she asked icily. "Filthy lucre?"

"Of course it's money!" Freitag butted in again, losing patience. "He's been on the Gestapo's payroll for a year. A nice little side-line, you might say, to supplement his lousy Abwehr pension."

"Just bits of information, advice, joining dots, really," Curt blustered to play down his role.

"And the punch-up on the zeppelin?" Klara recalled. "Purely for show? For my benefit?"

This time Freitag let Curt reply. "Don't flatter yourself. We had dozens of witnesses in that lounge. Not one of them would believe I'd just cut a deal with Herr Freitag." He looked away, admiring his own performance, then turned back. "Not even you."

Klara found this sudden sneer to be chilling. Was it a flash of the real Curt Schultz, unmasking his hateful cruelty? She'd wondered all along about his reasons for following her to Britain. Recently, he'd made a good fist of professing his affection – no, more than that – his love for her. Was any of it real, or all designed to dupe her?

It was as if Freitag had read her mind.

"You know, we had to remind my friend here who he was really working for." He grinned at Curt, who looked forlorn again. "What his real priorities were. He seemed to be getting a little too close to you for comfort, Gretel. He needed to focus elsewhere."

So, the attack at Amble had been a ruse, intended primarily to scare Curt, not her. Thinking back, Klara could believe that Curt had been the driver's target. It also explained, perhaps, why there had been no subsequent attempts on *her* life.

Klara rubbed her eyes again. She was feeling more alert by the minute, despite the dull ache in her head. She was desperate to know exactly what was in the four oil drums. Were there others, besides these? Where was Freitag taking them?

Another thought nagging the back of her mind sprang to the fore. Freitag and Schultz clearly wanted her under their thumbs, so they knew where she was, what she was doing, and preventing her from making any investigations of her own. Simply separating her from the ES2 removed much of her independence at a stroke. Freitag was aware of her English identity, cover, address. He and Schultz did not trust her – had never trusted her. But they were unaware she was working for MI5: had he known, Freitag would not have spared her life.

As they drove on, the light fading, Klara raised her knees under her chin. A purple bruise had blossomed below her right knee. She noticed for the first time that the oil drums were strapped to the van's inner wall, not standing freely. Under what she hoped was an unfazed exterior, her mind was racing.

***

You made a neat job of painting over the Swanson logo on the Morris Minor van, Bob 'Crusher' Cracknell congratulated himself. By the time he'd finished, it was lustrous black all over.

You couldn't tell where Swanson's identity had been obliterated, which had compounded his satisfaction.

Now, as darkness began to fall on Monday evening, 19 August, Bob wondered how many of the dozen bombs they'd assembled, with pride as well as care, had already been placed in situ by the big German. Given his contacts at the garage, Bob had not needed to be asked twice to provide petrol and oil drums. He'd stored them in one of the trenches used when repairing cars, covered with a galvanised steel sheet, bolted to the concrete. The spivs on his crew had asked no questions.

Harry Jarvis had been as good as his word. Incidentally, where was Harry? The weasel seemed to have disappeared. But so far, he'd paid Bob every month to help keep the business liquid. "Our friends in Berlin would not want the garage to go under before Operation Funk, which is so critical to our cause, now, would they?"

In addition, the cash he'd received from Christopher Talbot, for submitting MI5's redrafted versions of his occasional reports, had meant the payroll and suppliers' invoices could be settled promptly. Staff and suppliers alike had stayed loyal. One of the spivs – they didn't think he knew about their two-bit sidelines, but of course he did – now spent most of his time in the little office, administering the business. He'd shown a flair for it – very enterprising he was – and customers had kept driving in.

Bob realised, of course, that he was playing for two sides at once, taking shillings from the Germans and the British. The former side was a dictatorship, the latter a democracy. Bob was less concerned with the moral dilemma of his position than with his ability to do whatever was necessary to support himself. God, he deserved a break!

He must have been eight or nine – no more, because his mam was still alive – when he'd come home from school and recounted the tale of Moses sending twelve tribal chieftains to explore the Land of Canaan, when the Israelites were in the wilderness following their exodus from Egypt. Could the Land of Canaan be their new Promised Land? The story had captivated young Bob. Who were these chieftains, if not spies?

A term later, Good Queen Bess – Queen Elizabeth, the last of the Tudors – had despatched spies throughout Europe to report on the threats of invasion.

His mam had commended his enthusiasm, delighted that something at school other than fighting fired his imagination. A year later, she was dead. He remembered her sweet scent, but his memories of her face and voice had faded. Knocked out of him, perhaps, by blow after blow in the ring.

The point was, he told himself, that spying had been part of human civilisation from the very beginning. It may not be spoken of, but for thousands of years it had been there, betrayal below the surface, deception in the shadows. The trick was to make the most of any opportunities, while turning a blind eye the rest of the time. Isn't that precisely what everybody does? Had always done? Foolish to deny it, pretend anything different.

Bob had no qualms about his decisions, motives, actions. The Germans seemed satisfied with the reports he'd sent on the radar research at Acklington; MI5 seemed satisfied that he'd fed disinformation to the enemy and got away with it. Two satisfied customers, job done.

It had taken him three weeks to recover from the battering he'd received at Betty Maxwell's house. Or whatever her name was. He was still suffering more headaches than he'd had before. He massaged the back of his neck: ah, that felt better.

Having signed over the Morris Minor van – old branding blacked out – to Herr Freitag, Bob had been allocated a new task on Operation Funk. He was to take the Rover 10, the car used by Alf, and drive it in and around the city of Newcastle. A decoy driver, while Freitag went about his business near the coast. He'd known it was risky – not that, as with that man Talbot, he really had much choice – but the risk of getting caught, of being knocked out, had always made him feel more alive.

He was to vary his times and routes over several days this week, and he'd planned carefully which areas he would visit when. Today he completed two circuits of the Town Moor before heading into the northern suburbs, as requested passing the Carlton picture hall in Milburn Avenue and the Sycamore Grove B&B in Cookson Street. He'd heard no air raid sirens but had seen one RAF Hurricane on patrol.

Tomorrow, he would tour the docks and quays. Every day, remnants of the Heinkel that had ditched on the Tyne were fished out. Several riverside taverns had souvenirs mounted on their walls, and a local paper had run a readers' poll to determine the most impressive exhibit salvaged to date.

Bob thoroughly enjoyed driving. The sense of freedom, the infinite choice of destinations, at least in theory, felt empowering. Behind the wheel he could think things through, work them out in his mind. He was still surprised that he'd opened up to that man Talbot, especially after Talbot had exploited his vulnerability and made him supply carefully doctored information to Harry's network. Admittedly there was a degree of self-interest in so far as it might make Swanson's arrest more likely, as well as the fees he gained. But somehow Talbot had convinced Bob that he wouldn't really harm him, that he could safely do business with him.

This evening, as Bob headed south again through the dark city towards the Town Moor, he had a sudden premonition of impending disaster. A strange feeling – his flesh crawled. Another after-effect of the bang on his head? His brain playing tricks? He checked his speed, slowing well in advance of a roundabout ahead.

A police car entered the roundabout from the opposite direction. Two officers in the front. Bob took the second exit, straight ahead, going in the direction from which the police car had come. He accelerated gently out of the roundabout and continued along the quiet road. In his mirror, he was startled to see the police car loop around the roundabout, double back and follow immediately behind. What could...

The police car's headlights flashed twice. The officer driving made an exaggerated show of jabbing his index finger to the left, towards the roadside. He was thrilled to have spotted the

Rover to which he'd been alerted on a regular check-in with the station from a blue police call box.

There was nothing for it. His sanguine mood foundering, Bob pulled over and waited.

— 22 —

Tripwire

Again, it was Nils Larsen who noticed him first, from the back of the Ford 8. Having left the ES2 crash site, they'd passed RAF Acklington and had just begun a circuit of the research station when he cried out. Christopher Talbot brought the grey car to an abrupt halt.

The body of a man lay face down in the wild grass at the roadside. He was clad in army uniform with an old LDV armband, the jacket unbuttoned, one side flapping in the evening breeze. Sixsmith rolled the body over, clasped a wrist.

"He's alive!"

Talbot crouched beside Sixsmith and together they heaved the man into a sitting position against the nearest tree trunk. Below his ginger hair, an oval-shaped lump had sprouted on his forehead. He came to reluctantly, eyes bleary and unseeing at first.

"What…? Who…?"

"You're safe now," Talbot enunciated slowly, squeezing the man's hand. "You're a Local Defence Volunteer? Home Guard?"

Realisation dawned. The man nodded gratefully, looked around, getting his bearings, suddenly concerned that his attackers may still be watching. He gave a plaintive cry and felt the lump on his head.

Talbot gave him a card and he focused on it easily enough, sitting up a little straighter.

"I'm Private Yates, Home Guard. My company keeps watch on this area." Wearily, Yates waved a hand, encompassing the radar research station and the airbase.

"Oh." He patted his left breast, felt under his open jacket, looked crestfallen. "My Webley's gone." His service revolver was a .455 calibre Webley Mark VI with a six-round cylinder. "It was fully loaded," he added ruefully and shut his eyes.

"Did you see who coshed you?" Sixsmith asked. "Were they after anything apart from your gun?"

"It's all right," Talbot cut in. "I think the answer lies just over there."

Sixsmith and Yates followed the line of his gaze to a cluster of trees ten yards away, practically touching the research station's perimeter fence. On the other side of the fence stood two pairs of masts, part of the Chain Home network, a wall of sandbags cloaking their base.

On this side of the fence, partly concealed by the trees, were two upright oil drums, painted black. Jensen and Larsen were poring over them in the receding light, fingertips on the square plates screwed hard and fast to the casing.

"We need a bomb disposal unit," Talbot said, "most urgently."

In fact, an Explosive Ordnance Disposal team from the Royal Engineers arrived within twenty minutes, much sooner than Talbot had thought possible. Sixsmith had found Archie Livingstone listening to the wireless in the gatehouse at the RAF base. He placed a telephone call to the Royal Engineers and was advised that teams of sappers were already in the area. Not long after he'd returned, an army Bedford truck rolled up.

Three months ago, in May that year, responsibility for bomb disposal had been assigned to the Royal Engineers, the corps that provided construction and demolition support to troops in combat. All too rapidly, it was gaining experience in the specialist field of bomb disposal: twenty unexploded devices had been dealt with in June, a hundred last month, double that number so far this month, not quite three weeks into it. Initially, twenty-five bomb disposal sections had been created, but Talbot knew they were proliferating like ink on blotting paper. He thought there might already be more than a hundred of them within the corps, and many were in action this evening.

Lieutenant Bellamy, who jumped out of the Bedford truck, looked younger than his twenty-six years. A civil engineering graduate, he had attended a Royal Engineers' Officer Cadet Training Unit, after which he received an immediate commission.

He was followed out of the truck by Sergeant Sharp. A decade older than Bellamy, he was an outstanding analytical engineer but not primarily a leader of men. He'd completed his engineering degree at Cambridge in the same year, 1919, as George 'Hoppy' Hopkinson. Two privates also emerged from the truck, lugging toolboxes.

"You're from the Security Service?" Lieutenant Bellamy began. His voice was deep, belying his youthfulness.

Talbot introduced his team of four, from Britain and Norway.

Bellamy continued, seemingly without drawing breath: "You'll know we've been in the region all afternoon, plenty of boots on the ground. You may not know why."

Talbot waited.

"A highly alert WAAF in the operations room at RAF Bentley Priory noticed a pattern of German activity from first light this morning," Bellamy explained. "Gloria Hastings is her name – I do hope she's in line for a commendation."

He signalled to the two privates, Bowes and McGrath, who took their toolkits to the oil drums, alongside Larsen and Jensen.

"What she identified was a series of German bombers, usually two at a time, coming to our east and south coasts and dropping their payloads – none of which exploded."

"None?" Sixsmith repeated. "So, it can't be mechanical failure or sheer rotten luck?"

"These bombs are delayed-action," Bellamy advised. "Set to explode when their timers reach zero."

Talbot's expression was deadly serious. "Their targets – the Chain Home radar installations? And they will all go off at the same time, yes?"

"You've got it. We have scores of units working on this right now, up and down the country. The Luftwaffe is attacking our coastal radar. Actually, one bomb that we know of exploded on impact at Sheerness in Kent. Made a dreadful mess, a few injuries, none life-threatening. The masts were out of action for a few hours, up and running now, I believe."

"When will the rest of them explode?" Talbot reiterated.

"Zero hour is noon tomorrow."

"So, the oil-drum bombs being planted are – what – back-ups? Reinforcements?"

Bellamy nodded. "A way to be doubly sure of blasting our radar. Two lots of bombs at once, from the air and on the ground. Means they're determined that CH will be knocked out one way or another tomorrow, leaving us no way of reading the skies."

"That's been a pre-requisite for the invasion all along," Talbot said. He was stunned by the evident scale of this Nazi operation. Had they under-estimated the Nazis' ambition? Had there been a failure of British intelligence to gather even a whisper of the bigger picture? No doubt, in due course, MI6 would follow up such questions with its agents and informants in Germany.

"Quite so," said Bellamy. "Gentlemen, our time is getting shorter. If you'll excuse me…"

He strode to the oil drums, whose steel plates had been loosened, exposing the innards. Larsen and Jensen shone torches inside, while Bowes and McGrath worked with their tools, the former calling out his actions for the latter to copy precisely.

Meanwhile, a police motorcycle arrived. On his own initiative, Archie Livingstone had called the police to deal with the wrecked ES2, which Sixsmith had mentioned, and the attack on Private Yates. Talbot pointed the officer towards the ditch where the motorcycle lay and turned back to the twin defusing procedures unfolding before him. The privates had steady hands, although Talbot noticed the beads of sweat pricking McGrath's forehead.

"The Germans call this sort of device an SC bomb," Bellamy whispered to Talbot. "Stands for *Streng Cylindrisch*. Thin-walled, general purpose, cylindrical explosives."

"Sir." McGrath attracted the attention of Bellamy, who was immediately at his side.

"The fuse is fixed on this side of the bomb casing," McGrath informed him, his voice clear and authoritative. He pointed into the torchlit space. "It's secured by a small plate, here. I suggest we screw a hook into the plate to dislodge it, then extract the fuse through this aperture."

Bellamy inspected the bomb's entrails – assembled locally in recent days? – as Jensen adjusted the angle of his torch beam. As explosive devices went, this one, while containing gallons of fuel, capable of causing massive fire and blast damage, did not appear to be particularly sophisticated. It could have been rolled into place by a couple of strong men with the aid of a trolley.

"Very good," he said with a nod of approval to McGrath. "Carry on."

One after the other, McGrath communicating every step to Bowes, the privates set about defusing the bombs. From their toolboxes, they each selected a small steel hook and began, turn by turn, to screw them into the top of the plates that secured the fuses. Bowes dropped his hook and they all heard it clatter through the drum before landing on a thin plywood shelf inserted to separate the timer, fuse and detonator from the fuel below. Lieutenant Jensen, who had been holding his breath, gasped for air, and muttered an apology for swaying his torch beam.

The police motorcyclist returned. He parked by the Bedford truck, where Talbot, Sixsmith and Bellamy went to speak to him. Sergeant Sharp sat in the army truck, consulting his maps.

The privates produced a ball of string from their pockets and looped a length of twine around the hooks they'd inserted. Ignoring the ticking alarm clocks, they twisted out two small screws holding the plates in position and pulled the strings taut.

Biting his lower lip, McGrath tugged his string. The plate slid towards him, leaving the loosened fuse to sag. With a pair of pliers, he gripped the fuse, snapped it cleanly in two and brought out a length of it, dangling like fish bait from the pliers.

Larsen gave a small cheer.

Bowes followed suit, tugging the string with matching force and sliding the plate away from the fuse. As he reached in with his pliers, a wasp landed on Jensen's left ear, and he wafted it away. Suddenly, Bowes's view inside the drum went dark. As the blades of his pliers closed over the fuse, he did not see the black fibre, thinner than thread, that stretched through the mechanism behind the fuse. It was a tripwire. When the pliers touched it, before they could make the cut, it triggered an explosion, over-riding the ticking clock.

The blast was huge, the ground shook. In addition to petrol, this bomb had been spiked with quarter-inch steel ball bearings, hundreds of them.

***

An hour later, the acrid stench of burning clung maliciously to the air. As the last ambulance departed, Talbot surveyed the scene of devastation. He felt numb, sick, cold, and longed to hug his daughter. Privates Bowes and McGrath had both died instantly, as had Lieutenant Jensen, all three literally blown to pieces. Captain Larsen had suffered severe injuries – the probable loss of his left leg, shrapnel wounds to head and chest – but it was hoped that he would survive.

The others, further away, happened to have been luckier. Cuts and grazes, ears ringing, dust and grime in their hair, shoes, pockets, even under their collars. Sixsmith, having seen a blinding flash, found himself knocked to the ground by an invisible fist. His chest was sore, his hands were bleeding, but he knew how fortunate he was to be alive. The police officer also had bleeding hands, while his motorcycle was a write-off.

Several tree trunks were scorched and a gap of twenty yards had been punched in the perimeter fence. Members of 72 Squadron were standing guard while arrangements were made for new mesh to be instated overnight. The CH masts had survived – the sandbags helping to absorb the blast – but the legs on two of them had buckled and required urgent attention. The Acklington station would be off-grid for a few hours, repaired by tomorrow morning.

Lieutenant Bellamy jumped down from the tailgate of the Bedford truck, whose side was heavily pockmarked by ball bearings. Its windscreen, cracked but not dislodged, was covered in a film of earth and dust. He'd spent the last fifteen minutes 'on the blower' to headquarters – on a military radio, whose transmitter and receiver were housed in a double-doored metal case bracketed to the inside of the truck. There were a dozen valves, knobs and dials to co-ordinate, but Bellamy was an expert. His hair was flattened where he'd worn the headphones.

"The information from Yates, our Home Guard friend, was useful," he reported to Talbot and Sixsmith. "Confirming, I think, that we're on the right path."

Yates had provided a detailed description of the black van, a Morris Minor, in which his assailants had arrived. In the blast, he'd caught some shrapnel in his shoulder and his hearing told him he was under water. He'd been taken to hospital, accompanied by the police officer who had further questions about the attack, and his wife was already on her way there.

Talbot watched Bellamy closely. Even in the darkness, it was plain that his posture had sagged. The loss of two sappers and the Norwegian lieutenant weighed heavily upon him, body and soul. He looked haggard but put on a brave face.

"We issued a description of the van," he continued, "and it caught the late edition of a couple of evening papers. Calls came in from a farmer, whose son had seen the van from his tractor, and a fisherman changing his nets."

It was apparent that the man named Freitag, accompanied by at least one other person, was, as anticipated, driving south.

"There are two more sets of masts on the Northumberland coast, before you reach the Tyne and Wear conurbations and Yorkshire," said Sergeant Sharp, approaching with his map. "It's reasonable to assume that they're taking each one in turn, planting their crude, booby-trapped bombs along the way."

"Agreed," Talbot said coldly but calmly. "We know where those masts are. The first is outside the village of Lynemouth, the second is on a reef at Blyth. Its name is Crab Law."

"There's not a moment to lose," Bellamy urged. "The sergeant and I will accompany you, in case any more bombs have already been planted and require defusing."

Given the appalling loss of his men barely an hour ago, and the signs of shock – paleness, shallow breathing – evident when Bellamy spoke, Talbot felt this was admirably brave.

"What about the unexploded Luftwaffe bombs?" he asked.

"As I said, we have other teams working on those. Headquarters agreed with me that the oil drum devices are an equally urgent priority tonight."

Talbot and Sixsmith, relieved to have the Royal Engineers' support, helped to clear the truck's windscreen of debris, then hurried to the Ford. Twenty-five minutes later, they reached Lynemouth, a village three miles north-east of the mining town of Ashington, and Talbot slowed to a crawl. The army truck loomed large in his mirror.

Sixsmith peered left and right along the side streets of terraced cottages. No sign of a Morris Minor van…

"Wait!" Sixsmith called out. When he breathed in, the pain in his chest spiked.

Talbot stopped, likewise the Bedford truck behind him.

"Up that little street by the corner shop." Sixsmith pointed through the darkness.

He got out and hurried painfully across the road into the side street where, thirty yards along, a Morris Minor van was parked. He stared through the driver's door window, blast cinders tumbling from his hair and nose.

"Here, use this." A couple of paces behind, Talbot produced a torch like the ones Jensen and Larsen had used to illuminate the sappers' work. He would be sure to enquire about Captain Larsen's condition and, all being well, arrange a hospital visit post-surgery. If possible, he'd take Lucy. Perhaps she and Larsen's daughter, Sigrid, might strike up a correspondence, become pen friends?

On the front passenger seat of the van lay a flask, a map, a pair of sunglasses. Through the rear-door windows, Sixsmith made out half a dozen rolls of carpet. After a few seconds, he extinguished the torch, stretched his back.

"Yates gave us the first two letters of the registration number, and these are different," Talbot observed, laying a consoling hand on his colleague's shoulder. "And this van looks midnight blue, rather than black. What do you think?"

Sixsmith groaned. "You're right, it's not our target. Sorry, gentlemen." He was addressing not only Talbot but also Bellamy and Sharp, who had joined them in the otherwise deserted street.

"No problem, better safe than sorry," Sharp muttered.

They regrouped at their parked vehicles. To their left – east – across a bank of dunes was an extensive beach. The tide was out, and the waste coal strewn across the sand sparkled like diamonds in the moonlight. The masts stood a hundred yards beyond the village, on grassy land before the sand dunes. Talbot imagined Lucy seeing them as the long limbs of monsters whose upper bodies were lost in the night sky.

"Let's keep going." Bellamy rubbed his hands, still grimy after the explosion. "Freitag and company are either here in Lynemouth, or they've been and gone, leaving their lethal calling cards behind."

Sixsmith shuddered and rubbed his chest, where the sharp pain was getting worse. He joined Talbot in the Ford and they continued towards the masts. Two white gulls, pecking at the body of a mouse in the road, squawked their disgust at the disturbance and left it to the very last moment to flee.

23

Hawkskill

They passed a telephone kiosk – empty – and a letter box with a bicycle propped against it. Sixsmith winced as the car bounced over an uneven patch of road.

Approaching the masts, Talbot pulled over again.

"What's wrong?" Sixsmith fretted.

"Flat tyre, I reckon."

"Lord, what a moment for that to happen!" An ill omen if ever there was one. Suddenly Sixsmith froze and stared at Talbot, who read his mind.

"We were only away from the car for – what – a minute in that side street? No one could have tampered with it without any of us seeing or hearing. Besides, the army truck would deter vandals, wouldn't it?"

"Maybe."

"It's an accident! Just one of those unfortunate things." Talbot stopped short of accusing his colleague of paranoia. "Or maybe a ball bearing from the explosion got lodged in the rubber. Are you all right?" He cast a worried glance at his colleague.

"I think the blast might have cracked one of my ribs. I'll live."

They abandoned the car and clambered into the back of the Bedford truck, facing one another on the side benches. It was a rough, lumbering ride, their only viable option. Sergeant Sharp was at the wheel. Out of the village, woodland proliferated on their right, thickening the darkness.

"What are those shadows?" Bellamy demanded suddenly. "Black shapes flitting across the road up ahead – did you see them?"

"Yes, sir."

Sharp was already braking. As soon as the truck stopped, Bellamy let Talbot and Sixsmith out.

"We may have spotted them. Two men crossing from there," Bellamy pointed towards the sandbagged base of the masts, "heading over there." A less precise gesture to the trees on their right. "Good place to conceal a black van, eh?"

"Our immediate priority must be to check for new bombs," Talbot said. "But keep an eye out for that van."

We really need *two* vehicles, Sixsmith thought bitterly but said nothing more about the Ford.

In the black van, Klara Falke peered out of a rear window. When Freitag had removed two of the oil drums, sliding them carefully, one by one, on to the steel trolley, he'd snarled: "Gretel, you'll be shut in here on your own for a few minutes. I advise you not to move about in case you disturb a critical piece in the drums. Better to keep perfectly still."

"It feels airless, it's been a warm, muggy day." She'd invented a protest on the spur of the moment. "And I may need the toilet."

Freitag had thrown back his pumpkin head as if in raucous laughter. "No chance," he'd retorted and hastily shut the doors. A padlock was snapped across them before Freitag joined Curt Schultz, wheeling the trolley over the road.

In the curtained window of a wood cabin beside the masts, a dim blue light flickered. Freitag crept to the door and took out the Webley revolver with British bullets that he'd taken from Private Yates. Without a sound, he turned the door handle and stepped inside. Background music from a wireless set smothered the click as he shut the door. Two men sat at a desk against the far wall, their backs to him, gazing at oscilloscope screens. One wore headphones. Freitag approached him and snatched the headphones so hard that the cable tore out of its socket. Instantaneously, both men wheeled round.

"Hey, what the—"

"Who the heck—"

"Your shift has finished early, gentlemen," Freitag shouted, brandishing the Webley. "But stay exactly where you are."

With the heel of the gun handle, he smashed the oscilloscopes. One blow to each proved enough. Then he ripped the two telephones on the desk out of their sockets.

"Who are you?" one of the men repeated, less confidently this time.

"I told you, you're off duty," Freitag insisted. A new track faded in on the wireless. "This little outpost is now closed, do you understand?" The tiniest pause. "You see your clock on the wall there?"

Both men looked at the large clock that kept accurate time but, they now realised, with a rather noisy second hand.

"If you emerge from this cabin before thirty minutes have elapsed, you will be shot. Don't call my bluff on this matter, I am sure your lives are worth more to you than that. Just sit out the time, be patient, be silent."

Feeling queasy, the men regarded the muzzle of the revolver, then each other. They turned obediently to face the smashed screens. Within two seconds, Freitag had shot them both, sitting ducks, in the back of the head. The two cracks almost merged into one, he was so quick, and the bodies collapsed simultaneously in their chairs, leaving a sticky red spray on the wall and desk.

Dummköpfe! Did you really think I'd let you go in half an hour to raise the alarm? Freitag thought to himself. He liked many things about this proud yet self-effacing, pragmatic yet sentimental country, which was clearly pulling together, over cups of tea, at war time. As the government's motivational poster urged: 'Keep calm and carry on'. Yet some aspects of British life were alien. He could not comprehend a land of such tolerance and trust – these men were gullible, naïve, and it had cost them their lives.

He was about to switch off the wireless when a solo violin distracted him. The track was *The Lark Ascending* by Ralph

Vaughan Williams. Not merely music, it was sweet poetry and to Freitag it underscored that there was beauty in the world.

He turned off the desk light as well as the wireless and took the key from the inside lock. Stepping outside, he locked the door, pocketed the key and strode over to the sand-flecked grass, where Curt Schultz was setting the timer in the second bomb at the far side of the sandbag wall. They could be observed from the beach, but not the road.

Freitag's pulse was steady, his cheeks were not flushed – outwardly he gave no indication that he had just murdered two people in cold blood. He felt no guilt: what mattered was his cause and maintaining the absolute self-belief that he would achieve it.

"Do you need help?"

Schultz shook his head and screwed the steel plate into position. "All done. Noon tomorrow – kaboom!"

Freitag neither liked nor respected Schultz. He had shown himself to be a mercenary with no true convictions. How could such a feckless man be trusted?

And yet, he had shown initiative earlier, just after they'd left Acklington. He'd asked Freitag to stop at a telephone kiosk – he had an idea. Freitag had stood at the heavy red door, straining to hear what Schultz was saying while keeping an eye on their van, where Klara was out cold. Schultz, as Stephen Fletcher, called Mrs Purnell at Silverbeck. Freitag did not realise that the voice that answered was Andrea Crawford's, her friend from Alnwick.

"Sorry, dear, she's in the kitchen. Would you like to wait? Oh, all right, I'll give her a message, that's fine. What is it, dear? You and your sister are going to Scotland for a few days, is that right? A friend has invited you to stay? How nice. You'll enjoy exploring the Highlands, at their most glorious at this time of year. Now, before I forget, can you let Evelyn know that her colleagues from MI5 have been looking for her? Yes, I'll repeat that for you, is the line not very clear? Her MI5 buddies, she needs to get in touch with them. They wouldn't tell us what about, of course, they were too high and mighty for that, if you ask me. And then the police came round, because apparently her motorcycle was found in a ditch near to an RAF base. Quite the mystery! Well, that was all they said, but you could tell they weren't giving us the full story. Nothing like. Evelyn led us to believe she was a teacher, you see, but it turns out she isn't. I'm sure I'm not supposed to say anything, but she's evidently a high-flyer in MI5. Keeping us safe from those terrible Nazis. Who'd have guessed it? That was quite a revelation, I can tell you. As if there isn't enough upset in this house just now with poor Gary…"

Schultz had replaced the receiver without saying goodbye. He looked away from Freitag, tried to digest what he had learned. *Klara working for MI5?* That had come as a bone-chilling shock – he would have to think through the implications. *When…? How long…? What had she revealed…?* He wouldn't tell Freitag straight away – that would be signing Klara's death warrant, and he couldn't bear the thought of it. Composing himself and forcing a thin smile, he withdrew delicately from the kiosk.

Yes, Freitag had to concede, Schultz had done well to lay breadcrumbs suggesting that the siblings were in Scotland. He said he'd left a map of the Highlands in Klara's attic room at Silverbeck, too.

He had done an excellent job assembling the bombs, aided by Crusher Cracknell, from the materials acquired by his film society team, and priming them in situ. Provided he didn't let him out of his sight, checked everything, Schultz was an extremely useful asset.

"Come on, let's go. One more location on this run, then we'll reload and head further south."

Schultz followed him to the van. As Freitag unlocked the rear door, it swung wide open. In a blur, Klara leapt out, a caged animal unleashed, and was sprinting along the straight road towards Lynemouth before either man reacted.

Schultz spoke first: "We'll never catch her." Was that a hint of admiration or desperation in his voice?

"Of course we will." Freitag left no room for doubt. Keys in hand, he climbed in behind the wheel. "Are you coming?"

Schultz got in and Freitag threw the van into a tight turn. They soon spotted Klara, sprinting at top lick, once dashing into a side street before doubling back to the main road. Freitag stayed with her, pumping the accelerator, getting ever closer.

"Don't run her over, will you. Please!" Schultz gasped, unsure of Freitag's intentions. An acidic taste clogged his throat. He'd heard a gunshot from the cabin by the masts but, banishing his darkest thoughts, decided not to question Freitag. He'd emerged calmly humming to himself and that was the state of mind Schultz wanted him to retain.

Once he got ahead of Klara, Freitag whipped the wheel to the left, blocking her path. He slammed on the brakes, front wheels bumping over the kerbstone on to the pavement.

"Go and get her!" When Schultz hesitated, Freitag added: "Before I do."

Schultz stepped out to find Klara jogging on the spot. His leaned in to speak privately and his fair curls brushed her forehead.

"You're not going to run off?"

She resisted the urge to say that she'd only been trying to delay them, to give the men who would surely be pursuing them more time. Instead, she replied: "You know me, I can't stand to be cooped up like that. It's horribly uncomfortable."

"I'm sorry, but you'd better get back in. Now."

"How about swapping places?" She did not attempt to conceal the sarcasm. "Your turn to ride next to the bombs."

"Don't worry, the timers aren't set yet."

"What a relief! You always were mechanically minded, weren't you? You must be delighted with your handiwork tonight."

"Our country is at war, Klara. Our duty is to gather intelligence and sabotage enemy infrastructure." He thought back to last year. "I think you and I knew on the zeppelin, a feeling in our bones, that the British did have radar. I deeply regret that our pilots had to find out the hard way that we were right. In his own way, Herr Freitag regrets it, too. I suppose I'm only trying to atone for the lapses on Operation Bloodhound."

Klara snorted, said nothing. She could see Freitag's thunderously impatient face at the wheel.

"If Admiral Canaris thinks he can weaken the war effort, he is dead wrong," Schultz went on, more broadly. He was almost talking to himself now. "The Führer *must* win. If he doesn't, his dream and legacy, Germany's destiny, will lie in ruins."

So, Schultz adhered well and truly to the side of barbarism. She hoped he would live long enough to regret it, feel some shred of remorse. She let him shut her in the back and sat cross-legged as far from the oil drums as she could wriggle. Schultz got in beside Freitag, who glared at him as if to say: What took you so long?

"Go easy," Schultz said soothingly, "everything's fine."

Freitag reversed down the road, rewinding the yards along which they'd followed Klara. He pulled over by a clump of trees opposite the masts.

"Come with me," he said to Schultz. "I want to check the drums."

"Why?"

Freitag, already out, did not answer. Schultz followed behind.

This time, Klara stayed where she was. She'd bought precious minutes for her MI5 colleagues – would they count? At this stage, for her to disrupt Freitag's progress any further would be a risk too far.

Freitag unscrewed the steel plate from one drum and, with a tiny torch, checked the internal connections. Timer, detonator, fuse, all in order. No tripwire on this bomb.

Schultz said: "These explosions will show the British and their allies that we can penetrate their defences, execute large-scale attacks, strike at will." He smiled pitilessly at Freitag. "Now, time is short, we should go."

Freitag signalled his agreement. Yes, on this operation, he grudgingly admitted, Hansel had done well.

***

In the darkness, the two men crossing the road, returning to the van, was the motion that caught Lieutenant Bellamy's eye in the Bedford truck. Now, standing at the roadside, the four of them – Bellamy, Sharp, Talbot and Sixsmith – conferred about their next steps.

As they did so, another truck pulled up behind theirs. Out stepped two privates and a sergeant from the Royal Engineers. A brief exchange ensued. Bellamy was delighted that it had been agreed at headquarters that Bowes and McGrath, the sappers killed in today's blast, should be replaced immediately. The atrocity would not stand; their work would continue.

"A Godsend," Bellamy said, introducing the new men to his colleagues. The sergeant, Tom Milne, gave each private a reassuring pat on the back, then drove off.

Sergeant Sharp and the privates inspected the oil drums. The tide was a long way out and they settled into their painstaking work to defuse them.

Bellamy, Talbot and Sixsmith returned to their truck and drove south, following – they hoped – Freitag.

"If that was Freitag, leaving the drums, we're only a few minutes behind," said Talbot, willing the lieutenant to speed up. "The next set of masts are, what, ten miles from here?"

"A little less," Bellamy replied, taking a tight right turn. Half a mile further on, another ninety-degree bend, after which they saw in the moonlight the monochrome lines of a level crossing.

"Hawkskill Crossing," announced Sixsmith. "The spot is renowned for birds of prey and long ago the name stuck."

Bellamy peered ahead. "I can make out half a dozen cottages and a post office for sorting letters off the mail trains," he noted. "The gates are padlocked across the road, there must be a train coming."

"And just in front, do you see?" Talbot cried excitedly. "A black van waiting at the gates. It is black this time, isn't it? A Morris Minor? There have been no junctions or side roads. That *has* to be our target."

Behind them, the road was deserted. Only one vehicle was ahead – the van, stopped at the gates. Years ago, the gates had been painted in red and white stripes, but most of the colour had flaked off the wood.

"Sometimes," said Sixsmith, taking shallow breaths, "you have to wait for two or even three trains to pass before someone comes out to let road vehicles through. Mostly goods trains at this time of the evening."

"We must intercept them before the gates open," said Bellamy. "We may never get a better chance." He switched off, removed the ignition key.

Talbot agreed. "But we must assume that Freitag is carrying more bombs and that he'll kill if he has to." He thought of Klara's description of the Gestapo officer as a dangerous psychopath. Could Klara herself be in the van, in danger?

He stepped down from the cab, followed keenly by Sixsmith. The van had no lights on, and even moving stealthily around to the side they saw nothing through its windows.

Bellamy watched from behind the steering wheel, making a mental count of the Lee-Enfield No.1 rifles racked at the rear of the truck. Every time he blinked, the faces of Bowes and McGrath flashed before his tired eyes. Grieving, he reflected, was always a solitary ordeal.

Talbot drew level with the black van's near-side passenger door. He was about to knock on the window when, panther-like, the van leapt forward, filling his throat and nostrils with burning rubber.

It smashed into the first set of gates, which shattered into pieces that spun in the air and clattered on the rail track. It was travelling faster on impact with the gates on the other side. They too were ripped out, fragments strewn about the track.

Instinctively, Sixsmith and Talbot ducked for cover. By the time they stood, moments later, there was neither sight nor sound of the van.

Composing himself, Sixsmith began to remove the largest pieces of wood from the crossing. He bent at the knees and tried not to stretch his body. As he stacked an armful, he heard Talbot shout: "Warren – *run!*"

The nose of a steam locomotive was yards from him, closing fast. He dived off the track, the wood spilling and splintering under the wheels of the speeding engine. A shrill whistle screeched. It was a northbound repair train, pulling a crane and heaps of sandbags and finally an ambulance carriage bedecked with large red crosses. It had missed Sixsmith by seconds.

No sooner had it passed, and the swirling smoke cleared, than another train thundered over the crossing, southbound. This engine was pulling sleeper carriages, occupied by railway staff touring the network to instruct colleagues in air raid precautions.

"Warren?" Talbot screamed.

Sixsmith did not answer but used Talbot's shoulder to lever himself off the ground. His chest was in agony. Bellamy was out of the van, kicking more wood from the track.

No more trains were due and an irate, elderly man with poor posture appeared from the blacked-out end cottage. Presumably the keeper of Hawkskill Crossing, he surveyed the wreckage and sought to blame the man nearest to him – Lieutenant Bellamy. When Bellamy turned, he saw the Royal Engineers uniform and fell silent.

"Why don't you get this crossing replaced with a bridge?" Bellamy, ever the engineer, suggested. "There's plenty of space and the road could be straightened out a bit in the process."

Dumbfounded, the keeper could not speak. He returned to his cottage, banged the door shut.

Bellamy, Talbot and Sixsmith clambered into the truck, Sixsmith entering last to conceal his pained expression. A dairy van with the ponderous slogan 'Delivering your milk and milk by-products' had pulled up behind them, queuing to traverse Hawkskill Crossing – or what was left of it.

Bellamy nosed slowly forward, shards of wood giving them a pitted ride. He was mortified that Freitag had slipped through their fingers.

But, for the Chain Home network, the clocks were counting down. At noon tomorrow, Britain's radar defences would be blown to smithereens.

24

Crab Law

Bolting from the van a few minutes earlier, Klara quickly got her bearings. Even in the darkness, she'd recognised that they were in Lynemouth, driving south. She felt crushed that Freitag had escaped the army at Hawkskill Crossing. So near, yet so far. He'd timed his getaway to perfection, seconds before the train sped through. Such actions risked all their lives, but he would not have given that a second thought.

She'd followed the routes to the Chain Home stations on her ES2 many times in the last eight months, and she was sure where their next stop would be. Where the two remaining oil drums were destined to explode.

The next masts were in Blyth, an industrial coastal town in south-east Northumberland, a dozen miles north of Newcastle. She recalled Albert Hess chatting about the place as they glided over it on the return leg of their zeppelin flight. Britain's first aircraft carrier, HMS *Ark Royal*, was built in Blyth's vast shipyards in 1914. He'd also said that half a million tons of coal were exported from Blyth every month. This coal, and the reams of Scandinavian paper imported into Blyth for printing newspapers, were now the targets of German torpedoes.

Like Amble, Blyth had two distinct harbour areas. To the north were the shipbuilding yards, slipways as wide as avenues, fish quays, staithes and warehouses. Just offshore lay a broad ridge of rocks, partly covered at high tide. It was on this ridge, named Crab Law, that the Chain Home masts had been erected. Cemented into trenches excavated over a single weekend, they were surrounded by iron railings shrouded in blackthorn bushes which thrived in sandy soil and salty air.

The south harbour accommodated Blyth Submarine Base, as it had done in the Great War. From Blyth, the Royal Navy's Sixth Submarine Flotilla patrolled the Dogger Bank shallows of the North Sea and escorted incoming convoys. It also engaged in intelligence gathering, combing the busy Skagerrak area to observe the routes used by German maritime traffic. A large explosion in Blyth harbour would disrupt the flotilla's operations as well as damaging the radar system.

Via the film society, Klara had submitted a report on the submarine base earlier in the summer. The final, MI5-approved version stated that it posed no challenge as most of the flotilla's nine U-class vessels were undergoing lengthy repairs or refits in dry dock on the Tyne. The disinformation campaign bloomed.

In the Morris Minor van, Freitag and Schultz were silent, as was Klara, each absorbed in their own different thoughts. Freitag's instincts told him that, with the British army close behind, he should lie low and let the trail go cold. There was time in his schedule – and he doubted that the British would expect him to stop, so he would do the opposite. He could buy himself a few hours to plant the bombs in Blyth without being disturbed and then collect more bombs from Swanson's garage for the next run south of Newcastle. He thought they'd not been followed since Hawkskill, but especially in the dark could not be sure.

He hoped Crusher Cracknell was still driving the decoy Rover around the city. A precautionary measure, but watchful, suspicious eyes were everywhere. He didn't care whether the authorities thought they were in Newcastle or the Scottish Highlands, the more red herrings they were obliged to chase up, the happier Freitag felt.

On the outskirts of Blyth, a timely opportunity. Passing a stone-fronted parade of clubs, inns and a dance hall, they saw a Lyons café, rows of pastries filling its window.

"There was a café – was it open?" he demanded of Curt Schultz, whose mind seemed elsewhere. "Hansel, what did you make of it?"

"I think it was open, yes." Schultz collected his thoughts quickly. "Some of them stay open twenty-four hours, this one maybe because there's a naval community nearby." He and Klara had travelled to so many places of strategic interest in recent months, including Blyth. "Lyons' cafés usually have grand interiors, although I haven't visited this one before."

Freitag executed a U-turn, swerving to avoid a hexagonal pillar box. Headed 'J. Lyons & Co. Ltd.', the café had an enamel sign over the door promoting Lyons' tea: 'A packet for every pocket'. In the car park to the rear, not visible from the road, there were a couple of bicycles, a Hillman 14, and two vans – an electrician's and a grocer's. Freitag parked as far away from the road as possible.

"Stick with me," Schultz hissed to Klara as he let her out. His cheek momentarily brushed hers and she recoiled as if his flesh were poisonous.

He faced Freitag. "We should go in separately. If our descriptions have been circulated, it'll be as a group of three – two men and a woman."

"I'd already thought of that." Freitag took out a flat cap and covered his head, the peak low down over his eyes. Then he pulled his jacket inside out – it was reversible – and put it back on for a checked look. "I'll go first. Don't be long, do you understand?"

When Schultz and Klara entered the café a few minutes later, he was sipping black coffee at a table with his back to the wall and an unrestricted view to front and rear. He'd kept his cap on and they couldn't see his dark eyes. A handful of other tables were occupied, the liveliest by a group of six men in naval uniform. They were served at their table, whereas everyone else went to the counter. Another table, at the front, was absorbed in a game of dominoes.

Klara and Schultz took a table for two near the submariners. Schultz brought them coffee and cake, which they devoured hungrily and felt better for it.

Klara, facing the door, saw someone – a man – enter and immediately retreat. Head bowed, he kept his disfigured face from her. He had white hair, that was all she could tell. He did not reappear, and she thought no more of it.

She went to the lavatory, washed her hands and face, combed her hair. When she exited, Freitag was standing sentry-like outside the door. At the last moment, he stepped aside to let her by.

Though she felt fresher, Klara was tired and her head still ached. Almost 11 p.m. Gingerly, she leaned her head against the wall and closed her eyes. She did not know how long they would remain there, off road – would the British army truck continue south? – but at that moment she welcomed the respite.

Some while later, a young woman with a brown holdall entered and approached the counter. Clearly, she was known to the staff. Eyes shut, Klara half-listened. The woman was a volunteer at Blyth's lifeboat station, on her way home having varnished the boat. It was a task she'd undertaken regularly in the last year, a male colleague having departed. She took a quiet seat at the back.

It was nearly 5 a.m. the following day, Tuesday 20 August, when Klara jolted awake. Something was irritating the back of her neck and shaking her shoulder... It was Curt Schultz, but not as gently as he could – should – have been. Four empty coffee cups stood on the table, the dregs dry. The submariners had departed, the lifeboat volunteer, too. Freitag was not in the café, either.

"Dawn within the hour." Schultz helped her to focus. "Come on, there's much to do before first light."

In the car park, they found Freitag in the electrician's van, reversed in beside the Morris Minor. Schultz's surprise must have registered in his face because Freitag ceased what he was doing – strapping the two oil drums inside – and hopped out.

"I thought you'd approve, Hansel," he smirked, removing his cap. "I've traded our old van for this one. It will help to throw the British off our scent. Do you understand?"

"But this van is marked Matlock & Sons – Electricians," Klara objected. "Why on Earth would Mr Matlock exchange it on the spur of the moment for an unbranded one?"

"He was somewhat hesitant at first," Freitag admitted. "But he came round. I'd noticed him playing dominoes in the café, you see, his brown coat, and when he got up to leave, I followed him out. You were asleep, Gretel." A look of pure scorn. "In the end, he was very co-operative. Even helped me put our oil drums in here and his equipment in there." He waved a hand casually in the direction of the Morris Minor. Too casually.

"So, he's still here?" Klara said.

"Oh, he'll be around somewhere. Now, it's time we departed."

Freitag turned his back to close the doors of Matlock's van. Klara darted past him to the Morris Minor and pulled the rear-door handle. Unlocked, it sprang open. Inside, on a jumble of tools and cables, lay a male body. The eyes and mouth were open but completely still; the neck was purple and blue. He had been strangled.

Klara glared at Freitag. "The co-operative Mr Matlock, I presume?"

He strode up to her. Before she knew what was coming, he struck her hard across the face with the back of his right hand.

Feeling dizzy, Klara stumbled two steps backwards. She cried out but was determined to stay on her feet. Her right cheek was on fire and both her streaming eyes felt ready to burst from their sockets.

He took another pace towards her. "Today is the climax of a vital Gestapo operation," he snarled. "Which will be successful. You will not step a solitary inch out of line, or you will end your days like Matlock. Do you understand?"

"That's enough!" Curt Schultz shouted. "Klara, come here."

Numb from the slap, Klara approached him shakily – anything to get away from that monster. With a clean handkerchief, Schultz dabbed her eyes and wiped a trickle of blood from the corner of her mouth where, without realising, she'd bitten her lip.

"This will hurt you more than it will me, yes?"

Something about the way he used the words she'd uttered to him in his cabin on the zeppelin made her flesh crawl. It was on that flight that he had duped her, taken her for a fool, and double-crossed Admiral Canaris too. She walked off, opening and closing her jaw, rubbing her stinging cheek.

Freitag drove away, Schultz alongside him, Klara in the rear compartment, as before. With the first hints of a new dawn colouring the eastern sky, they passed a park, mostly dug up for vegetable allotments, and independent shops – a baker's, a greengrocer's, a butcher's – where later in the morning queues would form.

In north Blyth, Freitag headed for the harbour, he and Schultz on constant look-out for army trucks or the police. Lining up the wheels with the narrow pier, he edged past crews of trawlermen boarding their boats. The few who looked up, seeing an electrician's van making for the eye-sore radar masts, ignored it completely.

At the end of the pier, a concrete ramp laid for the diggers and cement mixers installing the masts remained in place. Freitag executed a seven- or eight-point U-turn, the rear doors finishing up at the head of the ramp. Klara noticed that Schultz did not once look back to see how she was faring as they lurched backwards and forwards on the brink.

Having checked the tidal charts more often than he'd care to admit, Freitag was the first out. Crab Law stretched into the darkness on his right – the tide creeping in, still a long way out. In the distance stood a mine shaft and, a little nearer, the thin steeple of St. Bartholomew's Church at Newbiggin Point. Closer still, a lighthouse known as 'the High Light' cast a pale beam across the reef.

Since Klara had last seen them, the blackthorn bushes around the base of the masts had thickened into a full hedgerow. She decided that the screens displaying the radar signals from the masts must be located somewhere in the submarine base to the south, connected by cables buried under the rocks.

When Schultz opened the rear doors, he avoided eye contact with her. He climbed in, loosened the straps around the oil drums, unfolded the steel trolley and passed it out to Freitag, waiting at the tailgate. Freitag wheeled the first drum down the ramp, irritated that the trolley had chosen today of all days to develop a squeak. He heaved the drum into place, shuffling it as far back into the hedgerow as it would go, with the steel plate facing outwards. Returning for the second drum, he watched a herring gull land on the heavy-duty barbed wire that coiled along the rocks, parallel with the pier.

"I'm going to drive back to the road that leads down to the harbour," he said thoughtfully. "I saw at least one outside tap to access a water main. I will pierce the pipe, flood the road, delay other vehicles. It will look like a leak."

"Good," Schultz commended him. The more obstacles they created to buy time, the better – even if Freitag's impromptu idea sounded rather improbable. "I'll be as quick as I can here. The timers will be set for high noon."

"No, they won't," came a different, deep voice from the shadows. "This is your high noon, and your career as a Nazi saboteur is over."

***

The white-haired man, late sixties, who stood on a jetty off the edge of the pier, frowned as he watched the British army officer step out of the shadows, armed with a Lee-Enfield No.1 rifle. Was the officer alone? It looked so, yet seemed unlikely.

The man had arrived in Blyth late yesterday and pulled in at the 24-hour Lyons café, the only one open for miles. As soon as he crossed the threshold, he saw Evelyn Fletcher drinking coffee with another man, sitting with his back to him. He knew the identity of this man and had wondered if he might be with her. But he didn't want her to see him – she would have recognised him at once as Alf, although it had been eight months since they'd met. So, he turned unseen on his heels and even now, he was sure no one knew he was on the jetty.

Alf was transfixed by the incident unfolding a few yards before him. A grizzled lion, observing, stalking in obscurity, although streaks of warm, yellow light were brightening the sky by the minute. The army officer had interrupted the two men from the electrician's van. They froze on the spot, captured prey, regarding each other in dismay, fury, defiance, what? From the shadows, he didn't have a clear view of their expressions.

Freitag was wondering whether this British officer had been in the truck they'd eluded at Hawkskill Crossing. If so, he'd been following them deliberately and must know they were out to destroy the Chain Home masts. And here he was, creeping up on them like a ghost in the night.

Freitag was convinced he'd been right to spend a few hours resting. Not only was there time in the schedule but, above all, he needed Schultz to be bright-eyed and alert for his finger-sensitive task. No margin for error. Reichsmarschall Göring would be proud of his diligence, thinking of everything. But he was getting ahead of himself. He still had to deal with this British intruder.

In his pockets were the Walther pistol, with which he'd parachuted into Scotland, and the Webley revolver he'd taken from Private Yates. All six chambers were loaded. In his right-hand pocket, away from the soldier, Freitag's hand enclosed the Webley so tightly that his knuckles were white.

"Please get out of the van, Miss," Lieutenant Bellamy ordered. "Stand together, all three of you, that's it."

Having shuffled to the edge of the tailgate, Klara could not resist a last look at the drum left inside.

"Don't worry about that one," Bellamy asserted. "We'll deal with it imminently."

Klara jumped down and stood next to Schultz, who shunned her.

"If any of you is armed," Bellamy declared, "place your weapon on the ground immediately. Doing so may save your life."

Talbot and Sixsmith appeared at Bellamy's side, backing him up. Sixsmith was still clutching his lower ribs.

His eyes locked on the confrontation, Alf risked a glance around him. Crab Law glowed in the rising sun, which was melting the shadows and he shuffled closer to the pier. An early-rising member of the Observer Corps was walking his Cocker Spaniel by the sea prior to his shift, oblivious to the events playing out by the masts. Otherwise, all was still.

Talbot took out his service revolver. He had only ever fired it on a shooting range, but his aim was firm.

"Herr Freitag," he said. "You have at least one handgun that belongs to a Home Guardsman – you took it from him yesterday."

Klara and Sixsmith swapped brief glances while he mouthed a few syllables – "You'll be OK" or "It's all OK" – to reassure her. Her eyes lingered on his mouth, the imperfect row of teeth, a fraction too long.

Freitag, senses heightened, noticed the exchange, read the look they shared. Something didn't smell right. Sixsmith and Klara knew each other, possibly even *liked* each other. Could this mean…? Surely not. Did Schultz know…?

Stepping back, Freitag reached slowly inside his jacket. "You wanted the pistol, yes?" he grunted to the tall civilian who had known his name. These men must be from the British police or security service, probably the latter. If they knew his name, they'd know a lot more about him too. The net was closing in – he must act fast.

Suddenly Freitag was pointing the Webley at Klara's face. But he was watching Sixsmith, and the flare of alarm in Sixsmith's eyes, overpowering the pain in his chest, betrayed him.

"How long have you been working for the British, Gretel?"

Klara felt paralysed. Staring at the unblinking hairless head, she said nothing. To her left, looking confused, Sixsmith almost mouthed: "Gretel?" She had never mentioned this.

Now Freitag was watching Schultz. Immediately, he received the confirmation he was seeking. Schultz squirmed and looked embarrassed – his eyes rolled, shoulders slumped – but not remotely surprised.

So, Schultz had known that Gretel was a traitor, Freitag was sure of it. Inside him, the rage began to boil.

"Here, catch!" He tossed the Webley to Schultz.

"I'll take that!" Talbot extended his left palm.

Bellamy aimed his rifle at Schultz. "Don't do anything stupid, just hand the gun over."

Freitag acted as if the British trio were not present. "Shoot her," he instructed Schultz, an index finger pointing at Klara. "Sacrifice her now. Or I will kill you."

Schultz lifted the Webley. It shook in his fingers. No longer the handsome team leader Klara had met in Berlin, he was terrified and seemed to shrivel before them. Every trace of swagger had deserted him.

"Shoot her!" Freitag's voice was now a bestial roar. The range was point-blank, even with an unsteady hand Schultz couldn't miss.

"Don't shoot!" Sixsmith howled, one arm raised.

He was almost drowned out by Bellamy's simultaneous cry: "Drop it!"

"Five," said Freitag.

Klara watched him, the demons controlling him, mind and body.

"Four."

"Hands up!" Bellamy screamed at Freitag.

"Three."

Sixsmith felt an urge to shield Klara. Talbot, who had read his mind, laid a staying hand on his shoulder, causing him anguish.

"Two."

Tears seeping down his face, the ruined Schultz gazed at Klara. She had always been his weak spot, but now he felt his life ebbing away and almost fainted. The gun shook uncontrollably.

"Klara, I–"

"One."

In a slick, speedy movement, Freitag dropped to one knee and pulled out his Walther. He fired once into Schultz's forehead. Schultz's eyes rolled back, and a line of blood trickled down the bridge of his nose. Sixsmith watched the lifeless body crumple, the lower legs the last part to collapse.

Seconds later, when he looked up, Freitag was not kneeling but rolling like a log to the pier's edge and the four-foot drop on to Crab Law. He landed on the barbed wire but managed to roll off it on to the rocks with minimal rips in his clothing.

Klara snatched the Webley that had slipped from Schultz's fingers and raced down the ramp, springing athletically over the rockpools and strips of seaweed.

Bellamy lowered his rifle as Klara bounded into his line of fire. He ran along the pier to find a new position, ducking as Freitag fired a loose shot in their direction. Bellamy realised that Klara, Webley in hand, was closing on Freitag with every stride.

Talbot ran to the blackthorn bushes, the towering masts glinting in the early sunlight. He crouched low, away from the drum, and lined up a shot at the back of Freitag's head, more than thirty yards distant.

Sixsmith, taking small breaths through his mouth, stayed on the pier with the body of Curt Schultz and the remaining drum in Matlock's van. *Had he given Klara away...? If she didn't survive this...*

Freitag could not help himself. Red mist clouding his senses, he felt compelled to stop the moment he heard Klara, as if an invisible magnet had control. She had been an irritant in his life for far too long, and now he knew that she was a traitor.

Klara stopped running ten yards from him. They circled each other for perhaps fifteen seconds, seemed longer. Klara versus Freitag, Webley versus Walther. He came to a halt facing the pier, her body shielding him from Talbot and the lieutenant. They stood in silence, their gun muzzles trained on each other's hearts.

A dog barked. It was the Cocker Spaniel at the water's edge, on the return leg of the morning walk. Both Klara and Freitag blinked. She thought he might run, use the distraction to take a chance and race away. But no, he regained his composure immediately and the Walther didn't move.

He wound himself up to yell: "You are not a patriot. You are a traitor, an enemy of the Third Reich. You deserve to *die!*"

Klara stood her ground but realised she was very afraid. She knew she had too much to live for. The moment he finished his parting shot would be the moment he'd fire and kill her.

"And finally, you face your executioner!" His usually sunken eyes were bulging and manic, his face twisted into a snarl. "Do you understand?"

Now, Klara, *now!*

Suddenly Klara's frightened mind played tricks on her. Oh, Lord… She was transported back four years to the Olympic Games, the final round of her shooting event. She was leading the field with one shot to go when the hammer of her gun jammed. This was the first time since then, apart from a few rounds on British practice ranges, that she had held a gun. For one petrified moment, she could think of nothing but her gun jamming.

Surely *this* gun, the Webley, would fire when her life depended on it? Shards of doubt about her predicament, what she was capable of, jabbed her head.

Now, in this instant, it was him or her.

Klara blinked, her mind cleared. She focused on the monster who had her in his sights and held her nerve. *I will not be your victim.* The Webley's rear notch in line with the tip of its long barrel, she squeezed the trigger. Had he fired at the same time, or had she got in first?

The unmistakable whipcrack of the hammer releasing and the gun firing came a second after her right arm rebounded into the air. A red hole opened in Freitag's chest and he staggered backwards, almost losing his footing, staring at the wound in disbelief.

He still had some presence of mind. "Gretel, you've…"

An eruption of red froth in his mouth smothered his words. Engulfed in pain and shock, he managed to raise the Walther once more. But his fingers were sticky from barbed-wire cuts that he had not even noticed, and his arm juddered. Like a drunkard, he staggered on the rocks and choked, propelling a red waterfall down his chin. His eyes felt heavy and weary.

A second, larger bullet hit Freitag full in the face and blew the left side of his head off. He toppled over, a tree felled, as the boom of the shot split the air. Klara dropped to one knee and looked back at the pier.

It was Sergeant Tom Milne of the Royal Engineers, holding a Lee-Enfield rifle, who had delivered the *coup de grâce*. He was one of the finest young marksmen in the army, but this was the first time he had fired at a living target. As he lowered the rifle, his stomach performed a somersault.

Milne and the two privates had driven to Blyth to deal with an unexploded bomb in a crater near the submarine base. Unflappable, the police were evacuating homes within an assumed blast radius, and the submarine base itself had adopted a state of the highest alert. No one was allowed on or off site, and extra guards were posted on the roof and at every entrance and exit.

Talbot left his vantage point by the blackthorn bushes and ran towards Freitag's body. Klara got there first. The body lay on its back. The right eye, the only one remaining, stared at them obstinately. It was wide open, as was his mouth, a lake of blood. The surrounding rocks were splattered with gory remains. A velvet crab, scarlet eyes glowing atop its hairy body, scurried from a rockpool across Freitag's outstretched palm, homing in on a starfish in another pool.

Talbot curled an arm around Klara's shoulders.

"You're not injured?" he asked as Bellamy approached from the pier. Feeling his robustness failing completely, Bellamy turned his back on this mutilated body.

No physical harm, Klara thought. And given the horrific deaths of Schultz and Freitag, witnessed close at hand, she was relieved quite suddenly to feel a greater sense of inner peace than she'd known for a long time. Now, perhaps, the intimidation that she and, in particular, her father had endured would cease. While people were capable of astonishing kindness and astonishing cruelty, she knew the latter would always be corrosive and demeaning.

Watching from Matlock's van, Warren Sixsmith breathed slowly to calm his pulsating heart, and held his ribs. Oh, how very brave was this gorgeous woman, how strong-willed and unflinching. If only he could, how he longed to give her a massive bear-hug, take those dimpled cheeks softly in his hands and kiss them. To be, as she herself had once dubbed him, her guardian angel.

"When you need help, I will help you," he would promise her one day, and mean it. "I will be by your side, to look after you. The best days lie ahead."

He could imagine her staying in his heart forever, but how did she feel? He had an idea for a gift which he looked forward to sending to her – but he would take it steadily. For the last century or more, English gentlemen had been bred not to grandstand their emotions, but to preserve a stiff upper lip. Which of the two instincts, he wondered in his own case, would gain the upper hand?

Sixsmith acknowledged Tom Milne, rifle shouldered, as he approached shakily. The image of that direct hit on Freitag's head would never leave Milne, who gazed at his Grana wristwatch without registering the time.

Neither they, nor any of those huddled around Freitag's corpse, were aware that Alf had abandoned his hiding place on the jetty. It was never meant to end like this, he'd castigated himself. As the morning sun rose, Alf was long gone and none of them would see him again.

25

Goodbye Klara

Christopher Talbot spent the following Tuesday lunchtime, 27 August, on Newcastle's Town Moor. He was sitting on a rather uncomfortable bench in sight of the bandstand, from where the trenches gouged by Karl-Heinz Weiss's Messerschmitt were plainly visible. In fact, while he'd been there, a gang of workmen had arrived to cordon off the scarred area for relandscaping.

On the bench beside him lay a manila envelope stuffed with a plump folder. Facing down protests from his daughter, he'd disregarded the sickly feelings of guilt and spent much of yesterday, Bank Holiday Monday, reading the contents of the folder, having promised to return it today.

It recorded the on-going joint investigation by the police forces of the county of Northumberland and the city of Newcastle into the attempt by an obscure branch of the Gestapo to destroy Chain Home in the north-east. It listed the multiple murders and other crimes on British soil of which the late Ulrich Freitag was suspected, pending further enquiries.

Other forces in England were assessing similar operations in their own regions. Talbot had just received in the post a cutting from the *East Anglian Daily Times*. It was a report on an unexploded Nazi bomb, successfully defused near the perimeter of RAF Bawdsey, part of 11 Group, Fighter Command. It included a posed, smiling photograph of a married couple, Tammy and Alana MacPherson, hard-working members of the station's staff. Tammy was evidently stooping to fit into the frame.

First on the scene, Tammy, forty-seven, had taped off the locality to prevent anyone from stumbling into danger until the ever-dependable Royal Engineers appeared from over the hill. Tammy and Alana were off to enjoy a jolly day at Brooklands racing circuit but would be back promptly. Thank you both for your service, keep up the exemplary work!

The Royal Engineers' bomb disposal teams had coped extremely well. Their race against time continued until the last minute – twelve noon, last Tuesday – and beyond. Only five explosions were reported on that day – three oil drums, in South Yorkshire, Norfolk and Kent, and two Luftwaffe bombs with faulty timers in Pevensey and Rye, Sussex. There were a few injuries but no further loss of life, and the affected Chain Home posts were down for no longer than six hours.

The folder contained a cautionary note, typed in red capitals, stating that there may still be some undiscovered ordnance by the more remote rural masts that had not yet detonated. Nevertheless, the PM was thrilled that the Nazis' sabotage mission had been thwarted. He would write to every army company, police force and government agency that played a part as soon as possible.

MI5 would continue working with the police to dismantle the Nazis' network of agents, proxies and informants that had spread like pus. They raided the Sycamore Grove B&B and the courier trawler in Amble harbour. With co-operation from the staff at the Odyssey, police officers had already arrested several members of the film society, among them Alice Young, Walter Dodds, Neil Sinclair and Jack Redfern.

"I'm not an extremist, I just want my world to be different," Alice had commented philosophically. "But I suppose, in the game of life, everyone has their entrances and everyone has their exits." The custody officer had not known what to say.

Further arrests were pending: Duncan Caldwell and the hapless Sonia Stobart were next.

Of Harry Jarvis, there had been no trace for weeks. But a handwritten note stated that a man answering his description, with a limp, had recently taken a steam packet, RMS *Teresa*, on the long-established route from Southampton via Lisbon to the Guanabara Bay seaport in Rio de Janeiro. While many steamships had been commandeered as troop carriers, Talbot knew that the ports in Brazil remained busy.

It later transpired that the passenger who may have been Harry had used Red Cross travel documents in the name of Bernard Harper. Such documents were intended to assist the movement of legitimate refugees, but at times the system became overwhelmed and papers were issued to some who, by rights, should not have had them. Reports that Mr Harper and two men in their sixties – one with a scarred face – were met in Rio by a pallid Professor Doktor Lukas Osterhagen were also unconfirmed. Further information was due from an FBI special agent, Sam Linklater, who was following up the case with reliable sources in the United States.

Karl-Heinz Weiss and the entire crew of the Heinkel bomber that ditched in the Tyne were despatched, after their hospital check-ups, to a prisoner-of-war camp in Oldham, Lancashire, where, it was envisaged, they would see out the war. Talbot would later learn that Weiss was transported to a camp in Canada, where food was more abundant and there was less chance of escapees making their way back to Germany.

One page was devoted to the Norwegian officers, Captain Nils Larsen and Lieutenant Tor Jensen (deceased). Their unstinting support and bravery were commended. Talbot reckoned the page was an edited version of a paper submitted to the police by Warren Sixsmith, whose heavily-bandaged cracked rib was slowly on the mend.

Larsen's post-operative recovery was progressing better than expected. Talbot had been able to visit him in hospital on Saturday with Lucy, who had written an introductory letter to Sigrid and was scouring each day's post for a reply.

The biggest surprise was the section about Alf, the driver who had met Klara on her arrival in Northumberland. At least part of the sketchy biographical note must have been provided by MI6.

In 1884, when Alf was ten, he was seriously injured in an explosion outside King's Cross station. A bombing campaign, conducted by the Fenians in favour of an independent Irish Republic, targeted London's infrastructure and led to the formation of a Special Branch in the Metropolitan Police. That day, including young Alf, nine people were taken to hospitals in north London. Alf awoke in the next bed to Robert, another streetwise ten-year-old with similar blast injuries. They were to become lifelong friends. And co-conspirators.

Having learned of the extreme lengths to which organised campaigns could aspire, the lads gradually set about subverting the British class system, which they felt disadvantaged their families and friends. At first, their activities were relatively minor – vandalism, petty theft – but the adrenaline rushes were powerful and addictive. They acquired forged copies of Scheduled Occupation Certificates and claimed they were steel workers to secure exemption from military service in the Great War. Instead, they assisted spies of the Imperial State of Germany – the Second Reich – working in Britain to gather intelligence.

They were utterly sickened when a telegram sent to Berlin by one of the Germans was intercepted by British Intelligence and he was executed by firing squad in the Tower of London. This only fortified their resolve.

Robert and Alf became known in Berlin by the codename 'Ralf', which very few officials knew embraced two Englishmen, not merely one, and their identities remained secret for many years. By the late 1930s, they had professional handlers, who specialised in embedded sleeper agents, in an arcane department of the abounding Abwehr. Alf – 'the Driver' – and Robert – 'the Collector' – were two of the Abwehr's most trusted men in Britain and both had assignments in Operation Trawl. They evaded capture and the report in the folder conceded that, by now, they could have been spirited away to anywhere in the world.

Like all who experienced it, Talbot would never forget the summer of 1940. He hoped Klara was enjoying her time in

London, where meetings about her future career in MI5 were taking place at the keen request of the same officers who had arranged her defection last year.

"Hello."

Talbot's train of thought was snapped by the arrival of a policeman with a custodian helmet, bulging breast pockets and three stripes on his upper arms.

"Good afternoon, sergeant."

Jonathan Hedley grinned as he sat on the bench, the plain envelope in between them. He was still getting used to being addressed as sergeant, having only secured the promotion last week. He and his lovely wife, Lorraine, were delighted, not least because of the extra income so soon after their nuptials, and he couldn't help but wonder whether this man from MI5, with whom he'd worked well, had put in a good word.

"Your folder, with many thanks." Talbot tapped the envelope with his middle finger.

"No problem." Sergeant Hedley spoke quietly, even though his words were covered by the sounds of workmen installing barriers. "The investigation continues, of course. Lots of strands, lots of leads, lots of people involved."

Three Spitfires flew overhead on patrol. The summer sunlight bouncing off their canopies was dazzling.

"There's been a development," Hedley said furtively, adjusting his helmet, "concerning one member of the film society. I heard about it today, although the incident occurred on Friday, before the long weekend. The fellow in question is Crusher Cracknell."

Talbot raised an inquisitive eyebrow. "Oh?"

"He was being transferred between police cells, purely routine. The van picked up another man on remand, moving him to the same locale. An altercation occurred in the back of the van, a rather serious one."

Hedley looked at the ground where a dry cow pat had attracted the attention of some lively beetles.

"And?"

"And I'm afraid Cracknell is now facing a murder charge."

"Murder? In police transport? Who was the other man?"

"Well, it was the most extraordinary coincidence. You remember the garage where he worked? The manager had dipped his fingers in the till and left his staff in the lurch. He was arrested recently in Hampshire."

"I do remember, yes. Cracknell was only too eager to tell me all about him. Maurice Swanson was his name, wasn't it?"

"That's right. The late Mr Swanson really made Crusher's blood boil."

"Far be it from me to put words in your mouth, but could it have been self-defence? No deliberate intention to harm, just a reckoning that got out of hand?" Grudges could be awfully dangerous, Talbot reflected.

Hedley let the concepts of murder, manslaughter and self-defence swirl in his mind as birdsong trilled in the background. His instincts told him it was better to see events as they really were and let justice take its course, but he was still inclined to take account of Talbot's suggestion.

"Time to go," he declared at last, rising to his feet. He picked up the envelope. "It's been a privilege," he beamed at the MI5 officer, holding out his right hand.

***

The stick bombs had exploded between two spectacular venues in London's West End: the Warner Bros. picture palace and the Hippodrome revue theatre, both in Cranbourn Street, which led from Charing Cross Road into Leicester Square.

Klara Falke entered the square from the west, the far side. She felt revitalised in her new outfit – a short-sleeved, blue dress, tight at the waist, and sturdy Oxford shoes – which was both comfortable and chic. Clothing would not be rationed until June 1941. Leaving Wardour Street, she passed the headquarters of the Automobile Association, fully intact, and took a seat in the square's gardens, where a swing band and singers were performing live.

Time out, try to unwind. She was getting better at relaxing, shedding tension from her neck and shoulders, and she let the music wash over her.

In the last few days, the Luftwaffe's bombing campaign against English towns and cities – civilian targets – had further intensified. The outcome of the Battle of Britain hung precariously in the balance. Central London was bombed daily, although you wouldn't know it from the merry throng in Leicester Square. Allied servicemen and women as well as civilians were letting their hair down, gyrating to the band music, allowing themselves a precious escape from the grind of air raids, black-outs and rationing. Giggles ripened into squeals when someone stepped too close to the spray from the Shakespeare statue and marble fountain that formed the square's centrepiece.

Klara replayed the lurid events of a week ago at Crab Law. She believed that Curt Schultz's feelings for her were genuine to the end, but he was weak-willed and confused and had let himself be corrupted by uncompromising men in the Gestapo. She had shed no tears for Curt. He'd needed to be liked too much. If truth be told, she'd spent longer fretting about the fate of little Kevin, whom she'd encountered at Alnwick station, than mulling over Schultz's place in her life. She'd written to the chaplain who had helped to register the evacuees on the station concourse, asking what he knew of Kevin's whereabouts.

Was it too much to want from life everything that mattered to her? Part of her craved anonymity, to blend in, observe, assess. But there was part of her, too, that longed to push boundaries, compete, agitate.

She'd always maintained that being single was preferable to an unsatisfactory relationship. Deep down, though, she desired a soulmate, as Katarina had found in Harald. Someone to laugh with forevermore, to look at her the way Schultz had sometimes done, unconditionally, deeply committed, as if nothing else in the world mattered. But for real this time, without the hidden agendas that twisted Schultz's heart. Freedom, loyalty, respect and love were all based upon truth, so it could never have worked with him. Meanwhile, life would go on.

Klara had witnessed the best of humanity, for example in her family and Olympic athletes, and the worst of it in Nazi fascism. Naturally she enjoyed living in a land where individual liberty was valued, where citizens were free from despotic powers to speak their own minds, create their own destiny. How fragile, yet how precious, was the flame of freedom. How vital it was, now more than ever, to reject oppression and defend liberty.

She could only imagine the reactions of Hermann Göring and the Gestapo and Abwehr spymasters to the news of her defection, the deaths of Freitag and Schultz, and the destruction of the film society's intelligence gathering network. They would take pains to sidestep any blame.

Would they attempt further sabotage missions to damage Chain Home? If so, the signs did not bode well. The Abwehr's Operation Trawl had been appropriated by Department G of the Gestapo and spun into a failed attempt to thwart Chain Home. More recently, Operation Lena had begun disastrously. Klara had heard that a spate of German agents sent to Britain had been identified with ease and arrested. One had journeyed from Stavanger by seaplane and dinghy, made landfall in Scotland, and promptly revealed an incredible lack of knowledge of British currency when trying to buy a train ticket. Another agent had sought to buy a pint in a pub before opening time! The litany of basic woes was so long that it hardly felt like a professional Abwehr operation at all.

She would enjoy speculating about what on Earth had gone wrong, and why, with Katarina and Harald. Thrillingly, arrangements had been made for them to meet in mid-September in Geneva, where Katarina was to undergo a kidney transplant operation.

Klara must find out whether, as she suspected, Warren Sixsmith had expedited the arrangements. She was, perhaps, a little surprised to find herself looking forward quite so much to seeing the gallant Mr Sixsmith again. Just thinking about him had put a smile on her face, energised her whole body. He was kind and chivalrous, less conflicted and less complicated than Curt Schultz. But was she ready to let anybody in? Despite their mutual attraction, could she fall hard for Sixsmith, find profound joy and build a long life with him? In the end, she'd only learn about a new relationship, an enchanting new dance, by throwing herself into it.

Sixsmith had sent a gift to her, heavy to lift but a delightful surprise. It was a *Times Survey Atlas of the World*, containing more than a hundred maps. The flyleaf contained a personal message just for her – a first in her life. Neatly written in blue ink, it brimmed with encouragement: "My dear Klara, as Shakespeare put it, the world is your oyster! *Bon courage* for all your future endeavours. Fly high and believe in yourself, as I do in you. Ever yours, Warren."

She found herself smiling. Was this at the prospect of Warren in her life, or at another line of thought involving her German family?

Katarina's illness had made Klara even more determined to live every day to the full. She recalled her father telling his precious daughters more than once that if they pushed with every sinew for something they passionately believed in, they'd be well-nigh unstoppable. For as long as my heart beats, she vowed, I shall still live, I shall still love.

Spying was, necessarily, a lonely profession, requiring her in part to live a lie. She accepted that her friendships would sometimes be deceptions – she had to conceal as well as charm – and did not feel punishing shame or guilt. But she would hate lies to become normal currency in other parts of her life, and one day, no doubt, she would have had her fill of the seemingly boundless deceit and treachery of the secret world. For the time being, espionage had got under her skin, and to play a part in preserving lives in safety, well, that was a very worthwhile, urgent adventure, wasn't it?

Whatever clashes she encountered between belief and doubt, reality and imagination, Klara reaffirmed her commitment to stay true to herself. She couldn't solve every problem, but she could always defend what she held dear – her family, her instincts, her principles of freedom, security and peace. Her identity lay not in her name – every day, brides changed surnames when they married – but in her underlying personality and conduct.

In MI5, she would retain the name Evelyn Fletcher – *Auf Wiedersehen*, Klara. She had always needed a purpose in life, and she relished her revitalised purpose now. Reinvention on her own terms. History told of many exiles who notched up great achievements in arts and sciences in their adopted lands, and she would give her all to every secret assignment.

Meanwhile, she hankered to renew her acquaintance with the sympathetic Hanna Lippert, who lived in Hamburg and shared her passion for motorcycles. Had Hanna's father tried as hard as hers to dissuade her from ever getting on a motorcycle in the first place? So far, she'd kept the idea of a reunion to herself – and of course it wouldn't be safe for her, a defector, to return to Germany – but this would become an itch that needed to be scratched.

Having spent the morning in protracted meetings at MI5, Evelyn longed to catch a film in the afternoon. Just off Leicester Square was a newly renovated picture hall, only three hundred seats, with a steel-reinforced basement used as a bomb shelter by taxi drivers. It was the first London venue acquired by Carol and Charles Rycroft, Harry Jarvis's relatives, who had disowned him. Their expanding circuit now embraced five picture houses. This afternoon, the London Odyssey was playing a re-release of the fantastical entertainment *King Kong* starring Fay Wray. The tale of a gargantuan beast, more capable of feeling emotions than his human captors, was a reminder, if she ever needed one, not to judge a book by its cover.

Evelyn glanced at a clock on the square's north terrace and at the mounds of twisted metal, shattered bricks and mangled concrete in the street to the east. Despite the presence of ARP wardens and police constables, some boys with grimy knees and socks around their ankles were using the bombsite as a playground, arms outstretched, Stuka dive bombers in human form.

No sooner had Evelyn stood up than a couple in battledress khaki uniforms sat on the vacated bench. As she exited the gardens and strode up to the Odyssey, she had a clear sense of new beginnings in her life, personal and professional, and it thrilled her.

She savoured the sight of a caterpillar of children, books under their arms, curling through the square towards the library in St. Martin's. She herself had always adored reading. At their age – about the age she'd been when her mother died – she'd devoured tons of titles from her father's shelves. Reading was her loyal, insightful guide through childhood and adolescence; the bug had never left her.

It was a long-held aspiration to write her own memoirs – partly, she sensed, for the cathartic release. One day, she would walk in her own distant footsteps, recounting her life story through times of strife as a daughter, sister, Olympian, spy, who knew what chapters came next. Let no one ever tell her there were heights she could not reach – how knowing was that message from Warren Sixsmith! She just hoped, when she looked into her heart, that she could say she'd made a positive difference.

Of course, to assuage the qualms of her current employer, she might embellish the facts with veneers of fiction, teasing her readers. But given the surname of her birth, *Falke* – Falcon, she had already deposited in the back of her mind a working title:

Warbird.

Afterword: A new world order

Warbird is a work of fiction set in the first year of World War II. It is not intended as a source of historical reference – masterly books for that purpose continue to proliferate. All the events, characters and organisations depicted in *Warbird* are either created by the author or used fictitiously.

Nevertheless, as you, dear reader, will know, the premise of *Warbird* is factual. Some of the characters who inhabit the story not only existed but influenced the course of history, while some incidents are inspired by actual occurrences.

There was, for example, a zeppelin spy flight over England in 1939 to investigate the Chain Home masts. The RDF (radar) technology was, as outlined, developed secretly by Robert Watson-Watt and his brilliant team of boffins. Astonishingly, the German scientists on the airship misinterpreted the signals and General Wolfgang Martini, the Luftwaffe's head of radar, did not realise the extent or the implications of Britain's radar at the outbreak of the war. He confirmed as much personally to Watson-Watt, who later befriended him. Martini narrowly escaped trial for war crimes at Nuremberg.

The coal-exporting towns and cities of north-east England were identified as Luftwaffe targets and bombing raids in 1940–41 caused hundreds of fatalities. Later in the war, the region was largely spared further incursions; German losses were far higher than they'd anticipated.

Luftflotte – Air Fleet – 5, which encountered resolute RAF resistance when it flew from Norway in August 1940, was never again an effective fighting force. At the end of that month, the fleet's residual aircraft were merged with Luftflotte 2, based in France.

It does nothing to diminish the utterly humbling bravery of the crews in the Battle of Britain – 'The Few' to whom so much is owed by so many – to reflect that they were aided by Sir Hugh Dowding's admirable, but perhaps less well known, system of radar detection and observation. This, at the time, was Britain's essential secret weapon.

Nor does it diminish the Nazis' repulsive atrocities to reflect that their regime did not command the full support of all those highly placed within it. Admiral Wilhelm Canaris, for example, head of the Abwehr in 1935–44, came to be regarded as a subversive conspiring to undermine the Führer and his henchmen. Charged with treason, Canaris was convicted in an SS court in 1945. He was executed at Flossenbürg concentration camp, Bavaria, where even the SS acknowledged that conditions were 'hard'. Thousands of prisoners died there of brazen inhumanity: malnutrition, brutality, lack of hygiene and medical care.

In the Holocaust of the 1940s, six million European Jews were systematically murdered by the Nazis. Millions of others, including Poles and Slavs, were declared *Untermenschen* – sub-humans. What did it mean to be human at such a time?

Canaris's associate, Herbert Wichmann, in charge of *Abwehrstelle* Hamburg, one of the top posts in the German secret service, was an arch critic of the Führer. Operation Lena was a controversial, rare disaster that contributed little to the planning of the invasion of Britain. After the war, the British manoeuvred Wichmann into a key role in rebuilding Hamburg's shipping industry. MI5 described him and his circle as 'good Germans, bad Nazis'.

From late August 1940, the Luftwaffe relentlessly bombed British airfields. On 30–31 August alone, the RAF lost fifty aircraft to the Germans' forty-one and came perilously close to being overwhelmed. Hitler's decision to switch the bombing away from airfields to morale-sapping civilian targets in British cities allowed Fighter Command to regroup at a critical moment. Mass bombings, including fifty-seven consecutive, dreadful nights of 'Blitz' attacks on London, continued for months. Every night of the Blitz, the capital's deepest Underground stations sheltered hordes of civilians.

The Battle of Britain represented the first significant defeat for the formidable Nazi war machine. Losses were high: more than 2,500 German pilots and aircrew were killed or listed as missing, while a further thousand were captured or imprisoned. It was a vital early turning point in the war. Operation Sealion was suspended in mid-September 1940, and formally cancelled a month later.

Crucially, the Luftwaffe never achieved air supremacy over Britain. Victory by the RAF rendered the invasion of Britain much less likely. It made Hitler prematurely turn his attention, and that of the Luftwaffe, to the brutal invasion of Stalin's Russia (Operation Barbarossa). Although the war still had five years to play out, the Nazis' fate was arguably sealed at that point. Millions were slain in the Soviet operation, in which Germany was eventually defeated.

Perhaps the Nazis' single biggest failure in the Battle of Britain lay in their acquisition and analysis of intelligence. Senior officials, who did not properly understand Fighter Command's systems, under-estimated its capabilities, preferring the narrative of their own invincibility. They did not know their enemy well enough.

Supported by the resolute Dowding, Watson-Watt's radar technology greatly helped the RAF to win the Battle of Britain. After numerous short extensions to his tenure, Dowding left Fighter Command in November 1940 and finally retired from the RAF twenty months later. He died in 1970 and his ashes lie buried in Westminster Abbey.

In March 1941, Max Aitken – Lord Beaverbrook – made Watson-Watt a member of his '1940 Club'. There were only ten members: those who had made the greatest input into the successful outcome of the Battle of Britain. In 1942, Watson-Watt was knighted, and later emigrated for a while to Canada. In 1956, he was caught in a radar trap and given a speeding ticket. Reportedly he told the bemused Canadian police officers: "If I'd known what you were going to do with it, I'd never have invented it!"

If the Battle of Britain, like so many others, was won by small margins, the work of Tilly Shilling was momentous. Her fuel restrictor disc, preventing Spitfires and Hurricanes from stalling, was of enormous value to Fighter Command. A thrill seeker who raced motorcycles at Brooklands, Tilly blazed a trail for women in engineering.

The Royal Engineers, responsible for the disposal of all bombs except those on RAF airfields or in crashed aircraft, dealt with around two thousand devices every month in the year 1940–41. Most, though not all, were bombs dropped by the Luftwaffe that did not explode. With little formal training available, much learning took place – fast – on the job.

Sir Vernon Kell, the first Director of Britain's Security Service known as MI5, had not prepared the service for a Second World War, despite having led it successfully in the 1914–18 conflict. Too few staff were grappling with a massive increase in workload. By spring 1940, the torrent of vetting requests averaged eight thousand per week.

In June of that year, the new prime minister, Winston Churchill, insisted that K be replaced as Director General by Brigadier Oswald 'Jasper' Harker, who served in the Indian Police before joining MI5 in 1920. He lasted only ten months in the top job. His successor, Sir David Petrie, implemented the much-needed reorganisation that made the service more efficient and led to considerable intelligence successes in the 1940s. MI5's 'double cross' strategy – turning enemy spies in Britain into double agents who fed false information to the Nazis – contributed to the success of the D-Day landings in June 1944. The strategy was overseen by MI5's cunningly named 'XX' or Twenty Committee.

Thousands of SS officers and Nazi sympathisers fled Europe for sanctuary, evading justice, in South America. Hundreds of thousands of German immigrants already resided in Argentina,

Brazil and Chile. Nazi scientists with special technical expertise were accepted in other countries too.

In 1945, the victorious Allied powers apportioned Germany into four zones, occupied by the USA, UK, France and the USSR – the Union of Soviet Socialist Republics. After the zones were agreed, relations between the USSR and the three Western countries soured to such an extent that the German Federal Republic (West Germany) came into effect in 1949, with the Soviet-occupied zone forming the German Democratic Republic (East Germany).

Likewise, Berlin itself was sliced into four zones. In August 1961, the infamous 96-mile-long *Mauer* – Wall – was cruelly erected by the East German dictatorship. It was the ultimate symbol of the Iron Curtain divide between east and west, communism and capitalism.

The West German capital was Bonn until the country's reunification. It was in November 1989, a few years after the *perestroika* (reform) movement and *glasnost* (openness) policy had seeded, that the Wall was breached and torn down. The scenes of jubilation as thousands crossed freely were broadcast around the world. Just eleven months later, the Bundestag voted to restore the seat of national government to Berlin.

In August 1945, the United States dropped two atomic bombs on the Japanese cities of Hiroshima and, three days later, Nagasaki. Intelligence reports had highlighted Japan's determination not to surrender even when the war in Europe was over. The cities were engulfed in blinding flashes of light and heat, up to $7,000^0$F at ground level. Tens of thousands perished. By mid-August, Japan had surrendered, effectively ending the Second World War. It has been reported that no newsflash in modern times triggered such overwhelming celebration.

Many of the supra-national organisations of today's world, such as NATO and the EEC (now EU), were formed as a reaction to the traumas of the war and to counter-balance Soviet expansion. Their over-arching aims were to foster peace, co-operation and freedom in the new world order.

While the post-war, nuclear world had a very different complexion, conflicts endured. The 'Cold War' struggle for supremacy between the blocs of east and west, the two opposing spheres of influence, lasted for more than four decades of the turbulent twentieth century.

More recently, in the twenty-first century, it is clear that solving complex matters affecting public health and climate change, for example, demands global co-operation. And yet numerous on-going rivalries still seem rooted in Cold War dogma.

Constituted after the Russian Revolution, the USSR dissolved in December 1991. Its fifteen republics, including Estonia, Moldova, Ukraine and Russia itself, were granted self-governing independence with the support of USSR President Gorbachev.

Tragically, in February 2022, land war returned to Eastern Europe when Putin's Russia invaded Ukraine after years of aggression in the Donbas border region. The liberal democracies of the West were again forced to confront barbaric tyranny. Russia's justification – to 'denazify' its neighbour – was regarded by many as grotesque.

With bitter irony, the bombed-out scenes of destruction were reminiscent of Germany's invasion of Ukraine starting in June 1941. Back then, the Nazis targeted the Jewish community: in just two days of September 1941, 33,771 Jews were reportedly massacred by the SS in the Babyn Yar ravine, Kyiv; many more thousands in the subsequent two years.

Russia's 'special military operation' of 2022 was widely considered an assault on democracy itself, on the stable principles that had upheld post-war peace. The Ukrainian people resisted with honour and bravery, their spirit indomitable. Millions were displaced, found refuge abroad. Punitive economic sanctions were imposed on Russia by many nations; Ukraine's Western allies pledged to support the country until the fight was done.

On 8 March, Ukraine's lion-hearted President Zelensky addressed the UK House of Commons via a video link and cleverly invoked Churchill: "We will fight to the end at sea, in the air. We will continue fighting for our land, whatever the cost. We will fight in the forests, in the fields, on the shores, in the streets."

With Russia a pariah, moral disgust heaped upon it, attitudes to the defence of Europe shifted. Had the West become overly comfortable and complacent? A new world order began to emerge: democracy aligned against autocracy. European countries sought to lessen their reliance on Russian-supplied oil and gas. Olaf Scholz, Germany's Chancellor (since December 2021), declared the moment a *Zeitenwende* – an epochal turning point. Germany dramatically reversed its post-war foreign policy and announced more spending on defence, including extra funding for NATO and upgrading its own armed forces. In May 2022, Finland and Sweden applied to join NATO after decades of neutrality. Their stated aim was better to protect their populations in the face of stark aggression.

Even today, history casts a long shadow across our ever-shrinking, digital, dangerous, beautiful world. As Churchill eloquently put it, 'The farther back you can look, the farther forward you are likely to see.'

The perpetual quest to settle how we human beings co-exist rumbles on.

About the author

Mark Batey was born and raised in Newcastle upon Tyne.

As a student at Pembroke College, Cambridge, he chaired the college film society, and after five years in advertising he forged a career in the film industry.

This included three years at the BFI and two decades running the trade association for UK film distributors – the pivotal companies that acquire, promote and release films to audiences.

He wrote stories from childhood. Throughout his career, he scripted articles, speeches and reports, and is thrilled to have turned latterly to longer-form narratives.

His first book, *Grace*, a life story of Northumberland's sea-rescue heroine, Grace Darling, was published in January 2022. It was reviewed in *The Ambler* (in Northumberland) as 'well-researched, informative, exciting and complete', and attracted further five-star write-ups. *Warbird*, an historical adventure set in 1939–40, a hundred years after *Grace*, is his second book.

He splits his time between London and Northumberland.

Lightning Source UK Ltd.
Milton Keynes UK
UKHW041821041122
411662UK00003B/49

9 781915 229168